PRAISE F
PREV

THE PER

"An enticing hook and compelling st

—*Kirk eviews*

"This page-turner builds to a breathless conclusion."

—*Publishers Weekly*

"Gritty and intense to the max!"

—*RT Book Reviews* (4½ stars)

LIVE TO SEE TOMORROW

"Johansen builds the fires of intrigue with each moment, each turn of the page, and each stroke of her masterful pen."

—*Affaire de Coeur*

"In a genre laden with macho, action-hero figures, Johansen's shrewd and steely female operative is as tough as they come."

—*Booklist*

"In addition to being a thriller master, Johansen excels at seeding in paranormal elements that kick her stories into a new gear. Top-notch and absorbing!"

—*RT Book Reviews* (4½ stars)

SIGHT UNSEEN

"The stellar team of Johansen and Johansen is back with the next installment of this clever and terrifying suspense series . . . Filled with frightening twists and terrifying turns, the book ends on a cliffhanger. The reader's heart will be racing the entire time, so waiting for the next book is going to be difficult!"

—*RT Book Reviews* (4½ stars)

"The Johansens do a page-turning job of tying up all the loose ends in this complex cat-and-mouse game, but they always manage to leave one thread dangling: just the kind of ploy designed to keep loyal series fans eagerly anticipating the next installment." —*Booklist*

"A thrill-a-minute, chill-a-minute thriller that keeps readers on the edge of their seats. Each character is minutely defined and believable; the good guys, the victims, and the executioner. Iris Johansen and her son Roy Johansen are true masters of page-turning terror guaranteed to shock and awe you." —*Reader to Reader*

CLOSE YOUR EYES

"Gripping . . . The authors combine idiosyncratic yet fully realized characters with dry wit and well-controlled suspense that builds to a satisfying conclusion."

—*Publishers Weekly*

"Mind-blowing . . . The scenes with Adam and Kendra ooze sexual tension, making this thriller a titillating delight." —*Booklist*

"Intrigue at its best!" —*Reader to Reader*

SHADOW ZONE

"A sexy thriller peppered with enough science and mysticism to make any beach seem a little more exotic."

—*Kirkus Reviews*

"In this adrenaline-accelerating tale of a high-stakes, high-seas conspiracy, the Johansens adeptly juggle multiple points of intrigue, smoothly balancing the prerequisite whirlwind pacing with plausible, even restrained, personal relationships." —*Booklist*

STORM CYCLE

"A fast-paced romantic thriller . . . action fans should be satisfied."
—*Publishers Weekly*

"A pulse-pounding adventure intricate enough to satisfy tech-savvy geeks and hard-core adrenaline junkies alike."
—*Booklist*

"Enormously exciting . . . escapist thrills of the highest order."
—*RT Book Club*

"With the authors' trademark research, fast-paced action, and charismatic characters, *Storm Cycle* will blow you away."
—*The Oklahoman*

"Breathtaking." —*Star-News* (Wilmington, NC)

SILENT THUNDER

"Bestseller Johansen and her Edgar-winning son, Roy, collaborate on their first thriller with entertaining results."
—*Publishers Weekly*

"Gripping." —*Booklist*

"[In *Silent Thunder*] . . . you'll be rewarded with a bumpy roller-coaster ride as you try to separate the good guys from the bad."
—*Rocky Mountain News*

"Talent obviously runs in the Johansen family . . . The duo has no difficulty weaving in fascinating technical details with the explosive action of this nonstop stunner."
—*RT Book Reviews*

"*Silent Thunder* [is] another grab-you-by-the-throat dash that pulled me along on a frantic chase for a deadly puzzle piece."
—*BlogCritics* magazine

ALSO BY IRIS JOHANSEN

The Perfect Witness
Sight Unseen
(with Roy Johansen)
Live to See Tomorrow
Silencing Eve
Hunting Eve
Taking Eve
Sleep No More
Close Your Eyes
(with Roy Johansen)
What Doesn't Kill You
Bonnie
Quinn
Eve
Chasing the Night
Shadow Zone
(with Roy Johansen)
Eight Days to Live
Blood Game
Deadlock
Dark Summer
Quicksand
Silent Thunder
(with Roy Johansen)
Pandora's Daughter
Stalemate
An Unexpected Song
Killer Dreams
On the Run
Countdown
Blind Alley
Firestorm
Fatal Tide
Dead Aim
No One to Trust
Body of Lies
Final Target
The Search
The Killing Game
The Face of Deception
And Then You Die
Long After Midnight
The Ugly Duckling
Lion's Bride
Dark Rider
Midnight Warrior
The Beloved Scoundrel
The Magnificent Rogue
The Tiger Prince
Last Bridge Home
The Golden Barbarian
Reap the Wind
Storm Winds
The Wind Dancer

YOUR NEXT BREATH

IRIS JOHANSEN

St. Martin's Paperbacks

YOUR NEXT BREATH

For information address St. Martin's Press, 175 Fifth Avenue, New York, NY 10010.

Library of Congress Catalog Card Number: 2014040835

ISBN: 978-1-250-06946-7

Printed in the United States of America

St. Martin's Press hardcover edition / April 2015
St. Martin's Paperbacks edition / October 2015

St. Martin's Paperbacks are published by St. Martin's Press, 175 Fifth Avenue, New York, NY 10010.

10 9 8 7 6 5 4 3 2 1

CHAPTER 1

BOSKAR, RUSSIA

The woman's throat had been slashed.

She must have been killed at least twelve to fourteen hours ago. The expression frozen on her face was one of horror and bewilderment as she stared up at the ceiling of this little house that she'd worked so hard to make home.

There was a name scrawled in blood on the stone floor beside her body.

"I thought you would want to know, Hu Chang," Ivan Lagoff said to the man standing beside him, staring down at the corpse. "No one else has seen the body. I'll have to notify the police, but you're the one who helped Catherine Ling set up Olena Petrov in our village." He added hesitantly, "It could be troublesome for your friend Catherine?"

"Yes. Very troublesome. You were right to call me." He reached down and touched the gold chain with Catherine Ling's name on the ID plaque shining against Olena Petrov's gray sweater. "The police might not understand and ask Catherine awkward questions. Neither of us would want that to happen." He gently took the chain from around the woman's neck. "So we will make sure that it will not. You did not see this chain, Ivan. You found the body and you assumed it was a burglary."

Ivan's eyes widened. "That would be a lie. I could get into trouble. I checked the house and it appears nothing was taken."

"Then it might be wise to cause a little disarray and not be sure that nothing was stolen." He paused. "And when I leave, you should get soap and water and scrub out that name written in blood on the stones."

"I cannot do that." Ivan's eyes were fixed on the gold chain. "And you should not take that chain. The police would say that it's evidence."

Hu Chang nodded. "But evidence of what? So often the obvious turns out to be false and causes only confusion. You did not see this chain." He turned toward the door. "You did not see me. You do not mention Catherine Ling's ever having had anything to do with Olena Petrov. Do you understand?"

Ivan nodded slowly. "I understand. But I'm the head of this village, the *Lurah*. I have a duty. You ask a lot of me, Hu Chang."

"But I also gave a lot to you, Ivan," Hu Chang said softly. "Do you remember the night you promised me anything if I'd only keep your son on this Earth? I asked nothing at the time. I'm asking now. The life of your son surely has more worth than this simple favor?"

"It's not simple." But Ivan did remember that night. The local doctor had given up on his Niki, but there had been rumors about the powerful properties of the brews and medicines created by the physician, Hu Chang, who was visiting him. Hu Chang had only come to their village because of the rare herbs found in the nearby forest, but Ivan had thought he might be a gift from God. He had gone to Hu Chang on his knees. And by morning, his

Niki was on his way back to health. "Perhaps for you, not for me."

"After you've done what I wish, it will seem much simpler. A small gift in exchange for a gift beyond price."

For a moment, Ivan looked down at the dead woman. Then he went to the sink and got a bucket of water and a brush. "I'll do it." He knelt on the floor beside Olena's body. "I . . . liked her, Hu Chang. In the years she was here in our village, she was always cheerful, always helping with the neighborhood children. She never talked about herself, but I thought she might have once been a teacher. Was I right?"

"No. You were wrong. She was a whore." Hu Chang shrugged as he saw Ivan's shocked expression. "But that was another life, and you should remember the life she chose, not the one that was chosen for her."

"I will try." He moistened his lips. "That chain with Catherine Ling's name must be some kind of gift or present. It's strange looking, isn't it? Sort of like a military dog tag. I never saw Olena wear it." He avoided Hu Chang's eyes as he started to wash the name scrawled in blood off the stones. "And Olena could have been the one to write this name . . ."

Ling.

The name was already beginning to blur with the vigorous use of soap and water. He scrubbed harder, avoiding Hu Chang's eyes.

"I've heard Catherine Ling can be quite deadly. She would not have reason to be angry with Olena?"

"You see, you are asking questions." Hu Chang opened the door, his voice was nonetheless lethal for its softness. "Which causes me to be most unhappy. Make sure no one else has reason to question my friend Catherine, Ivan."

SANTIAGO, CHILE

Pain!

It was a trap!

Robert Jantzen felt the blood pouring from the wound in his chest as he started to run.

Footsteps behind him. Not in a hurry. They knew he was going down.

The hell he was.

He reached in his pocket and pulled out his phone.

Venable. Get to Venable.

His hand was shaking as he dialed.

Venable picked up immediately. "Jantzen?"

"Trap. They were waiting for me. I'm at the dock. Chest wound—bleeding."

Venable cursed. "Try to find cover. I'll get someone there to help you. Don't hang up. We'll trace your location."

Cover?

Jantzen looked around: warehouses, boats at the piers, bars in the distance . . . He knew he'd never make it to any of them. He wasn't running any longer, he was barely staggering.

And those footsteps were getting closer.

But Venable knew where he was and wouldn't let him down. Venable never left an agent in jeopardy or considered him expendable. Jantzen still had his gun. Maybe he could manage to get behind some of those crates up ahead and hold out until Venable came through for him.

He forced himself to break into a run again, this time toward the crates.

He heard a laugh.

Three shots.

He pitched forward as the bullets tore into his upper back and lungs.

Dying. He was dying.

He was lying facedown but he saw the brown boots of the man who stopped beside him.

"Venable won't help you. *She* won't help you. You're a dead man."

His hand . . .

Something cold and metal was being wrapped around his hand.

Everything was blurring, but he forced himself to focus. He could see the gleam of the gold chain of the dog tag that had been forced into his hand.

Dog tag?

Yes, and the name . . .

Catherine Ling . . .

LOUISVILLE, KENTUCKY

"I feel ridiculous." Catherine Ling scowled at her reflection in the hall mirror. The small hat she was wearing was a confection of scarlet and black chiffon and was the closest she'd been able to come to flattering her long dark hair and golden complexion. But it was still the last thing she would have worn given a choice. "And you're getting entirely too much enjoyment out of this, Luke."

Her son Luke's dark eyes were gleaming with mischief as he stood back and tilted his head critically. "You look beautiful, Catherine," he said solemnly. "All fluffy and soft. Kind of like that photo I saw of Queen Elizabeth."

"I'm going to get you for that."

"And after all, it's Kentucky Derby Day," Luke's tutor, Sam O'Neill said. "I've been trying to teach Luke all the cultural ramifications of the different American holiday events. Since this race occurs on our doorstep, he seemed particularly interested. So I went into detail about it."

"Including these idiotic hats women wear to the race." She glanced at Luke. "And he jumped on it."

"You went along with him," Sam murmured.

Because she was always glad to see Luke full of mischief instead of soberness. It had been a slow road back for both of them this last year. She and Eve Duncan had only recently been able to free Luke from Rakovac, the Russian criminal who had kidnapped him when he was only two and held him captive for nine long years. The violence and horrors Luke had gone through she could only imagine. She was just grateful that Rakovac had failed in his attempt to make Luke hate her and blame her for everything Rakovac had done to him. They were still on tentative ground, as demonstrated by the fact that Luke still called her Catherine, never Mother. But they were growing closer all the time. "I was trying to be a good sport. But I think this is a little too much."

"On the contrary, no embellishment is ever too much for you, Catherine. You wear everything boldly and with superb style."

Hu Chang!

She whirled to see him standing in the doorway of the library.

"Luke is right, that splendid confection is more a crown for a queen than a hat." He smiled. "But it's far more Kate Middleton than Queen Elizabeth."

"What the hell are you doing here?" She glanced at Luke. "Did you have anything to do with this?" She wouldn't have put it beyond him to arrange this surprise for her. Hu Chang had been Catherine's best friend from the time they had first met in Hong Kong when Catherine was only fourteen. But during these last months, Luke and Hu Chang had become both great friends and master and pupil. At times, Catherine didn't know if the envy she felt at the closeness of their relationship was over Luke or Hu Chang.

Perhaps it was both. Gazing at the two of them, young Luke with his shining dark hair and brown eyes that were sometimes wary, sometimes curious and full of vitality, and Hu Chang, who was seemingly ageless and totally fascinating, it was difficult to know which one she loved the most. Or which one most exasperated her.

But Luke was grinning and shaking his head. "I only e-mailed him about your new hat. That's all. Hello, Hu Chang. I'm glad to see you. I thought you were still in Tibet."

"And I may go back. There's much work to do there. But I felt the need to see you and Catherine." He looked at Sam O'Neill. "I was able to get into the house with surprising ease, Sam. The library window was left unlocked. You are supposed to be Luke's security chief as well as his tutor. Have you not been doing your job?"

"And have you reason to check up on me, Hu Chang?" Sam asked. "I go around every night and make sure all locks are secure. I don't expect to have anyone trying to burgle the house in the middle of the day." He shrugged. "But then, you always do the unexpected. I'll go and put on a pot of tea to get out of the line of fire."

"That would be excellent." Hu Chang turned to Luke. "Why don't you go with him? I taught you how I like my tea while you were staying with me in Hong Kong. I've not had a suitable cup since your mother insisted on taking you to this place where horse races are more important than the cultures of a thousand years."

"Horse races are interesting." Luke's eyes were narrowed on his face. "And are you trying to get rid of me, Hu Chang?"

"Of course. I have private things to say to Catherine.

We may share them with you later, but that will be her decision." His gaze went to the pouf of scarlet and black chiffon on Catherine's head. "But anyone who could talk Catherine into wearing that bit of beautiful nonsense has a tongue of silver. You may have no problem talking her into baring her soul to you."

"It made me smile." Luke was grinning again. "And it made her smile. Catherine doesn't smile enough." He turned and moved down the hall after Sam. "You were with her a long time, Hu Chang. You should have taken care of that."

"So now the pupil is teaching the master?" Hu Chang said, amused.

"You taught me that everyone can learn," Luke said over his shoulder. "All this wisdom and mystic stuff is fine, but it's not everything . . ."

Hu Chang was smiling as he turned back to Catherine. "He is changing, growing. I find it exciting. I think you must give him back to me soon."

"And I think you're crazy. I did without him for nine years. I'm having enough trouble just making a friend of him, much less having a mother-son relationship." She made a face. "You manage to hypnotize him. You hypnotize us all, Hu Chang."

He bowed slightly. "Not you, Catherine."

He had in the beginning, when she was only fourteen, before she had been recruited by the CIA. It was a time when they had been fighting street gangs and crooked magistrates and all the wickedness of Hong Kong. Even his appearance was mesmerizing. He was wearing his usual black trousers and tunic that were cut with faultless elegance. His dark hair was shoulder length and shone from the sunlight streaming into the windows of the foyer. His cheekbones were high, his eyes night-dark, and he always appeared totally ageless. He had told her he was Russian and Mongolian but looked neither, except for those dark eyes. He was a little above middle height but appeared taller, and she had seen him perform amazing feats of strength and skill. But it was his mind that had kept her intrigued all these years. He had traveled the world and studied dozens of philosophies and accepted parts of them. He had his own moral code, but he would not answer to anyone for anything he did. And she never tried to judge him. He had saved her life. She had saved his. When you had a friend as remarkable as Hu Chang, you only accepted and were grateful.

Except when he tried to steal your son from you. "Keep your hands off Luke, dammit."

"I said soon, not immediately." He gestured to the library. "Come and sit down. I've found that Luke is not above eavesdropping. I've lectured him on the lack of honor involved, but he blames it on being raised by criminals and raiders. He said that eavesdropping could sometimes prevent punishment."

"And that could be true. Rakovac put a gun in Luke's hand when he was only a small child."

"And Luke could be clinging to that excuse because of an insatiable curiosity and the desire to control his own life." He shut the door. "Either way, it's understandable. We must just cope with it. I do not want Luke involved at the moment."

"Why not?" She tensed. "And why didn't you come to the front door, Hu Chang?"

"I wanted to make sure that you and Luke were safe. Sam O'Neill is ex-CIA and usually more than adequate as a guard. I just didn't want him to get too complacent. I regard you as a treasure, and treasures must be kept polished and away from all harm."

"Bullshit. Why did you put Sam on the spot? Sam's not complacent. I wouldn't have hired him as Luke's tutor if I couldn't trust him."

"But I must trust him, too," Hu Chang said quietly. "I thought I made that clear. I have both an emotional and scientific investment in Luke. And an overpowering emotional investment in you, Catherine." He reached in his pocket and drew out his phone. "And I do not like what has been going on for the past week. I've been trying to keep it from you until I could find a solution. But the problem is escalating, and it troubles me." He dialed up his photos. "And it will do more than trouble you." He added quietly, "Sorrow, Catherine."

She took the phone. "What the hell are you talking about? I've not got any idea what—" She broke off as she looked down at the photo. "Olena?" she whispered. Blood. So much blood.

Shock. She couldn't breathe. She felt as if she'd been kicked in the stomach. That look of frozen horror was unmistakable. Nightmare. This was a nightmare.

"Dead? She's dead?"

"Throat cut. No sign of robbery. You can see your name written in blood on the floor beside her."

She swallowed. None of it made sense. The only thing clear was that Olena had been murdered. "Was she trying to tell me something?"

"No. I believe her murderer was the one telling you something while making it as difficult as possible for you."

"Olena." She rubbed her temple. "I can't quite take it in, Hu Chang. I thought she'd be happy now. She didn't deserve this. All her life was pure hell until these last years. From the time she was a teenager she was serving tricks on the boat docks in Hong Kong. She started on drugs just to keep from cutting her wrists. But she was good to my mother, she was good to me. She'd share food with us. And she kept the men away from me until I was old enough to take care of myself."

"I know, you told me."

"I did, didn't I?" She shook her head to try to clear it. "I thought she'd be safe in that little village. After I went to work for Venable, I thought I'd cut the ties to that old life. But there was still Olena, and I didn't want to leave her in that hell."

"And you didn't," Hu Chang said gently. "We found a place for her, you got her off the drugs and gave her a chance."

"And she still died with a cut throat," Catherine said bitterly. "Just the way it might have happened on the docks in Hong Kong."

"But she had those years you gave her, Catherine. And Ivan said they were happy years."

"She should have had many more years. She wasn't much more than fifty." She drew a deep, shaky breath. "Who did this, Hu Chang? Why? How can we get him?"

"Three good questions. I have no answers." He took the phone and dialed the photos down. "Not for Olena. Not for Jantzen."

Her eyes widened. "Jantzen?" Shock on top of shock.

"He is also dead. I did not take these photos I'm going to show you. Venable sent them to me because you were involved, and he thought you should be advised. I take it you worked with Jantzen?"

She nodded. "We worked several drug busts together in Caracas and Quito. He's a good guy. I liked him."

"A good friend." He nodded. "As good a friend as a loner like you permits herself." He handed her the phone again. "With the exception of my humble self."

She flinched as she saw the photos of Jantzen's body torn by bullets. "He had a wife and a kid. He was always talking about how smart his little girl was. What happened to him?"

"A trap. He called Venable and told him that the meeting with the informant was bogus. They knew he was CIA." He paused. "And they knew his connection with you." He pulled out a small box and handed it to her. "This was wrapped around his hand when they found him."

She opened the box and pulled out a fine gold chain. But it had a circular ID plaque hanging from the chain with her name engraved on the surface. "Dog tags? I don't wear dog tags even when I'm in the jungle. Certainly not gold ones." The metal felt oddly warm in her palm. This strange chain had been held by Jantzen, and she had the feeling that some of his vitality lingered. God, his poor wife, Laura; what would she do now? It was easy to say that everyone survived, but how? "I need to call his wife."

"She hasn't been informed yet. Venable wanted to explore the reasons why he was targeted, so that he had something concrete to tell her."

She looked down at the dog tag. "What can he tell her about this stupid dog tag? It doesn't make sense."

"Neither does this." Hu Chang pulled out another gold dog tag. "Olena was wearing it. Ivan said it looked like a gift. They're both eighteen-karat gold and very fine workmanship."

"No coincidence," she whispered. "Halfway across the world but no coincidence."

"That was my thought when I received word from Venable." He paused. "And I received another message from him right before I arrived here. There are no photos yet, but he's just heard that a Kirov Slantkey was shot in the head while riding his motorcycle in Moscow. Venable said you'd know."

"Yes. Slantkey was the informant who told me Rakovac was holding Luke in Russia after he was kidnapped.

It narrowed down the search area. I was very grateful to him." She leaned back in her chair. She felt weak and confused and unbearably sad. Get it together. Something bad was going down, and she had to identify and stop it. "Three deaths. All connected to me?"

He inclined his head. "I would wager that Slantkey will have a piece of gold jewelry with your name on it."

"Which could have either incriminated me or sent a message."

"I believe it was the latter."

"Why? I did care about all those people, but it's not like they were family."

"Not like a son," Hu Chang said softly.

Luke.

Panic raced through her.

"That's why you were checking security. You think he's in danger?"

"I think someone does not appreciate you. Extreme bad taste, but it's very evident. He's spelling it out for us in gold."

"Then why not go after me? I should be the target."

"We won't know that until we're told. Or we discover for ourselves." He was studying her expression. "You are as upset as I thought you'd be. I think I will allow you a few minutes to get over the first shock. I cannot give you more because I believe we have little time."

"I'm fine," she said jerkily. "As fine as I can be, considering that good people are dying all around me."

"Shh. Just take those few minutes."

Perhaps he was right, she was terribly upset and sad and angry. And frightened because it was clear Hu Chang believed Luke might be next. Take those minutes and try to gather her strength and mind to find answers.

She leaned back and was immediately assaulted with memories of Olena. She had been too far gone on the drugs to furnish Catherine with affection during those early days on the dock. But she had shared food and what little protection she could. And when Catherine's mother had died of an overdose, she knew Olena had shared her pain. So different from Jantzen, who was strong and kind and able to control his own life.

Until the night when that control had been shattered by those bullets.

"Okay." She drew a deep breath. "What's happening, Hu Chang? You've known about this for at least a few days. You've had time to think about it. Right now, I'm having trouble thinking at all."

"Understandable. Pain tends to obscure." Hu Chang tilted his head thoughtfully. "It appears that you must be the primary target. But why are these other kills thrown at your door? I believe I see a pattern here. It's like a circle. On the far outer rim is Olena Petrov, who helped you when you were a child. Then Jantzen, who was part of your life after you became an agent with the CIA. Then Slantkey, who helped you to regain your child. The circle is narrowing, becoming more intimate."

And Luke was the center, the heart of that intimacy, she thought with a chill.

And not only Luke.

"Whoever did this knows me very well. He'd know about you, Hu Chang."

"Without doubt. For I have made myself indispensable to you." He smiled. "But because I'm so essential, I will be one of the last to be chosen to bid adieu to you."

"You think it's going to go on." She moistened her lips. "So do I. It's crazy, but I can see that weird circle you're drawing, and it's scaring me."

"It's supposed to scare you. That's part of the plan. You're supposed to be afraid, to dread, to anticipate, to suffer with every death." He gazed at the gold chain in her hand. "It's a plan that has been well thought out, even to those expensive little trinkets he's using as a calling card. Do they have any significance for you?"

"No."

"Then we look at them as just that, a calling card. However, I may be able to trace the purchaser if I use my contacts."

"Then do it," she said unevenly. "I want this over quickly."

"But your enemy does not. He's making a ceremony of it. Taking away your support and the people you care about one by one."

"There have only been three so far."

"I believe there will be more. We must try to mitigate or eliminate the harm." He took out a notebook and pen from his pocket. "But I have to know who those targets will be, Catherine."

"I'm supposed to make you a list? How can I do that?"

"I'm sure that the person who killed Olena Petrov has a list." He added, "But the circle is narrowing, and you may not have to list everyone from your past. Just your present. The names that come easily to your mind."

Catherine shook her head. It was positively macabre, choosing who you had to worry about dying because they were part of your life. Macabre and dark and wrong. She started to write quickly. A few minutes later she handed the notebook back to Hu Chang.

He glanced at the names. "The usual names I knew you would choose. Luke, O'Neill, myself, your young friend Kelly Winters, our charming Chen Lu, Erin Sullivan, Eve Duncan. A few omitted that I would have guessed you would have included."

"You said anyone from my present who comes easily to my mind. Those I omitted can either very well take care of themselves, or there would be no obvious connection."

"Such as Richard Cameron?"

Cameron. Hu Chang's mentioning his name jarred her. Probably because she tried not to think of him at all. Their only encounter had been months ago but it had traversed both Tibet and San Francisco. They had both been involved in trying to rescue journalist Erin Sullivan and been forced to work together. Cameron was the security chief of a powerful secret conglomerate whose actions were often at odds with Catherine's job with the CIA. A situation that had made for strange bedfellows.

Strange, erotic, bedfellows that had made Catherine feel almost helpless to resist staying in that bed or following Cameron when they had parted. And that helplessness had only served to show her that she had been right to refuse to go with him.

"I haven't seen Cameron since San Francisco, and he was never a part of my life," she said.

"Debatable. But I agree he can take care of himself." He closed the notebook. "And we have to hope that our list is the same as the killer who appears to be stalking you has."

"That's not good enough," she said fiercely. "I won't sit here waiting for him to pick off another person I care about. I have to find out who he is and go after him."

"Absolutely." He got to his feet and handed the notebook back to her. "So why don't you make another list of all the people who hate you and have the resources and contacts to carry out a vendetta this elaborate. In the meantime, I will go and talk to Luke and Sam and tell them why we've been so rude as to ignore them."

"You're going to tell Luke about this?"

"Of course. Your instinct may be to protect him from knowing he's a target, but that's a mother's instinct and has no basis in reality. He may be only twelve, but he's led a life that has rid him of any hint of childhood. How can he protect himself if he doesn't know that danger is out there?"

"I'll protect him. Sam will protect him." He was looking at her. "Okay, tell him. But he'll only worry about me."

"And so he should. It's a son's duty, and he must learn things of that nature." The door closed behind him.

She leaned back in the chair.

Dammit, she was sad and shaken and didn't want to have to handle this crisis that was looming over her.

And over Luke.

She looked down at the photo of Olena Petrov. You didn't want to handle this either, did you, Olena? Such a terrible life, and we all thought it had turned around for you. It should have turned around. You shouldn't have had someone come into your home and take your life just because you helped me when I was a little girl. It's not right.

Jantzen. His little girl would never have him by her side again. Not right, either.

All of this scenario was wrong and ugly and looked as if it would continue if she couldn't find a way to stop it.

So do what Hu Chang had told her to do. Look deep and find the name of the person who hated her enough to destroy everyone around her in order to hurt her before he took her life.

She flipped the notebook open.

Think.

Not as easy as the other list.

She was CIA, and she had made many enemies in her career. She had grown up on the streets of Hong Kong, and those years had not been free of conflict.

Weed through her life, which had been violent and brimful of people who might want her dead.

Give Hu Chang his list.

And then go after the vicious son of a bitch who had killed her friends.

* * *

I think there are really only two possibilities," she said when Hu Chang walked into the library thirty minutes later. "One is Charles Corliss, who was a gun runner in the Middle East. He also had a hand in smuggling chemical weapons out of Syria into Iran. Three years ago, I was instrumental in busting up his sweet little deal with Iran and in the process put a bullet in his kneecap that caused him permanent disability. Venable told me he'd put a price on my head."

"And the other?"

"Tomas Santos. He was a kingpin drug dealer in Caracas and had a network of criminal organizations that extended from Venezuela to Mexico."

"Had?"

"We managed to find enough evidence and witnesses not too terrified to testify to put him away for twenty years. He's in a maximum-security prison in Caracas."

"Then why is he a candidate?"

"You said to find someone who hates me. Santos hates me."

"For putting him away?"

She shook her head. "I was one of the force who went to his penthouse to arrest him. He had a helicopter standing by on the roof to whisk him away to Iran, where he couldn't be extradited. He tried to get to it. We stopped him."

Hu Chang's eyes narrowed. "But that's not all."

"No. I shot and killed his wife, Delores Santos."

"An innocent bystander?"

"Innocent? Delores Santos stopped being innocent when she left the cradle. She was an active partner with her husband in all his drug trafficking and reputed to be as vicious as he was. At that penthouse shoot-out, she'd already taken down one of the local police detectives before I got off a good shot."

"And knowing your expertise, it was a very good shot."

"She died in Santos's arms. He looked up at me, and I'd never seen such hatred."

"Threats?"

She shook her head. "But I saw him twice during his trial, and there didn't have to be threats. The hatred was still there."

"But he's in prison?"

"That doesn't mean he couldn't manipulate things from inside. He had tremendous power and money stashed away all over the world. Dorgal, his second-in-command, was almost slavishly loyal and could have arranged the kills."

"Corliss or Santos? What's your choice?"

She shrugged. "It could be either."

"Gut instinct."

"Santos. Hatred. Plus I killed someone he cared about. Evidently, Delores Santos was his alter ego or something. Maybe he thinks this is a fitting way to punish me."

"It seems that could be a reasonable assumption."

"There's nothing reasonable about this. It's all ugly and crazy." She looked down at the notebook. "What did you tell Luke?"

"Exactly what I told you I would tell him. O'Neill is in the process of bringing in extra security from his friends among the ex-CIA elite. All will be well."

She prayed he was right.

"Those other names on that list," she said brusquely. "We have to protect them. Until this is over, I'd like Erin to leave Tibet and go to Chen Lu's golden palace in Hong Kong. Chen Lu has enough of a security force to make it fairly safe. Can you arrange it?"

"But of course I can. Erin Sullivan is very stubborn, but she has a great regard for my vast intellect." He smiled. "Is this what they called in the Old West encircling the wagon train?"

"That sounds very strange coming from you. Yes, approximately. I'll call Eve Duncan and give her a warning. If Joe's at the lake house, that will be security enough for her."

Hu Chang nodded. "Joe Quinn has a reputation for being very competent in that area."

"Exceptionally. He's an ex-SEAL and a police detective. That's an effective combination." She picked up her phone. "Get busy, Hu Chang. You forced me to mentally go over those scumbags who want to see me dead, and I'm tied up in knots. All these years, I've managed to block them out of my mind and forget them, but that's gone now. I can't have any other deaths."

"You're calling Eve?"

"No, not right now. I changed my mind. I'm calling Joe Quinn. He's a police detective with Atlanta PD, and there's no way he'll let anything happen to Eve. If I called Eve direct, she'd want to come here and help. The only help I want is for her to keep safe. Right after I talk to Joe, I'm calling Venable. I want to check on the status of Corliss and Santos."

"Wise." He turned toward the door. "And I will go call Chen Lu and tell her to circle her particular wagons and prepare for visitors."

"Good." Joe Quinn's phone was ringing, then he picked up. "Joe, Catherine Ling. Look, God, I'm sorry, but I have a problem, and you and Eve may become involved in it." She filled him in quickly. "If you can protect Eve without letting her know what's hanging over her, it might be a mercy."

"Eve and I don't play those games," Joe said quietly. "She wouldn't thank me." He was silent. "You're okay?"

"I'm fine. Just take care of Eve."

"No one will touch her," he said flatly. "She'll probably call you back. You're her friend."

"I thought as much. I just wanted to be sure that you were on top of it."

"I'll contact Venable and see if I can do anything to help out."

"If you do, it'll be from behind a desk or at your lake cottage. I don't want you more than a few yards from Eve."

"Bossy female." There was a hint of amusement beneath the grimness in Joe's voice.

"You bet. Bye, Joe." She hung up.

CHAPTER 2

Catherine took a moment after talking to Joe, then dialed Venable.

"I expected to hear from you before this," Venable said testily when he answered. "When I turned that information over to Hu Chang, it didn't mean I was opting out. Jantzen was a good man, and I'm mad as hell."

"Yes, he was, and so am I," Catherine said. "Any more news about Slantkey?"

"A gold dog tag with your name in the pocket of his motorcycle jacket. He's definitely one of yours."

One of hers. One of the victims killed in her name. The casual words were cold, the responsibility even more chilling. "Hu Chang told you about Olena Petrov?"

"Yes, definitely a pattern." He muttered a curse. "Jantzen was smart, he wouldn't have walked into a trap if the bait hadn't been presented with a cleverness that was impressive. It was a tip on an arms shipment that came out of the blue. It didn't have anything to do with the mission he was currently working on."

"And Olena wasn't clever at all. She'd made wrong choices all her life. Maybe she felt safe in that home we'd given her and just threw open the door for her killer. Either way, they were both victims, and I have to find the bastards who killed them."

"*We* have to find them," Venable said. "I told you, I won't let them kill my people and just walk away." He paused. "And you'd be hard to replace. It would be easier just to take the son of a bitch down."

"Sentimental, as usual. I'm touched." She and Venable had been together since she was fourteen and selling information on the streets of Hong Kong and he was a CIA agent trying to strike a balance between the British and Chinese. He had trained her, schooled her, but he had never pampered her. She was an agent and took her risks. She would have thought it bizarre for him to do anything else. The job was everything to Venable. "I'm glad we're thinking along the same lines. I came up with two names, Corliss and Santos. Give me an update on them."

"Good choices," he said dryly. "You pissed both of them off royally."

"Corliss?"

"He's off the list. He was killed in Pakistan over a month ago."

"Then, Santos. He's still in that prison in Caracas?"

"He was until three days ago."

She went still. "What?"

"He received a release because two witnesses who testified at his trial recanted their testimonies."

"Why didn't I hear anything about it? Santos is big news."

"Money, influence, threats. I'd make a bet both the witnesses and the judge who issued the release were scared shitless and wanted only to do what they were told, then fade into the woodwork."

"But you knew about it?"

"I was there at the prison when they let him go. I felt helpless as hell."

"Why didn't you tell me?"

"I was busy. I had an agent down. Jantzen was more important to me at the time."

"Do you know where Santos is now?"

"I tried to get a trace on him, but it was a no-go. We think he left South America but don't know where he was headed."

"What about Manuel Dorgal? He's practically Santos's shadow."

"He didn't meet him at the prison."

"No?" she said grimly. "He was probably busy with Olena Petrov and couldn't get back for the grand occasion."

"You've zeroed in on Santos?"

"Until I hear something different. Santos has been in that prison for two years, but the killings didn't start until he was certain he was going to get out. He didn't want to miss any of the fun. He's been plotting and planning, and now he's ready."

"Ready for you?"

"Eventually. Hu Chang thinks that he'll want to hit a few more people I care about before he gets around to me. I tend to agree. I saw his face after I shot his wife. He'll want me to suffer."

"Crazy son of a bitch."

"That goes without saying." She was trying to think. "But if he wants me to suffer, he's going to want to taunt me, to take credit. It's what I remember about his psychological makeup. He'll call me or send me an e-mail or something. Put a trace on all my electronic devices."

"Okay. But he's not stupid. We may not get anything."

"It's the only thing I can think to do right now. Except warn the people I care about. I just called Joe Quinn. And I told Hu Chang to get Erin Sullivan to go to Chen Lu's palace in Hong Kong." She frowned. "But that may take too much time. I don't know how much time we'll have. Erin's doing humanitarian work with the people in that village in Tibet. You have agents near there, and I remember that Les Caudell actually knew her. Can you tell him to keep an eye on her?"

"Why don't you call on your friend Cameron? He knows Tibet like the back of his hand. As I recall, there was a connection between Erin and him, wasn't there?"

"They're . . . close." Connection? That was both descriptive and an understatement when applied to Cameron and Erin. She had thought at first they might be lovers, but that was far from the truth. As security chief for the conglomerate for which he worked, one of Cameron's duties was to recruit brilliant, idealistic people to the global movement in which he believed. As a Pulitzer Prize winner, Erin fell in that category, and their closeness came from an intimacy based on Erin's gratitude to him for banishing the pain and terror of torture she was experiencing after her kidnapping by a warlord in Tibet. Soon, Erin had become caught up in the mystery that surrounded Cameron.

And Catherine had become caught up with both of them while freeing Erin from the warlord. Erin had become her friend. Cameron had become . . . she still didn't know what Cameron had become to her.

"And Cameron's not in Tibet at the moment," she said. "The last I heard he was in Copenhagen. Besides, Erin wouldn't want Cameron involved. She's very protective of him. Just tell your agent to keep an eye on her until she gets to Hong Kong."

"Okay. Anyone else who would be on Santos's short list?"

"I don't think so. Maybe Kelly Winters, who's at the College of William and Mary in Virginia. She and Luke are friends, and she spends weekends with us sometimes.

Assign someone to keep an eye on her." She paused. "I thought I was a fairly solitary person, but we touch everyone around us. When I was going over the list of possible victims, I found that out. Someone I might not consider as close, Santos could decide was worth killing." Her hand tightened on the phone. "I just have to find him soon. Get me phone numbers. Any way to trace him. Start searching, Venable."

"What do you think I'm doing? I'll get back to you when I know something." He hung up.

Santos. He still wasn't a definite, but he was emerging as a clear favorite. Time to go over his history and favorite locations to see if something popped out at her.

She Googled his name.

A newspaper article and photograph popped on the screen.

Slick black hair, Castilian features, sensual mouth. He looked to be in his thirties, but she knew he was forty-four. A rap sheet that was violent and terrifying. He dealt out vengeance with swift and cruel efficiency. He'd risen from the gangs on the streets of Caracas as a child to head the most powerful crime organization in South America. His corruption of the political systems in Bolivia and Venezuela had kept him safe and at the top of the heap.

Where are you, bastard?

He'd spent a lot of time on the Riviera. He'd had a home on the coast in Bolivia, but that had been confiscated by the government when he'd been convicted. He'd also invested in a castle in Morocco, where he and Delores had entertained royally. Had that been taken away from him, too? She'd have to check into it. Not that he would be there now. He'd expect her to be on the hunt. Wherever he was hiding out, it wouldn't be anywhere that was obvious. But he must have had other places that the government hadn't been able to track down. She doubted if he'd establish himself at any totally new place. He'd want the comfort and protection of his own goons around him.

But he liked the sun, as demonstrated by the choices he'd made in the houses she knew about. Sun. Sea. Areas where he could control his surroundings. Helicopter pads? More than likely. She'd start checking into that possibility.

If she had time before Santos started moving against the people she loved.

"I brought you your tea." Luke was standing in the doorway with a tray. "Hu Chang said he'd bring it, but I told him it was my job." He came forward and set the tray on the coffee table in front of her. "*You're* my job, Catherine."

"I keep telling you, it should be the other way around." She poured the tea. "You don't have a duty toward me. You've got our relationship all wrong, Luke."

"No, I'm starting to get it right." Luke sat down across from her, his back straight, his dark eyes holding her own. "It took me awhile after you took me away from Rakovac. I wasn't used to worrying or caring about anyone. It's still . . . hard for me. But I'm learning, Catherine. I won't let anyone hurt you. I can't do that." He grimaced. "Rakovac taught me all kinds of ugly ways that would prevent anyone from hurting you."

"I know he did." She felt the familiar rage soar through her. "That's why I killed him. And I wanted you to forget that ugliness, not use it for me."

"Too late. I've tried to tell you. I can't change, I can't be a normal kid." His face was pale, grave. "But I can be your kid. Just don't try to shut me out. Hu Chang told us about this Santos. I heard Sam on the phone, and he's trying to build a wall around me."

"Good."

"But who's going to build a wall around you?"

"At the moment, I appear to be last on Santos's list. Maybe I won't need a wall."

"And maybe you will. But you're not going to let me be there." He was suddenly smiling recklessly. "But maybe I'll be there anyway."

"No!" Panic was soaring through her. "Let me work my way through this, Luke. It will be more dangerous for me if I have to worry about you. Can't you see that?"

"But I want to—" He frowned. "Maybe. But I don't like—"

"Forget what you don't like." She reached out and touched his hand. "You and Sam take care of each other, so I don't have to be thinking about either one of you."

"Someone has to protect you."

"Hu Chang and I have gotten along very well for years protecting each other. You trust Hu Chang."

"But Hu Chang lets you do everything that you want to do. He says it's your right and privilege."

"Thank God," she said emphatically. "Which just goes to prove he's the wisest man either one of us will ever know. Doesn't that tell you anything?"

"It tells me that I don't think like him." He smiled. "And he would say that's my right and privilege."

"You've been around him too long," she said in frustration. "Promise me that you'll do what Sam tells you to do."

He was silent. "I'll have to think about it. Maybe until I can't do it any longer. If I see that no one is protecting you."

And, hopefully, he wouldn't be anywhere near her that he would be able to see that. But it just emphasized to her how quickly they had to catch Santos.

"Drink your tea, Catherine," he said as he got to his feet. "And call me if you need me."

"As a matter of fact, I do need you." She'd had a sudden thought. "Kelly. I'm having Venable assign an agent to watch over her, but I really want her with us." Kelly Winters was only sixteen, but she was superintelligent and thinking out of the box and being able to detect patterns that no one else could detect had earned her a place in her university's science think tank. But that also meant that she could be obsessive about her work. Not that being absorbed was usually bad for her. Hard work had saved Kelly after Catherine had saved her from being killed in the jungles of Colombia. "Can you persuade her?"

He shook his head. "She's working on a special project for her think tank. It's important to her. She said that it's innovative and a groundbreaker. Maybe in a couple days. Unless you want me to tell her that she should drop everything and come and take care of you. Then she'd do it."

"I'm tempted." She thought about it. Kelly's science think tank wasn't turning out just student projects. They were occasionally written up in prestigious journals. She hated the idea of letting Santos destroy that for Kelly. "No, I guess not. She's not actually family, and she isn't able to come to see us very often. She'd probably be low on Santos's list of priorities. And I already have her protected." She frowned. "I suppose she doesn't have to know about this until that damn project is finished. But do me a favor, keep in constant contact with her. Okay?"

"Sure. I've got a new game that's pretty cool. It should be enough to tear her away from that project occasionally. You know how she likes games."

"Thanks, Luke."

"You're welcome, Catherine." He moved a step closer to her. "I don't think you can use this now." He took the scarlet chiffon hat from the table where she'd tossed it and smiled down at it. "Too bad. I liked the way you smiled when you saw yourself in the mirror."

She made a face. "Because I looked ridiculous."

He shook his head as he headed for the door. "No, because it was something we were sharing. You taught me that sharing is good, Catherine."

She watched the door shut behind him. My God, she loved him. He had been damaged and suffered horribly from those nine years of captivity, but somehow he'd had the will to survive with a strength that often surprised her.

And exasperated her.

And scared the hell out of her.

KADMUS VILLAGE, TIBET

"Stop nagging me. I *am* hurrying, Les." Erin Sullivan stopped packing to frown over her shoulder at Les Caudell, the CIA agent whose helicopter had suddenly appeared fifteen minutes ago on the plateau above the village. "You can't just show up and expect me to drop everything and go with you. I had to explain to the elders and priests of the village that I wasn't abandoning them. They went through a hell of a time living under the heel of that monster Kadmus, who took over their mountain."

"So did you," Caudell said grimly. "Torture. Captivity. God knows what else. I'd say the villagers got off lucky in comparison." He grabbed her duffel. "And Venable does expect you to drop everything. I have my orders."

"Venable doesn't give me orders. He's your boss, not mine." But Caudell's urgency had impressed her in spite of her words. She had known Caudell for years while she was a freelance reporter traveling from village to village in these mountains. Everyone in those villages knew that Caudell worked for the CIA and was keeping an eye on the Tibetan-Chinese conflict. But he had never been obtrusive or involved any of the villagers in U.S. political shenanigans. He had watched and waited and reported.

She had never been able to do the same, she thought ruefully. She had become involved with the people and the mystical traditions of this austere land. There was such need and yet strength in these simple villagers. She couldn't see how anyone could turn away from that need. Still, she had grown to like Caudell over those years of contact. "And it's not as if there's any real threat to me any longer. I don't understand it."

"Okay, you don't want to listen to Venable. But Hu Chang was supposed to call you. Did he?"

"Yes, he said I had to go to Chen Lu's. Something about Catherine Ling's being in trouble." She followed Caudell out of the hut. "But it's all wrong. I should be going to Catherine, not Chen Lu. I tried to tell him that, but he wouldn't listen."

"You can call him from Chen Lu's palace and make him pay attention. Right now, I have to get you off this mountain." He was striding toward the helicopter a few yards away. "And if it will make you move any faster, it was Catherine Ling who said she wanted you under Chen Lu's protection." He opened the door of the helicopter. "Now will you—" He stopped as he saw a young priest in a yellow robe approaching Erin. "Oh, shit."

"It's just Kerak Li," Erin said. "He works with me at the orphanage. I didn't get a chance to speak to him. It will only take a moment."

"One minute," Caudell said.

Or as long as it took, Erin thought. She smiled at the young priest, and said in Chinese, "You'll have to take over for me for a little while. I've been called away." She bowed ceremoniously. "I know you'll be able to—"

Kerak Li's head exploded!

"My God!" Caudell pulled Erin to the ground and covered her with his body.

She couldn't breathe.

Shock. Horror. Sickness.

Another shot.

"Get off me," Erin pushed Caudell away. "Get under cover, Les. Get to the helicopter and—"

She saw blood blossom on the shoulder of his brown jacket.

"No."

She was on her feet, pulling him up and half dragging him the few feet to the helicopter.

A bullet burned by her cheek as it buried in the open door of the aircraft.

She pushed Les inside the cockpit and dove into the backseat.

Pain.

Her calf . . .

She struggled to shut the door. "Les, are you able to fly this thing? If not, can you tell me how to do it?"

He was already starting the rotors. "If the bastard doesn't shoot the gas tank . . . I'll drop off the mountain and worry about altitude later." The helicopter was plunging erratically even as he spoke.

Another shot.

"The shooter's on that cliff to the north," Les said. "We'll go south. Did he shoot you?"

"Just my calf."

"Bleeding?"

"A little." Actually, quite a bit. She was getting dizzy. Fight it. She couldn't let herself go unconscious. Les might need her.

And that shooter was still firing.

Stay conscious.

Help Les.

Oh, God, they both needed help.

The helicopter was plunging toward the rocks in the valley below.

She couldn't count on staying conscious.

They were going to die.

Unless she could get the help to stay alive.

Unless *he* could help her.

"Cameron!"

Erin Sullivan has reached Hong Kong," Hu Chang told Catherine. "But she's not at Chen Lu's palace yet. Venable is having her and Les Caudell taken there now." He paused. "There were problems."

"Problems?" Her gaze flew to his across the library. "What do you mean problems?"

"It seems that she was already targeted by the time Caudell got to her. There was a sniper."

Catherine's heart leaped. "Erin?"

"Leg wound. Caudell has a shattered collarbone. Unfortunately, a village priest was killed."

"My God."

"But Erin and Caudell are alive and will remain alive," he said. "They'll be safe with Chen Lu."

"Maybe." She felt sick. "I need to talk to Erin."

"I'll let her know that is your wish. Right now, it would not be wise."

"Because she's already been shot, dammit."

"And you're angry and want to reach out and punish Santos."

"You're damn right I do. I'm feeling helpless. That's not going to go on. What about that sniper? Can Venable catch him before he gets off the mountain?"

"There was no other helicopter except Caudell's on the mountain. That means the sniper's on foot or in a vehicle. It's a possibility we can catch him, but it appears to be doubtful considering the time lapse. Still, there may be an alternative. I will see what we can do."

"No, I'll see what we can do," Catherine said. "He's

our only lead, and I'm not going to let him get away." She got to her feet. "I'm out of here."

"As you wish. May I ask where you're going?"

"I'm catching the first flight for Hong Kong, then on to Tibet."

"May I suggest you wait until you talk to Erin? She told Caudell she wasn't staying at Chen Lu's. She's coming to you."

"No! She can't do that. I don't want her anywhere near me."

"That's not going to happen. She's your friend and feels she owes you a great debt. You saved her life."

"It was my job. I had to get her out of Tibet and away from that bastard, Kadmus." She looked him in the eye. "Or you would have done it yourself. I'm CIA. I was trained to do it. You might not have made it."

"Oh, I would have survived. But it's true that you're more competent than I at killing and mayhem." He paused. "But I would have had help from someone who is your equal, if not your superior. It was only fair that he be involved, since he was the one who brought Erin to my attention."

Cameron. He was talking about Richard Cameron. She couldn't argue that Cameron was a superb fighter as well as having other psychic talents that were fairly incredible.

And sexual skills that were absolutely mind-blowing.

Don't think of that. Her relationship with Cameron was in the past, and it had to stay in the past. They had been ships that passed in a night so tumultuous that it had shaken her to her core. Very dangerous. They had radically different beliefs, and she couldn't trust him to be anything but what he was—the Guardian. It was the name by which the villagers in Tibet had known him. A mysterious man who moved in and out of the mountains, taught by monks and fighters to be expert in many disciplines and who had incredible skills.

Hu Chang's gaze was narrowed on her face. "You've not heard from him lately?"

She shook her head emphatically. "Why should I have heard from him? We live in different worlds. The last I heard, he was on his way to Copenhagen. Probably to promote something totally illegal and revolutionary of which Venable would absolutely disapprove."

"It's possible."

"It's probable." She made a dismissing gesture. "And why are we talking about Cameron? He has nothing to do with this."

"No? Cameron has a habit of intruding on situations surrounding people he considers his own."

"You mean Erin." She frowned. "Yes, he does consider himself her protector. Well, he can just stay out of this."

"If he chooses." Hu Chang looked down at his phone as it buzzed. "They've arrived at Chen Lu's. Shall I set up a Skype on your computer for you to see for yourself that Erin is well?"

She hesitated. "Yes."

"Excellent." He took her computer and set it up on the desk. "It will give you comfort and permit you to expend a little of that anger I can sense in you."

"I just want to see that Erin isn't badly hurt."

"That, also." He was adjusting the input buttons. "It will just take a moment . . ."

"What do you mean you didn't take her down, Nagoles?" Santos said softly. "She was next on the list. It was one step closer."

"I had to move too fast," Carlos Nagoles said quickly. "That CIA agent was rushing her off the mountain. I had a bead on her when she turned to talk to some priest.

I would have had her if she hadn't bowed to the bastard. I shot the priest instead."

"Stupidity."

"I wounded her. I got Caudell in the shoulder."

"Not good enough."

"I'll go after her. You said you think Ling will send her to Chen Lu's palace?"

"It's very likely." Santos was trying to keep his temper under control. Nagoles was in an optimum position to go after Erin Sullivan, and he was usually competent. He'd been working for Santos for over eight years, and the kills had all been clean or bloody, whatever Santos preferred. He might have to get rid of him later, but he needed this kill. "I don't have to tell you that I won't tolerate another failure, Nagoles. I've been waiting for this for a long time. Everything has to go smoothly."

"It will. I had it all set up. It should have been easy. She had virtually no protection before Caudell showed up."

But it hadn't been easy, and it had to be because that bitch, Ling, had learned of the deaths and set up a stalemate to prevent any more. The thought sent the rage curling, searing, through Santos. She probably thought she had beaten him with this move.

As she had triumphed over him in that penthouse when she had killed his Delores. That sudden memory was like salt rubbed in a raw wound.

He couldn't let even a temporary triumph stand. He had planned too long, researched too deeply, while he was in that stinking prison. She had to be shown who was the master. "It's just going to be harder now that she has Chen Lu's security forces at her disposal. But you will do it, Nagoles. I won't have Ling think I've fumbled this kill."

"She won't. I'm already off Kadmus Mountain and on my way to the next mountain over, where you can arrange to send your helicopter to pick me up." He paused. "I won't disappoint you, Santos. Trust me."

"I did trust you. From now, on you'll have to earn it. I don't have to tell you what will happen if you fail me again." He hung up, turned to Manuel Dorgal, and said curtly, "She's still alive. He bungled it."

"You should have sent me." Dorgal smiled. "Never let an errand boy do an executive's job. I know how important Erin Sullivan's death was to move your plan forward. Do you want me to go after her?"

"No, I'm giving him another chance. I have another job for you."

"Whatever. But you're very tense," Dorgal said. "I brought you a pretty little sixteen-year-old when I came in from Caracas today. She may even be a virgin. Why don't you try her? It will relax you."

"Not now." He got to his feet and moved toward the French doors. He had to get out of here. The taste of this failure was bitter, and he needed to take it to his love, to share it, as he always had. "I'll talk to you later."

The sun was on his face as he moved down the garden path. Hot. Soothing. The heat was making the blood pump in his veins. Taking away the coldness of defeat. Making everything exciting and right for him as he hurried to her.

Just as she always had made it right.

I'm here, Delores. I'm coming to you. That fool, Nagoles, has upset me. I need you.

Then he was there, standing before the grand granite tomb that was covered with bouquets of fresh roses.

He immediately felt the easing, the feeling of coming home, of being welcomed into her arms.

It's only a slight delay, Delores. I know you would have told me to just kill that bitch, Ling. But I can't do that. She has to suffer for what she did to you, what she did to us. She mustn't die until she's suffered as much as I did when she took you away from me.

He looked at the names he'd written in black charcoal on the wall of the tomb. Slantkey, Petrov, Jantzen. He'd planned on adding Erin Sullivan today. Another surge of searing rage went through him. I didn't mean to cheat you, Delores. Forgive me.

I promise I'll make it right. But first maybe we should let Ling anticipate what's in store . . .

The Skype picture of Erin Sullivan was bright and clear and showed both the strain on her face and the blood on the front of her shirt.

"What's that blood?" Catherine asked sharply. "Hu Chang said that it was your leg that—"

"For heaven's sake, Catherine, it is my leg," Erin said with exasperation. "And it's only a flesh wound. I just bled a bit. This blood is from Les Caudell's wound. I had to help him into the helicopter. They're working on his shoulder now."

"And he'll be okay?"

"Eventually. Not for a long while. The pain was excruciating. He kept passing out on the way here."

Catherine bit down on her lower lip. "I'm sorry about this, Erin. I never dreamed that this would happen. It came out of the blue."

"Or out of the depths of hell," Erin said grimly. "A young priest was killed back on the mountain. He was only eighteen and was going to Hong Kong to study teaching. That bullet was meant for me."

"If you're looking for someone to blame, I come first on the list. I'm the prime target, Erin."

"That's what Hu Chang told me when he was setting up this Skype. Why?"

Catherine briefly went over both the facts and her own

suppositions. "I'm thinking it's Santos, but it could be someone else. Venable is trying to confirm."

Erin was silent, thinking. "Santos would have the money, power, and the killers needed to bounce all around the world as needed to accomplish those three kills. And the attempt on me wouldn't have been easy. I was working on a mountain in Tibet. Not the usual target for one of Santos's goodfellas. He had to be motivated."

"Santos can definitely motivate," Catherine said. "And he's not going to stop. He'll try again, Erin. Stay with Chen Lu."

"Not likely. Chen Lu's palace is beautiful, and she's wonderful, but I don't belong here. I'm coming to you, Catherine."

"Bullshit. Stay away from me."

"I can't do that. You didn't stay away from me when I was being tortured and hunted down like an animal."

"I was just doing my job."

"No, you weren't. It might have started out that way, but by the end, you were doing it because you wanted me to stay alive. Life is a great gift. I won't be cheated of trying to return the favor."

"Erin, I don't—"

"And I won't be cheated of the justice that sniper deserves for murdering that village priest. As soon as I make sure that Les Caudell is going to be okay, I'm on the next plane to you."

"That's not safe."

"Then have Venable make it safe."

"Look, stay there. I'm going to be on my way to Tibet to track down that shooter anyway."

Silence. "I don't think that will be necessary." A flicker of expression crossed Erin's face. "You don't have to do that."

"Of course, I do. He's my only lead to—" She caught

another flicker of expression, and her eyes narrowed. "Why won't it be necessary?"

"I don't think that sniper will be around much longer."

"Erin."

"Les kept blacking out on the way to Hong Kong." She moistened her lips. "And I don't know how to fly a helicopter. I had to find a way for both of us to survive."

Catherine knew what was coming. "So you asked for help?"

Erin made a face. "Cameron. I yelled his name like a banshee. Just the way I did when I was being tortured by Kadmus. I was praying he was still linked to me."

It was one of Cameron's bizarre and annoying psychic abilities to be able to go into a mind if he chose and either read or take control. He had been able to do that with Erin when she was being tortured, to keep the pain at bay. "You should have known he would be." She made a face. "He considers you one of his chosen ones whom he has to guard."

"Things could have changed. I never accepted what he had to offer. I was lucky he was there for me before when I needed him."

"And how did he help you this time?"

"I told you, I don't know how to fly a helicopter. Cameron came in and took me through every motion, everything I had to do to get us to Hong Kong. I couldn't count on Les. Though he did manage to land when we got to the city. Cameron was able to leave me about five minutes before that time."

"Came in" Catherine knew what that meant. Erin was telling her that Cameron had linked with her mind and virtually took over, as he'd done when he'd made Erin impervious to pain while she was undergoing those months of torture when she was being held captive by Kadmus. Cameron was probably the most skilled and talented psychic that either of them would ever encounter. Catherine had had experience with the psychics the CIA had recruited. She'd even attended a workshop in Rome to teach her how to deal with foreign agents who might possibly be able to read minds. None of Venable's parade of gifted psychics could hold a candle to Cameron. He was totally unique in that area. Not to mention having several other lethal talents that were exceptionally intimidating. "He took over right away?"

"Yes, thank God. He told me exactly what to do. I was pretty scared, Catherine."

"Since you were probably bouncing around on air currents and dodging mountaintops, I can see that you might be," she said dryly. "So you think that in between making sure that the two of you got safely to Hong Kong that Cameron was gathering information about how you got into that position?"

She shrugged. "Cameron always knew what I knew when we were linked before. This time I know he was angry. I could feel it."

"That doesn't mean he's going after that shooter."

"It doesn't mean he's not or sending someone else to intercept him. He has a good many men in Tibet." She added quietly, "It would be a waste of your time to come here. It's a very long trip, it will all be over by the time you get off that plane."

She was probably right, Catherine thought with frustration. Particularly if Cameron was as disturbed as Erin had said. No one could take action with more lethal efficiency than Cameron. "I don't want that shooter dead. I need information. Cameron will ruin everything."

Erin was silent.

What could she say? Catherine thought. They both knew Cameron would do exactly as he wished. "Can you reach him?"

Erin shook her head. "Only if I'm in need. Otherwise, the contact always comes from him." She paused. "Can you? Most of the time after the two of you came together before, he contacted you, not me."

"Because we were both in warrior mode trying to keep you alive."

"Really." Erin's brows lifted. "I suppose that was part of it. Try it. He might be willing to listen."

"I will." She grimaced. "It would be pleasant if I could just pick up the phone and call the blasted man. But he probably wouldn't answer his phone unless it suited him. And it wouldn't suit him if he thought I'd be interfering in what he thinks is his business. I *hate* this psychic crap. I've told him I don't want to deal with it."

"Evidently, you may have to." She looked over her shoulder. "I think the surgeon is finished with Caudell. I'm going to go and get a report. I'll call you later from the airport." She disconnected, and the screen went blank.

"I assume you are not going to Hong Kong," Hu Chang said, as Catherine closed the computer. "And that Erin is not being cooperative and obeying you. Unfortunate, but I've always told you that you can't run quite all the world to suit yourself."

"The pot calling the kettle," she said through clenched teeth. "And I needed Erin to do just this one thing, so I could stop worrying about her ending up dead." She added, "But she's heading for the airport as soon as possible. So we have to make it as safe as we can. I'll call Venable and have him assign an agent to her from the moment she leaves Chen Lu's palace."

"A commercial flight is not wise. Have him get her passage on one of the military planes heading for the States," Hu Chang said.

Catherine nodded. "And then you meet her flight and find a way to keep her as far away from me as possible."

"Not an easy task." He held up his hand as she started to protest. "But I'm superb at meeting challenges." He turned and headed for the door. "However, I believe I will leave the challenge posed by Cameron in your hands. Unless he proves a danger to you. Then I'm at your service."

Cameron was dangerous but not to her, she thought as the door closed behind him. To her he'd been more troublesome than a danger. Though their encounters, admittedly, had an element of threat to both her physical and mental well-being. Their sexual chemistry was too raw and wild, and he had made her feel possessed, almost . . . weak. She had never felt like that with a man before. It was one of the reasons she had been glad Cameron had been called away and out of her life. Not that she wouldn't have been able to handle it. It was just easier this way.

But Cameron was back, and nothing was going to be easy.

He was angry, Erin had said.

So what? She didn't need to worry about what he was feeling when her world was falling down around her.

Screw you, Cameron.

She punched in Venable's number to try to set up a way to keep Erin safe from that disaster.

Dammit, I'll do everything I can," Venable said sourly. "It's not easy to get a civilian on a military flight at the last minute. Get her to stay with Chen Lu."

"That's not going to happen. Keep her safe, Venable." Catherine paused. "Or Cameron will do it. You don't want him to intrude on your space. All your control will be out the window."

Silence. "Cameron is involved?"

"You didn't get Erin off that mountain without incident. You should have known he'd be upset."

"Ask me if I care. I've got more things to worry about

than whether your old friend Cameron is going to get in my way. It may be time to take him down anyway. The only reason I haven't done it yet is that his aims usually coordinate with the Company's."

"And you've found him annoyingly ghostlike when he's in action. Look, neither of us wants to have to deal with Cameron. So get Erin into the U.S. and keep her from being taken under Cameron's protective, big-brother wing."

"It might be possible." He knew damn well he'd do it, but he didn't want Catherine calling the shots. She had a tendency to always want to run the show. He hadn't known when he'd picked her up from the streets of Hong Kong and trained her as an agent that she'd be this dominant. Though he should have realized that when he saw how brilliant and intuitive she was in every aspect of the job. She was his best agent in the field, and he found it worthwhile to put up with her total independence—most of the time. "I'll assign an agent to her right away and try to set her up on a flight."

"Do that." She hung up.

Which sounded remarkably like an order, he thought. So much for letting her think she wasn't calling the shots. He turned to Agent Jed Stone, who was on the computer at his desk across the room. "I'm going to need passage for a civilian out of Hong Kong right away. Get me Colonel Radcliff."

"Right." Stone checked his directory and started to dial. "Would I be out of line to ask for a name? It's not for Agent Ling?" He grinned. "I'll volunteer to personally escort her. God, she's gorgeous. I picked her up from the airport in Atlanta once, and it was a memorable experience."

And Venable remembered how impressed Stone had

been. He was sharp and enthusiastic but young enough to be dazzled.

"Oh, she's memorable all right," Venable said. "And very magnetic. But I don't have to remind you that Jantzen just got killed because Ling got a little too close to him."

"Not her fault," Stone said. "I'm glad you're pulling out all the stops to protect her."

"The lift is for Erin Sullivan," Venable said curtly. "And, of course, I'd protect Ling. She's one of us. Do we have any more information about Santos?"

"Not yet." He broke away and spoke into the phone for a few moments. He turned back to Venable. "There's a plane leaving Hong Kong four hours from now. Okay?"

"We'll make it okay."

"Confirmed," Stone said to his contact on the phone and hung up. He looked at Venable. "Anything else?"

"No." He changed his mind. "Yes. Check and see what's the latest we have on Richard Cameron."

Stone accessed the computer. "Not much. He was under surveillance in Copenhagen, but he disappeared from there two weeks ago. We think he may be in Beijing."

"Oh, shit."

"A problem?"

"Cameron is always a problem. I'd hoped he was still in Europe."

"We have no record of his contacts in Europe. But then we didn't start shadowing him until he was in San Francisco." He frowned. "I wasn't with you in San Francisco. I was still in the Atlanta field office." He was reading the screen in front of him. He gave a low whistle. "He blew up a fireworks factory in the middle of the city and walked away without even being charged? Did we intervene?"

"No, Cameron appears to have much more influential

friends in his corner," Venable said sarcastically. "Which is why we may have to take him down. Too much power corrupts."

"What friends? I don't see anything here that spells out much about—"

"Because we don't know much. For years, we've just been hearing vague reports about Cameron from our agents in Tibet and India. It's all guesswork and trying to put vague stories together."

"So why are we even interested?"

"Because Catherine Ling is interested. Because Cameron got her and Erin Sullivan out of Tibet after Ling rescued Erin from that prison at Kadmus Palace." He shrugged. "It seemed impossible at the time, but he did it. When we went in later and started asking questions about Cameron, I became . . . intrigued. He appears to be some kind of bandit or warlord or mystic who moves from place to place in the mountains. He has commando units and sophisticated weapons at his disposal. There are rumors of kidnappings of young, brilliant technicians and a few killings of Chinese agents."

"Only rumors?"

"That's all anyone has on Cameron. Here's another one: He's supposed to be backed by a huge conglomerate that has world political ambitions and put him in charge of the security of their operation. He's known as the Guardian."

Stone chuckled. "Shades of Marvel comic books."

"Yeah, maybe. I'm glad you find it funny. Catherine Ling does not. The Agency was supposed to drop all protective services for Erin Sullivan when she arrived safely in the U.S. Catherine wouldn't do it, and she teamed with Cameron to give Erin protection."

"And it worked?"

"If you call blowing up half a block of prime real estate working. But Cameron managed to bribe his way out of trouble." He grimaced. "Which has a significance that's intimidating. I don't like anyone who has that kind of power. With backing like that, you can fund revolutions and hire armies. That's why I decided to take a closer look at Cameron."

"Why not let Ling investigate him?"

"I might, but not until I have something concrete to show her that he's a threat. She wasn't pleased when she had to do without our help in San Francisco."

"But she's only an agent, sir. You're her superior, and she should be guided by you."

God, he was young.

"Absolutely right. Next time you see her, remember to tell that to Catherine Ling."

CHAPTER 3

"Catherine?" Sam knocked on the door of the study, then opened the door. "Sorry to disturb you, but I have orders from Hu Chang." He smiled. "And I've learned that it's always wise to obey him. Otherwise, I tend to have egg on my face. He said you need an intervention." He came into the room and studied her face. "And this time I believe he's right on. You've been in here going over those Santos files for four hours. You need a break. Why not let me take a turn at the computer? You can rest your eyes and your brain and spend a little time with Luke."

She glanced out the window and realized it was already dusk. She had been so intent on researching Santos that those hours had flown. "Why didn't he come and tell me that himself?" She rubbed her eyes. "Is he with Luke?"

"No, he just left. He said to tell you that he was on his way to San Francisco to meet Erin's plane. He said something about meeting the challenge." He held up his hand as she opened her lips. "Luke's not alone. The extra agents I called in are here. I've told them that Luke's never to be left alone. They're very good men, Catherine. I've sent their qualifications to your computer, and you can check them out."

"But they're not Hu Chang, and they're not you. I want someone who *cares.* It could make a difference."

He nodded. "Okay, I'll go back to him right away. But there's no reason why I can't do research while I'm with him. Tell me what you need."

Why not let him help? She was getting more and more frustrated going at this blind. "I'm gathering info about Santos's possible residences, any of his men we can squeeze to tell us anything. Any weakness of any sort. He thought of his wife as a strength, but he was obsessed with her. That could also be a weakness. I'm looking into their relationship." She shook her head. "I don't know what I'm looking for. I just have to find him. I just need to *do* something."

"Got it." He smiled. "Now go to the kitchen and have a bite to eat with Luke. He's rising to the emergency and made you a fantastic lasagna straight from the freezer. Then go to bed and try to nap. It's better than being bleary and missing something you should catch about this Santos scumball."

Her brows lifted. "Is all this Hu Chang's orders?"

"Let's call it a combined effort." He turned to leave. "After all, I have to keep you sharp. Hu Chang tells me that I'm on your list of people who it would hurt you to lose and therefore a target. That makes it doubly important that you're in the best shape possible to get this asshole. It's sheer self-preservation on my part."

"Yeah, sure." She added quietly, "I'm really sorry, Sam."

"We'll get through it." He turned at the door and inclined his head. "And may I say I feel honored to be included on that list?"

Then he was gone.

And she was sitting there with stinging eyes staring after him. Sam O'Neill was a good guy, and she was lucky to have him in her life as well as Luke's.

And Santos wanted to take him away from her, too. One by one, he wanted to strip away the people she cared about and leave her in pain and defenseless.

No way.

But the reminder of that threat sent a bolt of panic through her. She wanted to reach out and touch, hold those she cared about tight and close.

Luke.

She jumped to her feet and strode toward the door.

She needed to see him, sit across the table from him, watch the expressions on his face, have him smile at her as he'd done over that silly hat.

It was going to be okay. She wouldn't let anything happen to him. Santos wouldn't put a finger on him.

But she couldn't stop the panic until she was once again with her son.

"Hey, Luke," she called as she moved down the hall toward the kitchen. "I've been promised lasagna. Did you make the garlic bread to go with it?"

Good night, Catherine." Luke turned at the door to his bedroom to look at her. "Sam told me you need to get some rest, too. Are you going to do it?"

"Sure." Then, as he stood there looking at her, she made a face. "At least, I'm going to my room and take a shower. I'll see after that if I can function efficiently. I'm feeling very frustrated, and I need to get a handle on this guy. It's not enough just to protect the people I love. I've got to get rid of him."

He smiled. "Like you got rid of Rakovac?"

"Exactly like that." Though all the psychologists would

have told her she shouldn't have told a twelve-year-old child that she would kill this man who had threatened them. Too bad. She had tried to wrap Luke in cotton to heal him and make him forget when she had rescued him from his kidnapper, but she'd had to give it up. Luke had grown up with Rakovac, a monster who had abused him and tried to make him into a murderer and thief, too. He understood life and evil more than most adults and had told her that if she had not killed Rakovac, he would have done it. "Don't worry. I'm going to keep you safe, Luke."

"I'm not worried." He grinned. "But I'm absolutely not going to let Sam come in and sleep in his sleeping bag in my room. And not any of those other guys, either."

"Did Sam suggest that?" Catherine smiled, too. "It's not a bad idea, but he should have known you wouldn't go along with it. Don't blame him. I made it pretty clear that I wanted everything that could be done to be done. So don't be surprised if you find him out here in the hall when you come down to breakfast."

"That's okay." He looked at her door across the hall. "Because then he could watch out for you, too." He paused. "This Santos is a real bad guy?"

She nodded. "Sorry, Luke. I seem to have stacked the cards against you when I brought you into the world. Every time you turn around, you're facing one of these ugly crooks I have to get rid of." She tried to smile. "No PTA or Soccer Mom for you. Maybe the next reincarnation."

"You'd do that if I wanted you to do it. But it would be boring. I like you better as a soldier or cop. CIA is kind of like both." He opened his door. "I just have to get you to let me help you . . ."

And that was her greatest fear, she thought, as she watched the door close behind him. She could surround him with guards, but they would do no good if he slipped away from them. Only one solution. Just find Santos and get him out of their lives.

She turned and went into her own room. Take a shower. Get a short nap. Then back to work.

But first she'd try to call Cameron again to tell him to keep his damn hands off that shooter . . .

"Wake up, Catherine. I'm in a hurry and, dammit, you keep interfering."

Cameron, she realized drowsily. A very impatient and annoyed Cameron.

She opened her eyes.

Not her bedroom, she realized. Cameron was playing his mind games and furnishing her with the setting of his choice. But it wasn't a firelit library as he'd done with her before. There was a fire, but he appeared to be in some sort of cave. He had a cup in his hand, and she could see the steam rising from the black coffee. He was dressed in a black leather jacket and jeans and was leaning against the craggy stone wall. Dark hair, high cheekbones, wonderfully sensual lips, and blue eyes that appeared icy against his deep tan. Tall, lean, with possibly the most beautifully muscular body she had ever seen. Hell, he was beautiful, period.

And she had better stop thinking that because one of his more annoying psychic gifts was the ability to read minds if he chose. She didn't want to give him any more ammunition than necessary when he was so angry with her.

"And you think I'd use it against you?" He frowned. "Maybe you're right. I'm mad as hell that you didn't tell me right away that there was a problem. You waited until Erin was forced to do it."

"It was my problem. I was handling it. Venable sent an agent to get Erin."

"I know all that. It didn't work out too well, did it?"

"No," she had to admit. "There was no time. It was the best I could do, being half a world away from her. Could you have done any better?"

"Maybe." He grimaced. "Maybe not. I guess you did okay."

"No, I didn't do okay. She almost got killed. The best I could do wasn't good enough. Do you think I don't realize that?"

His gaze narrowed on her face. "And you're feeling guilty and responsible."

"Yes, about her and everyone else who is unlucky enough to be my friend." She glared at him. "And get out of my mind. You promised me that you wouldn't do that to me. Keep your word, dammit."

He shrugged. "I'm out now. It's always tempting. I did slip when I first joined you. I get reckless when I'm angry." He suddenly smiled. "But only with you. Sometimes it frustrates me not to know which way you're going to jump. Though I always hope it's going to be into bed with me. You're the exception to every rule, Catherine."

Sensual and erotic memories were flooding back to her as she stared at him. She could feel the heat tingle through her body, tightening the muscles of her stomach, causing her breasts to swell. She could remember lying naked on his lap, his fingers moving inside—

"I've missed you, Catherine," he said quietly. "I don't remember ever missing a woman after I'd left her. But I missed you. I wanted to come back and show you how good we could be together."

"Sexually?" she asked. "No argument. But life isn't only sex, and we're hardly compatible on any other level. I told you when you were running off to Copenhagen that I wasn't going to go with you and be your mistress. I'm CIA. I have a job to do." She looked him in the eye. "And

that job might be to go after you and take you down someday. We don't think alike, Cameron. You believe the world is trying to blow itself up and going to hell. You want to prepare a new civilization by hiring superbrains, stealing knowledge, and storing it away so that we'll have something to go back to. Me? I believe you may be right, but I'm going to work my ass off to try to keep that blowup from happening. Don't get in my way."

"It might be impossible not to do that." He tilted his head. "But we're both warrior stock, Catherine. We'd probably enjoy that, too. The idea . . . stimulates me. But then, everything about you stimulates me. I'd wake up in the middle of the night and want you there beside me. Do you remember my mouth on—"

"It's over," she said curtly. "And the last thing I want to think about right now. I have more important concerns."

"What can I say? I'm only a man, and there are no more important concerns than sex. Well, maybe long-term, but never on the current scale." His smile faded. "Okay, let's get down to it. Why did you phone me four times?"

"Why did you ignore me four times?"

"I don't like cell phones. I was irritated with you, and I wasn't ready to make contact."

"You mean in your own special way, where you have all the advantages?" she asked sarcastically. "But you slipped up, that's a very crude set you've created for me. Was it supposed to bring up thoughts of rough, tough cavemen?"

"No, I wasn't in the mood to play games. I just brought you to where I am."

She went still. "And where is this cave?"

"Tibet."

Her heart skipped a beat. "I thought you were in Copenhagen. Didn't your committee send you there?"

"That was an easy problem to solve. I went straight from there to Beijing."

"Why? Did they have a few brilliant computer whizzes you wanted to 'liberate'?"

"Perhaps. Whatever I was doing is classified, Catherine."

She dismissed the question. "Venable will find out. So what are you doing in a cave in Tibet?"

"I'm waiting for a helicopter to land to pick up our shooter. He's on a plateau about five minutes from where I am."

She inhaled sharply. "You found him?"

"I sent my men out questioning and searching the minute I got Erin to Hong Kong. I put an urgent on it. And I boarded a flight out of Beijing within the hour." His brows lifted. "Would you expect anything else? Erin is one of mine. No one is permitted to touch her."

"I'm afraid she doesn't accept that designation," she said dryly. "She's an independent journalist and belongs only to herself, not to you, not to your committee."

"And we respect both her independence and her vision. It's what made her a Pulitzer Prize winner. It's what made us have an interest in acquiring her for our project."

"She turned you down, Cameron. She doesn't want to be part of your 'perfect' future world."

"Not at the moment. But as she becomes more discouraged and disillusioned at what's happening around her, she might change her mind. She came close a few months ago." He shrugged. "If she doesn't, so be it. I still chose her, and I have to protect her. It's my job."

"As the Guardian?" she said mockingly.

"It's what I am," he said simply. "It took me a long time to decide I'd accept the responsibility. I take it seriously."

"I'm sure you do. Everything from killing and blowing up fireworks factories to rescuing idealistic reporters from the bad guys." She changed the subject. "Does this shooter have a name? Venable hasn't been able to trace him yet."

"Carlos Nagoles." He smiled teasingly. "And my techs were able to track and identify him within eight hours. It's wonderful what you can do without government red tape. He's a killer for hire who works principally out of Hong Kong and Beijing. Very efficient. Very expensive."

"You're sure he's the sniper?"

"Quite sure. I don't make mistakes like that, Catherine," he said gently.

"I thought he might have ties to the South American drug cartels."

"And he might, but he's freelance." He paused. "You thought he might be connected to Santos."

Her eyes widened. "How do you know about Santos?"

"Erin didn't know enough about what was going on with you, so I had to tap Hu Chang. I would have gone to you, but I was pissed off that you hadn't told me yourself." He paused. "I'm still pissed off."

"And, of course, Hu Chang told you everything he knew."

"He's a wise man. He wanted to enlist all the help he could to protect you. But we'll go into that at another time." He straightened. "I have to leave. I hear the helicopter. By the way, when we intercepted the message from the pilot to Nagoles, he mentioned that he'd been sent by Santos to pick him up. If you had any doubts it was Santos who was targeting you, that should put them to rest."

"Wait. Do you have help to take Nagoles down?"

"It's only a helicopter pickup. Nagoles is hiding in the rocks near the plateau. When the helicopter lands, he'll surface, and I'll have him."

"Is that a no?"

He got to his feet. "I'm touched by your concern."

"Cameron, listen," she said urgently. "I don't want this Carlos Nagoles dead. I want to ask him questions."

"I thought that might be why you were trying to contact me." He was heading for the cave opening. "I don't promise you anything, Catherine. Santos's errand boy piloting that helicopter will definitely go down. Nagoles? He tried to kill Erin. I'm not going to let him get a chance to do it again." The glance he gave her over his shoulder was cool, narrowed, and razor sharp. "If you're lucky, I might place a few questions to him. Emphasis on might."

"Damn you. I need to—"

But the cave was suddenly gone.

And so was Cameron.

She was only surrounded by the shadowy darkness of her familiar bedroom.

And Cameron was somewhere on that mountain in Tibet, running toward the shooter.

And she wanted to be with him.

Who knew what kind of firepower the pilot on that helicopter would have?

Why was she worried? Cameron was totally remarkable and could certainly take care of himself.

And the bastard had refused to give her any reassurances about Nagoles. Cameron would do things his way and to hell with what she wanted. Which meant that she might lose her chance to get the information she needed about Santos's location. So it was ridiculous for her to feel anything but anger at Cameron.

And stupid of her to still want to be on that mountain with him.

* * *

Cameron could feel the blood coursing through his veins as he ran down the rocky path to the plateau. Seeing Catherine again had made every sense come alive. Long, dark hair, sleek and shining, a slight tilt to those dark eyes that were bold and fierce and brimming with life against the gold of her skin. A mouth that was shaped as beautifully as the rest of her features. A slim body that was still sensual, sexual as well as strong. He loved her strength as much as that sexuality. In spite of his anger, she'd had the same explosive sexual effect on him as she'd had from the moment he'd met her. Sex and obsession. As Guardian, it wasn't wise for him to form obsessions, but Catherine had definitely become an obsession. That was why he'd resented the fact that she'd not come to him for help when she'd been targeted. She had left him out, and it angered him . . . and hurt.

Stop thinking of Catherine. There was work to be done.

His gaze raked the clusters of rock ahead for signs of Nagoles. By nature, he was a hunter, and Nagoles was fair game. Not only was he a killer, but he was a threat to Erin and Catherine. Besides, he didn't often get the chance to go one-on-one. To his infinite disgust, the committee regarded him as too valuable to the project to risk.

He could see the red-and-cream helicopter on the horizon. It was losing altitude, preparing to land.

Nagoles had still not come out of the rocks.

Wait.

Watch.

He dodged to one side for cover as he reached the rocks.

The helicopter was hovering.

Shit. There was a missile mounted on either side of the copter.

A complication.

Where the hell was Nagoles?

Then the helicopter was on the ground, rotors blowing snow in all directions.

"Here!" Nagoles was running through the boulders toward the helicopter, his right hand clenching on his rifle.

In a minute, he'd be out of the rocks and a few yards from the helicopter. That would be the time to take him down.

Just a little closer . . .

He carefully aimed his rifle at the door of the helicopter.

He'd do better to send the bastard straight to hell, but Catherine wanted information. He'd see if he could get it for her without damaging his own agenda.

Nagoles sprinted into view, only four yards from the helicopter.

Now.

He pulled the trigger.

Nagoles screamed as the bullet hit his back. He stumbled and went down.

Blood on the snow.

Cameron could hear the pilot cursing as he started to lift off.

And his second act would be lethal.

Move.

Cameron dodged to the right, just as a missile exploded and shattered the rocks where he'd been only seconds before.

Get in position for another shot. Fast. If that pilot gained altitude, he'd have a clear shot of anyone on the ground below him.

He was already ten feet off the ground when Cameron reached a boulder and rested his rifle on the surface and aimed at the helicopter.

Fifteen feet.

He aimed five feet above his actual target.

Gas tank. Take out the gas tank.

The pilot swiveled the aircraft around, spoiling the shot.

Aim again.

Now.

He pressed the trigger.

The helicopter exploded into a fiery ball as the gas tank blew.

Cameron moved to the edge of the plateau and watched as the flaming remnants of the aircraft fell out of the sky to the valley below.

Nagoles groaned on the ground behind him.

Cameron turned and looked at him.

Bleeding. Snarling. Trying to crawl to reach his rifle.

Conscious enough to want to kill.

Therefore, he should be conscious enough for Cameron's purpose.

Before he made sure that the bastard was never a threat to either Erin or Catherine again.

"Hello, Nagoles, I'm Cameron." He squatted next to Nagoles and shoved the man's rifle farther out of his reach. "We have to have a chat. You need to pay close attention, because I have a terrible temper, and that could bring you intense pain . . ."

The shooter's name is Nagoles," Catherine told Venable as soon as he picked up. "Cameron's men tracked him down. And he's freelance, not one of Santos's usual goons. But that doesn't mean he doesn't have information that I can use." She added in frustration, "If Cameron will give me the chance to get it out of him."

"Cameron?" Venable wasn't pleased. "Where is he? I'll send agents to intercept him and make sure we get our hands on Nagoles."

"Fat chance. Cameron is being protective, which means that Nagoles is a dead man. I just hope that he deigns to get me some of the information that I need before he sends Nagoles to hell."

"Where is he?" Venable repeated.

"Tibet. Don't send anyone near him. You know that Cameron and the CIA have been dancing around each other for months. You don't want a confrontation with him unless it's over something important to global security. Not about some drug dealer trying to take an agent out."

"I'll do what I please, Catherine. We want Santos back in custody on a charge that will stick. Or we want him dead. You're important to us, but there are other motivations. Once Santos is finished with revenging himself on you, he'll turn his attention to rebuilding the empire we tore down. So Cameron can keep his hands off anything to do with Santos, or I'll have to take him down."

"Good luck." She hung up.

The last thing she wanted was for Venable to go after Cameron. As she'd said, so far their encounters with Cameron and the committee had been glancing blows, not worth extending their full strength. He was more a figure of mystery, an enigma, than an enemy. But that could change in a heartbeat, and where would that leave her?

Why was she even questioning? She was an agent, and she would do her duty and go after Cameron if given the command.

But the order hadn't been given, and she'd let Cameron deal with his own problems. God knows, she had enough to worry about at the moment. She would lie here and rest and try to sleep.

And hope that Cameron would call her back and tell her that Nagoles had given him a hint where she could find Santos.

She would not think of what she'd felt when she'd first

seen him in that cave. The shock, the erotic sensation that had electrified every muscle, the searing memory of the ways he had touched, probed, rubbed—

And she was doing exactly what she had sworn she would not do.

She drew a deep breath and let it out slowly. Relax. Cameron was being Cameron, and that meant totally his own person, stubborn, and unpredictable. Both his men and the committee under whom he worked regarded him more as crown prince than Guardian of the project. Which also meant he was arrogant as hell.

But she didn't have to accept that arrogance. She didn't have to accept anything about the man.

She closed her eyes.

Go away, Cameron. I'm through with you for tonight.

There's been a problem." Manuel Dorgal hung up the phone. "The helicopter we sent to get Nagoles crashed as he was attempting the pickup. According to the villagers in the area, they think it was shot down."

"What?" Santos's hand clenched on his glass. "Nagoles?"

"We don't know if he was on board or not. There wasn't much left of anything on the helicopter. Cinders. Nothing but cinders. We know Nagoles hasn't surfaced anywhere in the area. We haven't been able to reach him."

"And we don't know who shot it down?"

Dorgal shook his head. "No word on the grapevine. Nagoles was our only contact in the area, and he's disappeared. Maybe CIA? We know that Sullivan was taken away by a CIA agent. It would make sense." He frowned. "Though I don't know how they'd manage to get more agents there so soon to track Nagoles."

"Find out," Santos said grimly. "And find out whether Nagoles is dead or not. If he's not, kill him. He's been targeted, and I can't afford for him to be forced to answer questions."

"He doesn't know that much. You kept him out of the loop after you went to prison."

"Do you think I don't know that?" he asked harshly. "But Ling is clever. She might be able to tap something, anything, that would give her a hint about where to find me."

"There's a solution. You could take her out right now. All you have to do is toss an explosive through a window of her house, and everyone is dead."

"And admit that I had to hurry the bitch's death because she's getting closer to me? Would Delores understand that I stopped short of total victory over the woman who killed her? That I stopped before I could wring every bit of mental and physical pain from Ling?"

"Death is a pretty awesome victory. Delores is dead. You can't—" Dorgal stopped as he met Santos's eyes. He forced a smile. "You're right, of course. We'll work around the problem. I'll locate Nagoles or whoever took him down."

"Yes, you will." His gaze lifted to the portrait of Delores over the fireplace. "But this is the second time Ling managed to block me. I have to move quickly to make sure that she gets no satisfaction from it." He reached for his phone, his gaze still on Delores's smiling face in the portrait. "Which one shall it be?" he whispered. "Which one, Delores?"

What the hell do you mean by going to Joe and not directly to me?" Eve Duncan demanded when Catherine picked up her call the next morning. "Not good, Catherine."

"Sorry. I had to make a decision on how to protect you as quickly as possible. Joe was my answer."

"Not a good answer. Though I admit that he's notified everyone who has a stake in keeping me alive, and they're rallying around me. But that's me, not you. This is all about you. You risked your butt to save my life not long ago. Yet you think I'm going hide out in this lake cottage while some drug king tries to kill you?"

"I'm hoping you will. I'm not first on his agenda. Santos is going to go after the people I care about first." She sighed. "Think of yourself as bait. Joe can spring a trap and save you and me at the same time. Does that work for you?"

"No."

"I didn't think it would. But there's still value in the idea. Talk to Joe about it." She added firmly, "Because it's all you can do for me. Stay where you are. I'm not letting anyone who might be a target near me. Santos would love to kill someone I care about in front of me."

"Yeah, I've been doing some research on him. He's a nasty piece of work." She paused. "Is Hu Chang with you?"

"Not right now. He's trying to stave off Erin Sullivan from doing the same thing that you want to do. She's flying here from Hong Kong." She paused. "And she's already been wounded. Apparently, she was next on Santos's list."

"Is she okay?"

"Yes, but it could have ended differently. She almost ended up dead. *You* could end up dead, Eve." She shivered as she said the words. "Anyone who I care about, anyone I love. I thought I was pretty alone in the world, but I'm finding that I care about a lot of people. And that scares me. Santos has evidently spent a lot of time doing his research. I don't know where he'll strike next."

"Then I should be there to—"

"No, Eve. I don't need you. I have guards all over the place. Do you think I wouldn't protect Luke?"

"No." Eve was silent. "You call and tell me that Hu Chang is back with you, and I might wait. I'll give you until tomorrow."

"He may not be back by—"

"Tomorrow." Eve broke the connection.

Catherine grimaced as she hung up the phone. It was no more than she had expected. It was what Catherine would have done in the same circumstances. But she'd hoped that maybe Joe would be able to keep Eve from acting. Evidently, he'd had some success but not enough.

"Eve is upset?" Sam poured Catherine a cup of coffee before sitting down across the kitchen table from her. "You're lucky she's not mounting her trusty steed and riding to rescue you."

"I think Joe is holding the keys to the stable at the moment." She lifted her cup to her lips. "But that's not going to last long. Tomorrow. She doesn't like the idea that Hu Chang isn't here."

"And I'm chopped liver?" Sam asked mockingly. "I'm insulted."

"You shouldn't be. Hu Chang left you to guard Luke. That's a compliment beyond price."

"He also told me to keep an eye on you, or I would end up dying a very slow and painful death." He took a sip of his coffee. "And from what I gathered, he's fully qualified to make that happen. Is he really a master poisoner?"

"No, but he's magnificent at creating them. He's been known to sell certain of his poisons for fabulous amounts." She shrugged. "But only to those he chooses and who meet his code. I don't know if he started out as ethical as he is today. I've never asked him. He's my friend, that's enough for me."

"A strange relationship."

"Why not?" She smiled. "It goes with the territory. Hu Chang and I are both a little strange. Haven't you noticed?"

" 'Unique' is the correct word. Do you want breakfast?"

"Just orange juice. Where's Luke?"

"In the library. He was up at six and ate his breakfast then. He's playing an online video game with Kelly Winters. She beat him last time, and he's out for revenge."

"He'll have his work cut out for him," she said dryly. "You've met Kelly when she's visited here. She's not in that think tank at the university for nothing. She may be only sixteen, but she's extraordinarily intelligent."

"But so is Luke," Sam said. "They're a good match. He has trouble adjusting to kids his own age, but he has no trouble with Kelly."

"Because she's smart about people, too. I've tried to get her to come here to study, but she likes the professors at her school in Virginia." She shook her head regretfully. "Too bad. Luke really likes her."

"And so do you," Sam said softly. "It was like watching a family when she was here visiting. It was good for you."

"Of course I like her. She was my friend before she was Luke's. She's sharp and funny and has a wry sense of—" She stopped and drew a deep breath. "Oh, shit."

"What's wrong?"

"*I'm* wrong. I should have ignored the fact that Kelly would have to be brought here kicking and screaming if we tore her away from that project she's working on. I told Luke that Santos would have Kelly listed as low-priority since she wasn't family. But when I was talking about her just now, I realized that she might as well be family. And Santos has done his research, he'll know that she's not just

Luke's friend. He would have found out that I rescued Kelly in Colombia when she and her father had been kidnapped by bandits. He'll know I care about her, too." She reached for her phone. "I'm so damn stupid. I could get her killed." She dialed Venable. "She could very well be high on his death list."

"And she might not," Sam said quietly. "Stop blaming yourself. He can't be targeting everyone."

"But I don't know who he is targeting," she said unsteadily. "And it's driving me crazy. Who am I going to miss?" Venable picked up the call, and she spoke quickly, "Look, Venable, I need you to check on Kelly Winters's surveillance. I'm getting pretty uptight about having her out there alone. I'm going to call her myself later and see if I can't persuade her to let us come and get her. Don't let her go anywhere on campus without a tail, okay?"

"That goes without saying. If there were a problem, I'd know about it."

"Okay, so I'm paranoid. Just do it." She hung up.

CHAPTER 4

"I am paranoid," she said to Sam after she'd finished speaking to Venable. "I can't help it." She leaned back in her chair and tried to compose herself. "I guess that's all I can do right now." Her hand clenched on her coffee cup. "I *hate* this. I want Santos."

"So do I," Sam said.

"He has me on the defensive. I feel so damn helpless. All I can do is wait for something to happen." She moistened her lips. "Or someone to die."

"You're not helpless. Erin Sullivan is alive, and she wouldn't be if you hadn't acted."

"Even that wasn't a complete victory. A priest died in that village." She waved her hand as he started to speak. "But I can't think about that. I'll accept partial victories."

"And it probably pissed off Santos big-time. All of his elaborate schemes down the tube."

She smiled. "You're great, Sam. I'm actually beginning to feel a little optimistic."

"No, you're not. But you might be seeing things a little clearer. You're going to beat the son of a bitch, but you're probably going to have to go the distance before you do. Right now, you have the weight of all those lives on your shoulders. You'll feel better once you're on the offense."

"You bet I will." She got to her feet. "And I won't get there until I find a hook to hang him. I'd better get back to the computer. Not that I've found anything worthwhile yet. It will come." And she might have had that hook if she'd been able to talk to Nagoles. Think positive. Cameron had not actually refused her.

And she hadn't heard from Cameron since he'd run out of that cave after Nagoles. How did she know he was even alive?

She quickly rejected the thought. Cameron was alive. She wouldn't have it any other way. He was too clever, too trained in every form of combat, too much the complete warrior to be brought down.

And she somehow felt she would have known if he wasn't still on this Earth.

"I'll go check on Luke in the library, then go to my room and hit the computer to see if I can find that hook." She headed for the kitchen door. "There may be something in the files Venable sent me on Manuel Dorgal. Santos was in prison, but Dorgal was flitting around the world doing his bidding. It could be that one of those errands might be the purchase of a hideaway. It can't hurt to—" She broke off as her phone rang. She glanced down at the caller ID.

She stiffened. Hell and damnation.

T. Santos.

Shock and excitement exploded through her.

"Sam, call Venable and have him try to trace this call."

She punched the access button. "Catherine Ling. What do you want, Santos?"

"Your suffering. Your death," Santos said. "That might satisfy me. Or perhaps not, but it will have to do. Don't try to trace me, I have a protected phone and I won't be talking to you for long. I just wanted to touch base with you in case you're getting too smug. One destroyed helicopter. One inadequate fool who could not perform a simple kill is nothing in the scheme of things."

"Nagoles is dead?" Relief. Then Cameron must be alive. "Then I think it's considerably more than nothing to you that he was taken out. Things aren't going your way, Santos? What a pity. Get used to it, you son of a bitch."

"I've no intention of getting used to failure. I knew you'd cause me a few problems once you realized what I was doing. I'll work through them." His voice lowered to silky menace. "And I'll make sure your pain will only be the more intense when it's your turn."

"What a coward you are, Santos. Why not come after me directly? Are you afraid? It's easy to send your goons to kill my friends. Olena Petrov, a helpless woman in her home, Jantzen and Kirov by ambush. But it's getting a little harder now. Erin Sullivan should have been simple, but it didn't turn out that way. Why not cross any other targets off your list and let's see if you can take me down."

"Why should I do that? Because you're hurting," he said softly. "I can hear it. You're trying to mask it, but the pain is there. And that means I'm winning."

"The hell you are."

"I didn't choose those targets because they were easy. I chose them because they were your past. The woman who helped you as a child; Jantzen, your friend, who worked with you during the first years you were with the CIA; and Slantkey, who furnished you with information that set you on the path to save your son."

"What are you getting at, Santos?"

"Do you know what Delores was to me? Everything. My past, my present, my future. She was me. When you killed her, you tore my heart out."

"How dramatic."

"Bitch." He drew a harsh breath. "Go ahead, spit out your sarcasm. I'll remember every word you say. I have such ugly memories of you. You standing in my home with that gun in your hand, looking down at my Delores. After they put me in prison, I lived with that memory, and so I set out to find exactly who you were. I know more about you now than that CIA you work for. Past. Present. Future. It seemed fitting that I take those away from you, too. I divided it into phases. Past. Petrov, Jantzen, Slantkey. People whose death would cause you pain and regret but not deep sorrow." He paused. "The tip of the iceberg."

"Go on."

"The second phase—present. People who are in your life now, who've actually interacted with you in the last year or so. People whose death would bring you wrenching sorrow. Erin Sullivan was on that list." He paused. "You became very close when you rescued her in San Francisco. She went away, but you kept in communication with her. Warm, affectionate, communication. Phone calls, e-mails. I enjoyed every one of them. But there are so many others. It's really hard to choose. I know all about you and how to make everyone in your world jump through hoops. I was going to limit that phase to three, but I may have to expand it."

"You won't get the chance, you bastard."

"Third phase—future. I don't think I have to elaborate on that target, do I?"

Luke.

She didn't answer.

"He'll have to suffer excruciating pain, you know. I've been planning it in detail. You may go through as much agony as I did when you shot Delores."

"You can't convince me you felt anything for her. It's all ego with you."

"You're wrong. And every time someone dies, you'll realize how wrong. I'm sure you went over possible victims after you saw what was happening around you. There were more than you thought, weren't there? How do you decide where I'm going to strike next? It may not be who you think it will be. I have to look at all the ramifications of a kill and see if it has the effect I want. Who will it be? You'll know very soon, Catherine."

"You listen to me." She had to struggle to keep her voice steady and not show him the panic she was feeling. "I've got my people covered. You're not going to be able to touch them. And I'm not going to wait around and worry about how you're going to decide anything. I'm going after you. I'm going to punish you and everyone around you for killing my friends. And, if you even get near my son, I'll destroy you in the most painful way possible. That's your future, Santos." She hung up.

She leaned back against the wall, fighting for control.

Sam shook his head as he hung up his own phone. "Venable wasn't able to trace the call." He pulled out the kitchen chair and pushed her down. "You need a cup of coffee."

"No, I don't. I need to kill Santos."

"That can come next." He went to the coffeemaker and poured her a cup of coffee. "Nasty?" He brought her the cup. "Of course it was nasty. I heard it from your side. Did you learn anything?"

"Maybe. I've got to think about it." She took a sip of the hot coffee. "He's got this plan . . . Past. Present. Future. We're in present mode. He's going after people who are important to me that are currently in my life. That's why Erin was targeted."

"But you haven't seen Erin in months."

"Close enough for him, evidently." She rubbed her temple. "He has to have been having me followed and tapping my e-mails. He knew I'd been in communication with Erin." To whom else had she sent warm, affectionate e-mails?

Kelly Winters. Her name jumped first into Catherine's mind. Kelly was not only Luke's friend but Catherine's, and it had been natural to keep in contact with her while she was at college. Kelly and her mother had a very cool, distant relationship, and Catherine knew about loneliness. Would there be something in one of those e-mails to Kelly that would trigger a target?

"I have to go back and check any messages I've sent out to anyone within the last six months. If Santos would consider that the present." She set her cup down on the table. "I'll call Venable back and let him know Santos's plan and that Nagoles seems to be out of the picture. Then I'll call Hu Chang. I need to keep him up to date."

And she needed to talk to him and hear his voice. She knew that he was doing what was best in keeping Erin safe, but she wanted him with her. It was all very well for him to say that he could take care of himself, but it didn't keep her from being afraid for him. Hu Chang was her past, present, and, God willing, her future. He was her best friend and the one person who could banish the loneliness that was always with her. Those facts alone would make him a prime candidate for Santos's hit squad.

How do you know where I'm going to strike next?

Not Hu Chang. Please not Hu Chang.

She started to dial Venable.

Venable rang through before she made the connection. "Fill me in."

She briefly went over the conversation. "Principally threats and his grand plan. I think he wanted to make sure I knew he wasn't worried that we'd taken out Nagoles. And it must be frustrating not to be able to actually see the effect of a strike. I may be getting other calls from him if we don't pull him in right away. No way of tracing?"

"Not unless he's on the line a hell of a long time." He paused. "He said you'd hear soon about a new victim?"

"He might have been trying to scare me."

"Maybe."

There was a note in his voice that caused her to tense.

"Dammit, something's happened?"

"No, it's something that didn't happen. I checked on the agent monitoring Kelly Winter, and he said she slipped out of her morning class, and he lost her."

"Lost her? How could he lose her? She's a college student. He should know they're always on the move."

"I'm not making excuses. He knows he screwed up. He tried to phone her at the number we gave him. She didn't answer her phone."

"What about phoning Mrs. Smyth, the lady where Kelly boards? Maybe she went back home."

"We checked. She wasn't there. Kelly stayed the night with a girlfriend but left her house early this morning."

Catherine didn't like this.

Who will be next?

"Tell that agent to find her, Venable." She jumped to her feet and headed for the door. "And to stay with her. She's alone, and she doesn't even know she might be a target. Luke was playing some game with her earlier. I'll go see if he can contact her."

"I'll let you know as soon as the agent reports in." He hung up.

"Hi, Catherine." Luke looked up from his book when Catherine entered the library. He was sprawled on the couch, and she recognized the book as one of the chemistry books Hu Chang had sent him. "Sam said you were sleeping late or I would have shown you my new game. It's really cool. Even Kelly said that it was kind of a challenge. And she can be pretty snooty about—" He broke off as he saw her expression. "What's wrong? Hu Chang?"

"No, Hu Chang is fine." Naturally, that had been his first thought. Hu Chang had become almost as close to him as he was to Catherine. Mentor as well as friend. "You're not playing your game now. Why? Lose interest?"

"No." His eyes were narrowed on her face. "I lost Kelly. She'll probably check in later."

"She just dropped off the game site?"

He nodded. "You didn't answer me. What's wrong?"

She had to tell him. He'd keep at her until she did, and she couldn't lie to him. Besides, he might be able to help. "Maybe nothing. I'm worried about Kelly. When was the last time you talked to her?"

"Last night. When I called her to set up the game. I was kind of edgy and couldn't sleep. She was at some friend's house, Barbara . . . something. I was surprised. Kelly doesn't usually go out on school nights. But she said she needed a distraction." He added, "But she must be okay. She's been playing the game all morning until about thirty minutes ago. You want me to call her?"

"Please." Maybe Kelly would answer Luke. It couldn't hurt to try.

He was frowning as he dialed the number. Then he shook his head. "Her phone's turned off."

"Okay." She tried to keep her tone calm. "Keep trying, will you?"

"Why?" Then he asked, "Santos?"

"He may be widening his victim base. I should have arranged to have her brought here. Venable's agent can't locate her anywhere on campus."

"She might not be on campus," he said slowly.

"What?"

"I told you that she said she needed a distraction. When she gets upset, she usually goes hiking in the woods."

"The woods?" Lonely trails, shadows, an attacker could be behind any tree on Kelly's path. "What woods? Where?"

"I don't know. Somewhere near the campus. Once she mentioned a dam." He looked down at his phone. "But I don't like it that she turned off her cell."

"Neither do I. Why would she do that? Did she tell you why she was upset?"

"Yes." He raised his eyes to meet her own. "She said that she got something in the mail that reminded her what day it was. Not that she needed a reminder."

"What day is—" Then it hit home to her. "The day that her father was murdered while the two of them were being held by those kidnappers." Of course. Kelly handled the trauma of that day extraordinarily well for a teenager, but she had been a witness to that murder. She even blamed herself because her father had died protecting her. "What did she get in the mail?"

He shrugged. "I think it was a note. I didn't ask her anything about it. I had trouble even keeping her on the phone. I just talked about the game and your face when you were trying on that fluffy red hat. I wanted her to laugh."

"And did she?"

"Yes, she said she'd like to see it. But, like I said, she didn't stay on the line very long."

A note. What had been in that note? Who had sent it? She doubted that it came from Kelly's mother, who was too involved with her busy social life to bother to communicate with her daughter.

I know all about you and how to make everyone in your world jump through hoops.

Did Santos know that a disturbing note would cause Kelly to leave the safety of the campus, making her more vulnerable? Had he been waiting, planning to take advantage of this day?

Dear God, she was afraid he had.

"Catherine?" Luke was sitting upright on the couch. "She's in trouble?"

"I can't be sure. But she might be." She tried to think. "I have to go and make sure. You'll be safe here with Sam and the guys. I'll be back as soon as I can."

"I'm going with you."

"No!"

"Yes," Luke said. "Kelly is my friend. Maybe I should have made her talk last night. Maybe I should have told her what's happening here. It's hard to know what to do."

"I'll tell you what to do. Stay here and keep safe while I find Kelly and make sure she's safe."

He shook his head. "I can help. When we're in the woods, I might remember other stuff she's mentioned that will lead us to her." He got to his feet. "Hu Chang would let me go."

He was maddeningly correct. "Hu Chang is not me. I know you believe what you've gone through has earned you the right to be treated as an adult, and I'm trying, Luke. But this is different. We'll both be vulnerable out there while we're searching for Kelly."

He smiled. "I won't feel vulnerable. You're a very good agent, Catherine. You'll take care of me. And I'm not stupid. I'll take orders." His smile faded. "And if I don't go with you, I'll go alone. She's my friend. You know I don't have many friends. I don't understand the kids my own age, and they don't understand me. But Kelly's different."

She wasn't going to be able to talk him out of it. He'd do exactly as he'd told her he'd do. Worst-case scenario, he'd be out on the road alone. He and Kelly had both had tragedies in their lives that had shaped their friendship in the last months. Tragedy that had made Luke strong and robbed him of his childhood.

"Blackmail, Luke?"

He nodded. "It will be okay, Catherine. Let's go find her."

No choice. How to do it and keep him as safe as possible. "You do everything I say. You don't waver, down to the last syllable." She turned away. "Go get a map of the area around the university and find out where there's a dam that would be within hiking distance. Hurry."

"I'll get it for you." He was already at the bookshelves, checking for the atlas. "I'll google it once I get an overall view. Are you going to drive?"

"No, it would take too much time, and we'd be more vulnerable on the road. I'll have Venable send a helicopter to pick us up at the airport and drop us off at the campus. We'll take Sam along with us."

"To take care of me?" He frowned. "Okay. I guess you can't go all the way. I like Sam."

"Don't be swellheaded. Maybe it's to take care of me or Kelly." She was pulling her phone out of her pocket. "Change your clothes and meet me at the front door with that info."

Maybe it would be all right, she thought. Santos had reserved Luke and her for the final phase of his grand plan. He might not move on them even if the opportunity presented itself.

But "might" was a frightening word when connected with the life of her son.

And Kelly Winters might not be the next kill on Santos's list. He had said three or four would be targeted and made sure that he kept Catherine guessing. They might find Kelly in the woods just struggling to fight her sorrow and demons.

And there could be someone else on Santos's list that

he was going after while Catherine was occupied with keeping Kelly safe.

"You'll hear soon."

She couldn't wonder and worry about something that could happen. She had to go find the person who she knew was most vulnerable and without protection.

And pray that she had guessed right.

Joe, go away, dammit." Eve Duncan frowned at him across the room as she finished smoothing the clay on the reconstruction on the dais in front of her. "You don't have to be right on top of me. Go on the porch and call the precinct or something. You're practically drumming your fingers on that coffee table. I can't concentrate."

"Put up with it." He didn't look up from his computer. "Consider it the test of being a true professional. Tell that young boy whose skull you're working on that it will just take a little longer to get identified this time. What's his name, by the way?"

"Garrett." Eve always named the skulls she was given by law enforcement to sculpt an identifiable face. She might be thought the most talented forensic sculptor in the world, but it all came down to personalities as far as she was concerned. It made her feel closer, creatively and emotionally, to bond with those poor children who had been murdered or merely thrown away like so much trash. "He was found buried by the railroad tracks outside Chicago. Nine years old." She stepped back and wiped her hands on the towel beside the reconstruction. "And I don't want to slow down. I want to finish Garrett today."

"Because you want to clear the decks to go to Catherine." He looked up and shook his head. "It's not what she wants, Eve."

"No, she wants me to sit here and be safe. She put her

life on the line for me. I can't hide away now." She crossed the room to stand before him. "You know that, Joe."

"I know that I don't want you getting anywhere near Santos." He got to his feet. "He's one nasty son of a bitch. But I know I can't talk you out of it. So we'll just work our way through it." He nodded at the computer he'd laid on the coffee table. "I've been going through every record on Santos I can find. I imagine that Catherine is going to go on the offensive as soon as she thinks she's protected all the people she believes are vulnerable. Maybe we can get a little ahead of her."

And Joe would take any action possible to bring down Santos, Eve knew. He was the quintessential warrior, ex-SEAL, ex-FBI, police detective. She had first met him years ago, when he'd been working the case when her daughter, Bonnie, had been taken. They'd gone through pain and tragedy and come out on the other side with their love intact. "I bet we can." She slipped into his arms and laid her head on his shoulder. He felt so good. Strong. Gentle. Alive. Sex was always there between them, but it was wonderful that there was also comfort and love. Lord, she was lucky. "Catherine needs all the help she can get." She made a face. "Even though she won't admit it. At least to me. She's so damn independent that I want to shake her."

"No, you don't. You're just like her." He gave her a quick kiss and let her go. "You want to handle your own problems, then go out and save the world."

"Just my corner of it. Now, do I get rid of you while I'm finishing Garrett?"

"Only as far as the front porch." He headed for the front door. "I want to take a look around near the lake road anyway. I'll be within calling distance."

"What a surprise." She grinned as she turned to go back to her reconstruction. "I guess I can take that."

"Sure you can. When there's a bad storm brewing, everyone rallies around to batten down the hatches. You know I'm an expert at rallying."

"But are you rallying around Catherine or me?"

"Both. I'm excellent at multitasking." He opened the front door. "Lock the door behind me. I'll be watching, but you can't be too—" He broke off as Eve's cell phone rang.

She glanced at the caller ID. "Jane?" Jane was at her apartment in London, and Eve hadn't heard from her adopted daughter in over a week. This was a little too coincidental. She looked at Joe.

He nodded. "I called her yesterday. I was checking out the possibility of your going to stay with her until this mess was over."

"And have her rally around me, too?" Eve asked dryly.

"Why not? She's family. She wouldn't have it any other way."

"I would. Jane's only beginning to heal herself." Jane had only recently lost Trevor, the man she loved, who had been killed while trying to save Eve. He had been the love of her life from the time she was seventeen to the up-and-down passions of her young adulthood. Then, when she had totally committed herself to him, he had died to save her life. She had been totally devastated.

Eve punched the access. "Hi, Jane. No, I'm not coming to London. Joe was trying to make a preemptive strike."

"Good," Jane said. "I'm glad you're not going to London because it would be to an empty apartment. I'm calling from Hartsfield-Jackson. I should be at the cottage in about an hour."

"What?" She looked at Joe. "The airport. We were just discussing rallying around and battening down hatches, but I don't believe Joe meant for you to fly here to batten down these particular hatches."

"Then he shouldn't have told me about that slimeball who's causing Catherine and you so much trouble. You all appear to have need of a little battening." She paused before she said unevenly, "And I need to be with you, Eve. There's been too much death in my life lately. You tried to help me before, but I couldn't really accept it. But now I'm having trouble coping. I'm scared it's going to happen again. Let me come and try to put a stop to it before it begins."

"Jane."

"Okay, then let me help Catherine. I didn't really get to know her until we all teamed up to find you after you were kidnapped by that psycho. But she worked her ass off to get you back, and I loved her for it."

"So did I."

"But there was another reason I got to love her." Jane paused. "I never told you about the e-mails she sent me after Trevor was killed."

"E-mails?"

"I know, Catherine is tough and keeps most emotions buried deep. You'd expect her to let everyone else take their knocks and ride with the pain."

"Perhaps. Not necessarily."

"Well, I didn't know her that well. It's what I would have expected of her. But she knew how much I was hurting, and a few days after I'd gone back to London, I got the first e-mail. It was just a simple expression of sympathy for my loss. I thought that would be the end of it."

"It wasn't?"

"No, every day I'd get a few lines from her. Never demanding a comment or answer. Sometimes it was just to tell me what Luke was doing. Or that she'd heard from Hu Chang and Erin from that village in Tibet and what they were doing to help the villagers. A few times she shared a few memories of how she'd grown up in Hong Kong. Once she told me about a temple where she'd spent time with Hu Chang after she'd first met him and prayed for the soul of a young prostitute. She said that the priests believed the soul lived on, and she'd lit a candle to light the way. She said at the time she'd thought it couldn't hurt. No preaching. Just touching base every day to remind me that she was there, and so was the rest of the world. It made me feel . . . warm."

"Me, too." Eve swallowed. "I had no idea."

"No surprise. I'm sure she wouldn't want you to know she'd reached out to me in such a personal way."

"You wouldn't think e-mails could be that personal." Eve smiled faintly. "But I can see that it would be a medium in which Catherine would feel comfortable. She could touch without revealing her own vulnerability."

"I was feeling pretty damn vulnerable myself, and I wasn't analyzing Catherine's motives. I was just grateful. I'm still grateful, and I'm not going to let anyone hurt her or you. I'm hopping into a rental car and I'm on my way. Okay?"

"It appears it's going to have to be. Maybe Joe should come and—"

"Love you. Bye." Jane broke the connection.

Eve turned to Joe. "You shouldn't have contacted her. She has her own battles to fight. It's pretty clear she's still going through hell."

"I thought a limited involvement could be good for her. It might take her mind off Trevor's killing." He grimaced. "But I meant for us to go to her, and then I'd make a call to Scotland Yard and get protection for—"

"Since when did Jane ever know the meaning of limited?" Her gaze went to the portrait of herself that Jane had painted last year and Joe had insisted on hanging on the wall. She had sketched Eve in her blue chambray work shirt with the sleeves rolled up, her head thrown back laughing. It was a wonderful example of Jane's brilliant talent, and her agent had wanted her to show it. She'd been insistent because Jane was still a struggling artist, and she'd told her this could be a breakthrough. In spite of Eve's arguments, Jane had turned her agent down flat. Joe loved that picture. And Eve loved it, too, because Jane had caught all the joy that she brought into Eve's life. Jane had always been wary and afraid to trust because she'd bounced from foster home to foster home throughout her childhood. But when they'd come together, magic had happened.

No, love had happened.

And she thanked God she'd found Jane on the streets that day.

"You're right, I suppose," Joe said. "I should have known Jane would come running. I guess I was only thinking about you."

She felt a melting deep within her as she looked at him. She was always first with him and had been all these years. "Not only," she said softly. "As usual, you were trying to make everyone safe, everyone happy. Sometimes, we just don't cooperate with you and go our own way. It doesn't make what you do any less important . . . or less loving." She moved across the room and into his arms. "And Jane knows that you're doing what you think is right. She just has a few ideas herself on that score. We'll have to work together to blend those solutions together." She gave him a quick kiss. "She's renting a car. Could you maybe call airport security and have someone follow her here?"

"Sure." He reached for his phone. "But she should be safe. She doesn't even know Catherine that well."

"Better than we thought." She frowned. "It makes me

uneasy. Who knew that Jane would develop such an intimate long-distance connection with Catherine?"

"And did she?"

She nodded. "And all through the glories of e-mail . . ."

E-mail?" Hu Chang repeated Catherine's word with distaste. She had called him after they'd boarded the helicopter at the airport and gone over both Santos's call and the possible ramifications on Kelly Winters. "I have no liking for such technology. We've always disagreed on this. It has a tendency to cause too many problems."

"And it can be both wonderful and informative. Providing you don't have a vicious killer trying to break into your Internet mail."

"Which you do."

She tried to hold on to her patience. "I don't divulge FBI business. I don't say anything personal that I would be uneasy about revealing. How was I to know that Santos would be monitoring—" She broke off. "But I suppose that clinches your argument. I didn't know. I left myself exposed. I should cut off the e-mails."

"No, I said we disagreed. I didn't say that you should stop. Sometime, things that aren't wise can be necessary for the soul. You have trouble reaching out, and this can be a healthy outlet for you. The chances of this happening again after we dispose of Santos is minimal."

"Then I have your permission to continue?" she asked sarcastically. "How kind." Then she added wearily, "But I believe I'd be afraid of reaching out again. I'll have to think about it." She changed the subject. "Is Erin there with you yet?"

"No, she'll be arriving in about an hour." He paused. "If the arrival was not so imminent, I would be tempted to come and join you in Virginia. I do not like the idea of the way matters are sorting themselves out. I thought you'd still be at your house in Louisville when I was finished here. You may need my brilliant and invaluable assistance."

"We'll struggle along." She glanced at Sam and Luke in the rear seat. "I told you Sam is here, and so is Luke." She added dryly, "And I'm sure Luke believes he can easily replace you. He informed me that you'd have no problem letting him go find Kelly."

"Wise boy. You might have had a slight chance of getting him to not go with you if his friend had not been involved. But it was very slight. Do you have any idea where in the woods Kelly is hiking?"

"There's a trail that goes by Jefferson Dam in the woods north of the school. Luke said she mentioned a dam that she passed on her hikes, and that one is a logical distance. Six miles. There's another one to the south, but that's over twenty miles from the campus. I called the special agent at the university who is searching for Kelly and told him to grab a couple more agents and get on the trail." She paused. "But he talked to the girlfriend she spent the night with again, and she said that Kelly had left her camping gear in the garage and it was gone this morning. So she may be planning to camp out."

"If she stops for the night, you might be able to find her more easily."

"So will anyone else following her."

"True." He paused. "You're truly concerned that she might be the next target?"

"I don't know. Santos is clever, and he might have mentioned those e-mails to throw me off base or to torment me. It could be either one. And it certainly made me second-guess my list of possible targets. It could be anyone."

"And therefore increase the torment. Still, I do not like your situation. Santos is feeling angry, and his nose is out of joint by the destruction of his helicopter and the removal of Nagoles. That could mean that he feels the need to outdo his former actions to regain self-respect. I may have to make adjustments to ensure that your safety is—"

"Do not come here," she said flatly. "Take care of Erin."

"You've not had any recent word from Cameron? He might be willing to take over for me here. After all, he considers Erin his responsibility."

"I told you about my last contact with him. I wouldn't have even known that he was alive and had taken down Nagoles if I hadn't gotten that call from Santos."

"You're annoyed with Cameron."

"Yes, he's so used to working alone that he thinks it's perfectly okay to leave me in the dark."

"And the displeasure is mutual from what I gathered when he contacted me to find out what was happening with Erin and you. He also felt in the dark, and it did not go down well."

"Too bad. I didn't even know Erin was definitely in danger, and I had to move fast."

"And he did not consider that an acceptable excuse?"

"Excuse? I don't make excuses to Cameron."

"I believe it's time for me to close this conversation. If Cameron's help with Erin is not a possibility, I will explore other avenues. Your safety and that of Luke are my primary concerns. I will consider my options and get back to you." He hung up.

And Hu Chang would probably ignore her wishes and be on his way here within a few hours, she thought resignedly.

"We'll be landing in twenty minutes," Ernie Walker, their pilot, told Catherine. "I think there's a heliport for the university north of the parking garage. It shouldn't take you long to reach the woods from there. Unless you want me to circle the woods and try to—"

"The heliport will be fine. The other option could be a waste of time. I don't have any idea if there's anyplace else for you to set down."

"Whatever." He turned back to his instruments. "Venable said that I was to do anything you wanted me to do. You're looking for a young girl? Student?"

"Yes, sixteen years old."

"She must be smart to be in college."

"Yes." Smart and intuitive and pretty, everything you'd want in a friend or child. Yet she had lost her father to a murderer, and she'd never been what her mother had wanted in a daughter. In her short life, Kelly had never had the life that she deserved. But she'd made the best of it and tried to handle the fallout from the hand life had dealt her. Like this trip into the woods to distract herself. Keep busy, she would have thought. Keep the pain at bay. Don't remember the night she had watched her father die.

Catherine felt a hand grip her shoulder.

Luke's hand.

She glanced back at him. He was leaning forward and his expression . . . intent, thoughtful, gentle.

"It's going to be all right, Catherine," he said quietly. "You know that Kelly's smart, and she sees patterns and kind of feels things. That will help her. And we're smart, too. We'll find her."

She was unbearably touched. She reached up and covered his hand with her own. "You keep getting it wrong, Luke. I'm supposed to be comforting you."

"But things are piling up on you, and it's hard to see stuff." His voice was grave. "I know people die. I've seen it. I know things go wrong. But this won't be one of them. We won't let it."

"Of course we won't. But do me a favor. Don't get too much ahead of me in those woods when we're searching for her. You may not think I need to look out for you, but what about sticking close enough to look out for me?"

He chuckled. "Hey, are you trying to manipulate me, Catherine?"

"You bet I am."

"And doing a good job," Sam said, amused. "How can you refuse, Luke?"

"I can't." He took his hand away from her shoulder and leaned back in his seat. "The helicopter is beginning to go down." His dark eyes were shining with excitement. "It's all starting, isn't it, Catherine?"

"Yes." And Luke was ready to go with it, embrace the adventure, embrace the thrill of the danger. Luke was so much like her. His captivity with Rakovac had torn away any hope she would have that he would be a normal child. And if she hadn't been so concerned about both Kelly and him, she would have had the same reaction. Luke was still young enough to believe in his own immortality, and that could be fatal. "For us. I only hope it's not already started for Kelly."

CHAPTER 5

VIRGINIA

Was she being followed?

Kelly stopped on the trail and listened.

No sound behind her.

But she had heard . . . something . . . a few minutes ago.

A voice? The sound of breathing? Maybe it was only the wind in the trees.

Stop being paranoid. It's not as if she owned these woods. It could be another student, just trying to get away from the pressures of the classroom.

"Hello," she called. "Anyone there?"

No answer.

A chill went down her spine.

Because she knew someone was there.

She started walking down the trail again.

Quickly.

She reached for her phone.

Whoever was behind her could be a practical joker. Some kid who thought it would be funny to scare her. But there were always stories about students being attacked by creeps who hung out around the colleges. She'd call campus security and give them her location. She'd speak clearly and loudly, and it might scare off anyone following her. At least she'd feel less alone in this—

Her phone was dead.

She felt a bolt of panic. It couldn't be dead. Her cell had been fully charged before she'd started on her hike. She wouldn't have gone into the woods without taking the precaution.

It was dead.

And she was definitely hearing the brush moving somewhere behind her.

Okay. Smother the fear. It wasn't as if she was helpless. She had a Mace gun in her jacket pocket, and she'd had karate training last year after she'd been rescued by Catherine from those beasts who had killed her father.

I didn't expect this, Daddy. I was just so sad and wanted to get away by myself and think about you. I don't know what's happening, but I could use a little help if you have any influence where you are.

There was only one trail on this stretch of the woods. She couldn't turn and backtrack toward the college. She'd run right into the person who was following her. But after she passed the dam two miles up the trail, it split and circled. It would be a good place to lose herself in the shrubs and trees and take that other trail back to the campus.

It was getting dark, the trees casting grotesque shadows on the trail. She had meant to camp for the night when she reached the dam.

Her pace instinctively increased at the thought of how vulnerable doing that would make her.

No way.

Blood gleaming in the moonlight, seeping into the dirt of the trail.

A dark-clad body crumpled in the bushes.

Catherine's pulse stopped, then jumped with panic. In the half darkness, she couldn't tell if the body was that of a man or woman.

Kelly?

"Sam, stay with Luke. Cover me." She drew her gun as she ran toward the body several yards up the trail.

Not Kelly, she realized with relief as she drew closer. Dark hair, not fair.

But that dark hair was matted with blood. She darted into the brush beside the body and did a quick scan of the area before she came back to the trail.

"It's safe," she called to Sam. She knelt beside the blood-soaked body. "Male. Throat cut." Her hands moved inside his jacket and dark trousers. She drew out a brown leather wallet and ID and flipped it open. "Lawrence Weber. CIA. He must be the agent Venable sent after Kelly."

"Shit," Sam said as he came close. "Ambush. Poor guy."

"Yes." She put Weber's ID and wallet back in his jacket. "And whoever killed him didn't want him to find Kelly."

"Or interfere with what he wanted to do to Kelly." Sam shook his head. "How long ago?"

"Enough time for Weber to bleed out." She looked at Luke, who had come up the trail and was staring down at Weber. She had to get him away from here. It wasn't that he hadn't seen wounded and dead before while he was with Rakovac. She was the one who felt a passionate desire to protect him, keep him from ever going through that horror again. Right, she thought in self-disgust, so she had allowed herself to be railroaded into taking him here where he had every chance of doing it. She got to her feet. "Come on Luke. We've got to get moving. Sam, call Venable and tell him what happened and see if he can get the State Police out here to search the forest and find that killer."

"We can find him," Luke said quietly. He was looking down at the ground. "He'll be easy." He pointed to the pooled blood on the trail. "He walked right through that blood." He went a few paces farther. "See, he was wearing boots, and he'll leave traces of it wherever he walks."

"Yes, I see." Now she was worrying about Luke's being too callous.

Luke looked back at Weber. "He was CIA. One of the good guys. I think he'd kind of like the idea of pointing the way toward the man who did that to him, don't you?"

Not callous at all. "You may be right." She moved down the trail, the light from her flashlight picking out the bloody footprints. "And he'd also be glad that he could show us the way to find Kelly."

ATLANTA, GEORGIA

Home.

She was going home.

Jane MacGuire looked down at the clock on the dashboard of the Toyota rental car.

Fifteen minutes more, and she should be at the lake cottage, which had been home to her since Joe and Eve had adopted her when she was ten years old. As an artist, she had traveled the world, but she always came back because family was everything. But she didn't look forward to what was waiting for her at the cottage today. She had won the first battle with Eve, but that didn't mean that Eve would give up. She had always been superprotective and would try to find a way to keep Jane away from any possible danger.

But danger happened.

Death happened.

Death had happened to Trevor.

He had taught her to love and trust, then death had taken him.

Don't think of that right now. She had thought she'd worked her way through the first agonizing stages of grief in the past months. But all of a sudden it was back again, and her hands clenched on the steering wheel as she tried to push it away.

For God's sake, no more self-pity. She had come to help Eve and Catherine, and she didn't matter right now.

She took a ragged breath, and the pain was gradually fading. It would be back but maybe a little less in intensity.

"I'm trying, Trevor," she whispered. "I know you want me to go on. It's just hard sometimes. I can't find anything here for me any longer. It's all empty. I want to be with you. God, I want to be with you."

But she couldn't be with him, she had to stay alive and care for the other people she loved. "Okay, I'm over it for now." She turned on the radio and ratcheted up the volume. "How about some classic Beatles?"

It was starting to rain, and she turned on the windshield wipers.

Ten more minutes, and she'd be home with Eve and Joe.

Screeching brakes!

Startled, she glanced in the rearview mirror.

A black-and-white police car was careening over the six lanes of the freeway, the front left tire completely blown. It finally collided with a gray Lexus sedan.

Should she stop and go back and try to help?

There were several cars behind her already stopping and a pileup was just waiting to happen. The best thing to do was to probably call 911 and report the accident.

She hoped everyone was okay. What had that police

car hit that would have blown his tire like that? Joe would probably call and find out what happened and the condition of the drivers in those cars when she told him about it. She picked up her phone and began to dial 911.

Definitely not a good sign for a homecoming.

VIRGINIA

He was still following her, Kelly thought.

She hadn't lost him when she had made the circle turn at the dam and started heading back to the campus. She could still hear his footsteps in the brush behind her. She glanced over her shoulder, but he was still too far behind her for her to catch a glimpse.

If she could have seen him anyway. It was fully dark now, and she would only have been able to detect shadows.

Shadows. The whole world seemed to be full of shadows.

And why was he just keeping pace with her? Had she been right about the possibility that he was just trying to freak her out? Well, he was doing it. The darkness, the sound of him, the sheer fear of the unknown. She unconsciously moved faster.

Don't run.

That might trigger him to escalate his pace. Don't provoke any change in the pursuit. The closer she got to the university, the safer she would be.

Her hand tightened on the Mace spray.

Listen.

He either wasn't woods savvy, or he wanted her to hear him. She hoped it was the former. She had a certain amount of control as long as she could hear and judge his movements.

It was when she could no longer hear him . . .

Don't worry about that now.

Move. Walk.

Listen.

He's losing the blood from his shoes the farther he walks," Sam said. "I've only managed to pick up a trace in the last several yards." He shined his flashlight on the trail ahead. "Soon we won't be able to pick it up at all. We'll have to make a decision whether to—"

"We're almost at the dam," Catherine said curtly. "We'll have to go with the assumption that he's following Kelly and just follow the trail. It was what we thought anyway." But she had hoped that they would be able to zero in on Weber's killer long before this. It wasn't going to happen. She broke into a trot. "Forget about the blood. Just watch out for ambush and hurry like hell."

Kelly suddenly couldn't breathe.

Her heart was beating so hard it was painful.

She could still hear him, but something had changed. He was no longer directly behind her on the trail. He was somewhere to the left, in the thick brush and trees.

And he was moving faster.

She broke into a run.

For God's sake, don't fall.

The beam of her flashlight lit the trail in front of her.

Ruts. Twisted tree roots. Branches.

She dodged and darted.

Faster.

He was coming faster.

She tore off her backpack and let it drop to the trail as she ran.

He must be only yards away.

No, she could hear him breathe.

Only feet away.

A crash of rotted limbs and brush.

Keep control. Don't let him take her down.

She whirled and raised the Mace.

A blur of a long face, short brown hair, blue jacket.

And a long, curved knife in his hand!

She pressed down on the nozzle and shot him directly in the face with the Mace.

He screamed.

"Whore. I'll kill—"

Then he was blundering blindly forward, almost on top of her.

She dodged the knife he was swinging wildly.

She sprayed him again.

But the tip of his knife sliced the flesh of her upper arm.

Pain.

His weight was heavy as he brought her down, straddling her.

Spray him again.

Spray him again.

She struggled to get her hand with the Mace from beneath his body.

So heavy . . .

She lifted her knee and caught him in the groin.

He grunted, cursing, but he was half off her, and she could at least move her arm.

But his knife was coming down—

"Roll to the side. Now!"

What?

It wasn't the same voice as the one that had been cursing her.

But she realized the weight was almost completely off her now. She instinctively moved, rolled, as she had been ordered.

And saw the leather garrote that was wound around the

throat of the man who had attacked her. His hand was struggling, tearing desperately at the garrote. His other hand trying to pull a gun out of his jacket pocket.

And she saw another man in a black leather jacket who was standing behind him and twisting the garrote.

As she watched, the next instant, the garrote did its work.

Her attacker's neck snapped.

The man who had killed him turned toward her.

She instinctively, frantically, lifted her Mace.

"No!" he said. He held out his hands, palms up. "I'm not going to hurt you, Kelly."

"I don't know that." She scrambled backward. "I don't know who you are. I don't know anything. Stay away from me."

"Just put down that Mace and we'll be fine," he said quietly. "I have no intention of letting you spray that stuff in my face. But I don't want to do anything that would alarm you. Catherine wouldn't like it." He grimaced. "And we're already at odds at the moment."

She went still. "Catherine?"

"Catherine Ling. She's on her way to you right now. I just came in by the road north of the dam and got here first."

"You could be lying. How do I know who you—"

"Of course you don't know who I am." He inclined his head. "I'm Richard Cameron. Perhaps your friend Luke might have mentioned me?"

"Cameron?" She repeated. "Luke did tell me about you after he and Catherine came back from Tibet. He thinks you're cool." She moistened her lips. "But he's a lot like Catherine. He believes that if you have good reason, it's okay to—" She looked at the body slumped over on the trail, and finished—"do that."

"I had a very good reason tonight."

"Yeah, I guess so." Her grip tightened on the Mace. "But I don't know that for sure. What Luke believes might not be what I believe."

"True. But the fact that I saved your life should have some weight. Give me that Mace, Kelly. Don't make me take it."

"I think I'll just hold on to it for a while until I—"

He moved.

Lightning fast.

She had never seen anyone move that fast.

Two paces forward.

His foot struck the Mace and sent it spinning toward the side of the trail.

She lunged toward it.

But he was behind her, his arm holding her still. Strong. Dear God, he was strong. She couldn't move, and her helplessness was filling her with panic.

She struggled wildly. "Let me go."

"Just be quiet and listen. You don't need—"

Her elbow went back and struck him in the stomach. "Let me go, dammit."

"Yes, let her go, Cameron."

Catherine!

Kelly stopped struggling as she saw Catherine coming down the trail with a gun pointed at Cameron. Relief surged through her. "He said you were coming. I didn't know if I could trust him."

"I often have the same problem," Catherine said dryly. "What are you doing here, Cameron?"

"Dodging that spray of Mace at the moment." He released Kelly and stepped back. "Before that, I was trying to keep her from getting a knife in her heart. Stop being protective and put down that gun. Ask her."

Kelly ran into Catherine's arms. "I was so scared," she whispered. "I didn't know what was happening." She looked down at the man on the ground. "Why would he want to hurt me? Is he one of those serial killers or something?"

"No." Catherine's arms tightened around her. "You're safe. No one can hurt you now." She gave her a hug, then released her. "But we should get out of these woods. We didn't see anyone else tracking you, but there will be State Police combing this area, and I don't want to have to answer a lot of questions."

"Are they looking for me?"

"Yes." She glanced at the man on the ground. "And for him. He killed a CIA agent with that knife."

"What?"

"Luke will tell you." She glanced down the trail. "Here he comes now, with Sam. I ran ahead when I saw you—" She waved. "She's okay, Luke."

"I told you she would be," Luke said. He frowned. "But it was really dumb of you to turn off your phone, Kelly. Everything would have been simple if you hadn't done that."

"I didn't turn off my phone. It just went dead. And who are you to call me dumb?" She came toward him. Dear heaven, she was glad to see him. Catherine had always been the savior in her eyes, but Luke was her friend and had cared enough to come looking for her. Even those insults were welcome because they were part of their relationship and far away from the horror she had just experienced. "You're pretty stupid yourself to go trekking through these woods after me. If you'd caught up with that man who was chasing after me, I would probably have had to rescue you."

Luke made a rude noise. "No way. You should have—"

She interrupted. "And I just met your friend, Cameron, and he almost broke my ribs. Shows you what a good judge of character you are." She added, "Catherine says you should tell me what all this means. So stop being rude and tell me."

"Hu Chang would say you have no gratitude or appreciation." He was silent a moment before he said gruffly, "I'm glad nobody cut your throat, Kelly."

"Me, too." She smiled. "Now talk to me."

It would be all right, Catherine thought with relief as her gaze shifted away from Kelly and Luke. Luke would not treat Kelly as a victim and that would keep her from thinking of herself as one. It was the best thing for Kelly right now.

"I don't appreciate your pointing that gun at me," Cameron said softly. "It hurt my feelings."

"Bullshit." She shot him a glance as she fell to her knees beside the man Cameron had garroted. Dressed in jeans and black leather jacket, Cameron was every bit as powerful and sexual as she remembered. And his expression was just as mocking and challenging. "I didn't know it was you when I came down that trail. And, if I had known, I would still have pointed it at you when I saw that you were holding Kelly helpless. How did I know what you were doing?" She was searching through the pockets of the dead man. "What are you doing here anyway? For all I knew, you were still in Tibet."

"I was finished with what I had to do there. I flew out almost immediately. I was already only minutes from landing in Louisville when Hu Chang contacted me and told me you were on your way here. So I just picked up a helicopter and extended my flight plan a little."

"And you didn't think to let me know what had happened or if you'd found out anything from Nagoles that I—"

"I was planning on telling you eventually." He knelt beside her as she flipped open the wallet she'd taken out of the man's jacket. "Who is he? He was definitely not Grade-A material."

"He didn't have to be," she said harshly. "He only had to kill a sixteen-year-old girl." She glanced at the driver's license. "Raymond Shaw. Issued in Richmond, Virginia. Local boy. Probably not one of Santos's regular goons. That might have some significance."

"And that is?"

"I don't know." She looked through the rest of Shaw's pockets and pulled out only a Shell gas receipt and a phone. "We'll check the phone records, but it's a disposable pay phone. It probably won't help us." She held up a small device. "And this is a signal blocker that he probably used to take out Kelly's phone. Nothing else."

"He had a gun. He tried to draw it when I was disposing of him. He would have been smarter to shoot Kelly than to try to use that knife. He could have picked her off from behind those trees." He shook his head. "But some killers just like the thrill of the cut. Santos would have been displeased at his self-indulgence."

"Maybe he ordered it. It would have made her death all the more ghastly for me." She sat back on her heels and said jerkily, "And that's what he wants. Pain. Shock. Terror."

"He didn't get it this time." He put his hand on her shoulder. "Your Kelly is alive and well." He smiled. "And amazingly ferocious for such a fragile-looking young girl. I didn't want to hurt her, but I might have had to put her out if you hadn't come along."

Cameron's hand on her shoulder was warm and comforting. Strange. "Comforting" was the last word she would have applied to Cameron. When he touched her, it was always sheer erotic combustion.

"Evidently there's a time and a place. I find it strange too."

"Get out of my head, Cameron. You promised me."

"It was only a temporary fall from grace. I was concerned, and it caught me off balance. I had to make sure that you were safe when I reached the woods."

"Get out of my head," she repeated. She stood up. "I have to get Kelly out of here. She's been through too much."

"Are you taking her back to the campus?"

"Hell, no. I'm taking her home with me, where I can keep an eye on her. Just because we were able to save her this time is no guarantee that Santos won't send someone else."

"I have a helicopter parked at the heliport north of the dam. It will be closer than for you to go back to the university."

She nodded. "And I won't run into the State Police. I'll call Venable and tell him Kelly's safe, and I'm going home with you."

He smiled. "Oh, that will please him. I've been sensing a certain antagonism in his actions toward me lately."

"You can hardly blame him."

"I never blame anyone who plays fair. It just makes the game more interesting. When Venable begins to show his fangs, I'll rethink and adjust."

"And go after him?"

He didn't answer. "It shouldn't take us long to get to the helicopter." He turned and moved toward Kelly, Luke, and Sam. "Coming?"

ATLANTA, GEORGIA

It was raining harder.

Jane could barely see more than a few yards ahead of her.

The windshield wipers on the Toyota were having to

work overtime as she got off the freeway and turned onto the gravel road leading to the lake cottage.

Just go slow and don't slide off into that ditch already overflowing with water, she told herself.

And it would have been easier if that car behind her wasn't hugging her bumper and didn't have his bright lights on. That brilliant beam reflected in her rearview mirror was blinding.

Just concentrate on the road.

Only a few miles more.

But, dammit, turn off those high beams.

VIRGINIA

Catherine turned around as soon as they were airborne to look at Kelly in the back with Luke and Sam. "Okay? We'll be home soon, Kelly."

Kelly nodded. "It all seems like a bad dream or one of those screamer movies. It doesn't seem real."

"It was real enough," Luke said. "Why did you go tearing off like that? You said something about a note. What did it say?"

"Just a couple words. With deepest regret. And a photo from a newspaper with the story about how Daddy was killed."

"No signature? Postmark?" Catherine asked.

"No signature. Local postmark. I thought it was maybe a student in one of my classes."

"Do you still have it?"

"Sure, it's in my backpack. I dropped the backpack on the trail. But I picked it up on our way to the copter. Will it help if I show it to you?"

"It could. I'll check it out when we get home."

"Look, I should go back to school. I'll be missing classes. I'm working on a project that—"

"No," Catherine said firmly. "I'll make sure you're excused, and your project can wait."

Kelly nodded wearily. "I guess that's okay. It will have to be." Suddenly, her lips tilted with sly amusement. "After all, I have to take care of Luke. He's just a kid."

"Who wasn't the one who caused us all this bother," Luke said. "Running around the woods. Talk about being—"

"Break it up," Sam said. "It's amazing that the two of you can be so mature alone and like this when you're together."

Truly amazing. And very healthy, Catherine thought as she turned back around in her seat. She looked at Cameron. "So tell me about Nagoles. Santos said he'd disappeared, but he didn't know at the time if he'd crashed in the helicopter."

"He did not. You wanted me to question him."

"But you wouldn't promise me to do it."

"You should have known that I would."

"Why? You were angry with me."

"I still am, but that doesn't alter the fact that I'm involved."

"Did Nagoles talk?"

"Eventually. Not that he knew a great deal. He'd worked for Santos a number of times before, but he generally dealt through Dorgal." He paused. "He was the one who killed Olena Petrov, but Santos hired someone else to take down Jantzen and Slantkey. Santos wanted Nagoles available to do the Erin kill."

"All very efficient and well planned," Catherine said bitterly.

"Why not? He's had a long time to think about it." He shook his head. "And Nagoles didn't know where Santos is now. He was to pick up his money in Hong Kong. That was all I could get out of him about anything connected to you. Though I did ask him specifically about any jobs he did for Santos while he was in prison that struck him as unusual."

"And were there?"

"Only one. He was contracted to kill some doctor in Guatemala. A Dr. Jorge Montez. An example killing. Very bloody."

"And not that unusual for Santos. He's been known to dangle the heads of his enemies off the bridges of their home cities."

"But it seems Jorge Montez had a brother who was also a doctor. Eduardo Montez. Nagoles was given orders that on no account was he to harm Eduardo."

"No reason?"

"Nagoles just obeyed orders and asked no questions. It was safer for him."

"I can see that. Nothing else?"

He shook his head. "Nothing."

"I wish I'd been there to question him."

"Do you really think you'd have gotten more out of him than I did?" His eyes were glacier cold. "I'm not an amateur. You'll have to be satisfied. I was not about to let him live one more minute than I had to after what he did to Erin."

No, Cameron could be more ruthless than she could ever be. She was just frustrated that he'd not been able find out more. "Where is Nagoles? Santos said he just disappeared."

"They'll find him in a cave in the rocks if they look hard enough." He reached into his jacket and pulled something out of his pocket. "It was difficult for me to finish questioning him after I found this little trifle on him." He dropped it into her palm. "It made me exceedingly angry."

A gold dog tag with her name engraved on it.

Her lips twisted. "Santos's signature for all of his targets. He must have meant it for Erin. Very elaborate planning, even down to this macabre piece of jewelry."

"Son of a bitch."

"You *are* angry." She looked at him curiously. "Why?"

"It bothers me. I don't like anyone using you, dirtying you like that."

"Neither do I." She shrugged. "But as I said, it's just something he does with every target and—" She stopped. "Oh, my God."

"What?"

"*Every* target. He does it with every chosen target." She moistened her lips. "But there wasn't one of those dog tags in the pocket of that killer, Shaw, who went after Kelly. I was very thorough searching him, but there was no dog tag. Why with all the other people Santos targeted and not Kelly?"

His eyes were narrowed on her face. "I think you're about to tell me."

"Because she wasn't the principal target." She shook her head. "My God, she was only meant to be a distraction. Maybe someone to keep me occupied while he went after the designated target. Santos said to guess who was next on his list. I guessed wrong."

"Easy. Perhaps not. There's no doubt Shaw meant to kill Kelly. It could be that he screwed up about leaving the dog tag. I told you he wasn't Grade-A material."

"And why would Santos have someone who wasn't absolutely expert to do the job? That's not Santos. Maybe because Kelly was a last-minute addition to his plan. And Shaw used a knife, not a gun. You even said that wasn't as smart." She was going down the list, and it was leading her where she didn't want to go. "And Kelly said he trailed her for a long time in those woods. He wasn't in a hurry. He had to be stalling. Waiting for word to take her out."

"And you believe he got it."

"I think that he was told to get rid of her because they'd managed to make the target kill. I wouldn't be able to stop it."

"Who?"

"I don't know." She tried to steady her voice. "I tried to make everyone safe. Hu Chang is with Erin. Joe is taking care of Eve. But Santos is finding other targets. He's not just going after the ones I thought he'd kill. He told me that I could never be sure." She reached for her phone. "Maybe he's found a way to get to Erin or Eve. Or Hu Chang. I always think that no one can touch Hu Chang, but maybe Santos found a way."

"I doubt it. I've found that he's pretty well bulletproof. Who are you calling?"

"Everyone. I have to make sure that they're all safe. That maybe I'm wrong. God, I hope I'm wrong." She dialed quickly. "I'll start with Eve."

The car crashed into Jane's Toyota from behind!

Her head snapped back from the whiplash impact.

Crazy. That driver had to be crazy. It had to be deliberate. The road was treacherous from the rain, but that impact had intent behind it.

Crash!

He'd done it again.

Her Toyota skittered across the gravel, and she was barely able to keep it on the road.

Again!

And the driver of the car who hit her was drawing beside her on the road. Metal scraped against metal as his passenger door screeched against her car.

Jane struggled desperately to keep the Toyota on the road, but she was being pushed toward the ditch.

"Idiot!"

But he had to be more than just stupid. Deadly. She could see the driver only dimly through the pouring rain, but she recognized the body language. Tense, intent, every muscle aimed at what he was doing.

And what he was doing was shoving her into that ditch.

He crashed against the side of her car again.

And the Toyota went out of control, and she headed for the ditch.

She went off the road and into the water in the ditch.

Her head hit the steering wheel.

Pain. Dizziness.

The air bag deployed, whipping her back in the seat.

More pain.

Her horn was blowing. She must have hit that, too, she thought dimly.

Her driver's door was opening.

She dazedly raised her head.

Someone in a brown jacket was standing in the road, the rain pouring off him.

He was smiling.

And he had a Luger pistol in his hand.

She instinctively tried to reach over, to grab her handbag, and throw it at him.

The air bag got in the way, and the handbag fell to the mud of the ditch.

The gun fired, exploded.

Agony.

Her chest . . .

He was throwing something at her. Something gold . . . a chain . . .

It didn't matter.

Nothing mattered.

The pain was going away. The rain was going away. Everything was going away but the warm, golden light that was suddenly surrounding her.

And beyond that light was Trevor. Tall, strong, his blue eyes shining and full of love.

He was shaking his head, but she didn't care. She could see the love, feel the everafter that was there for them.

"It's okay, Trevor." She was running toward him. "Do you hear me? It wasn't my fault. I would have lived. I would have done what you wanted me to do. But this just happened. I couldn't help it." She was getting closer, and the golden light was around her, in her. Soon she'd be in his arms. "So you must be wrong. It must be okay that we're going to be together . . ."

CHAPTER 6

I'm fine, Catherine," Eve said. "So is Joe. He's right here." She was trying to be soothing since Catherine was obviously upset. But her own heart had plummeted when Catherine had rattled out that frightening suspicion about Santos's intentions.

"Jane." Joe was at Eve's elbow. "Jane's not here. She should be home by now."

"Call her." She said to Catherine, "I've got to go. Jane was driving here from the airport. We have to check on her."

"Jane . . ." Catherine repeated. "God, yes. Make sure she's safe." She hung up.

"No answer, Eve," Joe said as he hung up his phone.

"Call that policeman who was supposed to be following her." Eve was already shrugging into her rain anorak as she headed for the door. "We've got to go look for her."

"It's raining." He was following her down the porch steps. "It could have slowed her down. Maybe traffic . . ."

"I've been telling myself the same thing," she said jerkily as she jumped into the Jeep. "But I'm scared, Joe."

"So am I." He hung up the phone. "Particularly since I can't rouse that security black-and-white that should have been following her. That's damn strange. I'd call the precinct but . . . that can wait."

And Jane might not be able to wait, Eve thought as she tore down the gravel road toward the freeway.

Not if Catherine was right.

Not if that bastard had decided to target Jane.

God, she wished this rain would stop. She could hardly see anything ahead of her.

No, that wasn't true. She could see bright headlights ahead.

But not on the road.

The car was in a ditch, but the headlights were still blazing.

"Dear God," she whispered. She stomped on the accelerator, and the Jeep jumped forward. They were stopping beside the Toyota in the ditch in seconds.

"The driver's door is open," Joe said. "But I don't see the driver." He jumped out of the Jeep and ran toward the Toyota. "Maybe the driver got out and is looking for help. It's a poss—" He broke off as he reached the car. "No, she didn't get out."

Eve was beside him, looking at Jane pinned back against the seat by the air bag. Blood. Her chest was covered with blood. "Oh, baby." She knelt beside the driver's seat, tears pouring down her cheeks. "Jane . . ."

Joe had taken his pocketknife and deflated the air bag. He was examining the wound, trying desperately to find a way to stem the blood. "Shot in the chest, close range."

"Dead?" Eve asked unevenly. "Is she dead? Are we too late?"

"She's still alive," Joe said. His eyes were glittering with moisture. "But I won't lie to you. I don't think she's going to make it. She's dying, Eve."

Shock. Followed by overwhelming sorrow. She reached

out and touched Jane's hair. Then denial came, hard, fast, rejecting those words. "If she's not dead yet, we have a chance. I'm not going to let her die. I'll hold on to her until the last minute. You stop the blood. I'll call 911."

He nodded. "Yeah, you bet we'll give her a chance." He reached out and gently touched the curve of Jane's lips. "What the hell? I think she's . . . smiling."

LOUISVILLE, KENTUCKY

"I have to call Eve back," Catherine said as she got out of the car in front of her house after driving from the airport. "I've been trying to leave her alone. I didn't want to get in her way when she was trying to find Jane." She watched Luke, Sam, and Kelly go into the house before she turned to Cameron. "And I'm nervous as hell about what she's going to find. What she's already found. Eve wouldn't keep me waiting without knowing anything if there wasn't a reason."

"Then call her and stop fretting about it," Cameron said. "From what you've told me, Eve is too responsible not to keep everyone informed."

"I don't need your permission. I told you I was going to do it." Catherine was already dialing. The phone rang four times before it was picked up. "Catherine, Eve."

"I meant to call you," Eve's voice was unbearably weary. "Sorry. I've just been busy. Things are . . . bad."

"Jane?"

Silence. "We think she's dying. Shot in the chest."

"Oh, my God."

"They got the bullet out, but there are all kinds of vein and arterial damage that can't be repaired. She's in a coma." Her voice broke. "The doctors say that she won't wake up."

Catherine's hand clenched on the phone as waves of

pain washed over her. She seemed to be feeling Eve's pain as well as her own. "Specialists?"

"We're bringing in one from Houston. It might not help." She cleared her throat. "But then it might. I can't stop hoping, can I?"

"No. Look, I'm coming down there to be with you. What hospital?"

"St. Joseph's. But I have Joe, Catherine."

"And he's probably all you need. But I need to be with you right now. I need to be with Jane." Her voice was unsteady. "For God's sake, she may be dying because of me."

"Not because of you. Because of Santos." She paused. "But it will be good to see you. I'm kind of ragged, and Joe is feeling torn about whether to help Jane or me. He'll be glad to have someone around to strike a balance. Get some rest and come tomorrow morning. That will be soon enough." She stopped and had to compose herself before she could continue. "The doctors think she may linger for anywhere from a week to ten days."

"Okay, whatever you say. Tomorrow. God, I'm sorry, Eve."

"I know you are. Good-bye, Catherine." She hung up.

Catherine could feel the tears brimming as the waves of sorrow and regret overwhelmed her.

"Jane?" Cameron asked quietly. "Dead?"

"Not yet. Soon." She wiped her eyes. "Shot in the chest."

"If she's not dead, there's still hope."

"That's what Eve said, but she's having trouble believing it. I'm going down to Atlanta to see her at the hospital tomorrow morning." Hold on. Keep the pain at bay. Don't think of Jane in that sleep that would probably last forever. She started for the front door. "Now I have to make sure that Luke and Kelly are settling for the night and that Sam has told security to put Kelly under their protection."

"I'd bet that your Sam has already done it." Cameron followed her into the foyer. "You can't be responsible for everything, Catherine."

"Yes, I can. I'll accept responsibility for the whole world if it keeps the odds down that there won't be another death Santos tosses at my door." Her lips twisted. "You know about that kind of burden. You shoulder all kinds of responsibility your precious committee throws at you. After all, you're the Guardian." She turned to look at him. "But I suppose I should thank you for killing Shaw and saving Kelly. I might not have been there in time."

"And then again, you might. Kelly was putting up a good fight." He reached out and touched her hair. "But I'm still a little annoyed that you pointed that gun at me. You know me well enough to know I wasn't going to hurt her."

"I couldn't take a chance. You're always a surprise, Cameron." His touch on her hair was gossamer light, but it still sent a ripple of heat down her cheek and throat. She moved her head and took a step back. Ridiculous. It had to be a purely automatic response to him because at this moment she was hurting, and sex was the last thing on her mind.

"I'm having the same problem," Cameron was looking directly in her eyes. "I'm trying to be sympathetic and helpful, but the sex keeps getting in the way. It may always be that way. We'll have to work on it."

"No, we won't." She turned and went toward the stairs. "Because you don't even have to be around me. I can handle Santos." She started up the stairs. "Go and take care of Erin."

"You're dismissing me?" He shook his head. "I can't accept that, Catherine. Erin will always be important. But

I find I'm feeling very angry toward Santos . . . and possessive toward you."

"Possessive?" She looked over her shoulder. "The hell you are. I told you when you left me that wasn't going to happen. I'll never be your mistress, waiting for you to come back from trying to—"

"It doesn't matter," Cameron interrupted. "That can be settled later. Right now, the possession is centered on keeping you alive so that I'll have another chance." He headed toward the door. "Now I'll go and make sure I approve of Sam's security arrangements. I may have to bring some of my own men here."

"Sam is perfectly capable of choosing good men. I trust him."

"Does Hu Chang?"

"Of course."

"You hesitated for a second. Hu Chang and I think alike on most subjects. I'll do that check." He looked up at where she was standing on the stairs. "Make up your mind. You won't get rid of me until I want to go. And that won't be until Santos is dead. It will be easier for you if we cooperate. It would help to keep me from getting in your way."

"You won't get in my way. I won't let you."

He shrugged. "What will be, will be." He paused. "Expect a call from Santos. He'll think he's won this round and want to jab. It would have been total victory if Shaw had managed to kill Kelly, but Jane was evidently the prime target."

"And she's dying," Catherine said hoarsely. "Yes, he'd consider that a win."

"You're hurting." He frowned. "I don't like the idea of your being alone. Let me stay with you."

"I don't need you. And I'm not alone."

"No, you have a whole world of people who lean on you. Just once, lean on someone else."

"You?"

"Why not?" He shook his head. "What am I thinking? That's not going to happen." He opened the front door. "I'll leave the offer on the table. Anytime, Catherine."

She watched the door shut behind him.

Anytime.

She was too tired and upset to make sense of those surprising words. She started back up the stairs.

Stop at Kelly's room and see if she needed her.

Check on Luke and make sure he was okay after all he'd gone through in those woods tonight.

They were so young. Young and tough and thinking they could conquer the world. Yet there might be some kind of aftereffect for both of them. Maybe they would need to talk.

And she would have to tell them what had happened to Jane.

Another shock to add to all the others assaulting them.

Then she would go to her room and think about Jane and Eve.

And let the hurt overcome the control that she was struggling so desperately to hold in place. She'd stop being strong for just an hour or a night and release the sadness that was tearing at her.

See, I don't need you, Cameron. I can handle it . . .

She knocked softly. "Kelly? May I come in?"

"Sure. I was expecting you." Kelly smiled wearily at Catherine as she opened the door. She was sitting cross-legged on the bed, wearing one of Catherine's sleep shirts. Her blond hair was tied up in a ponytail, and she looked scrubbed and shiny and very young and vulnerable. "I knew you'd be worried about me. I'm okay, Catherine. I'm a little shaky, and I don't promise I won't have nightmares, but I'll get through it. I think Luke's okay, too."

"I just checked on him, and he seems fine. But then, Luke developed a lot of calluses while he was with Rakovac." She sat down in the easy chair beside the bed. "And I don't think you've ever managed to do that."

"No." She made a face. "But that's a lot your fault. You showed me that no matter how ugly it can be out there, there might be a Catherine to make it right again. Like tonight."

"I almost got you killed. I should have made you come here right away. But you were so excited about your work, and I wasn't sure that you'd be targeted." She shook her head. "Excuses. I made a bad call." She reached out and touched Kelly's hand. "Santos is so damned clever. He even used your father's death to make you more vulnerable. I'm sorry he made you go through that, too, Kelly."

"Did you think I wouldn't have remembered anyway?" Kelly swallowed. "Dad's always with me. That night they killed him is always with me. And all the therapists they ran me through didn't do a damn thing to change that."

"I know."

She nodded. "You always know. From the moment you took me out of that camp in the jungle and saved my neck, I knew that no one else would ever really understand. That's why I've always clung to you whether you liked it or not."

"I liked it." Her hand tightened on Kelly's. "I care about you."

"Sure. Why not? I'm one cool kid." Her smile faded. "These times when I come here to be with you and Luke make me feel like I have a real family. I can't lose that, Catherine. I can't lose you. You're so worried about me? What about you? Look, I can't just sit here and twiddle my thumbs and play games with Luke. I can't let this Santos scumbag kill you while I'm hiding out here. I've got to *do* something."

"You have your project at school. You can be working on it here."

"To hell with my project. You know what I mean."

"Yes, I do. I don't want to involve you, Kelly."

"Involve me, or I'll involve myself. I helped you find out where Rakovac was holding Luke, didn't I? I don't know if I can find Santos for you, but I can try." Her voice was suddenly urgent. "You know I don't have a clue why my brain seems to be able to see patterns in puzzles when no one else can. I never wanted it, but it's there. So let's see if Santos has a pattern that we can trace."

"Kelly . . ."

"Let me try." Her eyes held Catherine's. "Please, Catherine. I felt helpless in that forest tonight. I *won't* feel helpless about you. I need this."

Catherine nodded slowly. "Okay. Information only. That's as far as you get involved. What do you need to have to form a pattern?"

"Everything about Santos and everyone close to him. Venable should be able to get it for you, right? Surveillance reports. Background. Emotional affiliations. Anything unusual. Anything that's common practice for him." She shrugged. "Everything."

"I'll call Venable and have him send it out to Sam. It's a lot of information to go through, Kelly."

"I'll have Luke help me go through it and feed me facts. He's smart and fast, and he needs to be kept busy, too."

"You can say that again," Catherine said dryly.

"You can't blame him. He's a little confused about being thought of as a kid when all his instincts are telling him to protect you." She smiled faintly. "I understand those instincts."

"Me, too. But it doesn't make the situation any easier." She paused, then forced herself to go on. "You weren't the only one in danger tonight. Jane MacGuire, Eve's adopted daughter, was critically shot at the lake house in Atlanta. They don't know whether she's going to live."

"No," Kelly whispered. "Santos?"

Catherine nodded. "We think she was the main target. Evidently, you were to be a bonus."

She shivered. "Should I be insulted? Lord, I'm so sorry. Poor Jane. Eve must be going crazy."

"Yes, and frantically trying to find a way to save Jane. I'm going to see her in the morning."

"Do you want me to go with you?"

"No, I don't know what I'm going to face. Stay here."

"I'll do whatever is best for you. And for Eve."

"Thanks, Kelly." She got to her feet and leaned forward to brush a kiss on Kelly's forehead. "You're sure you don't need to talk about what happened tonight?"

"No, I'm good. Well, not good, but I can handle it." She watched Catherine walk toward the door. "You're going to leave us, aren't you?"

Catherine looked at her in surprise. "I told you I was going to the hospital in Atlanta."

"No, I mean afterward. You're not going to stay with us."

"I didn't say that."

"No, but you said that you'd have Venable send the information to Sam. Why would you do that if you were going to be here to receive it and give it to me?" She tilted her head. "And besides, your character pattern is to be aggressive and go for the jugular. As long as we were safe, you'd start working on carrying the battle into Santos's camp."

"Very perceptive," Catherine said ruefully. "Providing I can find a way to do that. First, I have to know where the hell Santos's new headquarters is located."

"I'll see what I can do to help." Kelly got into bed and

pulled the covers up around her. "But I have to study his patterns . . ."

"Let's hope his character is as transparent to you as you find mine." She opened the door. "Good night, Kelly."

"Good night." She turned off the bedside lamp, and her voice came out of the darkness. "And there's nothing transparent about you, Catherine. It's kind of easy to see the patterns in the people you love." She thought about it. "It's as if they're written on your heart."

"I can see that. But even then, the writing is more clear to you than most." She paused. "And have I ever told you that I love you, too, Kelly Winters?"

"I don't think so. Not the word 'love.' But that's hard for you. And it doesn't matter. From the beginning, I knew that Luke was your whole world. But I also knew if I worked at it long enough, you'd come around." She chuckled. "What's not to love?"

"What, indeed?" Catherine closed the door behind her.

Strange. She had gone into that room to comfort Kelly and come out with a warm sense of inner comfort herself. A little of the horror of Jane's attack had dispersed by sharing it with Kelly.

Along with a renewed anger at Santos and a gratitude that Kelly had come into her life that horrible night in the Colombian jungle.

Her last words came back to her. No, there was nothing that wasn't worthy of loving in Kelly.

And nothing that was not worthy of protecting from that bastard, Santos.

ST. JOSEPH'S HOSPITAL
ATLANTA, GEORGIA

"Hello, Catherine." Eve got to her feet as Catherine came into the waiting room. "Thanks for coming."

"Are you crazy? Where else would I be?" Catherine gave her a hug. "You look terrible. Did you sleep at all?"

"No. Joe and I are taking turns staying with Jane in ICU." She went to the coffee machine and got a cup of coffee. "We don't want to leave her."

"Is she any better?"

Eve shook her head. "But we expect the specialist later today. Maybe he'll be able to suggest something, anything." She sat back down and took a sip of coffee. "I've been sitting here thinking about Jane. So many years, so many special minutes. She was always more my best friend than a daughter. She grew up in foster homes and on the streets until we came together when she was ten." She shook her head. "Ten going on thirty. That was why she was so wary about relationships. It was hard for her to trust."

"She trusted you. She loved you, Eve."

"Yes, but she didn't let herself trust anyone else. Not until Mark Trevor. It almost destroyed her when he was killed. I don't think she wanted to live after he died." She drew a shaky breath. "I felt so helpless. I didn't know what to do."

"Neither did I." Catherine sat down and took Eve's hand. "And I should have done nothing. I liked her, and I wanted to help." She paused. "She told you about the e-mails?"

"Yes, it was kind, Catherine."

"It was stupid. Jane might not have even been on Santos's radar except for those damn e-mails."

"You couldn't know."

"That's what I told myself, but it doesn't help. I don't see how it could help for you, either. Santos couldn't get at you, so he took Jane."

Eve's lips twisted. "So I'm supposed to hate you?"

"God, I hope not."

"Even if that wasn't completely unfair, Jane was grateful to you for your kindness. That made me grateful to you." Her expression hardened. "But, oh yes, I'm full of hatred. I saw her lying in that car bleeding, and the hatred was there. I look at her dying in that ICU, and I want to kill." Her hand tightened on Catherine's. "But it's Santos I want to kill."

"I'll get him, Eve. I promise you."

"Yes, you will." She looked her in the eye. "Because I can't go after him, and neither can Joe. We have to be here for Jane. We have to try to find some way to keep her alive." She swallowed. "And if we can't, we want to be with her as long as we can. But Santos isn't going to get away with doing this. You're going to find him, you're going to kill him." She reached in her pocket and drew out the gold dog tag. "There's still blood on it. Jane's blood." She lifted Catherine's hand and put the chain into her palm. "When you kill him, you're going to give him his damn chain back and tell him where it came from. Do you understand?"

"Yes." Her hand closed tightly on the chain. "I'll do whatever you wish. I won't fail you, Eve."

"I never thought I'd ask anyone to kill," she said unevenly. "All my life, I've tried to fight those monsters who kill children and just throw them away. But Santos has to pay for what he did. I can't take a chance on his disappearing before I'm able to leave my Jane."

She meant before she lost Jane MacGuire, the child she had chosen, the woman who had become her best friend.

Catherine nodded. "I'll find him. And I won't let him disappear."

"Good. Thank you. Now I've got to go trade places with Joe." She gave her a quick hug and rose to her feet. "Why are you still here? Get going. I don't need you here. You know what you have to do."

"I want to see Jane."

Eve shook her head. "Relatives only in ICU. I'll tell her you were here. They say that some people in comas understand. I've been talking to her since they brought her out of surgery." She threw her empty coffee cup in the trash. "Reminding, pleading, challenging. You name it."

"Then tell her I'm sorry."

"And, if she could, she'd tell you what I did. But I'll tell her." She added grimly, "I'll also tell her that you made me a promise. She knows you keep your word."

"Yes, I do." Her gaze went to the door that led to ICU down the hall. "I see Joe arranged for a guard outside the unit."

"Of course, that's Joe. We have all kinds of security. Both the police and those plainclothes private detectives you sent last night."

Catherine went still, alarmed. "I didn't send anyone last night. Joe had better check—"

"Well, not you. Someone named Richard Cameron. I didn't see him. He told Joe that he was helping you with a few security matters, and we'd be completely safe. Joe checked the detectives out thoroughly. Their credentials were very impressive. They've been unobtrusive but are always there when any new nurse or doctor appears anywhere near Jane. They've even checked the IV meds." Her eyes narrowed on Catherine's face. "And Joe thought this Cameron could be trusted. Was Cameron telling the truth?"

"Will you be safe? Yes. The men who work for Cameron are always experts at whatever they do. Did I know about them? No. Cameron doesn't always tell me what he's doing." That was a massive understatement, but she didn't need to worry Eve with her conflicted relationship with Cameron. "But I'm glad for all the security I can get. Aren't you?"

Eve nodded. "You just made me a little uneasy." She moved down the hall toward ICU. "I'll keep you informed about Jane's condition. God help you, Catherine."

"No, God help Jane."

Eve looked over her shoulder, and her eyes were bright with moisture. "I hope she's not already with him. Joe said she was smiling when we found her. I thought maybe . . . he was right."

You weren't as long as I thought you'd be." Cameron walked toward Catherine when she came out of the parking-lot exit of the hospital. "I hope that doesn't mean your Jane MacGuire is worse."

"She's not my Jane MacGuire," Catherine said curtly. "She's Eve's Jane. Eve is the only one to whom Jane has ever allowed herself to be really close."

"Santos evidently believes she's your Jane," Cameron said. "Or she wouldn't have been a target."

"I like her," Catherine said. "I wanted to help her. Help her? Good God, look where she is now."

"Is she worse?" Cameron asked quietly.

"No, but she's no better." She started for her car. "What are you doing here? Don't you ever sleep? Eve said you were here in the middle of the night setting up security."

"I don't need much sleep." He fell into step with her. "I would have told you last night I was coming to Atlanta, but you were being a bit touchy about my interfering."

"But you did it anyway."

"Jane MacGuire wasn't dead. I wanted to make sure that Santos didn't arrange to complete the job."

"Joe had already set up guards."

"Good for him. But I prefer my people."

"You always prefer to run the show." She turned to him as she reached her car. "Look, I'm not arguing about your sending extra security. Send an army if you want to do it. Anything to keep them alive."

He smiled. "I'll keep that in mind. I don't believe an army will be necessary."

"I'm not sure of that." She opened the car door. "You didn't answer me. Why are you here?"

He was silent. "Jane was touch-and-go last night while I was setting up the security. I wanted to be here in case you needed someone."

"I told you I didn't need you."

"I'm a slow learner." He shrugged. "But since you don't need a shoulder to cry on, I'll offer you my services in another area." His voice was crisp as he continued, "Since I'm not going to go away, you might as well use me to bring Santos down. You may not need me, but I guarantee it will make his demise a good deal faster. This isn't the time for pride, Catherine."

"That's not why I—" She stopped. She wasn't going to tell him that it wasn't pride but the fact that she always felt on the defensive with him. Together with that disturbing awareness that interfered with everything she thought and felt on other levels. She was experiencing that heated, vibrant awareness right now.

"You know that what I'm saying is true," Cameron said. "Let me go along for the ride, and we'll wrap this up quickly."

"Who are you kidding? That sounds passive on your part, and we both know that you're never passive." She was staring at him, seeing the strength, the contained explosiveness. But that explosiveness needed only a breath to break free of all restraints. Hu Chang had once told her that Cameron was probably the most dangerous man either one of them would ever meet. From what she had seen in the past, that statement had proved true.

So why not take what he offered? Anything that would

keep Santos from any more killing was worth taking the risk of working with Cameron. She didn't want to owe Cameron a debt of gratitude, but she would worry about that later. "As long as you work with me and not around or behind me."

He smiled, his light eyes suddenly gleaming with mischief. "What about ahead?" He quickly held up his hand to avoid her response. "Only joking. I'll be very meek."

She made a rude sound. "That's not going to happen."

"You're probably right." He went around to the passenger side of the car. "Now that we've come to an agreement, I'll let you drive me back to Louisville. There's no use us taking two cars. I'll have one of my men drive my car back later."

"I'm surprised that you don't want your own wheels," she said as she slipped into the driver's seat. "You do like control."

"I can always steal yours if it becomes necessary." He got into the passenger seat. "And I've found there are some situations where submission can be pure pleasure. Haven't you discovered that, Catherine?"

She had a sudden searing memory of lying naked, Cameron over her, his hands moving in her with incredible erotic skill. Yes, she had been helpless, submissive then as she had never been before. And it had scared the hell out of her.

"You're not answering," Cameron said softly.

"Because this isn't about us or sex games," she said. "If you can't realize that, you can get out of my car right now."

"I realize all the nuances of our relationship, but one of those nuances is sex. It's bound to pop up now and then." He paused. "Now, what are you clenching so tightly in your hand?"

She opened her palm. "A gift from Eve."

"Jane's?" He took the dog tag and held it up to the sunlight. It glittered and turned in his grasp. "It has blood on it."

"Eve didn't want to wipe it off. She wanted Santos to see it when I returned it to him." She took the dog tag back from him. "When I killed the son of a bitch."

"I'd be delighted to do it for you."

"No." She jammed the dog tag into her jacket pocket. "I made her a promise." She started the car. "I'll do it myself."

"As you wish." He leaned back in the seat. "As long as Santos doesn't annoy me any more than he's doing right now. By the way, has Santos called you yet?"

"No, why are you certain he will?"

"Aren't you? He enjoyed tormenting you before by outlining his agenda for you. It sounded to me like it was going to be an ongoing indulgence."

He was right. She had been half expecting that call from Santos. "Who knows what he's waiting for? Maybe he's setting up another kill."

"Then we'd better go on the offensive." He took out his phone. "Now while you're driving, and I'm being submissive, I'll make a few phone calls that will push our agenda along a bit . . ."

The call from Santos came when she had reached Louisville and was pulling into her driveway.

She looked down at the ID. "Speak of the devil."

"Wonderfully descriptive. Yes, I did. Do you suppose I'm psychic?"

"Not funny." She put on the brakes, accessed the call, and pressed the speaker button. "Santos, you son of a bitch."

"You sound stressed, Catherine," Santos said. "Are you

upset that I was able to fool you? I admit I enjoyed working out all the details. I suppose I can hardly blame you for being stressed after spending the morning with your friend Eve. Did she tell you that she hated you? I doubt that even the best friendships could withstand a daughter's death."

"She doesn't hate me. She hates you. And Jane isn't dead. Neither is Kelly. You keep failing, Santos."

"Kelly Winters was not a designated target, she was merely a bonus I was going to allow myself. I just wanted to keep you busy and not thinking about other directions until I was certain that Jane MacGuire was a sure thing."

"She wasn't a sure thing. She's still alive."

"I knew that an hour after she was taken to St. Joseph's. She must be remarkably strong. I heard that she should have died before she reached the hospital. I was upset that she didn't die instantly, but that shot should have done the trick, so I can't really fault my man." He chuckled. "And perhaps it's better that she takes a little time to die. That agony is greater for Eve, and that will hurt you. That's why Jane MacGuire was my choice. It was a way to hurt you in a multitude of ways. I was going to send someone to dispense with her once and for all, but I decided to let her linger. I understand the doctors say she has no possible chance."

"She might surprise you."

"You don't really believe that. You're a realist. No, I did not fail with MacGuire. If I get impatient, I may decide to finish her off, but not before I wring every bit of pain out of your friend Eve Duncan." He paused. "But at the moment, I'm busy planning on another gift to hand you. Who do you think will be next, Catherine?"

"Why don't you tell me?"

"But then I wouldn't be able to enjoy the scenario

nearly as much. No suspense for you, no stabbing at the jugular for me. No, it's much better the way I'm setting it up."

"You don't know who you'll be able to take from me. I have them all protected."

"Circumstances change. You can't guard everyone all the time. Just when you think they're safe, they'll do something careless. Then I'll have them."

"Not if I have you first."

"You won't give up, will you?" He laughed. "But then I knew you wouldn't. That's what I told Delores. You'll fight and fight until the minute I take you down."

She tensed with shock. "You told Delores? She's dead, Santos."

"But she's always with me. You couldn't take her away. I wouldn't let you." His voice was suddenly harsh. "Delores is impatient, but I keep telling her the revenge must be complete. But I understand, I've only given her three souls to quench her need for blood. She'll be glad to take Jane MacGuire. Perhaps I'll reconsider waiting for the bitch to die on her own." He hung up.

"Quench her need for blood? He's crazy." She drew a deep breath before she hung up the phone. "I knew he was obsessed with his wife, but evidently, he's talking to ghosts."

"It shouldn't surprise you," Cameron said. "Santos is laying sacrifices at his dead wife's feet. Why not talk to her?"

"Because he's feeding his own desires and bloodlusts into what he imagines she'd say. That means he's really gone off the deep end." She opened the car door. "And there's no reasoning with someone who's schizoid." She grimaced. "What am I saying? There's no reasoning with Santos anyway. We just have to find him." She got out of the car. "You heard him, he's trying to make me frantic about who he's going to kill next. He wants to keep on playing his ugly game."

"You handled him very well."

"It didn't seem that way to me. He made me feel helpless. I didn't have any ammunition."

"Then we'll go after it and shoot him out of the water."

"Where? How? Have you found out anything about that Dr. Montez that Nagoles was hired to kill in Guatemala?"

"A few very interesting things. I'll tell you about them when I get a definite confirmation." He got out of the car and took her arm as they went toward the front door. "And they might have a bearing on Santos's ghost . . ."

I was going to call you, Catherine." Sam met them as soon as they walked into the foyer. "But then I decided I might as well wait until you got here. You're not going to like this."

"Very true," Hu Chang said as he walked out of the library. "And you're very wise to let me take the brunt of it. Good afternoon, Catherine." He nodded at Cameron. "I trust you were able to take care of the problem with Kelly Winters. I would have appreciated a different choice on your part as to which valuable target you were going to protect."

Cameron's brows rose. "I was already on my way to Catherine. You didn't object when I told you that was my intention."

"What the hell are you doing here, Hu Chang?" Catherine asked. "You're supposed to be protecting Erin."

"And that's why I'm objecting now, Cameron. Situations change." Hu Chang spread his hands. "I failed the challenge, Catherine."

She stiffened. "Erin?"

"Is upstairs talking to Luke and Kelly."

"I don't *want* her here with me. Dammit, you were supposed to find a place to hide her."

"I'm tired of hiding." Erin was coming down the stairs. "I told you that when I talked to you on the phone, Catherine. Why do you think I left Hong Kong?" She had reached the bottom of the stairs and gave Catherine a kiss on the cheek. "You and Cameron and Venable are always trying to keep me safe. No more. I'm responsible for my own safety from now on."

"Not when it's me who put you behind the eight ball," Catherine said curtly. "I just came from a hospital where Jane MacGuire is dying. I won't risk having to go through that again with you."

Erin's face clouded. "Sam told us about Jane. I'm so sorry, Catherine."

"Tell that to Eve. She's going through hell. If you're sorry, you'll let Hu Chang find a—"

"Hole for me to crawl into?" Erin interrupted. "I've told you that I won't do it. Drop it. And tell me how I can help you catch that bastard."

Catherine whirled on Cameron. "Do something. She's not listening to me. You have that . . . connection. Talk her into being sensible."

Cameron shook his head. "She's very stubborn. My dear Catherine, I wasn't able to convince Erin that she should join in preparing this wicked old civilization for a brave new world. And she halfway believed I was right. Do you think I can convince her that she should just let you take your chances?"

Catherine whirled back to Erin. "Look, Santos knows everything that I do. He's researched every target and knows everything about them, too. Everyone is being watched, and Santos is just waiting to make his move. He missed with you. We had a chance of getting you to somewhere he couldn't touch you."

"He missed with Kelly, too," Erin said. "So he can't be that good."

"She wasn't the target. She was a distraction. He didn't miss with Jane."

"Give it up, Catherine," Hu Chang said quietly. "We will accept and just go in a different direction."

"Santos will know she's here," Catherine said in frustration. "He was sending Nagoles to Hong Kong to make another attempt on her. Do you think he won't send someone here? This damn place is a treasure trove of the people I care about. Everyone here is a target."

"It's true that she would be an additional lure. But Santos will not know she is here. I was most careful." He smiled. "I slipped her in through the back and into the basement. You are right, this house is a treasure trove. Which is why the security is important." He turned to Cameron. "Did I see some of your men out there?"

"I thought it wouldn't hurt. I've also made sure they're supplied with detectors that will signal the presence of any explosive within a fifty-yard perimeter. My men will tour the neighborhood every hour and make sure that there is nothing new or threatening. The web is very tight, and there will be no possibility of a sniper infiltrating the area. The house will be as safe as a military bunker."

"Very good. As usual, you're very efficient, and it seems a prudent addition."

"I'm glad you're both in agreement," Catherine said sarcastically. "May I say that I'm still terrified that one bomb could take care of all of Santos's targets?"

"But no bombs will be permitted to be tossed thanks to Cameron's detectors," Hu Chan said. "Hence the magnificent security."

Erin smiled. "Hu Chan is right, Catherine. Give it up. I'm here for the duration."

She gazed at her helplessly. "It appears you are."

"Then how can I help?"

"Stay inside. Don't let anyone see you." She paused. "Santos said that I'd think that I had everyone safe, then someone would do something careless, and he'd have them. You want to help? You can keep Luke and Kelly from being careless. They're both supersmart kids, but they have the arrogance of the young. Sam can keep them busy with educational projects, but that can only last so long. You're a prizewinning journalist, you have stories to tell. Don't let Luke and Kelly become bored and get careless."

"I can do that." Her eyes were narrowed on Catherine's face. "But it sounds like you're not going to be around to help with that."

"Not if I can find a lead to Santos. I can't just wait for him to start killing again." She shook her head. "And you're not qualified to go after him with me. You're not warrior stock, Erin. We all have our own talents. You're brave, you have endurance galore, but you'd get in my way."

"I know that. Everyone has their own strengths." She glanced at Cameron. "But you won't get in her way, Cameron. Keep her safe." She turned and started back up the stairs. "And now I'll go back upstairs and start doing my own job. Take care, Catherine."

"I will." She watched Erin disappear at the top of the stairs before she turned to Hu Chang. "It would have helped if you could have persuaded her to—" She stopped. "I know. Why blame you when I just failed?"

"It's a natural reaction. You're tired and afraid and sick at heart." He stood aside and gestured toward the library. "Come and rest, and I will make you tea and sandwiches."

"I'll do that." Sam turned to Cameron. "You're staying?"

"No, I have to follow up on some information I just received this morning." His lips twisted. "We all appear to have our duties, don't we? Mine is to find that lead for Catherine."

"That doctor in Guatemala?" Catherine asked.

"Actually, he's an Argentinean citizen. It's the only lead we have. So I'll gather leads and prepare myself for battle." He moved toward the front door. "Since I've already failed in the comfort department. You found me completely unworthy, and Hu Chang will be much better received by you." He opened the door. "I'll let you know when I've found out something."

"Interesting." Hu Chang smiled as the door closed behind Cameron. "I can't decide if that was mockery or annoyance. Would you care to enlighten me?"

"How would I know? He's an enigma."

"Growing up as he did with having to cope with all those mental talents, it's natural that he would have developed certain barriers." He tilted his head. "Aren't you tempted to try to breach them?"

"No." She headed for the library. "I have enough problems without attempting to decipher all the complicated triggers that make Cameron respond."

"Oh, I believe that he responds to you in a very straightforward manner," he murmured. "Which is the reason that he was angry with you for shutting him out when Santos first struck."

"I don't want to talk about Cameron," she said as she dropped down in the huge burgundy easy chair by the window. "He takes entirely too much time and effort."

"And I promised you food, tea, and rest." He sat down across from her. "Because your pain is great. Would you like to tell me about Jane MacGuire?"

"I have to call Eve later and check on what the specialist told her. She wasn't hopeful." She paused, thinking. "And what can I tell you about Jane? I didn't know her as well as I'd like to. I've heard Eve talk about her, and I think she must be extraordinary. I only reached out to her because I knew that she was devastated about Trevor's death. I wouldn't have dreamed Santos would target her. I can see Erin or Luke or even Kelly. But Jane should have been safe from him." Her lips tightened. "It was those damn e-mails."

"And the warm heart that made you send them."

"A mistake." She shook her head. "I can't keep blaming myself. The mistake's been made, now I have to do damage control."

"No, now you have to relax and heal." He met her eyes. "We will sit here in silence for a while. Then we will talk of Chen Lu and her beautiful gardens, and that glorious, ridiculous hat that Luke made you wear, and Erin's good work with the villagers on that mountain in Tibet. Nothing hurtful, nothing disturbing. Understood?"

His eyes were almost hypnotic and his voice smooth and yet forceful. She felt surrounded, enveloped by the sheer presence of him. Warmth that was always his gift to her. Friendship that had been founded on shared experiences and years of exploring the depths of that bond. She could feel the tight knot inside her breast begin to loosen.

She leaned her head back on the chair and smiled. "It doesn't seem like such a bad idea. Where do we start?"

CHAPTER 7

It was going well, Santos thought with satisfaction as he leaned back in the deck chair and let the warm sun seep into his skin. Catherine Ling had tried to be defiant and scornful, but he had been able to tell that she was in pain. He had been right to let Jane MacGuire linger for a while. It had served to draw out the agony for Ling.

"You look pleased," Dorgal said as he dropped down in a chair beside Santos. "You enjoyed the girl last night?"

"She was adequate." Not like Delores. But no one was like Delores. But he'd had a bittersweet enjoyment of screwing the girl and remembering how amused Delores had been when he brought another woman to his bed. She would sit and watch them, then stroll over to the bed and caress the woman with gentle, loving hands. Then she would give her a lingering kiss while drawing her dagger from the pocket of her silk robe.

He remembered the anticipation he always felt as Delores glanced at him.

She would purse her lips in a mock kiss and blow it to him.

And stab the woman in the heart.

Dorgal shrugged. "I thought you might enjoy her more

than the last one. Do you want me to dispose of her, or are you going to try her again?"

"I'll try her again." He glanced at Dorgal. "But you didn't come down to the beach from the house to ask me about that little slut. What's wrong?"

"Maybe nothing." He paused. "You told me to tell you if there were any inquiries about Montez. I received word that there was a computer inquiry yesterday and one very recently."

He went still. "From what source?"

"We couldn't break the code. We're still trying."

"Ling."

"Possibly."

Santos muttered a curse. "Probably. Nagoles must have talked."

"He didn't know that much. We gave him only the name of the kill and where he could find him."

"But Ling would be able to take that information and run with it. She'd dig and dig until she found out something she could use."

"Then the logical solution would be to make sure the place where she dug would be barren. It shouldn't be difficult. After we killed his brother, Montez got the message. He swore we'd have no trouble with him if we left his family alone." He smiled. "He was scared shitless and took off running for the hills. Should I order he be taken out?"

"No," Santos said sharply. "I've told you before. I may need him. Can you locate him?"

"He has a mother and a sister in Guatemala City. I'll find him. What then?"

"Make sure no one else finds him."

"Then I'd better start moving on it." Dorgal got to his feet. "And Montez?"

"Bring him here. I've been uneasy lately about leaving him free out there on his own. I don't want to have to go looking for him when she needs him. And I don't want to risk having Ling find him and ask awkward questions. I don't like her knowing as much as she does." His lips tightened. "I wasn't expecting her to be able to reel in Nagoles and question him. Any more information about who took down the helicopter? CIA?"

Dorgal shook his head. "Not according to the priests in the villages. From what we've been able to gather, it was someone they call the Guardian." He shrugged. "But that could be religious mumbo jumbo."

"Mumbo jumbo doesn't blow up helicopters. Get me a name." He added, "And a connection with Ling or Erin Sullivan."

"Right." He moved down the beach toward the path that led to the mansion on the hill. "But first things first. You can't expect me to zero in on Montez while I—"

"I expect you to do what I tell you," Santos said softly. "Whatever I say, whatever irons you have in the fire at the time. Have you forgotten that? Perhaps this island living has lulled you into being a little too comfortable."

Dorgal tensed. "I haven't forgotten." He moistened his lips. "Of course, I'll see to it." He turned and strode quickly up the path.

Santos watched him scurry up the hill. Dorgal had been with him a long time and grown too comfortable with him. Delores had always told him it was necessary to occasionally keep Dorgal in order and apply the verbal whip. She was right, and most of the time he enjoyed the sensation of power it gave him.

But not this time. The news Dorgal had brought had destroyed the satisfaction he had been feeling after he had talked to Catherine Ling. He wanted that satisfaction back. He didn't want to sit here by the sea. He wanted to move on that bitch.

No. Control and patience. He would not destroy the master plan he'd created because he was impatient. It would be a disservice to Delores.

Yet would Delores really want him to delay that final revenge?

She had always opted for bloodletting—swift, cruel, painful.

And was this doubt he was feeling her message to tell him that she was getting impatient, too?

It's so hard, my love. I need you here to help me.

He could almost hear her scornful laughter drifting to him from her tomb on the hill. He could never expect softness or sympathy from Delores. It was part of her appeal for him that she was as sleek and dangerous as he. She was a glorious, shimmering mirror of everything he was or wanted to be.

Nothing was as good without her. Even that little whore he'd had last night had only brought back painful memories. He had told Dorgal he wasn't finished with her yet, but there was only one last act to perform.

He got to his feet and moved toward the path.

You know it won't be as exciting as when we finished it together. I have to play both roles. But I'll be thinking of you every minute when I do it.

And then I'll bring her to you, and she'll belong to you forever.

ST. JOSEPH'S HOSPITAL
ATLANTA, GEORGIA

Eve stared dully down at the caller ID on her phone. "It's Catherine."

"Do you want me to talk to her?" Joe asked gently.

She shook her head. "No. I promised her I'd let her know. I just haven't been able to pull myself together yet."

She punched the access. "Hello, Catherine. It's not good news."

"Shit."

"Dr. Basle just left. He was very thorough, very kind." She tried to steady her voice. "And told us exactly what the other doctors had already told us. A week to ten days."

Silence. "God, I didn't want to hear that. Can you find another specialist?"

"I could. Basle is supposed to be the best."

"That doesn't mean he's right."

"That's what I've been telling myself. I'm not giving up hope. I'll bring in a shaman or witch doctor if he tells me he can help. I'll hit the Internet and see if I can find any new drugs or procedures that have had success in other countries. You know that the U.S. is the last to approve new drugs. But Jane has nothing to lose now."

"No. If I can help, let me know." She added grimly, "I'll get you any drug in the world, legal or not. If Hu Chang can't create one or duplicate it, Cameron and I will steal it."

"First, I have to find one that has a chance of working. In the meantime, you know how you can help. Joe and I will take care of our Jane. Good-bye, Catherine." She hung up and smiled shakily at Joe. "Catherine is all set to raid the CDC if we want her to do it."

"I've been on the computer while I was back in ICU sitting with Jane," Joe said. "I haven't found anything hopeful."

"Neither have I." Her hand tightened on Joe's. "But we can't give up. There has to be a way." She leaned her head on his shoulder. "I was telling Catherine the truth. I'll do anything I have to do." She paused, then said deliberately, "Shaman or witch doctor or anyone else."

He stiffened against her. "What are you saying?"

"She's having problems with blood flow, damage to the

arterial system. Those doctors say the usual arterial graft won't work with her."

"For God's sake, I know all that."

"Who do we know that could possibly adjust blood flow? Who have we seen actually kill by causing the blood to hemorrhage and induce a heart attack?"

He went still, then pushed her away from him to look down into her face. "Seth Caleb? You want to try to get Seth Caleb here to try to help her?"

"I'd try to get the devil himself here if I thought he'd help her."

"Some people would say that Caleb's uncanny ability to manipulate blood flow has a certain Satanic base." He grimaced. "I understand he's been accused of being a vampire on occasion."

"Not to his face."

"No, Caleb is too intimidating."

"Besides, that's totally ridiculous. It might just be that he possesses some kind of simple magnetic force."

"You don't think that. You were worried about Jane whenever he was around her."

"But she wasn't worried. He saved your life once, Joe. And she asked him to help her find me when Doane kidnapped me. She trusted Caleb."

"Are you talking yourself into this? I remember watching him at Trevor's funeral. He was almost explosive."

She remembered that night, too. The dark fascination that always surrounded Caleb, the overpowering tension that he had generated. "Okay, he cares about her. But that could be a good thing."

"Or a very bad thing."

"For Pete's sake, he's not going to steal her soul or anything like that. He's rich, he's intelligent, and he has a certain . . . wildness. He travels around the world, but no one accuses him of anything that's particularly—" Or maybe they had. She'd better drop that argument. Caleb kept his private life very private. "He's been in and out of Jane's life for years. She's always been able to handle him."

"She's dying, Eve."

"Yes." She leaned her head on his chest. "So I may have to be the one who handles Caleb for her. If he needs handling. Maybe he'll just want to save her like we do. No strings attached."

He drew her closer. "Maybe he will. I'm not going to talk you out of it, am I?"

"No, not if he can help her. Maybe he can't. He's always been a wild card."

"Wild, period," Joe said dryly. "But I'm like you—if there's a chance, I'll take it. And I'll be the one to handle him if he causes trouble. Do you want me to call him?"

"No, I'll do it," she said quickly. She didn't want Joe and Caleb to go up against each other during a first encounter.

"Then I'm going to go back to Jane with my computer and try to find a reasonable alternative to Seth Caleb." He kissed her nose and moved down the hallway. "And compared to him, almost anyone is reasonable."

But not just anyone was able to do what Caleb might be able to do, Eve thought, as she pulled out her phone. She quickly dialed the number she'd looked up after she'd talked to Dr. Basle.

"Eve?" Seth Caleb's voice was wary as he picked up the call. "What an unexpected pleasure. How are you?"

"Not good," she said tersely. "I need you."

"How flattering. I don't believe you've ever expressed—"

"I should have said Jane needs you. She's been shot." She added baldly, "She's dying, Caleb."

Silence. "No." His voice was dagger-sharp, vibrating

with explosive force. "She's *not* going to die. I won't let her."

The sheer power of his words filled her with a strange fear, yet gave her hope. "Then come here and keep her from doing it. She was shot in the chest, and they've managed to take care of most of the damage. But there's some kind of blood-flow problem that they can't seem to fix. She's in a coma at St. Joseph's in Atlanta. They say she has no more than ten days."

"Ten days? Blood flow is damn tricky. It could be much less. You hold on to her. Don't let her go. I'm on my way."

"Where are you?"

"Edinburgh. I can be there in seven hours. You keep her alive until I get there." He hung up.

Keep her alive, she thought wearily. How was she going to do that?

Talk to her and hope she could hear her.

Tell her how much they loved her, how much they'd miss her.

Pray.

"Perhaps a little of all three, Mama."

Eve knew what she would see when she lifted her gaze at the soft child's voice. Curly red hair, seven years old, and the most glowing smile in the universe. Bonnie, leaning against the doorjamb and gazing at Eve with love and sympathy. Bonnie, her little girl, who had died so many years ago. Bonnie's spirit, who had somehow been permitted to remain behind to save her mother when she had been spiraling downward after her death.

Eve tried to smile. "I'm glad you came. I needed you today."

"I thought you would." Bonnie plopped down in a chair. "I would have come before this, but I wasn't sure . . . I thought you might need me more later."

"You thought she was dying."

"Yes."

"She is dying. Or that's what those doctors tell me. They could be wrong. Tell me they're wrong, Bonnie."

"I can't do that."

"Then tell me she has a chance."

She didn't speak.

"Sometimes you know things, don't you? You're a ghost." She smiled shakily. "You have contacts. I wouldn't mind if you'd wield a little influence."

"I would if I could." She shook her head. "It's hard. She wants to come to us."

"So did I. I still do sometimes. But I had to stay, and they gave me you, baby."

She smiled. "And you thought I was a hallucination for a long time. You weren't easy to convince."

"I didn't care if you were a hallucination or a dream or a ghost, just so you were here." She could feel the tears sting. "And now it's starting all over again. And this time I'm not sure if I'd ever get Jane back. You keep telling me that it doesn't happen often. So, dammit, she has to live. I lost one daughter, I can't lose another one."

"I know. Sometimes there are adjustments, but I can't even promise you that."

"Adjustments. I don't know what you mean."

She shook her head. "We won't talk about it. I can't give you answers, but maybe I can give you comfort."

"You always do." She leaned back in her chair, her gaze on the red hair, the glow, the shining warmth that had always been her special little girl. "And I don't mean to be ungrateful, but I'm hurting. I have to do something."

"And you are," Bonnie said gently. "You've called Seth Caleb."

"Will he do any good?"

"Maybe. He'll want to do good for her. I can't promise that he'll be able to do anything."

"Sorry. I won't ask you again."

"I wish I knew all the answers. I wish I could give Jane back to you. But all I can do is stay with you until right before Caleb comes. Will that help?"

"You know it will." To have the love, to see her Bonnie, to remember the days when she'd had her to hold close, before she was only a memory. "Oh, yes, that will help me, baby."

Cameron.

Catherine could sense him in the darkness of her room before she opened her eyes. He was sitting in a chair a few yards from her bed. "What are you doing here?"

"Watching you sleep. You're beautiful. When you're awake, you're all alertness and wariness, every muscle tense and ready. That has its own charm, but when you sleep, there's an innocence and a sensuality."

Heat.

Push it away.

"It can't be both. That's a contradiction."

He chuckled. "But so was Eve in the Garden of Eden."

"Why are you here?"

"Not for seduction. I realize that it's not the time."

It might not be the time, but just sitting there in the dark he was pure seduction. The strong, lean line of his body, the scent of him, the memory of him over her, in her. "I'm not going to ask you again."

"I wanted to tell you I've located Eduardo Montez. I thought you'd want to know."

"I do." She sat up in bed. "But it wouldn't wait until morning?"

"No, by morning we should be well on our way to meeting the good doctor. Unless you want me to go by myself?"

"You know better than that." She reached over and turned on the lamp on the bedside table. "Where is he?"

"I'm not certain. Not in Guatemala City, where his mother and sister live. He's still on the run from Santos. By the time we get to Guatemala, I should get an update from the head of the group I hire to do jobs for me in Central America."

"The committee strikes again," she said sarcastically. "Do you have special forces you can call on all over the world?"

"Almost." He smiled. "I'm still working on some countries. After all, I'm only one man."

"With unlimited funds and influence. It's no wonder Venable is getting nervous about the conglomerate."

"But the CIA has its own army and influence." His eyes were twinkling. "I'm just fortunate to be on my own and not strangled by red tape. I think Venable is just jealous."

"You might be right." She swung her legs to the floor. "You might have the opportunity to discuss it with him soon. Did you find out anything more about Montez?"

"Eduardo Montez has a general medical degree and three Ph.D.s in various other fields. He attended a university in Rio de Janeiro, Brazil, but his family is from Argentina. He spent most of his childhood and school breaks at a rancho in the hills outside of Buenos Aires."

"How did he end up in Guatemala? And why did Santos order a hit on his brother?"

"And the most pertinent question is: Why did he order that on no account was Nagoles to kill Eduardo Montez?" He got to his feet. "Which we will know when we come back from Guatemala."

"We'd better." She frowned. "Because I'm scared shitless about leaving here. Besides that hospital in Atlanta, everyone else I love in the world is in this house. Talk about putting all my eggs in one basket."

He nodded. "But you have the equivalent of a special forces army guarding that basket."

She shook her head.

"Not enough? What about the fact that you have Hu Chang to ramrod the security? He's both wise and ingenious. He wouldn't permit anything to happen while you're gone."

"He might not be able to help it." She grimaced. "I'm being negative. You're right, they're as safe as they can be."

"If it makes you feel any better, I think that the pressure will be diverted by our going after Montez. Montez is important to Santos, and he might consider him a threat if we got hold of him. He'll be concerned about what you're doing and how to stop you."

"Unless he decides to stop me by hitting at someone else close to me."

His expression turned thoughtful. "It's always possible. But I'd bet that the action will be aimed at us. The only exception might be if you frighten or anger Santos enough to make him strike out."

"Great." She headed toward the bathroom. "And the chances are that I'll do both before this is over. Something I won't be able to avoid—"

She inhaled sharply. He had reached out as she'd passed him and grasped her forearm.

Electricity.

She looked down at his strong, hard, beautifully shaped hand against her softness.

His fingers on her wrist, his thumb rubbing her forearm. "But maybe not in Guatemala." His lips brushed the hollow of her elbow. "We might be able to get back before you piss him off."

His tongue on the softness of her flesh . . .

"Let me go, Cameron."

"In a minute. I've been very good. Do you know how much I've wanted to do this?"

She only knew how much she'd wanted him to touch her.

"Or how often I thought of you in the summerhouse with your legs wrapped around me. It sent me into a fever, and all I wanted to do was drop everything and come back to you."

"But you didn't come back." Her breasts were swelling, tightening. The muscles of her stomach were clenching. She had to get away from him. She jerked her arm free. "And you shouldn't have come back. There's nothing here for you. I told you that when you left me." She moved toward the bathroom. Walk, don't run. Don't look back. "I'll be dressed in ten minutes. Providing you still want to go with me."

He chuckled. "Catherine, of course I want to go with you. I'll do my best to be good. Sex is at the top of the list of the things I want to do with you. But followed closely behind it is fighting the bad guys with you. It's very exhilarating." His smile faded. "And I find I can't bear the thought of Santos taking either one of those pleasures away from me." He turned and headed for the door. "Ten minutes. I've arranged for a plane and pilot to be waiting at the airport. I'll be downstairs in the foyer."

PEDRO AMADOS AIRPORT
OUTSIDE GUATEMALA CITY

"We're landing." Cameron came out of the cockpit and handed her a manila envelope. "Documents. You're Narda Seldano. Memorize the rest of the info before we get on the ground."

"Not much time," Catherine said. "If you had these

documents before we got on this plane, why didn't you give them to me before this?"

"I'm sure you're a quick study. I had to make sure that they were authentic and not traceable. I told Dario to verify and get back to me before we landed. He came through just in the nick of time."

"Dario?"

"Rafael Dario. He runs the group that is going to spearhead our search for Montez."

"Well, it was more of a close shave than the nick of time." She was already scanning the documents. They seemed fairly good, including the passport photo and driver's license. "I'm not sure I'd have much faith in Dario."

"He's a good man." He was buckling his seat belt. "A little unusual, but nothing wrong with that. I'd rather he take his time than give me bad service."

"And no one can say that you're not a little unusual yourself," she said dryly. "No wonder you're comfortable with him."

"You'll be comfortable, too." He was looking out the window as the Gulfstream's wheels touched down. "I see him waiting by that hangar. See how reliable he is?" His eyes widened as he saw the tall man he'd just indicated was now running across the tarmac toward the plane. "Maybe . . ." He tore off his seat belt and ran toward the passenger door and called to the pilot in the cockpit. "Stop the damn plane!" The plane had barely stopped moving when Cameron threw the door open. "What the hell are you doing, Dario?"

"Being inventive and brilliant." Dario threw himself into the plane. "And trying to save the life of the beautiful Catherine Ling. You can take care of yourself, Cameron, but it would hurt me to see her go down. Get this plane back in the air." He was breathing hard. "Not a safe airport, Cameron." He got to his feet. "And if you'd gotten off the plane at that hangar, anyone would have been able to get a shot at you from those foothills. Right here, the plane is out of range of any sniper bullet. At the hangar, you'd be vulnerable. And my information is that a shot would have a 92 percent chance of occurring at present. Someone knows that you're in town and doesn't like you."

Cameron headed for the cockpit. "You told me this would be a safe airport, dammit. What changed?"

"Situations ebb and flow. This one overflowed." He turned to Catherine. "I'm Rafael Dario. I'm delighted to meet you. You should also be delighted to meet me since I risked my life to save you."

"Should I? So far I'm not impressed by you, Senor Dario." It wasn't the truth. She might not be impressed by Rafael Dario's actions, but there was no way not to be impressed by his appearance. He was literally larger than life, standing nearly six-foot-five and as muscular as he was graceful. His dark hair was meticulously barbered, and his features were regular except for a nose that was long, hooked, and somehow made his face appear all the more appealing. "I'm sure that Cameron paid you very well to do that."

"Fantastically well." He grinned. "But I always have a choice. I believe I would have chosen your life even if the money had been a mere pittance. When I saw your photo in the dossier Cameron sent me to help in getting your documents, you reminded me of my mother."

"What?"

He nodded as he sat down and buckled his seat belt. "She was very beautiful, too. And I always felt safe with her. Not many people felt that way about her since she fought with the rebels in Colombia, and she was very, very good. And then, too, beauty often gets in the way. Don't you find that?"

"No."

"I think you're wrong. My mother had a lot to overcome."

"And did she succeed?"

"Yes, until the very end. She was ambushed. It took twelve men to take her down." The words were spoken with no expression. "But I regard that as also a success."

"So would I."

He smiled. "You see, that's why you remind me of my mother. I sensed it would be so. You understand that the—"

"Okay, we'll be out of here in a few minutes," Cameron said as he came out of the cockpit. "So where the hell are we going, Dario?"

"North. The hills. There's another private airport near the border at San Esposito that will accommodate jets. I wanted not to be too obvious about our destination, but now it's just a question of getting you to Montez in time." He got to his feet. "I'll go up with the pilot and give him directions."

"What do you mean, getting us to Montez in time?" Catherine asked. "In time for what?"

"In time to make sure he's still alive for him to do you any good." He was heading for the cockpit. "His sister, Lena, was tortured and butchered last night. If she knew where Eduardo is hiding, then Santos probably does, too."

"And is he hiding?"

"Yes, he took off for the hills with his brother when Nagoles was on the hunt for them. His brother was caught and killed, but Eduardo escaped. It's been presumed he's been hiding out in the rain forests ever since. No sign of anyone in pursuit."

"Until now," Catherine said.

"As you say," Dario said. "It seems you stirred up a hornet's nest. When Cameron engaged me to find Montez, I sent out men in all directions and found that there was a recent call out to capture him."

"Kill him?" Cameron asked.

"No, capture, underlined and very definite. I have an idea that Santos might have had a general idea where to find him but it wasn't a priority." His lips twisted. "But I lost a man at Montez's sister Lena's place. Alfredo Ruiz was shot when he ran into Santos's men searching her house. Montez's sister and my man, Ruiz, were killed without a second thought. Only Eduardo evidently was to be spared." He paused. "I liked Ruiz. I believe that I'll have to do something about evening that particular score."

"You said that Santos might know where Montez is hiding," Cameron said. "Do you?"

"Of course." Dario looked at him in surprise. "You said you wanted to know. I make my living by acquiring information, then acting on it." He looked at Catherine. "Like you. Your dossier said that you sold information in Hong Kong when you were very young. It's another sign of our kinship."

"I sold. I didn't act."

"But you would have if it had become necessary." He opened the cockpit door. "I will get you to Montez, Cameron. And then you will give me permission to kill the man who killed Ruiz. Agreed?"

"If we don't need him for bargaining," Cameron said. "If there's a problem, we'll negotiate."

"I find it hard to negotiate when one of my men has been killed. I choose them, I train them, I become close to them. They are mine."

Catherine chuckled. "That sounds familiar, Cameron. You should understand that philosophy."

"I do. That's why I hired you, Dario. But in the end, I'm the only one who gives the orders."

He shrugged. "We will see." He went into the cockpit.

"Not your usual obedient drone," Catherine said mockingly. "Clearly, Dario didn't get the memo about the committee or your being all-powerful when you hired him. I've seen how you're usually treated by the people who work for you. Lots of bowing and scraping."

"And you think I like it?"

"No, I think it exasperates you." The plane was starting to roll down the runway, and she looked out the window at the distant hills. Had there really been a possible shooter in that mass of green vegetation? "But I don't believe you're going to have to worry about it with Dario. You may have trouble controlling him."

"Then I'll get rid of him. But I've always found independent thought is better than a 'drone' mentality. If I can work with him, I'll do it." He glanced at her. "Have you changed your mind about him?"

"Maybe. He appears not to hesitate when it comes down to pulling the trigger."

"Literally and figuratively." He studied her. "But what is this kinship bullshit?"

"Nothing." She made a face. "He says I remind him of his mother."

"What?" He smiled. "If I didn't know who Dario's mother was, I'd think that was a very tired line."

"He said she fought with the rebels in Colombia."

He nodded. "Elena Dario. Very smart, very dedicated, very tough. Rafael Dario grew up in the jungles while they were dodging and raiding both the cartels and the government forces."

"But they finally killed her? He said it took twelve men to take her down."

"Yes. He was fourteen at the time, and he found out names and went after each one of those men. It took him three years, but he killed every one of them. After that, he left Colombia and surfaced in Peru. He was a mercenary for a few years, then formed a unit of his own in Guatemala. Since then, he's struck a balance between working for the local police and private organizations that aren't necessarily on the right side of the law."

"Like you."

"Like me. Do you expect me to deny it? What a waste of time. Law is defined by the particular country or party that's in control at a given time. It's much more sensible to embrace your own code and forget the rest of that nonsense."

"Venable would not agree."

"But you do," he said softly. "Deep in your heart, you know that I'm right. You walk your own path."

"Not as long as I'm CIA."

"Yes, we do have to get you over that hurdle."

"It's not a hurdle, it's a vocation." She changed the subject. "It's fairly clear that your probing around the Montez killing got a quick and explosive response. Santos may not have wanted Eduardo Montez dead, but he didn't want us to find him, either. You told me that Nagoles said his brother's death was an example killing. That meant it was to warn Eduardo Montez in the most terrifying way possible that he wasn't to talk or he'd be next in line." She frowned. "But he wasn't next in line. He's still out there, and Santos is being very careful to keep him alive. Why?"

"Information. Blackmail. Or he may possess a treasure Santos wants to get his hands on."

"But he didn't go after Montez for the past two years. Santos wasn't that eager."

"Not until he thought he might lose Montez. He wasn't going to tolerate you scooping him up. Interesting . . ."

"But you're the one who hired Dario. No hint of CIA this time. Now he's going to find out that you're the one interfering in his plans. Which means you're a target, too."

"My, my, how unfortunate. Remind me to worry about that."

"Well, I'll worry about it," she said sharply. "Maybe I shouldn't. It was bound to happen. But it's just one more—" She broke off. "I told Hu Chang that there was no reason for you to be a target and, if you were, that you could take care of yourself. But now there is a reason. I gave it to you."

"And you were also right. I can take care of myself."

She nodded. "Correct. I'm being foolish. You would have dove into this mess anyway the minute it was clear Erin was a target."

"Very foolish," he said. "But you persist in thinking that Erin was the primary reason. Not true, Catherine."

She wasn't going there. "Close enough. You were outraged that anyone would threaten her." She suddenly remembered something. "You even used the same word Dario used. Mine. One of mine. Good God, you're as possessive as he is. No wonder you hired him. You're just like him."

"Wrong." His face was suddenly alight with humor. "We have several serious differences in viewpoint."

"Such as?" she asked warily.

"On no account in this world would you ever remind me of my mother, Catherine."

CHAPTER 8

ST. JOSEPH'S HOSPITAL
ATLANTA, GEORGIA

Where is she?"

Eve straightened to attention in her chair as Seth Caleb blew into the waiting room like a category five hurricane. "Where do you think she is?" She got to her feet. "I told you that she was in a coma. She's down the hall in ICU."

"She's still alive?"

"Yes, same condition."

"Then I'll talk to you later, Eve." He turned on his heel. "I've got to see her."

"No." She stepped in front of him. "One: The doctors and nurses get touchy about having someone examine one of their patients. Particularly if they have no credentials. I've arranged to have the staff permit you visiting privileges at ICU, but do not step on toes. Two: Her security is so tight, one of the guards might take you down if you get too close to her. They even look at me and Joe suspiciously. You can't just blunder in there without advance preparation."

"I never blunder. I'll take care of the hospital personnel." He tried to go around her. "And no security guard is going to keep me away from her."

She reached out and grabbed his arm. "And is that supposed to help? By all means, let's cause a ruckus that will make—" She stopped as she felt the tension, the suppressed energy that was almost electrifying in the arm she was holding to restrain him. His dark eyes were glowing, flickering wildly in his taut face. It was an extraordinary face, surrounded by close-cut, dark hair; high cheekbones; full, sensual lips; and those eyes that were totally riveting and dominating and had always intrigued her. He was somewhere in his thirties, tall, muscular, with an almost catlike grace. She had never been able to decide if he was good-looking or not because the sheer power and fascination he projected was the only thing that mattered when Caleb was confronting you. As he was confronting her in this moment. Caleb was never cool or tame, but his fierceness was nearly tangible in this moment. She had told Joe she would handle him, but this was not a good start. Try to calm him.

Oh, to hell with it. She wasn't about to deal with Caleb's problems. They had enough problems of their own. "I'm not about to let you go into that ICU and cause Joe any more upset than he's going through right now. You know Joe. Face him with the kind of vibes you're broadcasting, and he'd automatically go into defense mode. We're both in a superprotective state about Jane now anyway."

"You phoned me. You wanted me here," he said harshly. "Now take me as you find me."

"No, I won't do it. Why should I?" She gestured to the chair next to her. "Now sit down, and we'll talk, then I'll let you go and see Jane. But not until I think you're ready."

"That decision was out of your hands the minute you told me she was dying."

"Not unless you want to knock me down to get past me.

And neither one of us thinks that Jane would want you to do that."

His hands were clenched into fists at his sides. "I need to get to her."

"And you will." My God, she had been aware of his savage anger and determination, but now she was seeing much deeper. Wild despair, hurt, incredible disbelief that this could happen to Jane, that he couldn't have somehow prevented it. "Now sit down and you'll be able to break free of me that much sooner."

He didn't move for an instant, then dropped down in the chair. "Talk to me. Get it over with."

"Okay, first I'll tell you why it happened and what we're up against. Because even if you manage to save her, the fight won't be over. You didn't ask me any questions, and I didn't tell you anything but the bare minimum to get you here."

"I didn't care. I still don't care. I just need to keep her alive."

"I'll be as brief as I can. But you *will* listen, Caleb." She quickly and concisely filled him in on the details that had brought Jane to this state. "That's why the security is so tight. Santos could decide to send someone to finish the job at any time."

"That won't happen." He repeated the name. "Santos. I'll remember. I can't deal with him right now. But I'll remember."

"That's not why I told you about him. I gave that job to Catherine. She made me a promise. You just have to have the full picture, so that you can do what you have to do."

"So you've given it to me. May I go to her now?"

"In a minute." She paused. "I think you should know something else. Santos may not be the only one you may be fighting to bring her back from that coma. When we found Jane in that car covered in blood and so terribly near death . . ." She paused. "It's crazy, but she was smiling."

Caleb stiffened. "And?"

"You know how depressed she's been since Trevor was killed. Almost suicidal."

"Jane's too strong for that bullshit."

"But maybe not too strong to accept what she deems as fate."

He was suddenly smiling recklessly. "Then I'll have to convince her to change her mind, won't I? Being killed by that son of a bitch, Santos, isn't her fate." He met her eyes. "And Trevor was never her fate. He can't have her."

"She loved him," Eve said gently. "He was everything she wanted in a man."

"Do you think I don't know that? Trevor had the good looks of a movie star, he was brave, he was intelligent. He was also gentle and civilized and a great guy who she could trust and live with in never-never land forever."

"That's a difficult combination to beat, Caleb."

"But I would have done it if Trevor hadn't been killed. I didn't get the chance. I knew it was going to be hell when he was dying." His lips twisted. "Do you know even then he was trying to protect her? He wanted me to take care of her. He wanted me to be *him*. There was no way I was going to do that."

"But it seems that you're going to have to do what he wanted anyway," she said sadly.

"My way. Not Trevor's." He got to his feet. "Are you going to take me to her or not?"

She nodded. "I'll come with you. I don't want you to disturb Joe any more than he is now. We'll leave you alone with Jane for a little while. Though I don't know how much good it will do with her in a coma."

"I'll still be able to reach her."

"How? As far as I've heard, you're no psychic."

"I don't need to be. I can control the blood. The mind and the blood interact on so many levels. She won't be able to hide from me."

"That still sounds very—"

"I've done it before with Jane. Of course, not precisely in this kind of situation. I was angry with her once and I— Never mind. Needless to say she was annoyed with me, but I definitely was able to get below the top layers of consciousness to what was underneath."

"I can imagine she was annoyed," she said dryly. "No wonder she's so wary with you."

"We're wasting time. Just take me to her and leave us alone. Jane and I don't need anyone else."

"Maybe you don't. But Jane is different. She cares about people."

"And you think I don't?"

"I think you care about Jane. That's the only reason I brought you here." She studied him. "And perhaps Trevor found something in you on the day he died that could be a salvation for Jane. Or maybe he saw what was coming and was hedging his bets." She shrugged wearily. "But right now, you're the only game in town for us. So I'll play it the way you want it played." She paused. "As long as I see no harm in it for Jane."

He nodded curtly. "And after I save her, you'll try to send me on my way. I understand it. I'm no Trevor. I'm not safe."

That went without saying, she thought as she stared at him across the room. She could almost sense the darkness and flames surrounding him. But there was also power and feeling so intense that it took her breath away. She could understand why Jane had always been drawn to Caleb. The difference between him and Trevor was incredible, but there was a part of Jane that reached out for adventure and danger and the mysteries of life. But that power Caleb emitted was giving Eve hope and lifting her spirits in a world of despair.

"I've never thought you were safe, Caleb." She moved across the room and followed him into the hall. "I'll deal with that later. After you bring my Jane back to me."

"No, after that it will be up to Jane." He strode quickly down the hall. "Just as it always was and always will be . . ."

You whisked me out of there as if you were afraid I'd deck him," Joe said as he gazed through the glass of the ICU room from the hall. "I told you that I wouldn't object to your bringing Caleb here. Not if he had a chance of saving Jane."

"You wouldn't object," Eve said as she watched Caleb pull a chair closer to Jane's bed and sit down. "But you would have interrogated him and made him more impatient than he is right now. You have a perfect right to do that, but Caleb is explosive, and I didn't want to cause a disruption. This is a medical facility. You have better things to do than cross-examine Caleb."

"For instance?"

"Talk to the doctors and nurses and run interference for him. Caleb is liable to do anything he wants to do at the moment. He's wilder and less disciplined than I've ever seen him."

"I couldn't judge," he said dryly. "You didn't let me stay around him that long."

"No, we have to leave him to it. Neither of us can help her." She stepped closer, tucking herself against his strength. "I wanted to stay in there, too. It was hard to go."

Joe slid his arm around her. "But we're together out here in the cold." He pressed his lips to her temple. "Come on. Buy me a cup of coffee, then we'll go and try to convince the medical staff that Caleb isn't as weird as we know he is. Maybe we can tell them that he's a psychologist trying a new technique to reach her in that coma."

"It's as good a story as any." Eve looked back at Caleb, leaning forward, holding Jane's hand, his gaze fixed intently on her face. His entire body and mind appeared to be focused, riveted, on her.

Heal her, Caleb.

Heal her body. Heal her mind. Heal her heart.

And then please don't turn around and destroy her.

"Eve."

She turned back to Joe. "It's going to be okay. We've got to believe that." She kept her gaze from returning to Caleb, sitting so close to Jane. "I was just wondering what he was doing to her . . ."

Disturbance.

Jane could feel it move her, jerking her from the path.

Darkness.

Flames.

Caleb.

No!

"Yes," Caleb said. "Why did you think I'd let you go?"

"Because Trevor's there, he's waiting for me."

"Too bad. He lost you. He even knew that he'd lost you as he was dying. He wasn't trying to take you with him. He knew better. He was trying to release you. But you're too stubborn to let him go."

"Not my fault. I'm in a coma. I'm dying, damn you."

"And not fighting it. Just meekly going into the night. Meekly? Not like you at all, Jane."

"It is if I want it to be," she said defiantly.

"Not if it's not what I want it to be. You've got a fine,

strong body, and I can make the blood heal itself. It won't be easy. Particularly since you'll probably be fighting me, but I can do it. I *will* do it."

"No, the doctors say you can't. They told Eve that it's not possible."

"And Eve told me that she's not going to accept a death sentence for you. Think about her, not yourself. She doesn't trust me worth a damn, but she told me to bring you back."

"She doesn't understand. I fought it, but it's okay if I give up now."

"Bullshit. You're coming back with me."

"The hell I will." She began spiraling downward toward the golden path that was ultrasmooth and had only one ending.

"You're wrong. It has a hundred, a thousand endings, and I can show you all of them."

"I can't hear you."

"Yes, you can. But I'll let you rest for a little while. So shall I tell you how it will be?"

"No, I can't hear you."

"First, I'll work on the healing. Santos messed you up big-time. I'll have to pull a few rabbits out of my hat before you'll be in any shape for that arterial graft. Then I'll work on bringing you out of that coma. I'll show you reasons to live that would make angels leave Heaven and come down to Earth."

"Delusions and hallucinations."

"Life."

Go deeper. Caleb's words were taking her away, making her think, making Trevor dim in the distance.

"You can't go deeper. I won't let you. But I'll let you stay where you are for a little while. You have to take what you can get. But you'll always know I'm here. It's not Trevor who is waiting for you, it's me . . ."

GUATEMALA CITY

"Catherine Ling is here, Santos," Dorgal said as soon as Santos answered his cell. "And she's not alone."

"Venable?"

"No, someone else. Alfredo Ruiz showed up when I was searching the sister's house for information. We disposed of him, but when we checked, we found out he works for Rafael Dario. I had our people check the local grapevine for who was funding them."

"Who is it?"

"Richard Cameron."

"The same man who took out Nagoles," Santos said. "He appears to be moving very swiftly to help our Catherine Ling. I believe we need to know much more about him and what he is to her." He chuckled. "She may have furnished us with another target. Wouldn't it be amusing if I can take a lover away from her? Just as she took away my Delores from me."

"I'm already working on finding out more about him. I'm tapping our informants in the CIA to see what they know about Cameron."

"Good. But that's not as important as making sure that Ling doesn't get her hands on Montez. The sister talked?"

"It took hours, but in the end, she told us he was in the hills near San Esposito. But she died before we could get an exact location. I had to tear her house apart to find any other information. That's why Ruiz found me there when he came looking for her."

"I'm not interested in this Ruiz. I want to know if you found where that weasel, Montez, went to ground."

"I have an address in a village close to the border. I'm heading there now. I've already sent word ahead to our men in a nearby village to move in and verify that Montez is still there." He paused. "But I'd bet Ling and Cameron are heading there, too. Dario is a very good man, with connections all over Central America. He might not have had to question Montez's sister. We tried to hire him several years ago, when we were hunting for one of the bastards who was skimming money on the coke deliveries to the U.S."

"He turned us down?"

"Dario said that he preferred not to be involved with someone who would not accept it when he was forced to say no on occasion."

"Damn right I wouldn't accept it. You should have cut his throat."

"It didn't seem worthwhile at the time."

"But now we have to deal with him. Dario might lead Ling to Montez."

"I'll take care of it."

"Yes, you will," Santos said softly. "This was supposed to be a simple retrieval, and now it's becoming a problem. Get Montez and bring him to me." He hung up.

But nothing was simple where Catherine Ling was concerned, Santos thought. He should have known that she would cause Dorgal difficulty. For the first time, he was feeling a hint of uneasiness at the thought of Ling's moving closer to Eduardo Montez. He didn't want him dead, but he might have to take him out rather than let Ling get her hands on him.

But that was a worst-case scenario. There were still many ways he could attack Ling and ward off her interference.

It will be fine, Delores. This is only a little bump in the road. Trust me. I'll see that you're protected from that bitch.

He had always protected Delores, from the time he'd first met her when she was sixteen.

She had been lush and beautiful and belonged to one

of his men, Javier. One night, he had found her in his bed and what had followed had been a sexual marathon that had still left him hungry for her. He'd known even then that he'd always have to have her.

"So good." She curled up closer to him and rubbed against him like a cat in heat. "I knew you'd be like this. I've been watching you. Javier didn't like it. He said if I cheated on him, he'd beat me."

"Screw him."

She laughed. "Not anymore. I'd rather screw you. I have other plans for Javier." She kissed him and whispered, "Would you like to hear them?"

"Yes."

"You send for him. We tie him in a chair and make him watch us make love. Then you remove his penis in the most painful way possible. Doesn't that sound exciting?"

He was getting hard just thinking about it. The blood, the pain, the emotional hell. "He must have really displeased you."

"Not really. He was easy to handle. But I don't like threats, and I'm through with him. He might cause trouble for us later. And I've watched you, and I know you like what I like. The blood. The terror." She raised herself on one elbow. "Don't you like the idea of making a man who'd had me into a eunuch? It would make me all the more yours." Her eyes were glowing down at him. "I knew from the moment I saw you that we were going to be together. I want to be only yours . . . except when we want to play a little. This would seal it, wouldn't it?"

"Sealed in blood." His finger outlined her nipple. His mind was full of the picture she had drawn, and his body was excited and ready. "And then we'll do a little more fine carving before we put poor Javier out of his misery."

"Poor?" She chuckled. "He'll deserve it. He's in my

way. He's in your way. I'm your woman. You've got to protect me, don't you?"

"Of course I do. Forever." He reached for his phone. "I'll call Javier."

Forever, Delores. I promised you forever. I won't let Ling steal it from you.

Santos has to know about this airport," Catherine said as she got off the private jet. She glanced around the ten or twelve hangars that had been well camouflaged from the air. "It's perfect for drug trafficking and within miles of the border."

"Which is exactly why he doesn't use it," Dario said as he jumped down to the ground. "The police keep a close eye on what goes on here."

"And that doesn't bother you?"

"Why should it?" He grinned. "I'm an honest businessman who contributes generously to the children-and-orphans fund of the police department. Plus a little on the side. They prefer dealing with me rather than the cartels. Their bribes are more generous, but I make sure that mine can't be traced. Occasionally, I'll take out a cop killer or a child molester, and I'm a hero for a while. In short, I'm very . . . comfortable for them."

"And very clever," Cameron said as he joined them. "But I don't need a hero at the moment. I need to know where I can find Eduardo Montez. He's in this village?"

Dario nodded. "That's the word I have." He nodded at the Jeep parked by the third hangar. "He's supposed to be living in the basement of San Marcos' church at the edge of the village. He's been there since he fled Guatemala City after his brother was killed."

"A church?" Catherine repeated. "A strange hideout."

"Not really," Cameron said. "Not when you know his

background. I told you that he had three other doctorates besides his medical degree."

"And they are?"

"Chemistry, mechanical engineering." He paused. "And theology."

"So he would feel very at home in a church. But the resident priest must be very lenient," Catherine said dryly as she got into the passenger seat of the Jeep. "Particularly if he had to confess to causing the death of his brother."

Dario shrugged. "Montez is a doctor. A doctor is a very valuable commodity in a small village like this. Father Gabriel might have been willing to balance the risk of hiding a fugitive from a drug cartel against that value."

"Or maybe the priest just wanted to save his life when he learned it wasn't the police who were after Montez," Catherine said. "It's possible."

Cameron nodded. "I'm not arguing. A priest is a priest. They don't have a secular mind-set. I was taught several disciplines by priests in Tibet. Anything is possible with them." He got into the Jeep, and added grimly, "But I'd feel better if Montez had chosen someone to shelter him who had a better chance against Santos." His gaze went to the small church nestled in the foothills. "Step on it, Dario."

"Go, Eduardo!" Father Gabriel's voice was urgent as he threw open the door of the small spare bedroom. "Now. I just received a call from Carlo, at the restaurant in the village. Two men were there asking questions about me." He paused. "And about you."

Eduardo Montez wasn't even surprised. He'd known it would come sometime. He'd thought it would be before this. He leaped to his feet. "I'm sorry, Father. I didn't want to bring this down on you. You should have let me go when I told you about Santos." He was pulling on his jacket and grabbing the backpack and medical kit he always kept beside his bed. "How much time do I have?"

"Not long." He jerked open the door leading to the garden. "Go through the rain forest to the monastery, as we planned. I've told Brother Benedict to give you shelter."

Montez paused as he reached the door. "Come with me."

Father Gabriel shook his head. "I would only slow you down. I'm no longer a young man, and this arthritis is not—"

"Then I won't go," Montez said desperately. "You don't know what Santos's men will do to you. I told you, they killed my brother. For nothing, Father. For *nothing*."

"You don't know. It may have not been for nothing. God may have had a plan for you."

"I won't go without you."

Father Gabriel hesitated. "I'll go and hide in the village. Will that satisfy you?"

"No, but it's better than your staying here. Now. Hurry. Go now, Father."

He nodded. "As soon as I see that you've reached the forest. It's in your hands, Eduardo."

"Father, please, you have to—" He could see he wasn't moving the priest. Father Gabriel was only smiling as he gestured to the forest. "Very well, I'll go. Hurry. Please, hurry."

Montez started running through the garden toward the forest.

God, he's one of yours, protect him.

Please. Don't let me have killed another innocent man.

Smoke!

Not a thick, black smoke, but a mere gray wisp curling out of the upper windows of the church. Catherine hadn't even been able to see it until they were within a hundred yards of the church.

"Shit!" Cameron said. "Pull over, Dario."

Dario was already pulling to the side of the road. "There's only one car, and no one is in it." He ran toward the black Volvo parked in front of the church. "I'll wait for them to run out. You go inside, and see what—"

"I don't need you to tell me what to do, Dario," Cameron said. "Catherine, I'll go in the front door. You take the side entrance."

"Right." She was drawing her gun as she reached the heavy, ancient oak door. She threw open the door and stepped to one side to avoid fire.

Nothing.

But the smoke was now pouring out of the church, and it had turned black. She could barely see, her eyes were stinging.

Where was Cameron? He should be in the church by now.

Shots!

Straight ahead and to the left.

Someone was running down the aisle toward her.

A bullet splintered the wood of the pew next to her.

She fell to the floor and aimed at the dark-haired man in loose gray pants and white shirt whose gun was firing with every step he took.

The next bullet came too close.

Take him down fast.

She rolled to one side and took her shot.

He grunted, fell to his knees.

And then fell forward.

More shots, somewhere up ahead, near the altar.

Cameron?

She couldn't see anything for the smoke.

She jumped to her feet, held her breath, and ran toward the altar.

Cameron met her before she got there.

"Out!" He took her elbow and started running for the front entrance. "This place is going up like a tinderbox."

"The priest? Montez?"

"The priest is dead. He was lying up at the altar when I ran in the front entrance. I shot the man who had killed him." He threw open the oak door and ran down the stairs toward Dario. "But I didn't see anyone resembling Montez. Maybe the priest managed to warn him, and he ran out the back."

It made sense, unless another of Santos's men had spirited Montez away, Catherine thought. But that was doubtful considering the action that had been exploding when she and Cameron had run into the church.

So assume Montez had gotten away.

And go after him.

She ran down the steps and around the side of the church.

A garden with a small fountain.

A hundred yards beyond that garden, the rain forest, dense foliage, no houses.

Footprints?

No footprints at the rear door of the church that led to the garden.

But that didn't mean that there wouldn't be prints in the rain forest. The earth would be moist, saturated, and Montez would be in too much of a panic to try to erase those prints. He was a doctor, not a hunter or soldier.

She started toward the dense shrubbery that bordered the rain forest.

"It would have been polite to invite me to go along before you decided to disappear," Cameron said as he fell into step with her.

"I would have called you," she said absently. "I wanted to make sure that Montez was on foot and didn't have a car stashed in the back. He should have taken that precaution. But maybe it's somewhere in that rain forest. We have to move fast in case he—"

"We are moving fast. I told Dario to keep an eye out in case anyone else shows up in the village and to try to smooth things over with the local police and villagers. These people lost their priest and their church. They're not going to be pleased."

"Neither am I," she said wearily. "The deaths keep going on and on."

"But these weren't targeted because of you, Catherine."

"How do I know that? Cause and effect." She shook her head. "But I can't think of that right now. Santos wants Montez, so I can't let him have him. He might be of value to him, or he might know too much. Montez may be the key to getting to that bastard." She moved toward the forest. "So if you want to come with me, keep up, Cameron."

"I'll do my utmost to accommodate you." He was moving quickly, every step catlike, his gaze focused on the ground. "I believe that's not out of the realm of my capability."

He's not even trying to mask his footprints," Catherine said as she rose to her feet from examining a print four hours later. "I didn't think he would. All he wants is to move as fast as he can and get away. I'd judge we're about thirty minutes behind him."

"Twenty," Cameron said. "And he could surprise you. If he feels trapped, he might turn on us. He doesn't know who is following him, but he'll think the worst. He may not know about the priest's being killed, but his brother's death was a warning that he couldn't ignore."

"I know all that." She increased her pace and went

ahead of him on the trail. "So we'll be careful. There's no way that I want him to attack and have to take him down. He's got to know something about Santos that could be useful. Why else are we here?"

He didn't answer.

"But it might be better if we separated." She glanced over her shoulder. "And tried to—"

Cameron was gone.

The trail behind her was empty, and the only sign of his passing was the faint stirring of the shrubbery to the left of the dirt path.

Damn him.

Heaven forbid that he work with her instead of going his own way.

But it had also been her thought to separate, she thought grudgingly. She had just been about to tell him that they had to have a structure, a plan. And that plan could have involved going after Montez herself and leaving Cameron in the dust. It had occurred to her that a woman alone might seem less intimidating when she confronted Montez. It might keep Montez from panicking any more than he had already. The only thing that was important was getting Montez and making sure he wasn't too damaged to talk to her.

But Cameron had taken the initiative, and she didn't know what he would do if he reached Montez first. There was no one more chillingly intimidating than Cameron, which meant that she definitely didn't want that to happen.

She broke into a run.

Montez was directly ahead of her.

She could hear the crash of brush as he moved quickly, frantically on the trail.

She could hear his harsh, strained breathing.

But Montez was the only one she could hear. Cameron must be near, but, of course, she couldn't hear him. He was trained to be silent as a ghost on the trail.

Where are you, Cameron?

Forget him.

It was time to go for it.

She darted to the side of the trail into the brush. Then she covered the few yards to where Montez was plunging down the trail.

Identify and try to stop the fear.

"Montez! Stop. I'm CIA. I'm not going to hurt you."

Montez froze, cast a wild glance behind him, then started to run.

At least he hadn't drawn a gun on her.

She ran after him.

Five yards later, she tackled him.

"No!" He turned, struggling.

"Shh. I don't want to hurt you."

He froze, looking up at her. "Bitch." His fist struck her jaw.

Her head snapped back. Dizzy. She shook it to try to clear it.

So much for thinking he wouldn't be intimidated by a woman. It was clearly all too true.

"Sorry." She brought the edge of her hand down in a karate chop to his neck.

He went limp.

She sat back on her heels and drew a deep breath.

"Not very well done." Cameron was strolling out of the brush. "I was thinking I might have to step in, but that would have been very humiliating for you. He's obviously a rank amateur."

She got to her feet. "Where were you?"

"You obviously wanted to handle him alone, so I thought I'd let you do it." He knelt beside Montez and took his neck in his two hands and turned it back and forth, examining it. "This karate move was done expertly, and so was the tackle. Otherwise, you deserved that clip on the jaw. Too soft, Catherine."

"Which is why I didn't want you to—" She stopped and shook her head. "I thought there was a chance of not hurting him. He's already lost two members of his family and Father Gabriel." She shrugged. "It didn't work out." She knelt again and went through Montez's knapsack. "A wallet with ID and two hundred dollars' worth of quetzals. A few health bars and a bottle of water." She went deeper. "A quartz rosary, a prayer book . . ." She pulled out a hand-bound book with a yellow cover that was the worse for wear. On the cover the title was typed in large print. *Maggi.* "This is some kind of computer manual or book. It looks like something a college kid would have created for himself." She was flipping through the pages. "No text. Formulas, mathematics, chemistry. I can't make it out. Can you?"

He glanced at it. "No, but I'm not a scientist. And I'm more interested in what you allowed Montez to do to you." He lifted her chin and examined her jaw. "You're going to have a bad bruise. You only barely came out on top on this one."

"I'm fine." She felt a rush of tingling sensation and quickly leaned back, away from his hand. "Montez should be regaining consciousness soon. I have to find something with which to tie him while I talk to him."

"By all means. We wouldn't want him to clip you again." He got to his feet. "But I'll do it. I'm usually prepared for any eventuality, and if I'm not, I improvise. It's part of my training in Tibet with the monks. You stay with him and look alluring and helpless if he wakes up. Who knows? It might work the second time."

"I didn't intend to appear helpless," she said through

set teeth. "Only nonthreatening. There's a big difference as you—" She was talking to air. Cameron had vanished again into the forest.

But he would return and probably with as many gadgets and ingenious self-made devices as MacGyver on that vintage TV show. It wouldn't surprise her if he dug up a pair of handcuffs from somewhere, she thought crossly.

Stop it. She was just annoyed because she had not performed well in his eyes. They were both professionals, and she had not wanted to seem less competent than she knew she was.

What did it matter? she thought impatiently. Both she and Cameron marched to their own particular drummers. She answered only to herself or perhaps to Hu Chang. Certainly not to Cameron. She turned away from Montez and moved to the edge of the trail. Find wood and make a fire. She could do that while still keeping an eye on Montez and waiting for Cameron to come and dazzle her with his MacGyver-like ingenuity.

And then she would sit down and plan how she was going to tell Montez about Father Gabriel and his own sister, who were the latest victims of Santos. It would be ammunition to make him talk to them, but not one she would take pleasure in using.

Then don't plan, let instinct lead her to the right way to handle him.

If he could be handled. He was a man who was filled with panic and bewilderment, and that often translated to violence.

She touched her bruised jaw. For a student of theology, Montez had been less than Christian in his response to her.

She would just have to make sure she didn't turn the other cheek.

ST. JOSEPH'S HOSPITAL
ATLANTA, GEORGIA

He was there again, Jane realized with annoyance. Outlined in flames in the darkness. Sending out sparks that disturbed the serenity. She couldn't get away from him.

"No, you can't," Caleb said. "I'm glad you realize that. But I've never really gone away. I've just let you rest and get used to my being here again."

"I don't want to get used to your being here. I told you that before. I want you to go away."

"So you can go away? So you can go running back to Trevor? That's not going to happen. He doesn't want you, Jane."

"You're lying. He does want me."

"Not now. I'm not worried about him. He'll be on my side."

"He loves me."

"As much as he can love you. As much as you can love him. But there are all kinds of love, and you haven't tasted more than a sip. Trevor would want you to drain the cup. You know that, Jane."

"I don't know what you're talking about. I don't want to know."

"Too bad. Because I don't really care what Trevor wants. It's what I want that's important." His voice was velvet soft, insistent as a haunting melody. "And I want you to live, Jane. Not only will you live, but you'll reach out and embrace life. I won't have it any other way."

"You don't have anything to say about it. I'm dying."

"But you're better. I've been working, mending, helping you to mend yourself. I'm not there yet, but I'm closer. You're having trouble not being aware of me all the time. I'm behind you, pushing. Soon I'll be in front, leading."

"No."

"Yes." He smiled. "Give it up. I won't let you go. I'll sit here and work on that mending. And now it's time for you to think about something besides Trevor. So I'll slip in a few memories to blur him . . ."

She tensed. "Of you?"

"No, we've not really had that kind of relationship yet. Close, but not quite there. I'm looking forward to it." He chuckled. "No, I'll make those memories pure as the driven snow. Not at all what you'd expect of me."

"I don't expect anything of you."

"Then you should. You should expect everything from me. Because that's what you'll get."

"Certainly not anything pure or without—"

"Shh, what's more pure than the love of a puppy? Remember the day Eve gave you Toby? You were only a kid, weren't you? Remember the excitement, the pure joy of living? And all the time he's been with you, he's given you that same joy. But we'll start when he was a puppy and let you start reliving there. You were at the lake cottage, and it was only a little while after Eve and Joe took you into their home . . ."

He's mine, Eve? He's really mine?" Jane hugged the half-golden retriever, half-wolf bundle of fur closer to her chest. "Sarah sent him to me to keep forever?"

"As close to forever as it gets." Eve smiled. "She doesn't want him back if that's what you mean. She knew how much you loved her Monty and wanted you to have his and Maggie's firstborn. What are you going to call him?"

"I'll have to think. Maybe . . . Toby? He's so beautiful." Her eyes flew to meet Eve's. "I don't deserve him. I loved Sarah's dog so much that I wanted him to love me instead of her. That was bad, wasn't it, Eve? It was selfish.

But I'd never had anything that was really mine to love. And now she's given me this wonderful puppy of Monty's to be my own. Should I call her and tell her how bad I was? Maybe she'd want him back."

"I don't think that's likely," Eve said gently. "Sarah knows what a good home you'll give him. Because you've never had a home all these years, you know its value. And she'd understand that you'd need a dog of your own. Having something to love is very important."

Jane nodded. "And when you do, you should hold on tight and never let go." Her arms hugged the puppy closer. "That's what I'm going to do. Never, never, let go . . ."

CHAPTER 9

RAIN FOREST
GUATEMALA

"Who are you?"

Catherine's gaze went to where Montez was lying, across the fire from where she was sitting. "Awake at last? I didn't think you'd be out that long." She could see his muscles tense, and said quickly, "Don't try anything. Your wrists and ankles are tied. We thought it was a wise precaution considering that you decided to sock me."

"Who are you?" he repeated. "And who are 'we'?"

"I'm Catherine Ling." She reached in her jacket and pulled out her ID. "CIA. I know you're on the run from Santos. I don't have anything to do with him."

"Yes, you do. I know better than that."

"Do you?" Her eyes were narrowed on his face. "I'd like to know just how." She jerked her head to the right. "And 'we' includes Richard Cameron, who is leaning against that pine over there. He's responsible for finding some vines to tie you up so that you couldn't sock me again. He covered some strands of wire he had with him to keep them from cutting you. Not an entirely MacGyver-like solution, but I took what I could get."

"He's CIA, too?"

"No, a sort of civilian."

"Sort of?" Montez's eyes were wide with suspicion as he gazed at Cameron. "I've been around too many 'civilians' bought off by Santos. How do I know that he's—"

"You don't." Cameron strolled forward into the firelight. "You'll have to trust Catherine to keep me in line. I'm totally terrified of her."

"Shut up, Cameron," Catherine said. "You're not making it any easier for him."

"I don't intend to do that. I'm still a little pissed off that he clipped that lovely jaw of yours. You want to put him at ease? You do it."

"I'm finding it difficult trusting either one of you with my hands and feet tied like this," Montez said. "Was it you who were asking questions of Marco at the restaurant and sent Father Gabriel into a panic?"

Catherine shook her head. "No."

He inhaled sharply. "Not CIA? I was hoping—" He stopped. "Then why did you come after me? How did you know I was on the run?"

"The world didn't stop when you decided to hide away with Father Gabriel," Catherine said. "Santos didn't stop. He went after me, and when I became curious about your connection with him, it revived his interest in you."

"It didn't need reviving," he said bitterly. "I knew it was only a matter of time. I just hoped that they'd keep Santos in that prison for the rest of his life. Not likely. Even when they first arrested him, he was making deals and hatching schemes."

"Making deals?" Catherine repeated slowly. "What deals? I didn't hear about any deals."

"Forget it," Montez said shortly. "Why should I talk to you? I'm better off on my own. Santos hates you. Dorgal told me how much Santos hated you."

"Better off?" Catherine said. "I don't think you're doing so well, Montez."

"Or maybe he is," Cameron said. "It's the people around him that are suffering." His lips tightened. "The count is mounting. Tell him about the priest."

"Priest?" Montez stiffened. "Father Gabriel?" He inhaled sharply. "Is he all right? He told me he was going to hide in the village."

"He didn't make it," Catherine said gently. "He was dead when Cameron and I reached the church. Shot. We managed to take down the two men who did it, but it was too late for Father Gabriel."

"God in Heaven." Montez's eyes closed. "My fault. I told him that it wasn't safe for him to let me stay at the church. He wouldn't let me leave. He said that life gives second chances, and no one should know that better than I." He opened eyes glittering with moisture. "But he didn't have a second chance, did he?"

"And neither did your sister, Lena," Cameron said quietly.

"Lena?"

"Dorgal needed information. He thought she might be able to give it to him."

Montez turned pale. "She didn't know anything except that I was heading for this area. Nothing definite. And I was careful not to communicate with anyone after Santos killed my brother. She didn't *know*." He paused. "He killed her?"

"Yes," Catherine said. "I'm sorry for your loss."

"But being sorry won't replace her," Cameron said. "Or get revenge for her death. Only you can do that, Montez. Talk to us. Tell us why Santos is so interested in keeping you alive. Tell us why you and Dorgal had a chat about Catherine. That must have been about the time that Santos ordered your brother's death. Significant connection?"

Montez was silent.

"Listen, Montez," Catherine said. "Do I feel sorry for you? Yes. I believe you tried to break with Santos. I think you may be a victim. But I have victims of my own to avenge and protect. I've had three friends who have died, another is hanging on by a thread. My son's life may be on the line if I don't find Santos. I want to know everything you know about him." She held his gaze. "I will know it. I'll give you a little while to absorb your own personal tragedy, but one way or the other, you'll tell me what I need to know."

"You're threatening me?" His lips twisted. "I gave in to threats once, and where did it get me? I'm tired of threats. Look at you. You're such a beautiful woman. But you're probably as much a monster as Delores Santos."

"Catherine's not a monster," Cameron said softly. "And I'm irritated that you'd call her that. You don't want to irritate me, Montez."

"Drop it, Cameron. We've thrown some pretty rough flak at him." Catherine turned and pulled out the well-thumbed book with the yellow cover she'd taken out of Montez's knapsack. She pointed to the title *Maggi*. "What is this, Montez?"

He tensed. "What do you think it is?"

"I can't make heads or tails of it or I wouldn't be asking you. It looks like a bunch of chemical formulas."

"Give it to me. It's mine."

"What is it?" she repeated.

"You might as well give it to me. No one would understand it but me."

"I have a friend who might. Hu Chang would find it interesting."

"*Give* it to me."

"After we have a talk about Santos and how you can help me save the people I care about." She put the book back in her jacket. "And after I'm sure that it's of no value to Santos. I'm not giving him anything that he wants."

"I wouldn't give him anything he wants if I can help it," Montez said desperately. "I'll disappear. I'll dig down so deep, no one will be able to find me. All I want is to keep him from killing any more of my family. Let me go."

"I might be able to do that if I was sure that you couldn't help me find Santos. But I'm not sure that's true." She paused, her gaze on his face, waiting for any flicker of expression. "Have you ever been to the place where Santos has set up his new headquarters?"

Montez stared her in the eye. "No, I have not. I dealt only with Dorgal. I talked to Santos on the phone several times years ago, but that was before you managed to topple him and send him to prison."

"He didn't communicate with you while he was in prison?"

"No, everything was through Dorgal after that. Nor has Dorgal ever given me a hint as to where Santos's new compound is located. I knew that Dorgal was setting up a safe haven for Santos somewhere, but I hoped that Santos would stay in prison and not be able to use it."

"Safe haven," Cameron repeated. "How would you know what Dorgal was doing for Santos? It had to be top secret. Why would you know, Montez?"

Montez didn't answer.

Cameron's voice turned stinging hard. "Why?"

"Because I *had* to know. Satisfied?" A muscle was jerking in Montez's cheek, and his dark eyes held panic. "But I didn't want to know. I didn't want to know anything more. I could see where it was headed. That's why I ran away." His gaze flew back to Catherine. "And they let me go, but they gave me a warning."

"Your brother's death."

He nodded.

"But can't you see that it will just keep on? Your brother, your sister, Father Gabriel? How many deaths will you accept before you fight back?"

"I can see that if I don't take that warning, Santos will kill another one of my family. My mother is still alive, and so is my little nephew, Nathaniel."

"Everything you do is a danger to your family. You ran away, and your brother died. You stayed hidden, and they wanted to find you, so your sister died." Her voice was shaking with passion. "Do you think I don't know how that feels? Santos is threatening everyone I love, and it seems everything I do is the wrong thing. But your choice is to be a slave to that son of a bitch or fight him. You *must* know something, or Santos wouldn't have been afraid of having me find you."

"I don't know where he is," Montez repeated. "I can't help it if you won't believe me."

She did believe him. "Okay, but I think you can help us to find him. Will you try to do that? Look, we could set a trap for him if you'd consent to be the bait. Let Dorgal capture you and take you to Santos. We'll find a way to track you. We'll protect you and your family, and we'll make sure Santos never troubles you again."

"You're crazy. You expect me to trust you that much?"

"I hope you will." She held his gaze. "I'm telling you the truth. Can't you see it?"

He looked away from her.

"I know it's dangerous, but so is being on the run from Santos when any moment he might decide he doesn't need you. *Help* us, Montez."

He shook his head.

"I could persuade him," Cameron offered.

"No, it's not that simple. Didn't you hear me? I believe him. I don't want him hurt. We'll just stay here, and I'll try to convince him that—"

"I could do that, too." Cameron tilted his head. "Or go inside and attempt to find out why Santos wants him kept alive. Though he's so stubborn, there might be minor damage."

"Go inside," Montez repeated warily.

"Not unless there's no other way," Catherine said. "I told you, I don't want him hurt. He's suffered enough. We just need to make it clear to him what—"

Cameron's cell phone rang. He glanced at the caller ID and put it on speaker. "Dario."

"I hope you're moving very fast, Cameron," Dario said. "Because you may have company soon."

"What kind of company?"

"Dorgal. He must have been on his way to San Esposito and sent those two men who killed the priest on ahead."

"He's alone?"

"He was alone when he flew into the airport. He checked out the situation at the church, made a few phone calls, and two hours later he got reinforcements from over the border and a few local villages. By the time he started tracking you into that rain forest, he had twenty-two men."

Catherine muttered a curse.

"Is that our lovely Catherine?" Dario asked. "You won't be totally alone. I gathered together five of my own men, who are far superior to Dorgal's, and we're only fifteen, twenty minutes behind him. However, he has to be fairly close to you."

"Closer than you think," Catherine said. "We had over two hours' delay after we overtook Montez."

"Not good. Should we try to ambush Dorgal, Cameron?"

"No, not yet. Keep me informed. I'll get back to you." He hung up. "You heard him." He started putting out the fire. "Let's move."

"Untie me," Montez said. "Unless you want to serve

me up for Dorgal. He'd love telling Santos how you did that for him."

"No, we don't want to make it easy for Dorgal." Catherine unsheathed her knife and cut the vines binding him. "And we sure as hell don't want to have Santos get his hands on you. Which he will do if we don't move fast."

"Let me go," Montez said urgently. "You don't have to worry about me. I'll take care of myself." He jumped to his feet. "Look, if you hadn't caught me, I would have been all right. I spent months hiding in the rain forests before I went to Father Gabriel. I can do it again."

"With Dorgal on the hunt for you?" Cameron asked. "Personally, I would just as soon let you take your chances. But Catherine is feeling protective, so you go with us."

"No." His jaw set. "She says that she doesn't want me hurt. Let's see if she's speaking the truth. I won't go with you. You'll have to hurt me to make me do it."

He meant it, Catherine realized with frustration. "You're being a fool. Where could you hide?"

"I was heading for the Benedictine monastery at the far end of the rain forest. Father Gabriel made arrangements for me to stay there in case of an emergency. I won't let the monks run the risk of hiding me now. I'll find somewhere in the forest. But later, after Dorgal checks them out, I could make contact and have them find a safe place for me."

"He'll disappear, and you'll never see him again," Cameron said flatly. "We'll have it to do all over again."

But Montez wasn't going to help her anyway, unless she used force. She could see it in his expression, the tautness of his jaw.

Save him.

Let him live another day.

Hope that he'd realize that they were fighting the same battle.

"Then we'll do it again." Catherine turned and headed for the trail. "Okay, we'll let you go, Montez. But I want to do it right. We passed a stream a half mile to the east. You come with us. I want your footprints clearly heading east. Once we reach the stream, we can blur them and eventually lose the print. Then you take off south in the direction of the monastery. Cameron and I will make sure that you're not followed."

"How?"

"What do you care? You prefer hiding to confrontation." She was striding down the trail. "If you change your mind, I'll be glad to have your help."

"Taunting isn't going to make me do what you want," he said quietly. "You have your own agenda, just like Santos."

"No, but maybe this will help you to trust me." She turned to face him as she reached the stream. "Cameron has hired a very talented man who is every bit as deadly as Dorgal. His name is Rafael Dario. We'll have his men protect your mother and nephew from Santos. He'd protect you, too, if you'd allow it. But your family will definitely be protected. You can feel safe that whatever you do, nothing is going to happen to them."

"I'm supposed to believe you?"

"Believe what you wish. I've told you what I'm going to do."

"Why?"

"Perhaps because I'm not a monster like Delores Santos. Or perhaps because this isn't over, and I'll be back to ask you again to help us get Santos. Or maybe I'll call you and ask you if you've changed your mind." She scrawled her cell number on a card and gave it to him. "Or you can call me. I'll have Dario pick you up."

Montez's lips tightened. "I don't promise you anything."

"But I've made you a promise, and I'll keep it. Now get out of here."

He stood there looking at her, his expression a myriad of conflicting emotions.

"Go!"

He started to turn. "Maybe you're not like his Delores . . ."

"Thank you. I might remind you that I shot Delores Santos."

"Oh, yes, but you don't have to remind me of that." He hesitated. "I have friends. I'll know if you're telling the truth about having Dario protect my family."

"Good. Now get out of here before you ruin everything."

He hesitated once more, staring at her, then at Cameron.

Then he was gone.

"You rolled the dice," Cameron said. "Interesting. But I would have handled it differently."

"Get Dario on the phone and tell him to protect Montez's family."

"Oh, I will. But I'll also tell him to track down Montez near that monastery and keep an eye on him in case we need to talk to him again."

"That was going to be my next request." She slanted him a smile. "And I know you would have handled it differently. We have different skills and viewpoints. I believe him, and I think he has to come to us. But I also remember how patient you were with Erin when you were trying to recruit her. You aren't totally ruthless." She shrugged. "Besides, I still have that book he was so eager to get back."

"Keeping the book was the only thing that we agreed on. And the circumstances with Erin were different. I'm still angry with Montez for hurting you. I think it's going to take a long time for me to get over that." He shrugged. "We shall see. You get a branch and erase the prints Montez just made going back down the trail. I'll get busy blurring these footprints so well that we'll make Dorgal dizzy, and he'll end up back at San Esposito."

ST. JOSEPH'S HOSPITAL
ATLANTA, GEORGIA

"Progress?" Eve asked softly.

Caleb glanced up at Eve as she came to stand beside Jane's bed. "Yes and no. I think by tomorrow I might ask you to have that Dr. Basle have another look at her and reevaluate his opinion about the graft."

"Thank God."

"Yeah."

"So what's the no?"

"He might decide to do it before I can get her ready for it."

"Then we'll not bring him in again yet. We'll give her some more time."

"I don't have any more time."

She inhaled sharply. "That's not possible. All the doctors gave her seven to ten days. You've only been working with her for two days."

"I told you that they couldn't be sure of the time factor when the blood was concerned."

"But only two days? It should be longer than that."

"Yes."

Her hand grasped his shoulder. "Talk to me. Don't you sit there and give me one-word answers. Why is she going downhill?"

He twisted around to look at her. "Why?" His eyes

were glowing fiercely in his taut face. "Because of *me*. Because that's where she wants to go. Because she's afraid of what I'm doing."

"Then do something to change it."

"Do you think I'm not trying? No one knows better than you how stubborn Jane can be. Well, she's made up her mind, and she won't let go of him."

Her fingers dug into his shoulder. "Trevor?"

"Who else? I've been trying to offer substitutes. She loves her dog, her work as an artist, the beauty of the world around her. It's all important to her, but it's not enough." He got to his feet. "I'm glad you're here. I was going to come and get you anyway. It was time I brought in the big guns."

"And that's what I'm supposed to be?"

"You know you are. She loves you, she respects you, she'll listen to you."

"She's in a coma. I wasn't even sure that she was aware I was talking to her."

"She's aware. She was just shutting you out. She tried to do the same thing to me, but I wouldn't let her. So she started to go down deeper." He pushed her down into the chair he'd just vacated. "It's over to you now. I brought her halfway back. You keep her on the right track and away from Trevor."

"It sounds easy," she said bitterly.

"Easier than letting her go." His eyes were suddenly blazing. "Do you know how hard it is for me to leave her now? I want to do it all. But she won't let me that close to her." He turned on his heel. "So you do it, and I'll reach out as much as I can. Get busy."

Get busy.

It was an order she'd be glad to obey if she only knew how to start.

The only way to begin was to start in the beginning.

And hope that Caleb's certainty that Jane could hear her was right.

She took Jane's hand. "Caleb says that you can hear me and are just pretending and shutting me out. If you are, it's because you're confused. You wouldn't deceive me. We've always been honest with each other. Or have we? You told me that it was fine that we were best friends, and you didn't want to replace Bonnie as my daughter. Was it true? You'd been through so much growing up on the streets that I thought your defenses were too high for any other relationship. Hey, I was wounded and damaged, too. Maybe I accepted what you said because of that. I hope not. I was an adult, and you were a child. It was my job to give you whatever you needed." She leaned back in the chair, her mind going back to those years of watching Jane grow and change and become a woman. "But how I loved you. I realized how special you were, and you filled Joe's and my lives with joy. Can you feel that love, Jane? It's still there and as powerful as ever. I love you so much that I'd let you go if I thought it was best for you. But it's not best; you have so many things to do, so many loves to know. And even after all these years, we still have so much to learn about each other. You have to stay with me, and I'll watch you and love you, and maybe we'll come to understand why we were meant to be together. Okay?" She drew a shaky breath. "Are you saying yes? It's very hard to know without your opening your eyes and smiling at me. I really wish you would do that." Her hand tightened on Jane's. "Not ready yet? Then let's talk about Trevor. Caleb says that you want to be with him. Understandable. You've loved him since you were only seventeen. I remember you came back from Scotland and told me how dizzy he made you. You were young and not sure if it was anything deeper. We were sitting on the porch and looking out at the lake. And we talked about velvet nights, which was sex, then silver mornings, which might mean something deeper. I know you remember that night because we've talked about it since then, and it was important to you, too. But you realized something else as we talked about it, didn't you? Remember, Jane?"

Silver mornings . . . Eve put her cup down on the railing and sat down on the step beside Jane. "A relationship that changed the way you see everything?" She put her arm around Jane. "Fresh and clean and bright in a dark world. May you find that someday, Jane."

"I already have them." She smiled at Eve. "You give one to me every day. When I'm down, you bring me up. When I'm confused, you make everything clear. When I think there's no love in the world, I remember the years you gave me." She leaned her head contentedly back on Eve's shoulder. "Silver mornings aren't restricted to lovers. They can come from mothers, fathers, sisters, and brothers, good friends . . . They can all change how you see your world, too."

"Yes, they can."

They sat in silence for a long time, gazing out at the lake in contentment. Finally, Eve sighed. "I suppose we should go in."

Jane smiled. "Hell, let's not go to bed. Let's wait for the dawn and see if it comes up silver."

I'll always remember your smile that night," Eve said unsteadily. "It lit up your face, and it lit up my life. Because I knew that no matter what happened between you and Trevor, the love between us was going to go on. And when later you realized that Trevor was the silver morning that you wanted to fill your life, I rejoiced. When he was killed, I mourned."

"But I think you forgot that there are other silver mornings, and now you have to remember that night on the porch. Let me help you remember. Open your eyes. Come back to me."

Jane didn't move.

She repeated unsteadily, "Dammit, you come back to me."

Hold on, Eve. She's so close to you. She's almost there.

Caleb's gaze was zeroed in on Jane's face from where he stood outside the ICU.

He could *feel* the emotion Jane was experiencing. He'd been right to send Eve to do what he could not do. God, he'd wanted to be able to bring her back on his own.

But Jane was slipping back again.

"No!"

There was something in the background.

No, *someone* in the background.

Trevor, get the hell away from her. Let me take her. You're the only one holding her back. I know you don't want her to stay with you now. But you're having trouble leaving her. Let her see you turn your back and walk away.

Struggle. Pain. Resignation.

Gone.

Caleb's relief was mixed with a strange sadness.

I don't think I could have done it, Trevor. You always were the white knight.

Okay, Jane," Eve moistened her lips. "That was only the first foray. Let's try again. I'm not going to give up. I was just hurting and got a little frustrated when I couldn't—"

"Shh," Caleb was standing beside her. "You've won the battle. She's with you. She's just saying good-bye to him. She knows it's final now."

"She's with me?" Eve's gaze flew to meet his eyes. "Does that mean that—"

"It means I have a chance to make sure that Basle does his job. You can let go of her hand now. I'll take over."

"No . . ."

Both of their eyes flew to Jane's face at the mere wisp of sound. Her eyes were open, and she was looking at Eve.

"Oh, my God," Eve whispered. "You're awake, baby."

"You wouldn't . . . let . . . me go. Right . . . But hurts. Sorry." Her hand tightened on Eve's. "Stay."

"Of course, I'll stay. But Caleb needs to—"

"No."

"Yes," Caleb said. "But I'll draw up a chair to the other side of the bed. You can stay with her, Eve. But don't let her talk any more." He turned to leave. "I'll go tell the head nurse that she's no longer comatose, then go find Joe and give him the good news. Then I'll be back." He looked at Jane. "I'll always be back. I know that you're resenting me. I expected it." His lips twisted. "I've always been the black knight, never the white knight like Trevor. But I'm the one who will keep you surviving in this wicked old world."

"No . . . I'll . . . do . . . that." Her lids were closing again. "Can't let— You're all . . . fire and darkness . . . no silver . . . mornings."

"No?" He headed for the door. "Do you know I actually felt a twinge when you said that? I'll have to think about it and decide if I need to work on changing your mind. Take care of her, Eve. The minute the word gets around that she's out of her coma, it raises the possibility that Santos could move against her."

"We're on our way back, Hu Chang," Catherine said as soon as he picked up. "We spent the last seven hours dodging Dorgal and some of his goons in the rain forest near San Esposito. Our jet just took off from the airport. Is everything okay there at home?"

"Catherine, you texted me three times since you left here asking me that question. Why would it not be, with me in charge?" Hu Chang said. "And why would I not have sent you word if there were a problem?"

"Because you'd try to take care of it yourself. No sign of Santos's people?"

"No. But if they gave out signals, there would be nothing to worry about." He changed the subject. "You found Montez?"

"Yes, but he wouldn't talk, and we had to leave him down there temporarily."

"It isn't like you to accept a defeat. Most uncharacteristic."

"That's what Cameron said. He didn't approve." She added wearily, "But I believed Montez when he said that he didn't know where Santos is. In his own way, I think he's been struggling against him. And I didn't want to be the one to make him suffer any more than he has already." She paused. "How is Luke?"

"Upset that you didn't say good-bye to him."

"He would have wanted to go with me. That wasn't an option."

"I explained that to him and turned him over to Kelly. I was going to bring Erin in, but Kelly offers him challenges, and that's what he needs."

"If he doesn't persuade her to go after Santos with him," she said dryly. "It's definitely a possibility. He knows that Kelly helped to find him when he was being held by Rakovac. You know how brilliant she is at seeing patterns and connections when no one else can do it. It's almost an Einstein mentality. That's what she does at that think tank at college. Even Venable was considering trying to use her for some of his other cases."

"And will you try to use her?"

"She persuaded me to let her do what she could. I'm going to tap every source I can. If a situation arises where she can safely give us help, I'll ask her, not tell her." She changed the subject. "And speaking about tapping sources, I'm going to tap you, Hu Chang. I'm bringing you a paperback book I took from Montez. I think it's his own work. It's full of all kinds of the deliciously complicated chemical and mathematical puzzles and equations that you like. At least, it's complicated to me. You may find it child's play."

"Really?" He sounded fascinated. "Intriguing. I admit, like Luke, I'm desperately searching for a challenge. Let's hope that you're bringing me one that is worthy of me. Does this book have a title?"

"*Maggi.* Does it spark anything?"

"Not at the moment. I will think about it. When can I have the book?"

"I told you, I'm bringing it to you. You want the exact time? About six hours." She chuckled. "You're more eager to see all those calculations than you are to see us safely back there. I regret that you no longer look on me as a challenge, Hu Chang."

"You are always a challenge, always new, always fresh. But, unfortunately, you have no desire to explore the intricacies of the chemical rules of the universe and how to change them. That is why I had to turn to Luke to teach. He is coming along fabulously."

"No poisons, Hu Chang."

"Not until he is ready to accept the responsibility."

"No poisons."

He sighed. "One must furnish an entire picture. I will have to convince you of that someday. But there is time."

"I haven't heard from Eve. Jane?"

"Still alive. The last I checked with Eve, she had called

in Seth Caleb to come see Jane. It appears to be a last-ditch effort."

"Caleb." She remembered her encounters with Seth Caleb when they had been hunting and trying to save Eve last year. Dark, interesting, riveting, and totally focused on Jane MacGuire. She had heard strange rumors about his ability to manipulate blood flow, but she had not thought Eve would call on him for help. But perhaps Hu Chang was right, and desperation had led Eve down that path. "Yes, that's what it seems to be. I'd probably do the same if I were her. After I hang up from you, I'm going to call her."

"Give her my best wishes. I regret her sorrow. She is an extraordinary woman."

"Yes, she is. I'm hanging up now, Hu Chang. I'll see you soon."

"Yes, you will." His tone was absent, and she knew he was no longer paying attention. *"Maggi . . ."*

"Everything is status quo?" Cameron asked from his seat next to her as he looked up from his computer. "I won't say good, because that would be too optimistic."

"No escalation. But that may change once Dorgal reports back to Santos that he didn't gather Montez into his net. It would be too much to expect that his contacts won't have known that we were after him, too."

"But those same contacts will be able to tell him that Montez wasn't with us when we boarded this plane. Which means that he'll still be scouring that rain forest for him."

"Then we have to hope that Montez will be as good at hiding in the forest as he told us," Catherine said grimly. "Or that Dario will be able to keep a damn good watch on him."

"Dario will do his job." Cameron looked back down at his computer. "But you did make things more difficult."

"I believe you mentioned that."

"Edgy, Catherine?" He smiled faintly. "I just needed to make sure that you remember it wasn't my call if it blows up in your face. I admit I'm feeling a bit resentful that I wasn't allowed to be in control of the situation. It felt very strange."

"I imagine that's true. You're not accustomed to not being king of the mountain. But this is my problem, my mountain, and I didn't invite you to solve it for me."

"I believe I've been very good at taking a backseat. I disappeared and let you confront Montez by yourself." He tilted his head. "Then I stood by and watched him hurt you and didn't step in and gut him. That took a significant amount of restraint. You know, Catherine, I think that you came out way ahead of the game." He added softly, "But don't expect that to also be the status quo. I've been taught discipline, but I always have trouble applying those principles to you."

Status quo? Not likely. Cameron was always changing, innovating, doing the unexpected. Sometimes it was frustrating, often exciting, always disturbing. Yet it was true that he'd been amazingly laid-back and compliant when she'd been dealing with Montez. Compliant? What was she thinking? He was probably just biding his time before he stepped in and tried to take over the action with his usual lethal efficiency. But she was in no mood to argue with him right now. She was tired and discouraged. She had hoped for more when she had gone after Montez. "I'm going to call Eve at the hospital. The last thing that Hu Chang had heard was that Jane was still alive and Eve was trying anyone and everything to find a cure for her." She made a face. "Including a wild card that proves she's really desperate."

"I believe in wild cards."

"So do I, sometimes." She was dialing Eve's number.

"But I don't know about this one. I don't know about Seth Caleb . . ."

"We haven't been able to find Montez yet, Santos," Dorgal said. "There was interference, and things did not go smoothly." He added quickly, "But we're still searching. It's only a matter of time. You know I'll never give up."

"Why did things not go smoothly?" Santos asked harshly. "You had money, you had men. Montez had nothing. All you had to do was find him and gather him up."

"That's not entirely correct. Montez had Catherine Ling. We believe she made contact with him. I didn't tell you before because I hoped to have the situation resolved quickly and not bother you."

"Catherine Ling has Montez?" Santos asked slowly, spacing every word.

"No, she left San Esposito by plane with only Richard Cameron. But she was seen entering the rain forest where we tracked Montez. At one point, we saw three sets of prints but lost them in the forest. But I've just had a report that one of the trackers caught sight of fresh prints to the north that he thinks might be Montez's."

"Might be."

"Almost certain. And Montez is alone. Maybe he was on the run from Ling, too."

" 'Might.' 'Maybe.' I don't like those words."

"Look, there's no way Montez would talk to Ling. He's been hiding from us for two years because he was scared shitless. His brother and sister are dead, and he knows there might be more. He might not want to cooperate with us, but he's not going to talk. You said yourself he wasn't a priority unless you decided you needed him. That's why we didn't go after him before this."

"I know all that. But the reason I sent you is that I knew

Ling or Cameron had probably zeroed in on Montez. That made it a priority, dammit."

"I'll find him. I'll deliver him to you. Don't worry."

"I'm not worrying. Because I know you'll keep your word. We've been together a long time, and you've never failed me." He paused. "But Delores was always a little suspicious of you, did you know that? Naturally, I tried to convince her how wrong she was."

Dorgal had always known the bitch had never trusted him. It would have only been a matter of time before Delores would have been able to persuade Santos to get rid of him. "I only wish she'd lived so that I could convince her myself. She'd know how hard I've worked to do what you both wanted of me. She wouldn't doubt me now."

"It always took a lot to convince Delores. For instance, she would consider delivering Montez to me as a test." He paused. "So you'll continue to hunt for Montez and find him very quickly. You'll question him and make sure he didn't tell Ling anything. You wouldn't want to fail Delores."

She's dead. The bitch is dead, you prick. "Whatever you say. I'd better get to it. Anything else?"

"There will probably be a great deal else. Ling slipped down there to Guatemala and might have made contact with Montez. Even if she didn't find out anything from him, it was still a minor victory for her that she knew he was important to me. Thanks to you, I'm feeling on the defensive. So while you're busy doing what you should have accomplished already, I'll be looking north to see how I can make that small victory taste very bitter for her. Call me when you've located Montez, and I might let you make amends in the way that Delores would most approve." He hung up.

A bloodbath.

Santos was talking about a bloodbath, Dorgal realized. Delores had always gone for the jugular when the opportunity presented itself. And Santos was always only a breath away from savagery. Fear of arousing that bloodlust was one of the prime factors to his rise to the top of the cartel. He would be smooth and cool and clever, then suddenly release the demons. Dorgal had been around Santos too long not to recognize the signs that his composure was crumbling. It was surprising that it had not happened before. Only the obsession with his plan to make Ling suffer and its initial success had staved off his basic need to indulge himself.

And the only way to reinstate himself in Santos's good graces would be to pander to that part of him. Dorgal would go after Montez, but he'd designate one of his men to continue with the hunt if it stretched out too long.

He had to be free to find a way to attack Ling directly and be the hero. That would give Santos what he wanted.

Blood.

She's out of the coma?" Catherine repeated. "My God, that's wonderful, Eve."

"You bet it is," Eve said. "But she's not out of the woods. Dr. Basle is flying back for a reevaluation on the surgery. But Caleb thinks he'll go for it. The graft would be very delicate and extremely chancy."

"But 'chance' is the key word," Catherine said. "It would give her a chance that she didn't have before." She paused. "You're banking a lot on Caleb."

"Because he came through for me. Or for Jane. Or for himself. With Caleb, it's hard to guess why he's doing anything. But he's getting it done, and that's all that's important."

"No payback?"

"I'll worry about that after I'm sure Jane is going to live," Eve said. "Like I told Joe, I'll handle it." She added, "Right now, we're dealing with keeping her alive and security issues. We had to tell the hospital staff that she was out of the coma, but we're trying to downplay that we have any hope for the graft. Joe will keep Basle quiet, and we'll have to do a damn good job of acting appropriately depressed and desperate." She let out her breath in a shaky sigh. "Lord, I hope it's an act. For the first time, I'm actually feeling hope."

"Do you need me to come to you?"

"No, I have Joe." She added wryly, "And it seems we have Caleb, whether Jane likes it or not."

"As I remember, she was always wary of him. No gratitude?"

"Maybe later. She has too many mixed feelings at the moment. I think she knows she can't give Caleb an inch, or he'll take the world."

"But he gave the world back to her this time."

"She has mixed feelings about that, too. At any rate, I'm grateful, and I owe him. I just don't owe him Jane. Any news of Santos?"

"Status quo, as Cameron says. Montez may know something that can help, but his motives are complicated, and he doesn't trust anyone. But I'm hoping for a breakthrough." She paused. "And I still have the dog tag you gave me. I'll find Santos and give it to him."

"Do that. Maybe I should feel merciful now that Jane has a chance to live, but that's not happening, Catherine." She saw Caleb standing in the door of the waiting room. "I have to go. I need to get back to Jane."

"Give her my best. If you need anything, call me." Catherine hung up.

"Is anything wrong, Caleb?" Eve pressed the disconnect and shoved the phone in her pocket. "Is she—"

"Nothing's wrong." His lips twisted. "She just needed a break from me, and I let Joe rescue her. She'll feel safe and comfortable with him. She'll calm down, and all the tension will flow out of her . . . until I come back." He got a cup of coffee from the machine. "You were talking to Catherine when I came in? Any news of that son of a bitch?"

She shook her head. "Not yet. You sound as bitter as I am."

"Oh, yes." He took a swallow of coffee. "I haven't had time to think of anything but keeping Jane alive since I got here. But now I'm beginning to think of ways and means to castrate Santos, then tear him limb from limb." His voice was almost pleasant. "Jane usually disapproves of my savage streak, but this time she'll just have to suck it up." He looked Eve in the eye. "Somehow I don't believe you would disapprove of anything I'd choose to do to Santos. It's very personal for you."

"Terribly personal." She shrugged. "But you may have to stand in line. Catherine is very angry, and so are the people who care about her."

"I don't like to stand in lines." His gaze went to the ICU down the hall. "So much security . . . police, detectives. Practically tripping over one another. You'd think that would ensure there were no slipups, wouldn't you? That isn't always the case. People get overconfident and all it takes is one."

"You think Santos will come after her."

"Or one of his men. I'm starting to look very closely at everyone on the floor, to zero in on any possible Santos recruits. He'll almost certainly go on the attack if they think she has a chance of recovery. Don't you agree?"

"Yes. That's why we'll try to keep it from him."

"But Santos has deep pockets, and that buys information."

"You don't seem upset by the prospect."

"Let him come." He smiled recklessly as he tossed his empty cup in the basket. "Then I won't have to stand in line."

CHAPTER 10

"You didn't tell me you were going," Luke said as he came out of the library when Catherine and Cameron walked in the front door. "Why not?"

"It was the middle of the night and—" She stopped. No deceit. She wouldn't have appreciated it, and her son wouldn't either. "I was afraid you'd want to go along, and I didn't want to argue with you. I didn't know what I was going to have to deal with in Guatemala. I wanted you here with Hu Chang, so I wouldn't have to worry about you."

"But I worried about *you*." He turned to Cameron. "And you let her do it. I thought you knew that I wouldn't—"

"Get in the way?" Cameron finished. "Oh, I did. I know your potential. I wasn't much older than you when I was training in Guardian duties in the Himalayas. But I wasn't about to try to overrule Catherine when it came to you." He smiled as he glanced at Catherine. "It's your job to battle it out with her. But you'll have to be very patient and gentle. I'll be very annoyed if you manage to hurt her feelings."

Luke turned back to Catherine. "Why don't you trust me? Did I do anything wrong when we went after Kelly?"

"No. It wasn't that you did—"

"Stop interrogating her, Luke." Hu Chang came out of the library. "Hello, Catherine. If you'd let me know before you arrived at the front door, I would have had a discussion with Luke on diplomacy and kindness." He looked back at Luke. "Can't you see that she's tired and on edge? Clearly things didn't go as well as she hoped, and now you make her feel unworthy of meeting your needs. I'd advise you to think about her and not yourself."

Luke frowned. "Unworthy? That's not what I meant. You know that, Hu Chang. But she should have—" He stopped and then reluctantly smiled. "I'm sorry, Catherine. I was just— And maybe I was wrong, but so were you. But I would never try to hurt your feelings." He paused. "Things didn't go well for you?"

"They could have gone better." She reached in her knapsack and pulled out Montez's book and handed it to Hu Chang. "But maybe this will start to set things right. Montez was very nervous about my taking this from him. He said no one would understand it but him, but he didn't like it out of his hands."

"Another challenge," Hu Chang murmured, as his fingers moved over the rough, well-thumbed cover. "Unless Montez is of Einstein caliber, I refuse to believe he is correct. But his words hint of a certain originality, which may be intriguing." He turned and moved toward the library. "I will get to work on this immediately."

"Because you can hardly wait," Catherine said. "You're practically salivating."

"That's very crude," Hu Chang said. "And makes intellectual curiosity appear to be deceptively uncomplicated." He glanced at Luke as he stopped at the library door. "You will be courteous?"

Luke nodded. "I wasn't discourteous. I was just asking—" He nodded jerkily. "Okay. Maybe I seemed discourteous. I'll be careful not to do it again."

"Good." Hu Chang opened the library door. "Then you might make recompense by taking her up to your room and showing her the work you and Kelly have been doing while she's been gone."

"I've done most of the research. It's up to Kelly now."

"Then let's let Catherine go up and ask her for a report," Cameron said. "I need to tour the perimeter and check out security, Luke. I know Hu Chang and Sam have it well in hand, but I always feel better if I feel the reins in my hands. You can go with me." He smiled. "If you wish. Entirely up to you."

There was little doubt that Luke would do whatever Cameron wanted him to do, Catherine thought, as she watched Cameron exert that magnetism and charisma that was such a part of his character. She had seen it work before on his men, on strangers, sometimes on her. Usually he didn't even have to tap that psychic ability he possessed.

Luke hesitated. "I'll go." He came down the rest of the stairs. "Sam moved a few of the sentries around to different parts of the grounds and street. I'll introduce you to them." His eyes were suddenly bright, eager. "But I know Sam would think it was okay if you decided something different." He smiled at Catherine as he passed her. "Kelly doesn't need me now. She thinks she's beginning to see something in Dorgal's chart. She'll probably chase you out, too." He fell into step with Cameron as he opened the front door. "I asked Sam to let me check on the sentries by myself, but he wouldn't do it. He said that Catherine wouldn't like—" His last words were cut off as the door closed behind them.

Catherine stood there, gazing at the door. Stupid to feel this sense of loss.

"What do you expect?" Hu Chang asked quietly. "Cameron is a Pied Piper whose job it is to move hearts and minds. He's been trained to the task, and his natural abilities are enormous. Luke is very easy for him."

"I know that." She lifted her chin. "I'm surrounded by Pied Pipers. You're one, too, Hu Chang. Occasionally, I just feel a little shut out to be the only one who can't seem to reach Luke."

"You reach him. That's why he's fighting so hard to keep you safe. But you're in control, and he finds that . . . difficult." Hu Chang turned away. "Now forget about how easily Cameron lured the boy away. You know he did it to distract him and let you have a little time to adjust. By the time he comes back into the house, I'd judge that Luke will have a different mind-set . . . at least temporarily."

She frowned. "He'd better damn well leave Luke's mind alone."

"Only temporary. Go see Kelly." He smiled. "I have no more time for you." He lifted Montez's book. "I have *Maggi* to decipher." He closed the door.

She seemed to be having doors closed on her right and left, Catherine thought ruefully. All done for the best and most helpful of reasons. It shouldn't have bothered her. It was totally immature.

It bothered her.

So forget it, get busy. Open doors of her own.

Go up and talk to Kelly.

"You're back." Kelly was sitting at her desk and looked up from her yellow pad as Catherine came into the bedroom. "You look exhausted." She made a face. "And as if you'd gone through a war."

"Just a rain forest. I'm getting very tired of trekking through the wilds trying to save Santos's prey." She dropped down in a chair across the room. "I tried to clean up on the plane while we were flying back to Louisville, but I definitely need a shower. You'll notice I'm staying downwind of you."

"Yes, I noticed." Kelly smiled faintly. "But I also noticed you didn't bother to shower first before you ran in to see me. Does that mean the trip was not a success?"

"You could say that. Contact, but no information. I told Hu Chang to call Venable and add Eduardo Montez to your list. Have you got any information concerning him yet?"

"Just the bare bones. I haven't had time to study him." She frowned. "But there may be something odd about Montez. I can see . . . gaps."

"Gaps?"

"Spaces in his pattern as he was growing up in Argentina. Other spaces, when he was at the university in Rio de Janeiro." She shook her head. "And there would be long periods when he'd go to visit his uncle in the hills outside Buenos Aires."

"And that was unusual?"

"Some of those periods were when he should have been in school. Both in secondary school and the university. He was able to make the time up because he was a brilliant student, but it was still strange that his parents allowed him to miss school just to visit an uncle."

"What was his uncle's name?"

"Francisco Montez. I e-mailed Venable and asked for more information about him. He hasn't gotten back to me yet."

"I took a book from Montez's backpack that he evidently wrote himself. Lots of chemical and mathematical equations. I gave it to Hu Chang to study."

"I'll ask to see it after he finishes with it." She smiled. "Not that I think I'd be able to detect anything that he didn't. Luke would look at me with infinite scorn."

"Who knows? Maybe you'd see an answer to the break in the pattern." She changed the subject. "What about Santos? Anything that you noticed about him?"

"Besides the fact that he's a monster with no conscience? He enjoys torture and thinks of himself as being above any law. He was deserted by his father, raised by a prostitute mother, involved in gangs from the time he was eight. He hooked up with Delores Janvier when she was sixteen, and she appears to have become the center of his existence."

"I know that."

"I thought you would. She was fabulously beautiful and spent a fortune on clothes and makeup to stay that way. She clearly knew that was one of her prime weapons to keep Santos interested. But what I found very interesting about Delores was that he actually listened to her. His pattern seems to have been merged with hers." She paused, then said hesitantly, "I believe she may have been in control of the relationship."

"What?"

"I found that kind of weird, too, considering what a powerhouse Santos appeared to be to everyone around him. But as I went over the material, I noticed that several decisions and opinions that Santos stated were later changed to those that Delores advocated. And when questioned, he acted as if he'd never meant anything else. They went on quite a few vacation trips together, and it was always places that Delores chose. He not only loved her, he evidently respected her and wanted to please her above anything."

Catherine pounced. "What places?"

"Several islands in the South Seas, twice to Egypt, once to Moscow, Trinidad, Grand Cayman, Jamaica." She paused. "Buenos Aires."

"Montez. Was Montez still in Argentina at that time?"

"Yes." She added, "I checked that after I read the report on Montez. Though I don't know if they made contact with him or for what purpose. But as far as I could tell, neither Santos nor Delores ever went there again."

"What about Montez? Did he visit either one of them in Caracas?"

"Not according to Venable's surveillance reports on Santos." She paused. "But Dorgal visited Buenos Aires two months after Santos and Delores went there."

"Popular place."

"Not for Montez. He left Argentina and took his entire family to Guatemala City six months later. He appeared to have plenty of money and set them all up in fine style."

"Drugs?" she murmured.

Kelly shrugged. "You'd have to tell me. Santos's cartel could have had something to do with it. I haven't found the pattern."

"What else did you find out about Dorgal?"

"Very close to Santos, as you said. From the moment Santos was arrested, Dorgal was moving with the speed of light, talking to politicians and military. Then he disappeared under the radar, and no one knew where he was or what he was doing."

"Probably setting up Santos's new compound for the time when they managed to get him out of jail."

"Anyway, Dorgal surfaced again about six weeks later. He took over de facto for Santos, running his cartel while he was in prison. He visited him weekly, so the orders probably came directly from Santos."

"Did he visit anywhere else while Santos was in prison?"

"Trinidad, Curacao, Jamaica, several other islands in the Caribbean. Probably cartel business. Overnight visits, then he'd fly back to Caracas."

"Guatemala?"

"Only once."

The day he'd arranged with Nagoles to kill Eduardo Montez's brother and sent Eduardo running for the hills. "Anything else?"

She shook her head. "I only have what Venable gave me. I'm sure CIA surveillance is good, but that doesn't mean that Dorgal wasn't able to avoid it on occasion. Did I help at all?"

"I don't know. I'll have to think about it. Santos likes sunny places, and every location you mentioned is basking in sunlight. And that doesn't mean that he might not have boarded a plane or boat out of one of those countries to his own private domain."

"I'll think about it, too," Kelly said. "And I'll double-check every stop they made and see if I can detect a pattern. Though I haven't seen any sign of it yet."

"You've done very well." She got to her feet. "I didn't expect you to pull a rabbit out of your hat. I knew it would take time, and I only hoped you could give me a clue."

"I will. Maybe more than a clue." She leaned back in her chair and rubbed her neck. "We'll find him. It will all come together. I just have to relax and let the patterns form for me. It's probably all here on this pad. I only have to connect the dots."

"I can't even see the dots," Catherine said ruefully. "I'll have to leave it to you."

"You won't do that. You'll keep plugging along, just

like I am." She tilted her head. "And the reason you can't see the dots is that it means too much to you. You're over-thinking the problem. My professors say that I do that sometimes. I reach for complexity and ignore simple applications."

"At the moment, I'd embrace simplicity." She headed for the door. "And right now I'm going to embrace the simplicity of my bed and eight hours' sleep. Good night, Kelly."

"Good night." Her gaze was once more on her yellow pad. "You do that, Catherine."

"You, too," Catherine paused at the door. "Go to bed, young lady."

"I will." She didn't look up from the pad. "Those dots are bothering me. Eduardo Montez. All those gaps. What was he doing? They were supposed to be only visits. But I don't think that . . . I should be able to see something . . . Buenos Aires . . ."

Catherine's cell phone rang as she came out of her bathroom after a shampoo and hot shower.

Cameron.

"Is everything okay with security?" she asked as she accessed the call.

"Excellent. I didn't expect anything else, but it's always smart to make sure everyone knows that there will be frequent checkups. It keeps them on their toes."

"I'm sure Sam and Hu Chang are very good at that," she said dryly.

"But some of those men are mine. They tend to accept orders better from me." He paused. "You're in bed? You didn't sleep on the plane."

"I will be soon. I just had a shower. I needed that more than sleep. Luke's back in the house?"

"I just saw him go upstairs." He chuckled. "After he

went to see Sam in the kitchen. He told him that I had to stay here and asked which room he should give me. He didn't mention that he hadn't bothered to ask me if I was staying. He's quite a kid. I've had some officers who had less grasp of sentry placement or decision making."

"He was probably trained in a harsher school. And are you staying?"

"Why not? All the action seems to be centered here." He paused. "You're here."

"Only until Hu Chang deciphers that book, or Kelly connects her dots."

"Or Montez decides that he wants to give up being a pacifist and says that he'll help us. Not likely, Catherine."

"We're moving, we're not standing still." But it felt like standing still, she thought wearily. Yet at least some good things were happening. Jane was better and might live. Santos had not been able to kill any other people she cared about.

Shallow victories that could change at any moment but she'd take them. "Now I'm going to sleep and forget all the negatives. I'll see you in the morning, Cameron."

He was silent. "I didn't mean to be totally negative. I just have to be realistic."

"Your whole philosophy is negative. That's where we differ. You think the world is going to hell in a handbasket. I think there's a chance, and we have to reach out and grab and hold tight."

"I'm trying to grab and hold tight, just in a different way. I want us to be ready to come back from that hell." He added brusquely, "But enough of that. I do have some news that isn't totally negative. I called Dario, and he said that Dorgal's men are searching that rain forest from the mountains to the border and still haven't found Montez."

"The monastery?"

"They searched there, too, and roughed up a few priests

but left when they found nothing. Montez kept to his word and stayed away from there."

"I thought he would. He's already feeling guilty. He wouldn't want to endanger anyone else after Father Gabriel's death. He said he'd only contact them after it was safe."

"Which it definitely isn't at the moment. But Dario says that his tracker believes he knows the area where Montez might be hiding out. The foothills to the west are networked with dozens of caves, and he could be in one of them. Dario's heading that way now." He paused. "How is that for positive?"

"As good as we've gotten so far. You'll tell me as soon as he's confirmed Montez's location?"

"Unless it's the middle of the night. It won't do me any good to wake you if we're not moving on Montez. It will wait until morning. You need the sleep."

"Yes, I do. So do you. Are you going to bed?"

"Certainly." His voice was faintly mocking. "And I will sleep like a baby. It's part of the discipline I was taught. The committee did their best to make sure that I had the control that was needed to be their security chief." His voice lowered. "Though the discipline didn't include ignoring the fact that I'm horny as hell and can't stop thinking about you in that summerhouse with your legs wrapped around me. It's definitely bothering me that you're only a few rooms down the hall."

It was bothering her, too. His words were soft, silken, and they were causing the muscles of her body to tense. "Then maybe it's time you went back to your committee and took a refresher."

He chuckled. "It wouldn't do any good. You're the only one to whom the discipline doesn't apply. So I guess that I'll go take a shower, too. And it won't be a hot one. Then I'll look at the map of the cave area Dario e-mailed me and see if I agree with him. Good night, Catherine." He hung up.

And left her with that lingering heat and disturbing sexual changes that his words had brought. Forget the sexual implications, just remember what was important. Montez appeared to be temporarily safe. Cameron was here, and that automatically added an additional element of security.

Two positives.

Dry her hair, pull on her nightshirt, and go to sleep.

Don't think of Cameron; that was an automatic turn-on and distracter. If she couldn't drift off immediately, concentrate on Kelly and her bewildering mass of question marks and dots.

Or Montez and how to convince him that she was right and he was so wrong . . .

Holy Mary, Mother of God, forgive me.

Montez's fingers moved on the rosary in silent prayer. His heart was beating hard as his eyes stared into the darkness of the cave surrounding him.

Save me from causing any more deaths.

Forgive me, for I have sinned.

But wouldn't the sinning continue if he did what Catherine Ling asked him to do? She was as violent as Santos, and the killing would go on and on. Yes, she would still hunt and try to kill Santos, but he would not be involved. He had sworn to himself that he would go no further down that path that could be sending him to the depths of perdition, that he would be done with Santos forever.

But if that was God's will, why had he not kept Santos in that prison? Why had he sent him out in the world to test his resolve?

Because the resolve was wrong and mistaken?

Catherine Ling had seemed to be honorable and her cause just. Was that the message he should have taken away from their encounter?

Protect me from evil and ambition.

Deaths. So many deaths.

Agony was tearing through him as he thought of Father Gabriel standing at the door of the church and watching him run through the garden.

Forgive me, Father. I should have been wiser. I shouldn't have let this happen. I just didn't know what was right or wrong. Even you who were so much wiser couldn't tell me. You said that I had to rely on God to guide me.

But He's not guiding me.

I'm lost, and He's not showing the way home.

Holy Father, please, give me a sign.

"You're overthinking the problem."

Catherine's eyes flew open, pulled out of sleep, as she remembered Kelly's last words to her.

Not that she had been deeply asleep; it had been a restless slumber. She had been tossing and turning most of the night. But it had only been when that last thought of Kelly's had intruded that she had been jerked awake.

And she was wide-awake, she thought ruefully, as she sat up in bed. Okay, Kelly, I'll think about it and see how I can simplify. I'm tired of leaving it up to you and Hu Chang to connect your dots. She might as well concentrate since she wasn't sleeping worth a damn.

She got out of bed, went to the bathroom, and got a glass of water. She splashed water in her face and sat down in an easy chair with her computer. She pulled up the file Kelly had sent her and studied it. Fifteen minutes later, she was still as frustrated as when she had begun.

All the dots were still mysteries, all the gaps were not telling her anything.

She leaned her head back in the chair and looked at the computer screen. Smother that frustration. It wasn't going to help. Approach the problem from another direction. She didn't have the individual skills of Kelly or Hu Chang, so simplify as Kelly had suggested.

Simplify what?

Montez appeared to be an important key. Kelly was intrigued by him. Hu Chang was studying his book.

The book.

The only part of it that she might be able to decipher was the title. She accessed Google and typed in *Maggi.*

She sighed with discouragement as the answers started flowing on her screen. If she'd hoped to have an easy time, it wasn't going to happen. The primary answer appeared to be a European seasoning food product, and the examples seemed to go on forever. Then it skipped to Maggie and famous Maggies in entertainment and history. She used several other search engines and came up with basically the same result.

All right, expand the search. Connect the word to something else.

Buenos Aires . . .

Kelly's last words before Catherine had left her room.

She typed in Maggi and Buenos Aires and asked for the connection.

More exotic seasonings and where to find them in Argentina.

She scrolled down the screen.

She froze, her gaze on the entry that had suddenly appeared.

"Holy shit."

It could be nothing.

Or it could be the answer.

It was a start.

Her hand was shaking as she punched in the access.

God, please, let it be the answer.

Two hours later, she hung up the phone from talking to Venable.

She leaned back and drew a deep breath. She could feel the flush burning her cheeks and the pounding of her heart leaping in her chest. Calm down. It was more than a start, but it wasn't the entire answer.

But she could get that answer if she worked hard enough, then she'd have something with which to confront Montez. Arguments she could use to sway him.

But she had to have Hu Chang.

She got up from the chair, grabbed her clothes, and went to the bathroom. She came out five minutes later, snatched her computer, and left the bedroom. A moment later, she was opening the door of the library. Hu Chang was sitting at the desk, studying Montez's book. She'd known he wouldn't be able to leave it until he'd made significant headway.

She slammed the door behind her. "Anything?"

"Delighted to see you, Catherine." He gestured to the page he'd been reading. "Fascinating stuff. But I'm not ready to discuss it with you yet. I thought you were going to bed."

"Could you make heads or tails of it?"

"Yes, though Montez is right, it is difficult." He tilted his head. "May I ask why you're accosting me in the middle of the night?" His gaze narrowed on her face. "Never mind. You're practically lighting up this boring study. Excitement, eagerness . . . what else, Catherine?"

"Frustration. I need to know more."

"So you came to me." He smiled slightly. "An excellent choice. Who else can you count on for superior knowledge?" He leaned back in his chair. "On what subject?"

"I think you know. *Maggi.*"

"I haven't dealt with the title yet. I was too absorbed in the contents. But you evidently have been doing a little research when you should have been sleeping. So tell me about *Maggi.*"

"Maria Maggi. It's the name on a tomb in Milan, Italy." She dropped down in the visitor's chair beside the desk. "And the occupant was a very famous Argentinean countrywoman of Eduardo Montez." She opened her computer and pulled up the document she'd been studying. "A beautiful woman who caused a great deal of trouble in her day." She turned the screen around to face him. "You'll recognize her."

"Yes, indeed," he murmured, his gaze on the screen. "Eva Peron. Blond, beautiful, and ambitious to be the queen of Argentina. Perhaps the empress of the world. Would you care to tell me how she came to be the occupant of that tomb in Milan?"

"It was only one of her burial sites after her death. On this tomb, they even inscribed a different name. They were trying to hide her identity so that her corpse wouldn't be stolen or vandalized. It was a constant threat. She wasn't buried permanently for twenty-four years. She was an icon to the common people of Argentina. Political factions fought over possession of her body because they were afraid that her influence with the masses, even after her death, would sway their political futures. Her remains were transferred from place to place in Argentina, then Europe, so that her effect on the political process would remain negligible. Maria Maggi was the name on her crypt in Milan."

"And Montez was such a Peron fan that he named his work after her?"

"No, I think that he thought that it was a fitting name for his project." She met his gaze. "Didn't he?"

"Perhaps. But I'm interested in why you deduced that."

"I'm not Luke, Hu Chang. Stop playing with me."

"I would never play with either you or Luke. I just wish you both to stretch to meet your full potential."

She shook her head in exasperation. "Those equations logically indicate Montez was doing some sort of medical or chemical experiments, considering his education and training. So I asked myself what kind of experiments would Santos be interested in that would make him kill someone to keep Montez under his thumb?"

"And what did you answer?"

"That it wasn't Santos, it was Delores who was interested in what Montez was doing. It was Delores who had Santos set up Montez for a special duty. She was so intent on recruiting him that she went with Santos to see Montez when they visited Buenos Aires."

"Recruit him for what? And why? Montez had no remarkable medical credentials. He was trained as a general practitioner."

"For a reason. Everything he did was secret and strictly undercover. He was working on a very special project. He worked with his uncle in a lab in the hills and consulted with experts on his results only when he needed help. The Montez family was very careful after what happened to them during the Peron era."

"Uncle?"

"Kelly was intrigued by the amount of time Eduardo spent with his Uncle Francisco in the hills. It was one of her 'dots.' She was having Venable check on him. But after I found out about Maggi-Peron, I called Venable myself. I'd just got off the phone when I came down to talk to you."

"And the uncle was a doctor, too?"

"A pathologist. Brilliant and well respected in the small town where he served as coroner. But very little social contact, no published papers. He was said to be devoted to his nephew and was teaching him the family business."

"And that was?"

"He also had the only funeral home in town." She paused. "A business that had been in the family for almost a hundred years. It was a nice little funeral home, and he was very competent. So were his father and grandfather and great-grandfather, but, of course, their reputations couldn't compete with that of their distant cousin in Buenos Aires. Everyone knew that Dr. Pedro Ara was a pathologist without peer." She nodded at Eva Peron's photo. "He was the one chosen to embalm Evita Peron, the spiritual soul of Argentina."

"And I understand he did a fantastic job with very unusual methods for the time."

"Alcohol in the heel and neck. He and his assistant worked all night for perfect preservation. Which didn't please Peron's political foes. They would just as soon have tossed her in a ditch. They couldn't touch Dr. Ara, but there was a certain amount of persecution leveled at those close to him, including the Montez branch of the family. Particularly in less civilized towns in the hills. Deaths. Beatings. That's why the Montez clan made sure they never were exposed to the limelight again. They'd learned their lessons."

"But not enough to close up shop and stop embalming their clients evidently."

"Tradition . . . and the desire to prove they were as good or better than Dr. Pedro Ara and his world-famous embalming of Eva Peron." She grimaced. "And then Uncle Francisco found that Eduardo was an even more brilliant doctor than Ara. He set out to train him to develop even more innovative procedures and show everyone that the Montez branch outshone Ara in every way. When the family saw that Eduardo Montez had potential, I think they coached him, educated him, then helped him experiment and have his discussions with experts in the field. But you can't do that in complete privacy. Someone must have talked when Santos was asking questions." She added, "Or when Delores asked questions."

"On what subject?"

"Delores was vain. She was incredibly beautiful and did everything possible with makeup, clothes, and minor surgery to make sure that she stayed that way. I think that she had a horror of being ugly even in death. Heaven knows she'd seen and caused enough deaths to know what that looked like."

"Are you guessing?"

"Yes, but some of the places she visited might have been a search. She spent a lot of time in the tombs of Ancient Egypt and the Kremlin. Egypt might have been the first culture to work on preservation. Lenin is still wonderfully preserved in Moscow. It probably impressed her. What if she heard that Montez had developed an embalming procedure that was better than the one Dr. Ara used on Eva Peron?"

"Then, if she thought of herself as great a leader as Eva believed herself to be, she would have done anything to make sure she would have an even greater chance for many years of preservation." He nodded. "She was truly that vain?"

"From what I know of her, from what Kelly has found out, I'd say that she would have stolen Lenin's coffin if she thought she could have gotten away with it."

"Instead, she went after Montez."

"And he suddenly came into a lot of money and moved his entire family to Guatemala shortly after he met with Santos and Delores."

"They paid him for what? I believe Delores was in fine health until you shot her."

"Future insurance? Eva Peron had her entire funeral planned, down to having her hairdresser come in and bleach her hair after her death." She saw his brows rise, and she said in exasperation, "I don't *know*. How could I? It is guesswork." Her hands clenched. "But I'm close, Hu Chang. I know I'm close."

"I know you are, too," he said quietly. "And I do enjoy watching you move toward your goals. It gives me great pleasure to—"

"I'm not trying to entertain you, dammit." She leaned forward. "I came down here for help. Now I've told you what I know and—"

"Guess," Hu Chang corrected.

"Guess. Now you tell me what you know, you arrogant bastard."

"Well, I wouldn't actually say 'know,' although my calculated surmises are much more scientifically based than any you've—" He held up his hand as she opened her lips. "I'm getting there. And I admit that your insight has filled in several holes in my theory of what Montez was working on." He looked back at the photo of Eva Peron. "Poor woman, she was born a little too soon. Delores was much more fortunate."

"Hu Chang."

"Well, until you killed her. But even then she was planning on not letting that defeat her."

"You mean those equations are for an advanced procedure for embalming and preservation?"

"Yes and no. Think about the degrees that Montez earned and how they could apply."

"Medical, chemical, mechanical engineering, theology," she said impatiently. "And I don't want to think. Tell me. Yes and no. What's the yes?"

"Yes, there are chemical formulas in his book that are brilliant and innovative and probably concern an amazingly noninvasive form of embalming fluid."

"So I was right."

He smiled.

"Okay, what's the no?"

"He wasn't satisfied with just going a few giant steps further than Dr. Ara did with Peron. He decided that he could do much more." He paused. "Hence the degree in mechanical engineering. He wanted to address not only cosmetic preservation but something more permanent. Or not. Considering your beliefs. I found formulas using liquid nitrogen and a glycerol-based chemical protectant mixture. I'm almost sure that they were to be used as a cryoprotectant."

"Cryoprotectant?"

"Human antifreeze," he said bluntly.

Then she understood. "Cryonics," she said. "Delores planned on being frozen after death in hopes of being resurrected later, when medicine could take care of whatever had killed her."

"That's usually the purpose of people's choosing to be kept in cryogenic-storage facilities. There are many arguments about whether there would be too much damage to the body from the freezing or the chemicals injected. It appears that Montez may have been able to solve those issues."

"He did? How do you know?"

"I studied cryonics at one time. Preservation of life always interested me." He shrugged. "But then I gave it up and went another direction. Too sedentary for me. I prefer to extend the life of the living, not the dead."

"But Montez came close enough so that it would have had an instant appeal for Delores and Santos?"

"I couldn't confirm that without experimentation. But

his calculations are definitely more promising than anyone else's work I've studied."

Excitement was surging through her as she realized the possibilities. "He would have been a dream come true for Delores. An advanced embalming cosmetic procedure that would have preserved her youth and beauty. A cryogenic innovation that might bring her back from the dead someday. Still young, still beautiful." Her lips tightened. "Still the monster she was when I killed her."

"All of the above," Hu Chang said. "Santos probably promised Montez a fortune for setting up Delores's last resting place." His lips twisted. "Or perhaps not only Delores. Santos has sufficient ego and desire for self-preservation himself. Maybe it was also for him."

"But where did Montez set it up?" She was frowning. "Montez said that he didn't know where Santos had set up his new headquarters. Yet I'd bet that Santos would have wanted his Delores near him."

"Montez lied?"

"I don't think so." She reached for her phone. "But preparations would have had to be made immediately after Delores's death, so there would be no deterioration. Isn't that right?"

"Yes."

"So Santos wouldn't have let her be taken to the morgue."

"As I recall, he was relatively helpless at that particular moment."

"Maybe not." She remembered Montez saying that Santos had begun wheeling and dealing the moment he was arrested. She hadn't thought anything of it at the time. She began dialing her phone. "I'm calling Venable and asking him just how helpless Santos was that day."

"Don't you ever sleep?" Venable asked sourly when he picked up.

"Listen. Directly after Santos was arrested, was he making deals with the police and political bigwigs?"

Silence. "Maybe."

"You know. Tell me."

"It wasn't a bad deal. I'd have taken him up on it, too."

"What was the deal?"

"He offered up the location of two warehouses with close to a billion dollars in drugs and the names of the distributors. The only thing he wanted was for them to immediately release the body of his dead wife to Dorgal. He said he wanted her cremated. Of course, they took the deal. What good was a dead Delores Santos to them?"

"And no one checked to see if she'd been cremated?"

"Why? She wasn't important to anyone but him."

"She's important now. Thanks, Venable." She hung up and turned to Hu Chang. "She was turned over to Dorgal immediately. Supposedly to be cremated. So if there were injections to be given, it could definitely have been done. He paid very highly for the privilege of making sure Delores didn't lose her chance."

"But Montez had to be involved at that point. Preparation of the body. Insertion into the cryogenic coffin. Even if all the advance preparations had been made, Santos would have insisted Montez do the final."

"I know all that." She rubbed her temple. "Or maybe I don't. I'm not certain about anything about this. The only one who can give us the answers is Montez."

"And he won't do it."

"He's got to do it. He's my only hope. I'll have to talk to him again." She grimaced. "Without Cameron. Cameron and he are not compatible."

"And are you and Montez compatible?"

"More than Cameron. But I don't understand him. He should fight Santos."

"In a way, he is fighting him. Just by not doing as he wishes, by opting out of the deal he made with him. Not everyone is a warrior like you and Cameron."

"Cameron calls him a pacifist."

"Or merely a man struggling to keep his soul."

"What?"

"The third advanced degree. Theology. A strange major for a man who is fascinated by science and chemistry. Or maybe not so strange when you think that bringing back the dead could be breaking God's laws. A religious man might have a struggle to balance his ambition to strike new ground against his sense that he had sinned and could lose his soul."

His words hit home. Yes, Montez had exhibited all the signs of a man in the throes of crisis. Not only the guilt of the killings of those close to him but the agony of wrestling with his conscience before God. "You believe he was trying to find moral answers even as he was working on *Maggi*?"

"Don't you?"

"I guess I do." She lifted her chin. "But I can't let it matter to me. He's got to help me any way he can." She stared Hu Chang in the eye. "I asked him to let Santos capture him so that I could track him. I told him I'd keep him safe."

"If you could."

"I'd find a way to do it." She moistened her lips. "I won't let any more of the people I care about be killed by Santos. Even if I have to risk Montez. Let him wrestle with his demons after I kill the biggest demon of all."

"Very practical. Very Catherine." He chuckled. "Our Erin would suffer and agonize with him and try to find a middle ground."

"Which is admirable. I don't have time to risk agonizing with him. I have a son." She added deliberately, "And

I have you, Hu Chang. Neither one of you is going to die because Montez won't cooperate." She got to her feet. "We've got a better grasp on Montez's problems and the reason he's on the run. We have to assume that Delores Santos was never cremated and that Santos made Montez do what he was paid to do. But we still don't know where Delores's body is now. If she's with Santos, we may have the key to find him. Now I'll have to use it to get Montez to do what's right."

"You're going back to Guatemala?"

"If it's necessary. I planted a few seeds before I left Montez. I'll see if they take root. But I can't give him much time." She had the desperate feeling that time was running out. "I'll try calling him to make contact. Dario is keeping tabs on him. He'd let us know if he was in danger."

"And will Cameron go with you?"

"Perhaps. He says that I'm where the action is."

"And he doesn't have enough action in his life?" Hu Chang asked dryly. "Look deeper, Catherine."

She didn't want to look deeper. She was having enough trouble keeping their surface emotions in check. She knew the solution was to refuse to be with him.

It was a solution she didn't want to accept. Even though the competitive edge was always there when she was with him, she always felt safe. It was as if when they were together, nothing could beat them, nothing could take them down. And the excitement of dealing with the unknown was there every minute. Why give that up when he was always an asset in the trenches? "I'll let him know what we've figured out. He'll have to make up his own mind what he wants to do." She headed for the door. "But not before I try to get a nap. It's almost morning."

"But a bright day dawning?"

She smiled over her shoulder. "At least, it's not as dark

as it was when I went to bed last night. Together, we've shined a little light, haven't we, Hu Chang?"

"Always," he said softly. "That goes without saying. From the moment you found me when you were fourteen, the light came and never left us."

She stood there, looking at him, taking in the darkness and the light. Intelligence close to genius, wry humor, philosophy drawn from life and the study of the world's cultures. She remembered that first time when she'd run into his apothecary shop and thought that she was saving him from a street gang. Perhaps she had saved him, but he had also saved her a dozen times in the following years. What was just as important as the salvation he had given her was the barrier against the loneliness. "I've never regretted that day." She cleared her throat. "Let me know if you find out anything else from Montez's manual." She opened the door. "I'll tell Kelly what we've learned so that she can fill in a few of her dots and concentrate on where Dorgal might have really been going when he was island-hopping in the Caribbean."

"Excellent." He picked up the copy of *Maggi* again. "I'm not sure that I'll be able to find out anything else of value, but I will see . . ."

She wasn't sure that he'd be able to find out anything more either, Catherine thought as she started up the stairs. Unless you believed the value might lie in improving on Montez's formulas. That was entirely possible. Hu Chang not only created his own chemical magic, but often took others' dross and turned it into gold.

Though no one could call Montez's work dross, according to Hu Chang. It had been good enough to have Santos draw him into Delores's death fantasies. Montez had called Delores a monster, and she wondered if the judgment was based on the brief meeting he'd had with her or on the horror her vanity and ruthlessness had brought into his life. Perhaps a little of both.

Now that she knew the circumstances that had made Montez try to escape from the mistake he'd made dealing with Santos, perhaps she could use it to persuade him to help her.

She could only hope that he'd have had enough time to think about it before she made contact again.

CHAPTER 11

ST. JOSEPH'S HOSPITAL
ATLANTA, GEORGIA

I'll do it." Dr. Basle was frowning. "It will still be an extremely difficult operation, but she has a limited chance for success. I admit I didn't think I'd be saying this, Ms. Duncan. I thought you were desperate and this visit a waste of my time. I'm glad that I was wrong."

"And I'll be glad when you prove to be entirely wrong," Eve said. "When can you operate?"

"Within the next four hours." He looked back down the hall at the ICU. "It's remarkable, you know. The artery appears to be strengthening and healing itself. No other physician has looked at her?"

She shook her head. "Only family . . . and friends." That was almost true, she thought. Though Jane would not call Caleb a friend, Eve would accept him in that position for her. He had saved her, dammit. If that didn't let him into the club, she didn't know what would. "Nature is a wonderful and mysterious thing. When she came out of the coma, I thought you should take another look at her." She smiled luminously. "Thank you for coming."

He grinned. "Why do I feel that you and Joe Quinn would have come down to Houston and dragged me out of an operating room to put me on the next flight." He turned and started down the hall. "You can stay with Jane for a little while longer, then we'll begin the prep."

She watched him disappear into the elevator before she hurried toward ICU. Joe was coming out of the room when she reached it, and a broad smile lit his face. "Basle told you?"

She nodded and went into his arms. "Optimistic skepticism," she said, as her arms tightened around him. "It couldn't be anything else considering what he told us previously. But we know better, don't we, Joe?"

"I hope we do." He looked back at Caleb, sitting by Jane's bed. "God, I hope we do. Should we kick him out until after the operation? Jane rests better when he's not in the room."

"No, I think we should leave instead. Maybe it's better if he keeps her stirred up. All I know is that he's healing her, and I don't care how he's doing it." She linked her arm with Joe's and pulled him out of the room. "And he has a little more time to give Basle a head start . . ."

Why don't you go, too?" Jane asked Caleb as she watched Joe and Eve leave the room. "That doctor tired me out. I'm going to take a nap."

"Go ahead." Caleb smiled. "But I'm staying. You should be used to me by now."

That was an understatement. He had been so close to her mentally and emotionally during the last days that she almost felt he was a part of her. A disturbing part that she fought against but couldn't push away. "I don't need you here, Caleb."

"Yes, you do. My work's not done yet." He tilted his head. "Every minute counts. I think Eve senses that and wants me to have my chance at saving you. Otherwise, she'd be in here."

"I'm surprised she's not." She smiled crookedly. "Eve

is sure that you brought me back from the pearly gates. It's a done deal as far as she's concerned."

"You're wrong, she's still scared. She won't give up trying until you walk out of this hospital. She told me that before you were shot, you were getting better about accepting Trevor's death. It was slow, but you were on your way. But the attack came at just the wrong time. You reached out and grabbed at what you thought fate was handing you." His lips twisted. "And you're so damn stubborn, I had to pry you away from it. Now she's afraid you're going to slip back." He added deliberately, "No, not slip, turn back."

She wearily shook her head. "I won't do that. I know it's not going to happen now. That I can't let it happen. Eve's had enough tragedy in her life. I can't be that selfish. It was wrong of me."

"But so tempting," Caleb said mockingly. "You're right, it's not going to happen. If you take a step back, I'll be there to pull you forward."

"And I'll tell you to stay the hell out of my way. I'm in control now, Caleb."

"Not yet. That's why you've got to fight to get out of that bed. As long as you're lying there pale and sickly, I won't leave you. The only way to get rid of me is to get rid of all signs of illness."

"Then you can be sure I'll definitely work on it," she said grimly.

"I know." His smile faded. "You used to be only a little afraid of me. But that's changed, hasn't it?"

"I'm not afraid of you. I just don't like that you interfered with my life."

"Not your life; I interfered with your death." His voice was suddenly fierce. "Get used to it. That's one interference that won't go away. After you've beaten back this attack, there will be others. I won't leave you, I'll stand beside you, until every one of Santos's men is in hell. I'll never let death have you. I'll fight, and I'll win."

She was stunned by the sheer power he was generating. She tried to dismiss it, to ignore what he was making her feel. "You already won that battle. So just go away, Caleb. I don't want—" She stopped. As usual, his passion had sparked her own emotions to an equally high level, and she was saying things that even to her sounded unreasonable and self-absorbed. "I know I should be grateful to you for all your time and effort trying to save me. I *will* be grateful. Just give me time to become accustomed to—"

"Screw your gratitude. We both know that's not what I want. I saved you because I had to save you. Now be quiet and let me concentrate. Your Dr. Basle is arranging to have his staff prep you for the operation, but I've got to do my own prep before he takes over."

He was already concentrating, she realized as she studied his expression. She was being wrapped in that dark, pulsing flow that was both soothing and energizing. She smiled shakily. "No nap for me?"

"Basle will let you sleep. Right now, I've got work to do. Put yourself in my hands. I'll never fail you."

"Won't you?" She closed her eyes. "That sounded remarkably like something Trevor would say."

"I'm nothing like Trevor. I'll never be him even if that's what he wants. You'll have to take me the way I am."

"Or not at all."

"Shh. Worry about that later. Just a few more adjustments . . ."

Dammit, Basle should be finished by now," Joe said harshly. "How long is it going to take?"

"He said that it wasn't going to be easy." Eve took a drink of her coffee. How many cups had she had during these last five hours? "Think positive. He's being careful, and that takes time."

"And I shouldn't be this on edge and mouthing off." Joe grimaced. "Sorry. I'd just like to be in there and making sure that I couldn't do anything to help."

"And running the show," Eve said. "I'm afraid that you'd have to have a couple decades of medical education and experience to have Basle step aside for you." She glanced at Caleb, who was leaning against the wall; his intense gaze focused on the operating room. He had scarcely moved from that position during the last five hours, but she didn't sense that he was as on edge as she and Joe. "How about you, Caleb? I'd think you'd be the one to want to burst into that operating room."

He smiled sardonically. "Because I'm not as cool and controlled as Joe? You're right, I'm a savage when things aren't going my way. But this is going my way. So I'm just monitoring it, so that it continues on that path."

"You're sure of that?" Joe asked, his eyes narrowed on Caleb's face. "How?"

"I gave Basle a smooth road for the graft. I checked his credentials, and he should have no trouble doing it."

"I saw you talking to him before they brought Jane into the operating room," Joe said. "What did you say to him?"

"Do you think I threatened him?" Caleb's brows rose. "Why, I wouldn't do that. I needed his hands to be steady and skilled. I just introduced myself and told him that it was exceptionally important to me that Jane get through this operation with flying colors. He seemed to understand."

And that aura of hypnotic intensity and danger that Caleb always cast could not have helped but to make an impression, Eve thought. "I'm sure he did," she said dryly.

He shrugged. "That was only a preventative measure in case Santos had managed to get to him. There was the slightest possibility. And I checked out everyone in that operating room to be certain that everything would be safe."

"So did I," Joe said.

"I thought you would. It didn't matter. I had to be sure."

Joe stared at him for a long moment. "I still have problems with you, Caleb. But I'm beginning to think we may have a lot in common."

Caleb shook his head. "You have a few savage elements yourself, but you have much better control. You're one of the good guys, like Trevor."

"And what are you, Caleb?" Eve asked quietly.

"What do you think I am? Aren't we who we are perceived to be? Ask Jane."

"I prefer to form my own opinions. And Jane is on the defensive. But you may be right about perception being—"

The doors of the operating room burst open, and Basle strode out into the hall. Eve jumped to her feet, and she and Joe rushed toward the doctor.

He's smiling, she saw with relief. Thank God, he's smiling. "It went well?"

"Excellent. Better than I hoped. She'll have a few more nights in ICU, then I think we can move her to her own room."

"No." Caleb was suddenly there beside them. "Talk to him, Quinn. He has to put out a statement that the operation didn't go as well as he hoped, and she's still hanging on by a thread."

"I won't do that," Basle said. "It's not true, and besides, word would get out from the nurses and doctors in that operating room that it was a lie."

"Talk to him," Caleb said. "If you don't, I will. And I won't be worried about his hands shaking now. The minute Santos knows that she's on her way to recovery, it will give him a green light to send someone to take her out."

He was suddenly smiling recklessly. "Not that I might not enjoy that. But Eve wouldn't, and I wouldn't take a chance with Jane."

"Doctor Basle's right," Eve said. "It will be hard to keep the news from spreading in a hospital. It's a community in itself." She turned to the doctor. "But we've got to try. We need your cooperation."

"And we'll get it," Joe said grimly.

"You don't understand," Basle said. "It's not going to—"

"You deal with him." Caleb turned and moved toward the door of the operating room. "While I have a chat with the nurses and the assisting doctor. I'll bet they'll be much more cooperative."

Basle was looking warily after him. "Who the hell is he?"

"A friend of Jane's. I believe he introduced himself to you," Eve said. "And he can be very persuasive." She smiled at him. "I only hope that we can be just as persuasive. We need your help. Did I tell you how grateful I am that you saved my Jane? I know it's not fair to put you on the spot and risk damage to that wonderful reputation, but you'll understand after I explain." She took his arm and led him toward the coffee machine. "Let Joe and me get you a cup of coffee and we'll talk about it."

RAIN FOREST
GUATEMALA

"What do you mean you can't find him?" Dorgal tried to keep his temper. Juan Pablo was usually clever and an expert tracker, and he was the one Dorgal had chosen to take over the hunt for Montez. However, unless Pablo could show some active progress toward finding Montez, Dorgal would have to face Santos's rage and charges of incompetence if he left Pablo in charge. Then he would be stuck here in this damned rain forest instead of getting to a position where he could wriggle himself back into Santos's favor. "Have you gone back to the monastery and questioned those monks again? I can't believe they don't know something. Montez lived with a priest for almost two years. He's a religious nut."

"We searched the monastery twice. He's not there."

"Then tell me where he is," Dorgal said through his teeth. "The bastard's an inventor and a doctor, he shouldn't have been able to hide out in that forest for more than a few hours before you caught him."

"He's gone to ground somewhere." Pablo shrugged. "We'll find him eventually."

"Santos doesn't understand the word 'eventually.' If Montez has gone to ground, give him a reason to bolt out of his hole."

"He knows we'll gather him up the minute he does. What reason is good enough for him to risk his neck?"

"You have no imagination." Dorgal moved out of the shrubbery to the edge of the hill and gazed down at the red clay roof jutting out of the trees. "It may not be that hard at all."

Good morning," Cameron said as he watched Catherine come down the stairs. "You look bright-eyed and wide-awake today. I'm glad. Does that mean we can stop spinning our wheels?"

She stiffened. His words had been more attack than greeting and so was his demeanor. She could *feel* his impatience. "It's only been one day. Sorry you've been bored. You don't have to stay here, Cameron."

"The hell I don't. The minute I walk away, you'll be on the move." He grimaced. "Though I hoped to wrap this up sooner. I'm having problems dealing with my own minor affairs long-distance."

"The committee giving you a hard time? Of course they are. You're the crown prince to their chosen new world. You shouldn't waste your time on anything else."

"I've told you, I'm only the security chief. That's all I've ever wanted to be. And I've not consulted the committee about my private affairs. I just have to work around them." He made an impatient gesture with his hand. "You didn't answer me. When do we move? It's not like you to hesitate."

"I wanted to see if Kelly was going to come up with a possible destination." Her lips tightened. "But I can't wait any longer. Though she does think she's getting closer. It's something to do with boat rentals and gas consumption."

"Interesting. But I can see why you'd not want to wait for her to connect those particular dots. Montez?"

She nodded. "I'm going to call him and see if he's had time to think while he's been on the run. Using him as bait for a trap is still our best bet to get to Santos."

"And now that you know more about his dealings with Santos, you have more ammunition with which to persuade him." He paused. "The latest report I have from Dario is that he's sure Montez is in the cave area. But Dorgal is frantically searching for him and has increased his manpower. If you want to set him up, you'd better do it quick. His time may be running out."

"I'll call him now." She went toward the library. "Which was what I was going to do anyway."

"Only a gentle push to nudge you toward the way we both want you to go."

"Cameron."

He held up his hands. "I'll let you do it without hovering over you. I'll go see Luke and talk to him for a while."

She frowned. "You've been spending a lot of time with Luke."

"I find him interesting. He's on the verge of being something very exceptional."

"And he believes you're some kind of superhero." She had a sudden alarming thought. "You're not fooling with his mind?"

He shook his head. "I took one quick look when I first met him. That's all I needed. And I know he's off-limits as far as you're concerned."

"You're damn right he is."

"Besides, I can wait for him to get a little older before I make a decision about him."

"Decision? You will *not* try to recruit him."

He smiled. "No?" He turned away and started up the stairs. "We'll see. Go try to persuade Montez. If you get us on the road again, I won't have an opportunity to influence your son."

Which might be a very good thing, she thought grimly. Cameron exerted a tremendous charisma even when he wasn't using that psychic mojo. Well, he could just stay away from Luke.

But he was right, if he was kept busy at the violent tasks at which he excelled, he wouldn't have time to draw Luke into his web.

She pulled out Montez's number and quickly dialed.

Would he look at the ID and not answer?

It rang once.

Twice.

Three times.

Come on, Montez, pick up.

Four times.

Montez answered the phone. "I don't want to talk to you, Catherine Ling."

"Yes, you do. Or you wouldn't have picked up. You're

still on the run from Dorgal and his men, and you must be tired and a little scared. It's going to keep on. They won't stop. They'll never stop until I take Santos out." Her voice lowered with urgency. "Help me take him out. Then the running can stop."

"I told you that I'm opting out. I've caused too many deaths already. Go get him yourself."

"I will." She paused. "But unless I have an edge, I may not be able to stop him before he kills someone I love. He's been very quiet for the past couple days, and I think it's because he's concentrating on hunting you down. You're very important to him. Why does he need you? Surely, you've completed your work on Delores."

Silence. "I don't know what you mean."

"Maggi."

He inhaled sharply. "You're guessing."

"It started as guessing, but as my friend, Hu Chang, made his way through those equations, the guessing became a certainty. He's a brilliant man, and he said that you were also exceptional. That your cryogenic formulas might well do what you intended if the container or coffin in which Delores is held is as mechanically sophisticated as he thought it might be."

"How condescending," he said sharply. "My formula does exactly what I meant it to do."

She had stung him. Evidently, he was very defensive about his work. "I'm sure it does. And Hu Chang didn't mean to be condescending. I told you, he thought your work was exceptional. He appreciated the fact that you went a step beyond cosmetic preservation to actually preserve life itself."

Another silence. "You did work out what I was doing. I was hoping it would be too complex for you."

"It was too complex for me, not for Hu Chang. I was only able to contribute the research about Maggi and Eva

Peron's gravesite. You couldn't resist calling the project after her?"

"I'd heard about her all my life. My kinsman, Pedro Ara, was famous for his work on her. The entire world was in awe of his embalming technique after the two million people who passed by her casket in Buenos Aires saw how alive and beautiful she still appeared. Even after over twenty years of constant moving and poor treatment of her body, Domingo Tellechea, who was chosen by Juan Peron to prepare her for public display again, was amazed at how wonderfully Ara's initial embalming had held up. But Tellechea suffered the same persecution as our family after he repaired the damage. Yet Ara was still an inspiration to everyone in the family. Me, too. I worked hard from the time I was a boy. I wanted to be better, smarter than he was."

"And you were."

"Yes." His voice was bitter. "And you see where it got me. I should have left it alone. Not taken that extra step. They would never have heard of me."

"I know Delores and Santos came to see you in Argentina. They'd heard about your work?"

"I'd thought I'd kept it secret, but they knew. They visited me in my uncle's lab in the hills. They told me that I was the man they'd been looking for and started asking me questions. No, *she* asked me questions. Santos sat back and smiled and acted as if he'd bought her a present by bringing her to me."

"She was the one who was the most interested?"

"She acted . . . hungry. Beautiful, so beautiful, but she was excited and flushed and was drinking in everything I said. I admit I was flattered, but then I became uneasy. She made me tell her everything, then she turned to Santos, and said, 'He's the one. Get him for me.' "

"Threats or money?"

"Principally money. He offered me more money than I could make in twenty years. But the threat was there, too. He was going to give his Delores what she wanted no matter what it took."

"And exactly what did she want?"

"Forever."

"Eternal life? She couldn't have expected that."

"Why not?" he said scornfully. "She thought everything belonged to her, that she could reach out and take. Being frozen would only have been a stopgap. If they were eventually able to heal and bring her back to life, then she'd go for the next step, then the next. She was fascinated by Eva Peron. Every child in South America had heard tales about Eva. Eva is a folk heroine even after all these decades. Delores had read every biography, even devoured that Madonna movie they made about her life. She told me she could have handled Eva's career with Juan Peron better than Eva had done, but she admired her boldness. Eva's power over everyone around her was what led Delores to study her complete life . . . and death. She even tried to visit Eva's final resting place in Buenos Aires but couldn't get permission. Eva lies five meters underground in a crypt built like a nuclear bunker. The government wanted to be sure that no one would ever disturb her remains again. But that didn't stop Delores. It only led her to Pedro Ara, then to every distant branch of his family, and, eventually, to me." His voice was bitter. "I was to be her Dr. Frankenstein, but I mustn't make her look like the monster she was. She had to remain beautiful."

"Why was she so obsessed with it? She was still in the prime of life and supposedly in good health. She couldn't have known that I'd kill her a short time later."

"I asked her the same question. She said only fools didn't prepare for the worst-case scenarios and she wouldn't be defeated if a ten-ton truck happened to careen around the corner and hit her. She laughed and reached over and touched Santos's hand and said that whatever preparations she made for herself must also be done for him. They had to go on together."

Catherine felt a chill. Delores meant they had to go on together forever. What evil would they be able to spawn if their time was extended indefinitely? "How kind of her to include him." She moistened her lips. "So you took the deal."

"I took it. She was young. I thought she'd live for years and years. By that time, anything could happen that might change my obligation to him. He was a criminal. So was Delores. They might both end up dead or in prison."

"And then you'd be rich and free. What did you have to do for his money?"

"I gave them several vials of serum to be injected within four hours of death. I sold them the prototype of the cryogenic container that I'd built in my lab and instructions what to do with it."

"But that wasn't all."

"No, they made me promise to do the final preparations and come immediately when needed."

"And Dorgal called you when Delores was killed, and you kept your word."

"Of course I did. There wasn't anything else I could do. Santos would have ordered me butchered."

"No doubt about it." She paused. "But where did you go? Where was that container?"

"Not in her final resting place, if that's what you're hoping. I told you the truth, I don't know where Santos set up his new compound. I did the work in a climate-controlled warehouse outside Bogotá. It took me three days, but I did a job that would have made Ara green with envy. I did everything right. In the end, she was as beautiful as a goddess and has every chance to wake when the time is right for her. I was as proud as if I'd resurrected Mother Teresa. It was only later when I started to question myself and my work that I realized what I'd really done." He added hoarsely, "I'd become the Frankenstein Delores had wanted me to be."

She could hear the horror and agony in his voice. "And that's why you wanted to opt out."

"I *had* to opt out. Dorgal wanted me to stay with her, make sure that nothing would go wrong, spend my life attending that Plexiglas coffin. I took off and ran back to my home in Guatemala City."

"But Santos sent one of his contract killers after you."

"I'd already gathered my belongings and taken off for the hills by the time he got there. So he sent me a warning instead. He killed my brother and said it would only be the first death if I didn't come back when I was needed."

"In case there was a problem with the cryogenic unit."

"Yes."

"And you don't know where Delores's body was taken?"

"The last time I saw her was that warehouse in Bogotá." He paused. "I assume she's with Santos. He was very protective."

"Then help me to find him. He'll never stop searching for you, Montez. You know how this has to end. Help me to end it for all of us."

"If you hadn't killed Delores, it might have worked out without my having to be involved with them again."

"That's not fair and you know it. You made the deal. You took the risk."

Silence. "I know where the blame lies. I should never have interfered with decisions that belong only to God. I tried to do penance working with Father Gabriel tending the sick in San Esposito."

"And it only resulted in more deaths. It wasn't enough.

You know what you have to do. Cut off the head of the snake so that it can't strike at your loved ones, *my* loved ones."

"You're still trying to trap him," he said slowly. "What if something goes wrong?"

"Something has already gone terribly wrong. We'll put it right."

Silence.

"Look, I have people protecting your family," she said urgently. "You're the only one at risk, and I know that's no small concern. But you'll be doing what you should have done in the beginning. Fighting Santos instead of enabling him."

Another silence. "I'm not sure you're right. I'll pray about it and get back to you."

It was less than she hoped. She tried to contain her disappointment and impatience. "How soon?"

"I'll pray," he repeated. "And I'll look for a sign."

Positive. Think positive. "I know it's the right thing to do. I'll be waiting for your call." She paused. "But Santos isn't waiting, let's stop him before he makes another move."

"I have to think."

She kept her tone level. "Hurry, Montez. There may have been too much thinking and not enough action. Don't look too long for that sign."

"I have to be sure." He hung up.

"From what I heard it appears that Montez wasn't cooperating," Cameron said from the doorway behind her. "He's looking for signs?"

"Don't you know?" She pressed the disconnect. "I would have thought you'd have been tempted to do a little mental eavesdropping."

"I gave you my word." He smiled. "Besides, it wasn't important enough. I knew you'd tell me."

"Yes, he's looking for signs and praying." She frowned.

"But I think I almost had him. Evidently not. It's still a waiting game. So you can go back to trying to lure Luke into your camp."

"No, I can't. He dismissed me. He's busy doing some kind of research for Kelly." He came into the library. "So you're stuck with me, and we both need entertaining. Shall I lock the door?"

As they had locked the door of the summerhouse months ago, when they had first come together.

Damn him. She tried to take a deep breath. Her chest felt tight and her nipples hard and sensitive.

"I've been very good," he coaxed. "All duty and nose to the grindstone. So have you. Don't we deserve a reward?"

"No, that's not what this is about."

"Yes, it is. It's all how you look at it. It's about saving lives. But every second of life should be lived to the hilt." He was only inches away from her. She could feel his warmth, smell the spicy man scent of him. "I'm all into hilt. Remember?"

The muscles of her stomach clenched. She could almost feel him inside her. "You know I do." She kept her voice steady. "But I won't have sex with you, Cameron. Not here, not now."

"Pity." He leaned forward, and his tongue slowly outlined her lower lip. She could feel the blood tingle beneath the sudden plumpness the sensation brought. "I thought that might be your reaction with your son in the house. But I wanted you enough to take the chance." His hand moved lightly over her breast, then paused to rub, squeeze. Why couldn't she step away from him? She was leaning forward, wanting to tear off her clothes, to frantically seek more. "We both know it's going to happen. Now or later. But if you change your mind about now . . ."

Step back.

She couldn't let him touch her any more, or she wouldn't be able to stop it from happening.

Hard, so hard.

She whirled away from him and headed for the door. Get away from him. Get away from the way she was melting as he touched her. "I won't change my mind." She didn't look back at him. "I'm going upstairs to work with Luke and Kelly. Then I'll call Eve and see how Jane is recovering from the operation. I'll give Montez a little more time to call me, then I'm going back and tracking him down to see him. As I said, I think I almost had him. He only needs a little more push."

"So do you," he said softly. "But I can wait until we're on the plane going down to give Montez that extra little shove."

The intimacy of that picture of the two of them on that long flight caused heat to escalate. "Bastard."

"Impatient bastard," he corrected. "Life is too short. We can't afford to do anything but live for the moment. Now go do all those worthy, reasonable things that you've planned."

"I shall." She headed quickly for the stairs. She wasn't running, she told herself. The hell she wasn't. Cameron was the only man who made her unsure of her own ability to resist temptation.

She had almost let him lock that door.

Don't think of that long plane ride down to Guatemala.

This wasn't about living for the moment.

It was about making sure that no one ended up dead.

ST. JOSEPH'S HOSPITAL
ATLANTA, GEORGIA

Caleb was in the room again, Jane realized drowsily. They had kept her heavily drugged since the operation, and she had been going in and out of consciousness. Sometimes, she'd been aware of Eve, sometimes Joe, but always Caleb in the background, somewhere in the room.

But now he was once again in the chair beside her bed as he'd been so often before the operation.

"Don't play possum."

Her eyes opened. "I wasn't . . . playing . . . anything. Still sleepy."

"I told them you wouldn't need the drugs. They didn't listen to me."

"How . . . terrible. That they'd pay attention to the doctor's instructions instead . . . of yours."

Silence. "I believe you're smiling at me. How unusual."

"It must be the drugs. Even you're looking mellow to me."

"Mellow?" He tilted his head. "Then maybe I'd better take advantage of the moment while your defenses are down. Did Eve or Joe tell you that the operation was a success?"

"Joe."

"Good." He studied her face. "And you didn't fight its being a success. That helped to make it work. I was a little worried Basle might have an uphill psychological battle in spite of everything I did to give those arteries a chance to heal."

"No, I told you that . . . I knew I wasn't being . . . fair. Trevor knew, too. He turned his . . . back. I'll do what you all want me to do."

"That will do until we can bring you back all the way. I made the operating staff promise not to reveal your condition to anyone else. As far as anyone knows, your status is still critical."

"To keep someone from trying again? It . . . won't work."

He shrugged. "I don't think so either, but I had to try.

It will make Eve feel better." He leaned forward. "You know that I'll protect you?"

She could feel the dark intensity, the flames that surrounded him. But at this moment, they didn't disturb her. "Yes, I'm . . . not worried about that."

"You're not worried about much of anything," he said dryly. "I think now is the time I should probe a little, don't you?"

"Not honorable."

"And since when did you think I was honorable?"

"Never, but I think you have a . . . code. I just can't read it."

He chuckled. "Neither can I." He tilted his head. "And why do you think I'm so determined to protect you?"

"Sex," she said emphatically.

"Oh, I'm afraid of having my toy taken away?" He nodded. "Yes, sex has a good deal to do with it. Of course, you'd recognize that aspect. Anything else?"

She shook her head. "Can't read your code."

"But you could always read Trevor." His smile faded. "And when you couldn't, you knew what there was for you. You'll never know that with me because it just keeps building and changing."

"Don't want to talk about Trevor. Makes me . . . sad."

"Fine. So let's go back to what's important while you're still mellow enough to listen and comprehend. I'll be with you constantly until you're out of here. I'm expecting problems, and I'll not allow my work to be wasted. Whenever I tell you to do something, it will have nothing to do with what I eventually want from you. It will only be to keep you alive. Understand?"

"Yes."

"Believe me?"

"I think I do."

"And you'll do what I say?"

She was silent.

"Jane."

"Until I get out of this hospital."

He smiled faintly. "I couldn't ask any more. I'd be afraid you had brain damage if you hadn't qualified that." He got to his feet. "I'd like to stay for a while, but I don't want to push my luck. You understand, and you won't fight me. I feel lucky to be given those concessions. I'll go get Eve and Joe and let you relax for a while. But I'll always be close."

"I know." She stared at him. Darkness and fire and a fascinating sensuality. Strange that she felt no tension or threat at this moment. "I'm perfectly relaxed."

"The drugs. It probably won't last that long."

"Maybe not." What would it feel like to be comfortable and at ease with him all the time? She would probably never know. Even now, she was experiencing a faraway, tiny ripple of uneasiness. "Too bad."

He looked back over his shoulder. "Is it? We'll have to see as time goes on . . ."

RAIN FOREST
GUATEMALA

Smoke!

Montez woke from an uneasy sleep with the acrid sting in his nostrils. The cave was dark, but he could see a veil of smoke hanging on the air.

He jerked upright. Had the cave he'd found been discovered? Were they burning him out? He reached for his knapsack and crawled forward toward the cave opening. He stopped warily, his gaze searching the darkness of the forest.

Smoke all around, but there was no fire licking toward his cave.

And no one appeared to be in the trees near him.

So where was the smoke coming from? All he needed was a forest fire trapping him in this cave.

Find out.

If the fire was no threat to him, stay here. If there was danger, go on the run again.

Or go to the monastery if he judged that it was now safe from Dorgal.

He was sure Dorgal had ordered it searched already, but Montez still had to let time pass before he made contact. He would never forgive himself if other innocents died because he was scurrying for shelter.

No, not the monastery yet.

This cave was shelter enough and threatened no one but himself.

He moved cautiously out of that shelter and glided toward the trees.

His lungs were burning. He started to cough.

Ignore it.

Where was the fire?

To the west. He could hear a deep whoosh of crackling sound.

Find out where it was and in what direction it was traveling.

He covered his nose and mouth with his handkerchief and moved through the forest.

The smoke was thicker now.

The crackling louder.

And dread was beginning to turn him cold with fear. No, it didn't have to be—

Then he heard the screams.

And he realized what was on fire.

The monastery.

CHAPTER 12

Her cell phone was ringing, waking Catherine from sleep.

She jerked upright in bed and grabbed it from the bedside table.

Montez. Thank God, it was Montez.

"You've made up your mind?" she asked as she answered the phone. "I knew that—"

"Come and get me," Montez said hoarsely. "I told you that I'd ask for a sign. Well, I have it." His voice was strained with agony. "Sweet Mary, Mother of Jesus, I have it."

"Sign?" She was on her feet. "What sign? What's wrong, Montez?"

"They set the monastery on fire. I'm standing here watching it burn. Screaming. I hear the screaming. I think they locked the monks inside, but some must have escaped because I see a few running for the forest. But they're on fire. Burning—screaming and burning. I've got to help them."

"Listen, Montez. It's a trap. The minute you show yourself, Dorgal will pounce."

"They're burning up. Dear God, I can *smell* them. I've got to help. I'm a doctor."

"I can see that." She tried to think. "Stay away from the monastery itself. It won't help anyone for you to be trapped. I'll have Dario and his men rush over there and free anyone locked inside. Cameron says they're in the area. If you need to help any of those monks who ran into the forest, do what you have to do. Just try to keep Dorgal's men from catching sight of you. Okay?"

"If I can—" He hung up.

And Catherine was running out the door and down the hall to Cameron's room. "Call Dario and tell him to get to the monastery. Dorgal has set fire to it," she said when she threw open the door. "Montez says that he locked some of the monks inside."

Cameron didn't question, he was on the phone in seconds.

And Catherine was darting back to her room, tearing off her nightshirt, and throwing on her clothes. She dashed into the bathroom and splashed water in her face, then was hurrying back down the hall to Cameron's room again.

He was just hanging up the phone. "Dario's no more than eight minutes away," he said tersely as he got out of bed naked and started dressing. "I told him to release those monks and try to gather up Montez if he could find him. He's at the monastery?"

"In the forest trying to help the burn victims who escaped. It had to be a trap, Cameron."

He nodded. "And it will be a miracle if Dario gets there before Montez is caught."

"I know." She rubbed her temple. "I tried to warn him. But I knew I couldn't stop him. I wouldn't have stopped. You wouldn't have stopped. He talked about terrible evil and the sign he'd been given."

"No longer a pacifist?"

"He said to come and get him. I'm going to do it. I want to head for the airport and fly down there right away. But it may be too late."

"And it might not. Dario might get there in time. Or if Montez has already been captured, he might have been able to track them."

"To where? The nearest airport? What good would that do?"

"Don't be negative." He smiled. "I have a feeling that all is not lost."

"Feeling?"

Cameron was entirely too confident, she realized suspiciously. And Cameron was never confident unless he had a reason on which to base it. Who knew if that basis was something connected to the psychic ability he undoubtedly possessed. Though she didn't really believe he could read the future, she thought impatiently. But she didn't really know the extent of what he could do. He hadn't ever shared any in-depth information with her about his capabilities. "You wouldn't care to tell me why you have that 'feeling'?"

"I'm an optimist." He grabbed his jacket. "And, since you have a tendency to see right through me, I like to have the ability to occasionally surprise you."

"Occasionally?" She moved toward the door. "I never know what the hell you're going to do next. But if you're hiding something that concerns me, I'm not going to be pleased."

"My dear Catherine, I like the thought that everything that concerns me, concerns you. So the chances are that you'll not be pleased somewhere along the way." He followed her down the stairs. "I believe I'll keep my surprises to myself."

"As if there was any doubt." She stopped short as she

reached the bottom of the stairs. "Wait here." She turned and ran back up the stairs. "Luke . . ."

"Ah, you're not going to risk his being angry with you again?"

"I have to tell him . . ." And she wasn't looking forward to it. She had no time to argue. But she had been a coward before because she hadn't wanted to face Luke's almost certainly wanting to go with her. She wouldn't do it again.

She drew a deep breath and quietly opened his door.

Luke was asleep, curled up in a ball in his bed across the room.

"Luke?" she said.

No answer.

She moved across the room to stand beside his bed.

So deeply asleep, so beautiful in his tousled disarray, half boy, half young man. Dear God, she loved him.

And dear God, she was glad she had an excuse not to face him at this moment. She would only have been able to hurl the information at him before running back down to Cameron.

She glided over to his desk and scrawled a note on a Post-it.

Sorry. I tried, Luke.
Catherine.

He would know that it had been a halfhearted effort, but he would also know that she had listened to him and been here.

She turned and quietly left his room.

No pilot?" Catherine said as she climbed the steps of the jet and saw the open door of the cockpit. "The committee won't be pleased you're not taking a backup bodyguard to protect their golden boy."

"Too bad. As we discussed, I prefer to be in control, and I haven't had enough of that lately." He strode down the aisle. "It might have been tolerable if I'd had a sexual reward in view for putting up with being a passenger instead of pilot, but that's not going to happen. So come up to the cockpit and keep me company."

She nodded and followed him up the aisle. "Shouldn't we have heard from Dario by now?"

"Anytime."

Cameron got the call from Dario as they were about to taxi down the runway.

Cameron pressed the speaker and answered. "Montez?"

"Too late," Dario said. "We released the monks locked in the monastery. Three dead of smoke asphyxiation there. Then we found that monk Montez was trying to save in the forest. He was coherent enough to tell us that the man who had been helping him had been attacked and knocked unconscious by four men, who dragged him away into the forest. He heard rotors. Evidently, Dorgal had a helicopter waiting about a mile from the monastery. He's probably on his way to San Esposito to transfer aircrafts."

"Then you've lost him?" Cameron asked.

"I didn't say that," Dario said. "I said I was too late here. That doesn't mean I totally failed. It's just a postponement."

"Postponement to what?" Catherine asked.

"I called my people in San Esposito and told them to locate a plane that's being readied for takeoff. I told them to put a GPS tracker on the plane."

Hope flared. "We'll be able to trace Dorgal to Santos?"

"If that's where he's going," Dario said.

"Where else would he go?" Catherine asked. "He's taking Montez to where Santos needs him. Even Montez thought that Santos would keep Delores near him. He's taking Montez to Delores."

"You've lost me," Dario said.

Yes, Dario had not been privy to anything to do with Delores, Catherine thought. No time now to fill him in. "I mean we'll be able to track him to Santos. Don't try to stop him at the airport."

"I wouldn't anyway. I have only a few men there. Look, I've got to get back to that monastery. I'm trying to get help from nearby villages to take in those monks. Are you done with me?"

"Yes, right now," Cameron said. "Let me know if they manage to attach that GPS."

"Of course. But they'll do it. And I'll let you know the final destination." He hung up.

"He sounded very certain," Catherine said.

"And if they do, we'll get our shot at Santos," Cameron murmured. "So do we still go to Guatemala?"

"Probably not," Catherine said. "But we get in the air and head in that direction. We'll let that GPS on Dorgal's plane dictate our destination." She glanced at him. "As if you wouldn't do that without asking me."

"You've constantly pointed out that this is your show. Naturally, I'd ask you. Otherwise, you might cast me into outer darkness." He readied for takeoff. "Which terrifies me to no end . . ."

We've *got* him," Dorgal told Santos as soon as he picked up the phone. "I told you that I wouldn't fail you. We're heading for San Esposito Airport now."

"Why are you so pleased? It took you too damn long." Santos's voice was sarcastic. "All you had to do was pluck him up so that Ling couldn't get to him. He was just an interference, not an objective."

Dorgal tried to restrain his own impatience. Santos had obviously been sitting on his island, seething. It only reaffirmed his conviction that to maintain his own position in the cartel hierarchy, he had to give Santos the bloodbath he needed soon. "I realize that it took longer than we thought it would," he said soothingly. "I suspect that was Ling's fault, too. So the fact that we managed to get him was still a triumph. Not enough. But Delores will still have him as insurance, and it frees me to move on to more important items on your agenda." He paused. "That I believe you may have also decided are more urgent. Isn't it time you crushed Ling as she deserves? We can take out the people she cares about in a grand climax rather than one by one." He added quickly, "If that's what you want. If I'm reading you correctly."

Silence.

Dorgal was beginning to sweat. If he'd guessed wrong, Santos would have an unpleasant surprise waiting for him when they next met.

"You didn't guess wrong," Santos said shortly. "I don't think Delores would like Ling to live one more minute after all this trouble she's been causing. Let's put an end to it."

"Whatever you say."

"Grand climax . . ." Santos was mulling the concept. "I like the idea. But it has to be done right. I have to be able to watch her face when she realizes what she's losing."

"Of course," Dorgal said. "I'll make the arrangements. Most of the people who are on your list to exterminate are gathered like chickens in a henhouse. I've had information from my man watching Ling's place that Erin has recently been seen there, too. Jane MacGuire is the only one who we may have to go after individually. She's out of her coma and may be recovering."

Santos muttered a curse.

"But think of the agony of lost hope Ling will feel when we step in and kill MacGuire."

"You've told me that there are guards all around the hospital. Can you get to her?"

"I'll get to her. There's an orderly, John Chalce, with wonderful credentials and security clearance, who is permitted on her floor. Fortunately, he's also highly corruptible. So I'm sending Montez with Juan Pablo on that plane to you, and I'm heading to Atlanta to give MacGuire my personal attention. I've already started making preparations in Louisville for the major show. As you can see, I haven't been spinning my wheels while I was searching for Montez." He paused. "I hope that you approve and realize that I'll give you whatever revenge Delores would deem necessary."

"What *I* deem necessary."

Mistake? Who knew whether it was that bitch or Santos who seemed to be guiding the ship. It appeared to change from hour to hour. "That's what I meant."

"But not what you said." Silence. "Do you think I don't know you believe I'm crazy to have done all I've done for Delores? It doesn't matter. Not as long as you do as I order, as you've done in the past. If you don't, you'll end up dead with no magic coffin, no hope, and Delores and I will laugh at you as you decay into dust."

"I don't think you're crazy. That's totally untrue." He tried desperately to sound sincere. "And I'll do everything you wish and more. I'll be in touch, Santos." He hung up and drew a deep breath. Conversations with Santos were always perilous, no matter what he said. Anything could be taken the wrong way.

And anything that offended the bastard could end with fatal consequences.

But the bloodbath would not offend him. Not if Dorgal did it right.

Blood.

Pain.

And visible agony for Catherine Ling.

It was the right decision, Santos thought sadly, as he gazed at Delores's tomb. It was disappointing that the torture for Ling could not be drawn out indefinitely, but he couldn't bear the thought of her alive, thinking, hoping, moving. It was becoming torture when he entered this tomb and saw his Delores so beautiful but still, so still.

He took a gardenia from the bouquet beside the door and entered the crypt. He was hit by the scent of rotten flowers and rotten flesh. The body of the young whore he'd offered up to Delores lay huddled on the floor beside the clear plastic casket where she lay. He usually kept any sacrifice here at least a month, but after that he had one of his men toss her into the sea.

Not that he minded the stink. He was sure that Delores would not either. But room must be made for any other offerings. He moved to stand beside the glass coffin and gazed down at Delores.

Beautiful.

Vibrant.

Serene.

Montez shouldn't have made her serene. Delores was never serene. Maybe he should have Montez try to—

No, Montez had warned him that any change would be dangerous now that the creation was completed, he remembered regretfully. Oh, well, he would imagine that the serenity was Delores dreaming of him, of the things they did together, the things they would do in the future.

He put the gardenia on the glass. It would stay fresh a long time on that cold surface. "I've decided to get rid of this stupid whore and give you a more worthy offering.

Catherine Ling. It's time we started to punish her. Don't you think so, my darling?"

Serenity.

But beyond that serenity, beyond that cold beauty, was Delores smiling?

Catherine received a call from Kelly a few minutes after their plane crossed the Texas border. "Hi, Catherine. I'm pretty sure I've connected a major dot. We may be able to trace Santos."

"What? How sure?"

"I'm sure, but that's not saying anyone else would be. It's all theory and calculations."

"Cameron and I may be able to track him without your theory and calculations. We planted a GPS on the plane taking Montez to Santos's compound."

"Plane? Helpful, but you're not going to connect."

"Why not?"

"Because I'm figuring that there's no air access to where Santos is hiding out with his Delores. I believe that he has to take an aircraft to a nearby jumping-off place, then go by boat to the final destination. I'd bet it's probably a small island."

"Why would you think that?"

"Fuel."

"What?"

"I told you, Venable tracked down all of Dorgal's credit cards under his name and known aliases. You remember that I told you that Dorgal visited all kinds of Caribbean hot spots while Santos was in prison?"

"Yes."

"He was very careful. He didn't concentrate on any specific destination. And he changed credit-card use frequently."

"Use for what?"

"Motorboat rental and gas. The cartel probably has its own boats, but Dorgal wouldn't want anyone but himself in the cartel to know anything about Santos's location. It would have made him a target for a takeover by a member of his own organization or a rival cartel."

"I can see that." She was thinking quickly. "But Venable had credit-card records. Gas usage?"

"Yes. If you measure gas usage to and from each jump-off destination. Then you compare the results and map the distances, you can zero in on Santos's possible headquarters." She paused. "Or you could talk to Luke once you know where that plane is dropping off Montez and his guards. For the last day and a half, Luke's been working on possible scenarios for me.

"I'm not sure that he'd be willing to talk to me," Catherine said ruefully. "I'd better try to do it myself."

"He was very annoyed," Kelly said. "But he wouldn't let that interfere in the balance of keeping everyone alive. He's more grown-up than you think."

"No, just more than I want him to be," she said.

"Trust him, Catherine."

"I will. I'll throw myself on his mercy when I know where Montez ends up. Thanks, Kelly." She hung up and turned to Cameron. "You heard her. It's not as easy as we hoped."

"But that would have made the hunt so much less interesting." He glanced at her. "And it gives Luke a chance to save the day and make you proud of him."

"I'm always proud of him."

"Then it will make him able to enter your world for a brief moment or two. That may be of even more value to him. Why do you think he's fighting you so hard?"

"He thinks he's thirty years old instead of twelve."

"Maybe he is."

"Don't say that," she said sharply. "I won't have those years stolen from him."

"Then you'd better strike a delicate balance." He shrugged. "But who am I to offer advice? You'll do what you wish anyway. I just see Luke from a different viewpoint than you do."

"As a possible recruit," she said tartly. "No way."

"I wouldn't try to take him away from you," he said quietly. "I find myself wanting to give you fabulous gifts and offer you glittering worlds to conquer. Give, not take, Catherine."

She blinked. He meant it, she realized. For a moment, she didn't know what to say. "Really?" She looked away from him. "And take nothing in return, I suppose."

He chuckled. "I never claimed that." His cell phone rang, and he reached for it. "Dario," he said as he answered, "do we have a destination?"

"The plane landed in Port of Spain, Trinidad, ten minutes ago," Dario said. "I tried to scramble to have someone follow them, but they whisked Montez away with the speed of light. You'll have to have your people do a search, Cameron."

"Or Catherine's people," Cameron murmured. "She has one or two excellent operatives with whom she's just been in contact."

"Excellent? I can always use good people. Can I hire them away from her?"

"I doubt it. She's very protective of her sources."

"Then she should tell them not to focus only on Montez. Dorgal wasn't on the plane when it landed in Trinidad."

"What?" Catherine said. "Where is he?"

"He hired a private jet two hours after that flight left for Trinidad. The flight plan said New Orleans, but I doubt if that's where he'll end up."

"So do I." Catherine moistened her lips. "More likely Louisville. Or Atlanta."

"I'll use a little bribery and intimidation with the rental company and find out which one is the target and get back to you. I thought I'd warn you. Let me know if you have anything else for me to do."

"Just the continued surveillance and protection of the Montez family," Cameron said. "Now that Santos has Montez, at least he won't have that threat to hold over his head."

"No, just death and torture," Dario said dryly. "No threat at all. But I'll eliminate the only one I can right now. No one will touch his family." He hung up.

"Santos won't kill him. He believes he may need him," Catherine said. "And he may threaten him, but Montez will be able to fend off torture. He's smart, and he knows it's only a matter of time until we find Santos."

"You don't think he'll cave as he did before, when Dorgal sent for him to work on Delores?"

"You didn't hear his voice when he was looking at that burning monastery. He was sick and horrified at the destruction. Dorgal went too far. It boomeranged. He's in our camp now."

"If we can find a way to use him."

"And to find out where the hell he is."

"Oh, I have complete confidence we'll find him," Cameron said. "Have a little faith."

She gazed at him in annoyance. His tone had been as confident as his words. "Why are you this certain?"

"Kelly and Luke. Didn't I tell Dario that you had wonderful people?"

"And that's the only reason?"

"What else could there be?"

She shook her head. "With you, there's no telling." She

dropped the subject. "But right now, I'm more worried about Dorgal's heading back toward the U.S."

"And rightly so." His lips twisted. "But we always knew that Montez was only a temporary distraction. Now that he's scooped him up, it appears distraction time is over, and he's focusing on the main event."

"Evidently." Panic was pounding through her. "I have to talk to Hu Chang and Eve and warn them."

"It's not as if they're not expecting it to happen. They're prepared for it." He held up his hand. "I know that you still have to call, but suppose you phone Luke first. I'll set up Skype so that he can show us the general directions he and Kelly figured out from the gas usage."

She nodded. Of course, that was the smart thing to do. If they could take Santos out, then any plans Dorgal had would fall apart. But it still didn't stop her from wanting to turn the plane around and rush back home. "Do it."

Ten minutes later, she was looking at Luke's face on the computer screen. He was wearing a dark red shirt that made his hair appear darker than ever. He was not smiling. "Hello, Catherine. Kelly said that you need me."

I always need you, she wanted to tell him.

Get it over with. Try to clear the air. "And she told me that you were annoyed. You have a right to be."

A flicker of expression. "Yes, I do. You cheated, Catherine. You didn't want to have trouble with me, so you—"

"You're absolutely right." She tried to smile. "You intimidated me, and so I just paid lip service to what you wanted from me."

He frowned. "Intimidated? No one intimidates you, Catherine."

"You do. Why else did I chicken out? I apologize. Will you forgive me?"

He was still frowning. "I guess I will. But you should have—"

"Take me to task later. I need you to tell me about connecting those dots. Kelly said you've been working on a few scenarios to give me a general direction where I might find Santos."

He nodded. "More than a few. I went through dozens of gas receipts from every city in the Caribbean where Dorgal rented a motorboat. I checked out weather, wind current, tide for every trip, and gave the figures to Kelly to calculate how far the gas used would take Dorgal on that particular day." He held up an oceanic map chart with arching lines and scrawled numbers issuing from several cities. "And then I charted them all and their approximate distances from the origin point." He pointed to the sizable circle he'd drawn in the ocean. "There are dozens of tiny islands in this area, and I can't tell which one was his exact destination, but Kelly and I both think Santos's island is somewhere in that group."

"Dozens," she repeated. "But that's more info than we had before. We'll just have to be careful not to be seen when we're scouting around that area."

"And it may not be all that difficult to find," Cameron said. "What's the approximate mileage of your circle, Luke?"

"Maybe forty miles."

"Weaving in and out of those islands," Catherine said. "And I'm sure Santos is equipped with manpower and high-tech missiles on that island."

"We'll work it out."

"Yes, we will, but it won't be easy." She turned back to Luke. "Good job. No, exceptional job, Luke. This is a big help."

He smiled. "Yeah, Kelly and I did good work, didn't

we? It was kind of fun. Of course, she did all that high-tech stuff." His smile faded. "I hope it helps. I should be down there with you. You take care of her, Cameron."

"I wouldn't let anything happen to Catherine. You have my promise. Now I believe that she needs to speak to Hu Chang."

"Ah, I was waiting for my importance to be properly addressed," Hu Chang said as he came into view. "Though I have to concur that these young people did a fine and valuable job. I generally prefer that Luke concentrate on chemistry and the rules of—"

"Hu Chang, Dorgal left Guatemala and is probably heading toward you," she interrupted. "I don't know whether he's heading toward Louisville or Atlanta. We're trying to find out. Warn Eve. I think Santos will escalate now that he has Montez tucked away."

"It would appear likely. I have a feeling that the situation will turn even more nasty from now on," Hu Chang said. "I will take it under consideration and act accordingly." He paused. "You might make an effort to save Montez if possible. He has a fine mind, and I detest the idea of waste."

"I'll do what I can. Good-bye, Hu Chang." She broke the connection. "I want to be there with them." She closed the computer with a click. "He wants me to try to save Montez? What about them?"

"We have a chance at Santos," he said gently. "I know you're torn, but you have to—"

"Stop trying to comfort me. It's not like you. You don't have to tell me where I have to focus. Cut off the head of the snake. But what if we don't cut it off in time?"

"Okay, comfort over." He shook his head. "You don't have an alternative. So stop agonizing and start thinking how you're going to kill the son of a bitch."

"After we find him."

"No, Luke helped out there. Just work on a plan." He paused. "Or I will."

And if he took over, she'd have to fight like hell to regain control. He knew that would be a goad. Stop thinking about all she might lose if she didn't do everything right. Start thinking what she might win if she did.

"I'm working on it. Just get us to Trinidad. It's probably the closest place to the island, since they flew directly there from Guatemala. We'll follow the route Luke drew out of Port of Spain and hope it puts us closer than when Dorgal flew to one of those other Caribbean cities."

"Logical. Reasonable." Cameron glanced at her. "Did I scare all of that emotional trauma out of you by threatening to become a presence you might have trouble with?"

"Be quiet, Cameron." The emotion and panic was still there, but she was trying to keep it subdued. "You told me that I had to think, and that's what I'm doing."

"And it's probably the first and last time you'll ever do what I tell you to do."

She didn't answer, her mind was shifting, moving, probing. So many things to consider.

Find a plan.

Was Dorgal heading for Louisville or Atlanta?

And how could they keep him from more bloodshed?

She was searching desperately for a way to keep the people she loved safe.

And still manage to cut the head off the snake.

ST. JOSEPH'S HOSPITAL
ATLANTA, GEORGIA

"Hu Chang says that Dorgal may be on his way here or to Louisville." Eve hung up the phone and turned to Caleb, who was standing by the door of the ICU. "Or so

Catherine thinks. She told him to warn us. She'll call when she knows which one is his destination."

"Then there's probably good reason to pay attention." He glanced back at Jane in the bed across the room, talking to Joe. "Not that we aren't anyway."

"She's safe, isn't she, Caleb?" Eve's worried gaze followed Caleb's to Jane. "Dorgal can't get to her? She has all these guards Joe and Cameron arranged to watch her. Every one of the hospital staff who attend her has been checked out. Why would Santos think she'd be vulnerable?"

"Maybe because he has a giant inflated ego that's telling him that anything he wants, he can have." His lips tightened. "But he can't have Jane. He's lost her, and I won't give her back."

"Neither will I." Eve crossed her arms across her chest to ward off the chill. "I lost my Bonnie when she was only seven years old, and I almost lost Jane. I've always been able to deal with loss, but while I've been watching Jane struggling these last days, it's been tearing me apart. There's nothing more precious than your own child, and I want to reach out and grab and hold on." She smiled unsteadily. "You know, when Jane had to start traveling to promote her paintings, I thought that I was starting to lose her. In a way that was true, but only the way that children always leave their parents. She always kept in touch, she always came home. Not like my Bonnie. I was lucky with Jane, Caleb."

"She was lucky, too," he said quietly. "You found her in the streets, you took her in, you loved her. You were willing to sacrifice anything to keep her safe." He smiled as he touched his chest. "Even calling on someone who you don't really trust if there was a chance that I could help her."

"And you did."

"That's past tense. It's not over. I'd like to think it was. But I promise that I'll be the one to finish it."

"Excuse me, ma'am, would you please step aside? I have to get in to set up this equipment."

They both turned to see an orderly in white pushing a stainless-steel cart. He was in his late twenties with a sandy crew cut, freckles, and a polite smile. Eve vaguely remembered seeing him on the floor but couldn't recall his name. "Equipment?"

"Portable X-ray equipment. The techs are going to take them here in ICU." He grinned. "They'll be in and out in a few minutes once I get it set up. Okay?"

"Yeah, I remember its being done here before." Caleb was already on his cell, his gaze on the orderly's name tag. "Just let me verify the order." He talked briefly on the phone, then stepped aside. "Set it up, Chalce."

"Yes, sir." The orderly propped open the door and started to roll the cart into the room.

Chalce. Yes that was the orderly's name, Eve realized as she saw his ID badge as he passed her.

John Chalce.

CHAPTER 13

PORT OF SPAIN, TRINIDAD

And what's our next move?" Cameron asked as he taxied down the runway of the airport toward the private hangars. "You were entirely too quiet on the way here. Should I be worried?"

"By all means. Why should I be the only one?" She unbuckled and stood up as the plane came to a stop. "Something has to change, Cameron. We have to make it change." She tried to keep the tension from her voice as she moved toward the door. "I guess the first thing is to try to locate the island that—"

Her cell phone rang.

"My God," she whispered as she saw the ID. "Santos."

She punched the access. "What do you want, Santos?"

"Perhaps to rub a little salt in your wounds," he said silkily. "I haven't had the chance lately since you've kept me so busy hunting down Montez. You shouldn't have involved yourself in my personal business, Catherine. It made me angry and will make your punishment all the more painful."

"You were already hunting him when I stepped in and offered Montez a little help."

"Because you thought he might help you find me. Disappointed?"

"A little. But it just put off the inevitable." She paused. "And it was worthwhile to touch base with him to discover what a pitiful pair of fools you and your Delores turned out to be. My God, Santos, are you that much afraid of dying that you're clinging to life with—"

"Shut up," he said harshly. "You're the one who is a fool. Delores found a way for us to beat the odds and come out on top. There's nothing pitiful about us." He paused, struggling to regain his temper. "Montez told you?"

"No." Protect Montez and keep him from the brunt of Santos's rage. "He was too afraid of you to talk." That was true enough. "But I found his technical journal, and we figured it out."

"It was a magnificent plan, but Montez was too frightened to give us everything we needed from him."

"You mean his life in slavery to Delores?"

"She might need him again. That container is experimental. What if something went wrong?"

"She'd defrost?" she asked mockingly.

"Never. That won't happen, you bitch. I'll keep her with me forever." His voice dripped malice. "You're the one who's going to die, and soon. I'm going to be able to concentrate on making sure of that now. But I've decided that I'm too impatient to wait to see you dead. I'm going to offer you a deal, Catherine."

"A deal?" she repeated warily.

"I was planning on making you the last on my list of victims, but I'm going to give you the opportunity to let you go to the front of the line."

"What are you saying?"

"Why, that I'll not make you watch the deaths of your son and Hu Chang and the rest of those people who are so unfortunate as to be close to you. I'll let you step up to the plate and come to me to get what you deserve. Wouldn't you be willing to sacrifice yourself for your fine son?"

"You're crazy. Why should I do that? I'm keeping you from hurting them now. You won't be able to touch Luke. And I'll find a way to kill you before you get near him. Before you get near any of them."

"I'm near him now. I watch him. I see him smile. My men take photos all the time and send them to me. Such a handsome boy. I've only been waiting until I was less occupied with Montez to fully enjoy watching him be exterminated."

"You're lying."

"Am I?" He chuckled. "You sound desperate. It's strange that a vicious bitch like you can be so soft about a child. I believe you might actually take my deal if I can convince you how vulnerable you are. I will convince you. Time for another choice, Catherine. I'll show you I can reach out and kill, and no one can stop me."

"You're delusional, you bastard."

"And then if you come begging, I might decide to be merciful about any other kills. It might be enough to give you to Delores and watch you die . . . slowly."

"And it might not. You're all bluff. You've not been able to take one of my people since I found out what you were doing. We've blocked you, Santos. Now you think I'm going to come running and let you put me down? It's not going to happen."

"Yes, it is. But it seems I have to prove to you that you can't stop me no matter what you do." He hung up.

"That was something of a surprise," Cameron's gaze narrowed on her face. "And he managed to upset you."

"What do you expect?" She was shaking. "The bastard was talking about my son. He's not stupid. He knows how to strike where it hurts."

"And he thought he could manipulate you to take his deal," he said thoughtfully. "Interesting. Of course, it might have been a shot in the dark. Or he might have wanted only to show you that he could control you."

"I'm glad that you can be so cool about it. I'm having a few problems doing that."

"Oh, I'm not at all cool," he said softly. "I'm imagining all kinds of ways that I can hurt him that will take a long, long time. I didn't like the way he was playing you."

She felt a ripple of shock as she glimpsed beneath that composure to the savagery that lay below. She looked away from him. "And you immediately started taking him apart and seeing how you could bend the situation to suit yourself."

"To suit you, Catherine."

She felt a warm melting deep inside her.

She still didn't look at him. The moment was too fraught with raw emotion. "Then I appreciate the effort, but that's what I should be doing." She drew a deep breath. "Okay, it surprised me, too. Evidently, Santos's revenge isn't happening fast enough. He's never been a patient man, and he hasn't been able to move as quickly and efficiently as he'd like. His ego is probably hurt. That call might have been a sincere offer, or he might just have wanted to talk to me and vent his superiority." She was trying to think clearly. "But there might be something that I can use, some way I can turn it against him."

"I'm not liking the way you're thinking," Cameron said slowly.

"Why not?" She met his eyes. "That's exactly how you think, Cameron."

"That's different. Santos's offer was very personal and very deadly."

"And depended on an emotional breakdown on my part

to give him his chance to manipulate me and draw me into his lair." She paused as possibilities began to occur to her. "Which could have a hell of a lot of advantages."

"Catherine."

"You know it could." She held up her hand to stop him from speaking. "I have to take advantage of the fact that Santos is getting impatient. He'll make mistakes."

"Maybe."

"Probably. He's beginning to salivate at the thought of how he's going to kill me. Couldn't you tell?"

Silence. "Yes."

"That was hard for you to admit."

"Because I don't want you to use yourself as bait to reel him in."

"If I don't, I'd have to use someone else I care about. In the end, this is all about me. Now it's time I stepped up to the plate, as Santos said." She was thinking. "And we'll have Montez in place on the island. He might be able to help."

"He's not been much help in the past."

"I told you, he's changing."

"And you're willing to clutch desperately at that chance, aren't you?" He studied her expression. "Maybe 'desperate' isn't the word. You're excited. I can almost feel the vibes."

He was right; she could also feel the zing, the familiar breathlessness that always preceded action. "I won't count on Montez, but he might be a plus."

"He will be a plus," Cameron said crisply. "And I'll see that you can count on him. Now tell me what else you need to come out of this fiasco alive."

"We've got to make sure it's not a fiasco," Catherine said. "Because if Santos suspects that he's not in control, he'll order a mass execution even if it's a suicide mission.

He can't stand the thought that I might beat him." She was nibbling at her lower lip. "And the only opportunity we'll have is if Santos thinks he's been able to force me to do what he wants me to do."

"You mean if someone dies," he said baldly.

"Oh, God, no." She drew a shaky breath. "Look, I've got to think about this. Right now, let's go rent a boat and locate that group of islands Luke and Kelly zeroed in on."

"You'll get no argument from me," Cameron said. "I like the idea of an attack by sea much better than having you deliver yourself to that butcher's block." He reached for his cell phone. "A small motorboat, scuba equipment . . . I'll supply a few sophisticated pieces of electronic equipment myself."

"I almost forgot that your committee always keeps you supplied with the latest gadgets," she said dryly. "Shades of 007."

"His stuff's not nearly as high-tech as what our young scientists are bringing out these days." He smiled. "Microscopic but very effective." He gestured for her to precede him. "Doesn't that make you feel safe?"

"If your gadget can blow Santos to kingdom come before he can give the word to kill anyone else."

"Possible but not foolproof unless the explosion is set off within twenty feet of the bastard. I may have to smuggle a rifle onto the island and pick him off."

"Providing we find the island before Santos's men find us."

"Oh ye of little faith . . ."

What are you looking at?" Catherine asked, her eyes narrowed on Cameron's face. He'd been very quiet for the last ten minutes as they'd cut the motor and rowed silently among the dense, green islands. Twice he'd lifted the binoculars to his eyes. This last time he'd taken a long time before he had lowered them.

"Success," Cameron murmured. "And it's very sweet." He pointed to a verdant jungle of palms and brush on a small, hilly island. "Too much brush and trees for a helicopter landing pad but that would also keep any houses or compounds from being seen from the air." He paused. "Or any tombs that happened to be in the area."

"We've only been coasting along these islands for the last fifteen minutes. We can't be that lucky. That's not the only island with that much shrubbery."

"But it's the right one."

"Why?"

"Because Montez is there."

She went still. "What? How do you know? Are you guessing? Are you managing to home in on his mind or something?"

"I suppose I might try, but this seemed much easier."

"What seemed easier? What the hell are you up to?"

"Nothing." He smiled. "Montez is the one who's doing it all. I'm just receiving." He nodded down at the waterproof pocket of his scuba jacket. "And I've been receiving for the last five minutes."

"What's happening, Cameron," she said through her teeth. "Or so help me, I'll hit you with this oar."

"So violent . . ." He raised the binoculars to his eyes again. "I planted a microchip GPS in Montez's neck when I was examining him after you gave him that karate chop in the rain forest. It's fairly powerful, and I knew I'd be able to detect his location from at least thirty miles."

Her eyes widened in shock. "You bastard. Why didn't you tell me?"

"I was feeling a little irritated about not being in control. I wasn't entirely in agreement with your attitude with

Montez, so I decided I'd do a little advance prep in case I decided to break free and go off on my own." He lowered the binoculars again. "I almost did that a couple times, but I managed to be more patient than I thought I would."

"Patient? I never asked for your patience. I've just been trying to survive and keep people alive."

"I know that." He tossed the binoculars aside. "And I left that part of it to you. I've been guarding and biding my time." His eyes were glacier blue as they met her own. "But that's all over. I know where you're going with this, and I'm not trailing behind in your footsteps. We're together; you'll listen to me. If we argue, then I may go my own way, and you'll have to adjust."

"And if I don't?"

"You will because I'm damn good, and you know it." He slipped out of the boat and into the water. "Now stay here while I do a little reconnoitering on that island."

"Orders?"

"You won't argue about this one. If Santos caught you before you were ready to spring a trap, it would mean that he'd have Luke and the rest at his mercy."

He was right, she thought reluctantly. "And what about you?"

"He doesn't regard me as important in his plans." He pushed away from the boat. "I'd deal with it. I'll be back in forty-five minutes. If I'm not, go back to Port of Spain. I'll join you there."

"How will you—"

But he'd dove below the crystal aquamarine waters, and, minutes later, he was lost to view.

Thirty-five minutes.

No shots.

No sight of anyone on that strip of pristine beach.

But that didn't mean that Cameron hadn't been captured.

Anything could have happened to him on that island.

But it wasn't as if he were an amateur.

He's probably the most dangerous man either of us has ever seen, Hu Chang had said.

But he wasn't immortal, either.

Get back here, damn you.

Forty minutes.

What if there were video cameras on those trees?

It was possible.

Forty-two minutes.

Be safe, Cameron.

Come back to me.

How can I resist a touching invitation like that?

Relief surged through her.

You cut it close.

Because I wanted to savor all that heartfelt feeling you're broadcasting.

You've savored it. Now get out of my mind.

Just another minute. I'm enjoying it.

Out.

Laughter.

And the next moment, he surfaced beside the boat.

Blue eyes shining with mischief and recklessness.

And life.

Oh God, life.

He hefted himself on board and settled on the seat across from her. "You're being very revealing. I don't even have to try to read you." He reached for a towel and wiped drops of water from his face. "I . . . like it."

"Well, I don't." She picked up her oar. "Let's get out of here."

"Right." He started rowing until it was safe to start the motor. "Though there's not much chance of being seen from this side of the island. All the action is in the hills to the north."

"What action?"

"A small palazzo structure tucked under all those palms. There's a bunkhouse that would support maybe eight or ten men." He paused. "And a granite tomb farther up on the hill. Still protected from view from the air."

"Like a cocoon ready to come alive."

"Neither Santos nor Delores are butterflies. But Santos is definitely there. I didn't see him, but he's there."

"Montez?"

"He's being kept in the bunkhouse, under guard." He shot her a glance. "But I was able to inject a few words of wisdom to guide him in his dealings with Santos. I believe he'll go along with them."

"What words of wisdom?"

"Cooperation so that he'd have a certain amount of freedom. He already thought that you'd be coming for Santos, and I only told him to be ready."

"And he probably thought he was going crazy."

"No, but he might have believed he was hearing heavenly voices. Since I emphasized destruction of his archdemon, Santos, it was likely."

"All of that in forty-five minutes?"

"I'm very efficient. And I didn't want to be left behind," he added slyly. "You can be very ruthless. I knew you'd hold me to my word and not give me one extra minute."

She wanted to push him overboard. "We've found Santos. We could notify Venable and have him ready for a strike."

"But you have no intention of doing that. You can't control Venable's actions, and you'd be afraid he'd move too soon and endanger Luke and the others." He paused. "When we're ready for a strike, it will be my men. We won't have a problem of control with them."

"No, you've made it quite clear that you won't give up control for any length of time."

"But I gave it up for quite a while for you," he said quietly. "And I've never done that before for anyone."

And he'd done it because it was the only way that she'd accept his help. Which made it a gift all the more precious. Almost too precious for her to accept. "Should I believe you?"

He nodded slowly. "Oh, yes, by all means, believe me, Catherine."

Maybe she would believe him. For now, for a little while. It would be . . . nice to have that feeling that she was special to a man as unique as Cameron. The world right now was frightening and uncertain. He might change overnight, and that safety net would be gone. She would probably soon realize that she had no need or right to link with Cameron in any way.

But it wouldn't hurt to listen, to watch, to let him a little closer.

And hope the risk was worth it.

She looked away from him. "So what are we going to do now?"

"Over to you," he said. "I wouldn't presume to make a suggestion after taking over the action at the island. It's your turn."

"How very kind." She dipped her oar in the water. "Then we go back to Port of Spain, check into a hotel, you start getting your men down here and in position. We contact Dario and get his report on Dorgal's destination and decide how we can use it. Then we talk about what comes next. Okay?"

"Absolutely."

She smiled. "And you pretend that's not exactly what you would have done anyway."

He smiled back at her. "That's harder to do."

And in this moment, she didn't care.

It was enough to have him here beside her, smiling.

It was enough that she wouldn't be alone to face what was crashing toward her like a freight train.

Santos only miles from her, waiting.

Dorgal, who had to be stopped and eliminated before he could kill again.

If it was not already too late.

ST. JOSEPH'S HOSPITAL
ATLANTA, GEORGIA
11:05 A.M.

Move slowly, be casual, John Chalce told himself as he left the ICU. It was almost over, and everything had gone slick as glass. Now he had only to get down this hall to the elevator and take it to the parking deck.

"Hey, John, you're done a little early." Nancy Rodham at the nurse's station looked up from her computer. "How's your dad doing?"

"Great." He grinned. "Thanks for asking. I'm taking him down to Florida this weekend and see if he can shake that cough."

"You're a good guy." Nancy looked back at her computer. "I see that Basle has changed MacGuire's medication."

"Did he? I wouldn't know. I'm just a humble orderly, and no one lets me even get close to meds. Fine with me. I'd hate the responsibility." He punched the elevator button. Come quick, dammit. "She seemed a little groggy when I took the fresh blankets into her room." And slipped the tasteless poison Dorgal had given him into the ice water that he'd helped her drink. It had worked as quickly as Dorgal had said it would.

"She did?" Nancy frowned. "She's been doing so well . . ."

"Maybe it's my imagination." Eve Duncan and Joe Quinn were walking back from the waiting room toward the ICU. They were smiling. They wouldn't be smiling for long. Where the hell was that elevator?

At least that bastard Caleb wasn't with them at the moment. The doctor had called him away as John had entered ICU. Seth Caleb gave him the creeps. He was always at his shoulder, staring at him with those piercing dark eyes.

But not today. Today was John's lucky day. Everything had gone just right.

But it might all be going downhill. Eve Duncan and Joe Quinn had reached the door of the ICU. He could see Eve's forehead wrinkle in a frown as she looked at Jane MacGuire, lying in the bed across the room.

No. Too soon. Too soon.

The doors of the elevator slid open.

Yes.

He jumped into the elevator and punched the button.

As the doors started to close, he saw Eve Duncan stiffen. Her eyes widened. "Jane?"

And then she screamed.

Dead." Eve ran across the room, tears streaming down her cheeks. "Joe . . ." Her arms went around Jane's slack body. "No, it can't be true."

"What's wrong?" Nancy Rodham ran into the room. "The alarms just went off. Dead? You've got to be wrong. She was doing so well." Her gaze went to the machine. "Shit." She ran forward, picking up her phone she called the code. "You'll have to leave," she told Eve and Joe over her shoulder as she tore the cover off Jane. "We've got to try to save her."

"It's too late," Eve said, as the doctor ran into the room. Seth Caleb was right behind him, his gaze on Jane's face. "Leave her alone. Can't you see? You can't help her." The tears were still flowing, and her voice broke. "My Jane's dead."

CHAPTER 14

He still had time, John Chalce thought. It was going to be pure chaos in that ICU for the next five to ten minutes, and by that time, he'd be out of this parking garage and on his way to the airport.

He unlocked his Ford Escort and threw open the driver's side door.

"Hello, Chalce." Seth Caleb was suddenly beside the door. "In a hurry? Too bad. Because I don't think you're going anywhere."

"Oh, hi, Mr. Caleb. I've got to leave." John moistened his lips. "I just received an emergency text from my dad. He's not well, and he needs me."

"No, I need you more." He stared him in the eye. "And I want you to stick around."

Those damn dark eyes were almost hypnotic, John thought. And with all the ferocity of a forest animal. He could feel the sweat begin to bead on the back of his neck. "Sorry." He tried to get in the car. "Family, first."

Caleb slammed him against the car. "I'm sure Eve Duncan would agree with you. But not about your dear old dad. She's very concerned about her daughter. There's a big furor going on in ICU about Jane MacGuire. You wouldn't know anything about that, would you?"

He shook his head.

"I don't believe you. You don't know that they think she had a reaction to her medicine just when you left her room?" His eyes were blazing in his taut face. "She's dead, Chalce."

"I'm sorry." He tried to sound sincere. It was hard, with this beast looking at him as if he wanted to devour him. "She seemed like a nice lady. You seemed devoted to her."

"You have no idea." His voice was soft, silky, but totally deadly. "I promised her that she wasn't going to die, and here you come along and try to make a liar of me. That doesn't please me, John Chalce."

"You think I had something to do with it? Why would I do that?"

"Money. Drugs. A little of both? I don't care about the reason. All I know is that Manuel Dorgal got to you."

"I don't know any Manuel Dorgal."

"Yet I bet his name and number are on your cell phone."

"How do you . . ." He stopped. "That's not true."

"It's true. I took a long look at all the people trusted to care for Jane. You were high on my list of suspects. Let's check it. Give me your phone."

"No. You have no right to—"

But Caleb had already grabbed Chalce's cell from his pocket and was going through the directory.

"Why me?" Chalce asked. "Why would you think I'd do it?"

"You're so nauseatingly wholesome. That automatically sends up a red flag to me. In case you haven't noticed, there's nothing the least wholesome about me. I was going to steal your cell anyway, but you moved too fast today."

"Steal?"

"It's easy for me. I seem to distract people when I get near them." He nodded. "Here it is. Manuel Dorgal." He shoved the cell back to him. "I want you to use that phone right now."

"Why should I?" he said defiantly. "Why should I do anything you want? This is all guesses and lies."

"Why should you?" Caleb's hands were suddenly on his throat. "Because I'm very angry with you. Because you might live a little longer if you give me Dorgal. Tell me what you were supposed to do after you killed Jane."

"I didn't kill her."

"Don't lie." His hands tightened on John's throat. "That annoys me, and you don't want me annoyed any more than I am right now. Do you feel the blood pumping in the veins of your throat? So fast . . . Soon it will be even faster, and the pain will start."

It was starting now, and so was the panic. He couldn't keep his eyes from Caleb's. "I . . . didn't mean to kill her. Dorgal made me."

"Liar. Tell me what you're supposed to do."

"Leave the hospital and call Dorgal. He has orders to personally validate the death. I think he wants to take pictures or something."

"When?"

"Right away. Tonight. Though they might do an autopsy since the death was unexpected."

"Completely unexpected," he said grimly. "She was on her way back."

"I had to do it. I was afraid."

"You should be afraid right now."

He was terrified. He had never seen anything like the ferocity that Caleb was showing him. And the blood was pounding, choking him, causing his eyes to bulge in their sockets. What was the bastard doing to him? "Please . . ."

"I'm going to take my hands away from your throat.

You're going to make that call. You're going to tell Dorgal that everything went well, and she's ready for her close-up. You're going to sound absolutely normal, then you're going to hang up. Do you understand?"

He nodded. "Anything you say. And then you'll let me go?"

"Maybe. Maybe not. I might exchange one murderer for another. But you won't have a chance if you don't do what I tell you."

"I'll do it." He grabbed his phone from his pocket. "It was Dorgal who's to blame. It's not my fault." His hand was shaking as he dialed Dorgal's number. Two rings, and Dorgal picked up. "She's dead," John said. "No problem. I'm leaving for the airport now. Transfer the rest of the money into my account in Grand Cayman."

"You'll get it after I verify that you did the job." Dorgal paused. "You sound a little breathless."

"I've never done anything like this before. I'm glad it's over."

"I hate working with amateurs."

"Just give me my money." He hung up. He looked at Caleb. "Okay?"

"Good enough."

"Then let me go."

Caleb shook his head.

Panic. "You said that maybe you'd do it."

"You told Dorgal that you were glad it was over. Did you think how Jane might feel as she took those last breaths? You didn't care whether she lived or died as long as you got your money." His hands closed on his throat again. "But I care, Chalce. Do you feel how much I care?"

Blood pounding.

Heart pounding.

Was he dying?

Darkness.

4:22 A.M.

The morgue was cool, almost cold.

The lights over the three metal tables brilliant and glaring.

And on one table, a figure covered by a white sheet.

Dorgal moved quickly from the door toward the table.

Shoot the damn photo and get out of here. The place was beginning to stir, and he'd noticed that there was a light on in the small reception office across the hall. He wouldn't have risked going through with the damn verification if Santos hadn't insisted. He'd said that it would be more effective if he could show Ling a photo of the actual body.

And he would show MacGuire's body, and Santos would realize once more what a valuable asset Dorgal was to him.

Quick.

He flipped the sheet down and aimed his phone at that beautiful, peaceful face.

One picture.

Two.

Three.

Enough.

He jammed his phone back in his pocket and started for the door.

"Dammit, he's getting away, Caleb. Do something!"

Dorgal froze.

What the hell?

He whirled back around.

Jane MacGuire's eyes were open, and she was glaring at him. She said softly, "Surprised?"

He reached for his gun.

And tumbled to the floor as Seth Caleb sprang from behind one of the file cabinets and tackled him. "I was getting to it, Jane." His fist crashed into Dorgal's jaw. "I wanted him to get a little farther away from you."

"I didn't want to wait. I felt . . . violated."

"Bitch." Dorgal grunted. He was struggling wildly. "Chalce sold me out?"

"Not in the beginning. He didn't know. I switched the poison you so kindly provided him."

"Fool. I'll kill him. I'll kill *you*." He rolled sideways and broke free. Suddenly, there was a knife in his hand, plunging at Caleb. He made contact, but Caleb slid away. And then the knife was gone, skittering across the floor toward the door.

The door was opening, and the knife was being snatched up by the man standing there.

"Get off him, Caleb," Joe Quinn said grimly. "I want my turn with him."

"Not now. We still have a use for him."

"Tell that to Eve. She's had enough of this charade. She wants someone to pay."

"Later. Give me your cuffs."

Joe reluctantly tossed his cuffs to Caleb. "He took the photos?"

Caleb nodded as he cuffed Dorgal's hands behind him. "He was in a big hurry."

"Santos will kill all of you," Dorgal could feel the humiliation and fear tying his stomach in knots. Make a deal, then find a way to take them down. "He missed MacGuire this time, but he'll get her the next. If you want to live, you need me."

"Do I?" Caleb got to his feet and moved back toward the metal table where Jane MacGuire lay. "You're right. You wouldn't be alive right now if I didn't have a use for you." He looked down at Jane. "How do you feel?" he asked quietly. "Was it too much for you?"

"No." She looked him in the eye. "Not exactly where

I'd choose to spend the night. But it was necessary, wasn't it?" Her gaze shifted to Dorgal. "He's the one who gives the orders for Santos? He's probably the one who arranged for me to be shot in the first place."

"There's a good chance," Joe said. He looked down at the knife in his hand. "Maybe just a few minor but painful cuts?"

"No, not unless he doesn't cooperate." Caleb's gaze had never left Jane. "We've got to get her out of here. Eve's talked the doctor into ordering her to be slipped into an isolation room for the next couple days. Questionable, high-level contagion. Strictly limited access. As far as anyone but three members of the hospital staff on the ICU floor are concerned, Jane died of a drug reaction and remains here for the time being."

"High-level contagion?" Jane repeated.

"Atlanta has the CDC. Lots of bad stuff. Even the hospital staff would be scared," Caleb said. "A good choice."

"Thank you." Eve pushed open the door and came into the room. She scarcely glanced at Dorgal as she hurried past him on the way to Jane. "Hi." She gently pushed a strand of hair away from Jane's face. "How are you doing? He didn't hurt you?"

Jane smiled. "No, I just held my breath when I heard him coming toward me, as Caleb told me to do. But then I thought he might get away when he started hurrying out, and I ruined my death scene."

"She couldn't resist expressing her displeasure with me," Caleb said. "Only to be expected."

Eve looked at Dorgal for the first time. "I would have been worried about his getting away, too. After all Jane had to go through for us to stage this little drama, I would have jumped him the minute he got near her."

"I had to have the photos," Caleb said. "That's what this was all about, wasn't it, Dorgal?"

"We need to make a deal," Dorgal said. "Okay, you've got me, but I'm no good to you. Santos is the only one who can call off the killing."

"Are you offering us Santos?"

"I can't do that. Look, if you think that because you have me that you can bargain with Santos, you're crazy. He doesn't trust me. He doesn't trust anyone." He paused. "But I might be able to tell you where he's located."

"That's no longer a valuable bargaining chip. Catherine knows where his compound's located."

"Then perhaps I can persuade Santos to—"

"I don't believe that Santos is persuadable," Caleb said. "Let's call Catherine and see what she thinks, Eve."

Eve reached into her bag and pulled out her iPad. "I promised I'd call her on Skype when it was over anyway. She was scared to death something would go wrong."

"Skype?" Jane said.

"She wanted to see you," Eve said. "Because she knew that she'd probably be forced to see Santos's photos he received from Dorgal." She made the connection. "Catherine. Everyone's safe, and we've got Dorgal." She turned the iPad toward Jane. "You see, she's fine. In a few minutes, we'll be taking her to a safe room in the hospital and tucking her in for the rest of the night."

"Thank God," Catherine said. "I'm sorry, Jane. I seem to be always putting you on the spot."

"You're trying to get me out of this particular spot. Stop giving yourself guilt trips." Jane made a face. "And at least it was more interesting than lying in bed and feeling completely useless. Though when you called Eve and told her that you'd found out that Dorgal was heading for Atlanta and you thought that he and his henchmen were going to make another try at killing me, I admit I was a little shook."

"I was tempted not to even involve you," Eve said. "But

Catherine said that she needed a reason to make Santos think that she was so terrified that she'd turn herself over to him on the condition he wouldn't kill anyone else she loved."

"So I had to be involved," Jane said. "And preferably dead."

Eve shuddered. "Don't say that. This whole day has been a nightmare."

"You did a great job pretending that nightmare was real," Joe said. "Tears, near hysteria."

"That wasn't all pretense," Eve said curtly. "After Caleb zeroed in on Chalce as Dorgal's likely accomplice, I was terrified. I was scared to death that maybe Caleb hadn't managed to switch that poison he found in Chalce's apartment. That maybe we'd killed her."

Caleb shook his head. "I would never have left her alone with him if I hadn't been sure she was safe."

Eve shrugged. "I was running every bad-case scenario on the planet." She said to Catherine, "Anyway, Jane is safe. When Santos tells you that she's dead, it's a lie. We'll keep Dorgal from doing any more damage. Go play your game with him and blow the bastard out of the water."

"I'll do my best." She paused. "You've all been wonderful. When I called and gave you that hideous job to do, I wasn't certain that—" She stopped. "But I should have known better. You've never failed me." She smiled. "I'll call you when I know something. Or after I give Santos his gift from you. Take care." She hung up.

"What gift?" Jane asked, puzzled.

"Just a little remembrance." Eve turned to Dorgal. "I'm sure he knows what she was talking about. Perhaps we should give one to you, Dorgal."

"Maybe later," Caleb said. "He has a few things to do first."

"What things?" Dorgal said warily.

"First, you're going to e-mail those photos of Jane to Santos." He looked down at Dorgal's cuffs. "Or I'll do it for you. You appear to be incapacitated." He took Dorgal's phone out of his jacket, dialed up Santos, and texted, "Just a brief message. Chalce's mission verified. Know you'll be pleased." He pressed the send on the photos. "Death does please Santos, doesn't it? Sometimes it pleases me, too."

Darkness. Violence. Ferocity. All were in Caleb's face as he was looking at him. For the first time, Dorgal was afraid. "What are you going to do to me?" he asked hoarsely.

"I'm thinking about it. Nothing at the moment. I've got to go with Eve and see that Jane is safely settled in that isolation room." He turned to Joe. "Will you take Dorgal to my car and wait with him until I get through? Please don't kill him. I have a use for him."

"I'll try to restrain myself," Joe said coolly. "It won't be easy."

"Where are you taking me?" Dorgal asked. "We should deal. I have money."

"Blood money. I'm going to take you for a ride up the interstate to Louisville. I'm sure you have men there who are on watch at Catherine's home. You're going to identify every one and tell me what you have in mind for them if Santos decides to attack that house. You won't miss even one because I'll know."

"How?"

"Why, I'm a hunter. Violent. Ruthless. Deadly. Not at all a nice guy. Ask Jane." He turned and headed for the door. "I'll go get that bed we stashed in the other office and wheel it in here."

"Caleb."

He looked back at Jane. "What?"

"You *are* a hunter. You proved that tonight. We might

not have survived if you hadn't." She paused. "But that's not all you are."

"But you're not sure what else I am." He shrugged. "Maybe someday you'll figure it out. Or maybe not." He opened the door. "Why should I care? Enigmas are so much more interesting."

They did it." Catherine turned to Cameron, her eyes shining with excitement. "I can't believe it. They not only set up Santos, but they removed Dorgal as a threat. I only asked Eve to protect Jane and try to make it logical that I'd go along with Santos's suggestion to put myself on the chopping block."

"And they did much more." Cameron smiled. "Why are you so surprised? You've surrounded yourself with extraordinary people. It's natural they would behave in an extraordinary manner and go the extra distance." His smile faded. "But there's still a threat to Luke and the others. Dorgal might be forced to reveal Santos's plans to kill them, but all he has to do is leave out one element, and they're dead if Santos gives the word."

"He won't give the word." But his words had quenched her exuberance. Yes, everything had gone well, but they wouldn't be home free until Santos was dead. "Eve and the others have done their part. Now it's time for me to do mine." She moved over to the window overlooking the harbor. "I should be hearing from Santos soon. Shouldn't you be getting out of here? You told me that Dario and his men had arrived at the airport."

"I have some time. Dario is capable of equipping his team and arranging for transport to the island."

"But you don't like to rely on anyone but yourself." She smiled crookedly. "You're sure that no one can handle anything better than you do. It's that control thing."

"You mean arrogance."

"I used to believe that was at the bottom of it. Sometimes, I still do. But I'm leaning toward thinking that you have a king-size sense of responsibility that won't let you give up authority."

"Except to you."

"Which you still managed to skirt." She glanced over her shoulder. "And I'm thinking that responsibility is kicking in right now, and you're reluctant to leave me to my own devices. Get out of here, Cameron. You know I can take care of myself."

"Of course you can." He moved across the room toward her. "But I find I'm having a problem with letting you go right now." He stopped before her, and his hand reached out and touched her throat. "We could change the plan. Instead of Dario and I taking out Santos's men on the island. You could go with us, and we could—"

"No." She stared at him in exasperation. "You know that it's better and less risky for me to zero in on Santos. Divide and conquer, dammit."

"Conquer?" His hand tightened on her throat before it loosened and fell away. "Why am I having trouble embracing that concept? All I can think about is Santos cutting your throat after he finishes torturing you." He leaned forward, and his lips brushed her throat with infinite sensuality. "And not being able to do this ever again. So shortsighted of me."

My God, the feel of him. That face, those light eyes that told so much and yet nothing at all, that strength that she wanted to draw inside her until all the madness was over.

Then he was stepping away from her and moving toward the door. "So I'll just have to make sure that Santos doesn't have a chance to cheat me. Go ahead and play your game with Santos as Eve told you. I'll step in and referee if it gets too rough. Call me when Santos contacts you. It's the least that—"

Her cell phone rang.

"Or maybe you won't have to call me," Cameron said grimly. "Santos?"

She nodded, drew a deep breath, and punched the access. "You bastard. What kind of monster are you? Jane was helpless."

"You sound upset," Santos said mockingly. "But I tried to tell you that you couldn't stop me. How was your friend, Eve, when she told you about her dear, Jane?"

"How do you expect her to be? She's broken. She was so sure that Jane would live, then you did this . . . monstrous thing."

"Which was all your fault. I gave you the opportunity to persuade me to let her live." His voice dripped malice. "You could have said yes, and I would have told Dorgal to scrub the assignment. Though he would have been disappointed because he knows how much I wanted her dead. However, I gave him the pleasure of taking her photo after she was killed. I'm sending you a copy. So beautiful, so peaceful."

"I don't want to see it. The idea of Dorgal's gloating over—"

"You're getting rather throaty." His voice hardened. "You don't want to see her photo? Would you rather see a picture of your son? Only he wouldn't look peaceful or beautiful after I killed him. I have other more violent plans for him. There might not be enough pieces to put together to stage a photo shoot."

"Shut up!"

"Frightened? It's coming. I have it all planned. I wanted to pick them off separately, but I made contingency plans. He has a day, two at most, and he'll be dead."

"No!"

"Yes. Nothing and no one can stop it." He paused. "Except you, Catherine."

"You're bluffing."

"Jane MacGuire is dead. I warned you. Was that a bluff?"

Silence. "No."

"Then why should I bluff about your fine son?" He paused. "I'm sending you another photo, and I'd advise you to look at this one."

She felt a chill. "Why?"

"You'll know."

She heard a ping from her phone, and she accessed the photo.

Luke. Smiling.

But his head was in the sights of a rifle.

She inhaled sharply, and she didn't have to pretend the panic she was feeling. She had thought he was safe. How had he become a target?

Just take one chance, and I'll have them.

Luke must have taken that one chance.

"You're not speaking," Santos said mockingly. "I believe I've made my point."

She swallowed. "What do you want from me?"

"Justice. Revenge. Pleasure. Step into my parlor, and I'll have all of those things."

"And where is your parlor, Santos?"

"I believe you're getting close. Dorgal's men tracked you and Richard Cameron to Port of Spain after Pablo delivered Montez to me. Of course, it would take you years to find me. By that time, you will have lost all of the people you love and also your life. So sad."

She forced herself to look away from that photo. "I love my son. But you can't expect me to just let you kill me.

I'd have to know that I'll have the chance to save myself and him."

"By killing me?"

"Are you afraid, Santos?"

"Of a stupid bitch like you?"

"I wasn't too stupid to kill your Delores. She wouldn't be afraid to give me my chance."

He was silent. "No, she wouldn't. And I should have expected you to try to bargain with me."

"All I want is a chance."

"And maybe you'll have it. Or maybe not. Go to the docks and walk down to the warehouse area near Beetham Road. Don't bring Richard Cameron, or I'll give the word for the boy to die. Only you, Catherine."

"I'm going to bring a weapon."

"No weapon. I want you defenseless."

"Delores wasn't defenseless."

"No weapon." He hung up.

"You heard him, Cameron." She looked back down at the photo. "Dear God, Luke was within a heartbeat of having his head blown off. My home is surrounded by guards. Hu Chang wasn't even afraid to let him go with him to check on the sentries. How did they get a bead on him?"

"I don't know." Cameron shook his head. "My men said it was safe, too. The two blocks around your home were checked out, then sentries were constantly on guard. No one could have gotten this close to Luke."

"But they did. I've always known that the young think they're immortal, but this terrifies me. I may never let him out of my sight."

"And you'll lose him."

"But he'd be alive." She shook her head to clear it. "Okay, I know he was probably unprotected only for an instant. I can't even tell where the photo was taken. But it was enough . . ." She had to concentrate, but all she could think about was Luke. "It could happen again. Santos wanted to show me how vulnerable he was no matter what I did to save him."

"Everyone is on alert, Catherine. But when I leave you, I'll call Hu Chang and tell him that neither Luke nor anyone else is to leave the house until we tell them it's okay."

"Good." And she had to pull herself together if they were all to survive. "And nothing will happen to them. Not if we handle this right." She got her jacket from the closet. "No weapons. I expected that." She took off the ankle holster for her dagger and handed it to him together with her gun. "You were on the island. Can you find a place that I'll have access to them?" She made a face. "Providing I'm able to use my hands." She had a sudden thought. "The tomb. He's bound to take me there for one reason or another. Either to show me that I wasn't able to destroy his Delores or to kill me in front of her. Is there a place there where you could hide them?"

"I wasn't inside the tomb." He nodded. "But I was thinking that there might be action there, so I took a good look around. There's a large, oval, granite stone heaped with flowers outside the bronze door. I remember seeing gardenias . . ."

"Fine. Gardenias. I'll remember." She slipped on her jacket. "Don't follow me, Cameron. You get my boy shot, and I'll kill you."

"I know that." He stepped closer, and his fingers gently touched her cheek. "Nothing will happen to you or him, Catherine. I promise you." His fingers lingered an instant longer, then dropped away from her. He turned away. "See you on the island."

She watched him walk out the door. Her cheek felt warm where he had touched her. Not the searing heat of sex but something deeper, stronger, that made her stronger because of that fleeting instant of bonding.

She'd had a moment where she'd felt uncertain and weak, and he had sensed it and shown her that she was neither.

And now it was time for her to go and show Santos.

BEETHAM ROAD AND SOUTH QUAY

"Not a great neighborhood. I could have staged an ambush anywhere in the last two blocks," Dario murmured to Cameron as they moved along the alleys bordering the warehouses. "We should get closer to Catherine if you want to intercept."

"I don't want to intercept," Cameron said. "And if I got any closer, she'd know I was following her." His lips tightened. "Or someone else would know, and that can't happen. Catherine would not be pleased. She threatened to kill me."

Dario's brows rose. "Then you have a right to be careful. If she's like my mother, she'd keep her word. If you're not going to intercept or interfere, why are we following her?"

"I need to be sure that we haven't miscalculated. Santos almost certainly will send someone to capture her. That's why he told her to come here. But what if he decides to come himself and take her out on the spot?"

"Is that likely?"

"No, he's giving up a hell of a lot of torment by cutting down his victim list. He'll want to take his time with Catherine. But there's always a possibility. If Santos doesn't come, who will he send?"

"Juan Pablo. He's the one who brought Montez here. Santos uses him more than any other of his men except Dorgal."

"Would you recognize him?"

Dario nodded. "I've run into him a time or two in Trinidad and Jamaica. Pretty nasty. Do you want me to take him out?"

"No. I told you, I can't interfere."

"But you will if it's Santos and not Pablo."

He nodded shortly. "Then it won't be a capture, it will be a murder. And even if it's Pablo, I may have to intervene. Catherine is supposed to let them take her with only a token resistance."

Dario gave a low whistle. "And you don't believe she's capable of doing that? I tend to agree with you. She would find it impossible to give in meekly to Pablo. But that would make her resistance appear more authentic."

"If he doesn't kill her." His gaze was fixed on the brief glimpses he was getting of Catherine, who was almost two blocks ahead of them. She was moving slowly, warily, her head lifted as if she was listening.

Soon.

He could feel his tension growing as he waited for the attack to come.

The attack he couldn't stop.

If Santos was there, the attack would stop before it began.

Catherine would die.

And then Cameron would kill Santos before he breathed another breath.

More warehouses.

Shadows.

Crates.

Trucks.

Machinery.

It should happen here, now.

Catherine thought so, too. He could read her body language, the tension, the hesitation, as her gaze searched the darkness.

She was passing a huge crane.

Shadows . . . moving!

Leaping out from behind the crane!

Three, no, four men.

Catherine whirled and the heel of her boot caught one of her attackers in the throat. She leaped forward, and her fist plowed into another man's belly, and then her foot shot backward and caught the man behind her in the groin. He fell to his knees.

"Give it up, Catherine," Cameron murmured beneath his breath. He knew the instinct that was driving her. That was one of the primary reasons he had followed her. But these men had weapons, and she had none.

The man she had kicked in the groin was now on his feet and drawing his gun.

"Shit." Cameron drew his own gun.

But the man wasn't firing. The butt of the gun was coming down with vicious force on Catherine's head.

Her legs buckled, and she fell to her knees. The next moment, she was crumpled on the dock, unconscious.

The man who had struck her was cursing, and he took a step forward. He lifted his foot and kicked Catherine viciously in the rib cage.

"Son of a *bitch.*" Cameron's gaze was fixed on the man's face, memorizing every feature. "Who is he? Do you know him?"

"Juan Pablo," Dario said. "She was fairly incredible, wasn't she? I can see why you were worried. That was no token. But I think she made him a little angry."

"That's nothing to what he made me," Cameron said. He watched as one of the men picked up Catherine's limp body and carried her down the dock. He could feel the rage tearing through him. He had to forcibly resist the temptation to go after them. Stick to the plan. Go with Dario and his men to the island and bring Santos to his knees.

And slaughter that prick Pablo later.

CHAPTER 15

Pain.

"Wake up, bitch."

Catherine's head jerked as she was struck on the side of her cheek.

She tried to open her eyes.

Another blow, this one splitting her lower lip.

"I don't want you lying there like a zombie. Open your damn eyes."

Santos. It had to be Santos. Catherine forced her lids to open.

Santos's face was only a foot away from her own, and his eyes were blazing, his lips drawn back from his teeth like a feral animal. "Yes, that's what I want. Pablo shouldn't have hit you. I'm the only one who's permitted to cause you pain." He raised his hand and whipped it again across her face. "Maybe later. Maybe when I get tired and just want to watch your final throes of agony."

"How . . . dramatic. Was that supposed to intimidate me?"

He hit her again.

Okay, don't taunt him. She had to stop him from hitting her until she could clear her mind. Where was she?

Sand. She was lying on . . . sand. Darkness. Palm trees. She could hear the ocean's surf close by. She must be on the island.

Yes, there was a speedboat anchored a short distance away, and three men standing, watching Santos. She recognized one as the man she'd kicked. The other two she didn't remember.

How long had she been here? Had Cameron had time to get around to the other side of the island yet?

Ask.

"I don't remember anything after I was struck on the head. How long have I been here?"

"Too long. A couple hours. I thought Pablo might have spoiled everything. I couldn't wake you."

"I could have shot her." One of the men stepped forward. "I only hit her."

"Shut up, Pablo," Santos said. "I wanted her to be clear-headed and able to appreciate everything I'm going to do to her. Go on up to the tomb and wait for me."

She watched the man scurry up the beach. "Two hours. He must have hit me very hard. Though I'm sure you were ever so gentle about bringing me around."

He hit her again.

Two hours. It could be long enough for Cameron. She would have to see.

"You're suddenly very quiet," Santos said softly. "Are you feeling how alone you are? All your friends, and none of them can help you now." He reached down, grabbed her arm, and jerked her to her feet.

"At least I have friends," she said. "You have no one, Santos. No one cares whether you live or die."

"They care. Because I'm the one who says whether they live or die." He pushed her down the beach toward a path winding beneath the overhanging palms. "But now it's time for me to take you to Delores. You've kept her waiting. I meant to have more time with you on my own, but you've spoiled that." He shrugged. "Oh, well, perhaps I'll enjoy it even more thinking how she would feel when I begin on you. Delores was always more imaginative than I was when it came to discipline. She could stretch punishment out for days, and she would try so many new toys . . ."

"I'm sure that she was everything you say she was." She gave him a cool glance. "And I couldn't be happier that I blew her away. I wish she were alive, so that I could do it again."

Rage. Twisting, ugly, rage that contorted his features. "She is alive," he hissed. "You'll see. You couldn't kill her. You're not good enough. She fooled you. She fooled everyone. She's alive. She's only waiting."

"You're crazy," she said. "And Delores was just as crazy to lead you down the path toward such a bizarre scheme. It's all pretense and lies, and you can't even see it."

"Pretense? Lies? Was it a lie when I showed you that photo of your son? You didn't think so. I could sense your fear. Delores would have loved that moment." He smiled. "As she'll love the moment when I give the order for your Luke to be shot."

She stiffened. "I'm here. I'm the one you want."

"But I have to feel your pain. You keep it so well hidden that it takes a great deal to make you reveal it."

"That was a freak incident when Luke was targeted. Hu Chang takes good care of him. He'll find the man you've planted outside my home stalking Luke. I've told him not to let my son leave the house for a while. It might never happen again."

Santos laughed. "No? You think he's just skulking in the shadows and dodging your people? That photo was taken through a window while Luke was in his bedroom. I have a shooter in the attic of an old Victorian house over a thousand feet away. Donald Lambell is an expert marksman I hired in Iraq and he answers only to me. I didn't even trust Dorgal to know about him."

Panic raced through her. Oh, God, and the fact that they'd told Hu Chang to keep Luke inside had actually set him up for the shooter.

Don't let Santos see the fear that was tearing at her. He was waiting for a reaction. Don't give it to him. "And I thought that you and Dorgal were soul mates. Both tarred by the same brush."

"Delores never trusted him. Why should I? She's the one who hired Lambell in case I ever had to use him to take Dorgal out if he becomes too troublesome." He smiled. "So you can see, Lambell is my ace in the hole. If Dorgal's men can't make the hit, Lambell will do it. I called him last night and told him to be ready for the kill. So all your safety measures are going to be for nothing. As soon as I give the word, he's going to blow your Luke's handsome head off."

Catherine felt sick. He was so terribly certain.

And he could see what she was feeling in spite of every effort to keep it from him. "Yes, that's what I want from you. Horror. Your worst nightmare. No more photos. I might just let you get a Skype shot when he pulls the trigger. What a terrible feeling. And you wouldn't be able to give him his chance to live, as I gave Delores. No Dr. Montez for your son. No chance for him. No chance for you. It gives you a different perspective, doesn't it?"

"It makes me wonder if there's a hell that's horrible enough for God to send you to." She swallowed. "It won't happen. You'll fail, Santos."

"Shall I take out my phone and give the word?"

She didn't answer.

"You're frightened. I like that. But I'll wait until we're

with Delores to kill the boy. She was always one to appreciate the turn of the knife."

"She's dead, dammit."

"Only in your eyes. But you may change your mind when you see her." He gestured up the hill. "You see that granite tomb? Isn't it splendid? The finest black granite, the doors crafted of Italian bronze. Everything about it is meant to be a frame for a queen. My queen. You were so interested in Montez and what he was doing for me. Now you can see for yourself."

"Montez is here?"

"Of course. I would have had him killed in Guatemala if I hadn't wanted him as an insurance policy for Delores."

"And for you."

"Yes." He shrugged. "But I have no intention of needing his services."

"Neither did Delores."

"But she was always more cautious than me. I went along with her, and I'm glad I did. For her sake. I intend to live for a long, long time before I need Montez. But when I do, he'll always be here . . . waiting. Just as he's doing now. You see him standing there by the door of the tomb? I thought you should see that you'd failed with him, too. He came to me last night and told me that he wouldn't cause me any more trouble if I spared him and his family."

"Poor bastard."

"He's learned his lesson. Now it's time you learned yours, Catherine."

They had reached the tomb, and the sheer massiveness of the structure was overwhelming, Catherine thought.

Weapons.

Had Cameron managed to hide her gun and knife?

Gardenias. The scent of the ivory-colored blossoms drifted heavy and fragrant on the air.

She could see the large, oval, granite tray before the ornate bronze door, and heaped on it were the bouquets of gardenias. She couldn't tell if her weapons were stashed beneath them, but she had to assume that they were.

Or pray that they were.

How to get to them?

"Hello." Eduardo Montez stepped forward. "I told you that what you were doing was useless, Catherine. I couldn't fight against him, and neither can you."

Did he mean it? Cameron had been sure he'd influenced him, but she couldn't be sure. Had Montez finally caved to the pressure?

"Speak for yourself," she said jerkily. "I'll fight him until there's no breath left in my body."

"Which will be very soon." Santos chuckled. He took her arm and shoved her toward the tomb entrance. "Let's start the process right now. I guarantee seeing Delores will take your breath away."

"No." She stopped before the door and then spun around to stand defiantly in front of the gardenia tray. "I won't go and pay some kind of sick homage to that bitch," she said fiercely. "If you want to kill me, do it here."

"You will go in that tomb." Santos's face was flushed, and his eyes were glittering with rage. "You're going to know that you failed."

"The hell I will." Push him just a little more. "Screw you, Santos."

She spit in his face.

He made a sound of pure animal rage.

He backhanded her across the face with all his strength.

Pain.

Ignore it.

Use it.

She cried out, spun away, and fell.

Straight down into the granite tray of gardenias.

The scent of flowers was overwhelming as her face buried itself in the soft blossoms.

Dizzy. Her head was whirling from the blow. For an instant she couldn't move.

That was okay. He had struck her with such force, he would expect her to be stunned.

Her hands reached out blindly beneath her.

Where was it?

Cool metal . . .

Her right hand closed on the butt of her Luger. Too big. Too risky. She wouldn't be able to hide it in her jacket.

Her dagger . . .

She found it!

She flipped it under her jacket sleeve.

"Are you all right?" Montez was kneeling beside her, his expression concerned. "I told you not to fight him."

"Get away from her," Santos said harshly. "Get on your feet, you stinking whore."

"In a minute." She made a show of struggling to get to her feet. While pushing the bouquets of gardenias back over the gun.

"Call me whatever you want." She could feel the blood running down from her split lip to her chin as she finally stood before him. She glared at him defiantly. "It was worth it, you know. Has anyone else ever spit in your ugly face?"

He drew back his hand, then dropped it to his side. "I think you must want me to kill you. Do you? That would avoid having to admit that you're responsible for my butchering your son." He opened the bronze door. "But I'm not going to let you get away with it. You have to experience it all. Come in and see my Delores." He pushed her inside the dim interior. "And you'll see why I permitted Montez to stay alive."

She glanced at Montez over her shoulder. If she expected some sign of encouragement, she was disappointed. His face was without expression.

"You'll excuse the chill. Delores requires it. But it doesn't interfere with the décor. All the mechanics are in an underground room." Santos was turning on the gothic torchlight beside the door, and the dimness suddenly came alive. The flickering bulbs revealed a room that was magnificent in every detail. It looked like a cross between an Egyptian temple, with stately, gilt chairs and statues on malachite pedestals, and a Persian palace, with thick carpets that covered the cold stone of the floor. There were dozens of photos of Delores in gilt and bejeweled frames on the walls. "The lowered temperature cuts down on additional power needs."

And then Catherine saw Delores lying on what appeared to be a glass-enclosed pedestal in the center of the crypt. She was dressed all in gold, like an ancient pagan empress, her dark hair shining on her bare shoulders. She looked vibrantly alive and wonderfully beautiful. So alive that anyone might have expected her to open her eyes at any moment, sit up, and step out of that coffin.

And that's what Montez had planned, Catherine thought. In this moment, she could believe that it would only be a matter of time before Delores would be able to conquer the ravages of death.

And then all the evil and ugliness that was hidden behind that beautiful mask would return and come alive again.

"I told you." Santos's gaze was raking Catherine's face. "Now you know that you couldn't destroy her."

"I know that Montez did a fantastic job. I saw the Lenin

exhibit and studied Stalin's embalming. This far exceeds the skill they used." She turned to look at him. "But I *did* destroy her, and if necessary, I'll do it again."

"No!" His lips curled. "You fool. You can't touch her. I'll kill your son. Then I'll kill you and lay you on the floor beside her coffin. You'll rot there, while she goes on forever. I'll come and visit here, and Delores and I will laugh."

"I don't doubt you'd make the attempt, since you're completely wacko." She put her right arm half behind her as she took a step closer to the casket. "But I imagine she'd have problems with changing expressions, wouldn't she? Did Montez fix that, too? Let me take a closer look . . ."

"Don't touch that glass." His hand grasped her shoulder, and he jerked her back. "Keep away from her."

"Whatever you say." She moved her arm so that he wouldn't touch the dagger in her sleeve. "It sounded as if you wanted us to be best buddies."

"I don't want your foulness near her. Not until you're—"

Kaboom.

The explosion caused the tomb to shake.

Santos froze. "What the hell?"

He grabbed Catherine's arm and jerked her out of the tomb. His gaze flew up the hill.

Flames. Smoke.

The house that must have been Santos's residence was almost entirely destroyed, flames clawing the night sky. Pablo was giving orders to the two men with him as he ran up the hill toward the house.

Kaboom.

Another explosion.

The bunkhouse?

"Venable?" Santos screamed. "I'll kill that bastard, Pablo. He swore he wasn't followed to the island."

"Not Venable." She jerked her arm away from him. She

jabbed her elbow in his belly with all her force. He bent double with pain. "And Pablo didn't lie." She dove around the side of the tomb just as Santos fired a shot that ricocheted off the granite.

Another explosion down at the beach.

"Come back here, Catherine," Santos said. "Blow up everything in sight, and I'll still win. Because I'm taking out my phone. I'm dialing a number . . . In two minutes, your son will be dead."

"No." She let her dagger drop down her sleeve into her hand.

Position. Throw.

Aim for the hand holding the phone.

"You heard her," Cameron said from the road behind Santos. "She said no. It's not going to happen."

He dove forward and tackled Santos, knocking the gun from his hand.

Thank God.

Catherine moved from behind the tomb.

But Santos had his hands around Cameron's throat. Her hand tightened on her dagger.

Cameron kneed him in the groin, and when his grip loosened, he flipped him over his head.

Santos crashed against the side of the tomb and slid down to the ground. He lifted his head dazedly. Then as he saw Catherine, his face contorted with rage. He reached for his phone again.

She was on him in seconds, her dagger pinning his hand to the ground.

He screamed!

"No way." She bent down, and her eyes gazed fiercely into his own. "You're not going to touch my son. Not now. Not ever."

"The hell I'm not." He screamed again as he jerked the

dagger out of his hand and ran back toward the entrance of the tomb.

"Dammit, get out of the way, Catherine." Cameron's gun was aimed at Santos. "You're blocking my shot."

"Let him go." She watched Santos disappear into the tomb again. "He's not going anywhere. There's no back door to the tomb. He's trapped in there with his Delores. I'll go after him in a minute. Give me your phone. I've got to call Hu Chang."

"Why are you—"

"Now!" He took one look at her strained expression and tossed her his phone.

Her hand was shaking as she dialed Hu Chang. She started speaking as soon as he answered. "I can't talk more than a minute. Don't let Luke go to his room. If he's there, get him out. Dammit, I don't know where else in the house he'll be safe. Not near any window. Do you hear me?"

"I hear you. Now slow down and tell me why."

"No time. A Victorian house over a thousand yards from my house. The attic. A shooter named Lambell. Did you get all that?"

"I've got it. Are you safe?"

"Yes. No. Maybe. I'll call you when I know for sure." She hung up.

Safe. Luke would be safe.

As safe as she and Hu Chang could make him.

"Lambell?" Cameron repeated.

"A surprise from Santos. His ace in the hole. But I think Hu Chang will be able to block it." She was trying to catch her breath as she glanced at Cameron, then up at the burning hillside. "It appears you decided to blow up the island. Is there going to be anything left?"

"Very little. Dario is rounding up the rest of Santos's

men, and they don't seem to be enthusiastic about defending it." His gaze was fixed on her face. "Your face looks like it went through a nasty blast, too. Santos?"

She nodded. "He didn't like a few of my comments about Delores." Her gaze went to the crypt. "So he brought me here to join her."

"I thought this was where you'd end up."

"So did I. Delores was where it all started." Was it fate that had led Santos to run back into that crypt? She wondered. She had a strange feeling that it had been. "This is where I want it ended."

"I was wondering why you blocked my shot." Cameron's lips tightened. "And I noticed you said I, not we, will go after him. What are you doing, Catherine?"

"What do you think? This battle was always aimed at me, and I've got to end it. He killed, he wounded, he terrified people I love in the name of Delores. I'm going to punish him."

"Not without me."

"Don't be selfish; you practically blew up the whole damn island yourself. Leave Santos to me."

"Not without me," he repeated. He looked her in the eye. "Absolutely not."

And if she didn't accept that help, he'd go in after Santos himself. His entire being was poised, ready, glittering like the dagger with which she'd stabbed Santos. "Okay, I won't shut you out. But it probably won't be in the way you might prefer. Give me a couple minutes to get my breath, then I'll tell you what I need." She gazed at the bronze door of the tomb. He was in there waiting for her. She could feel his waves of hatred, the frustration, the bloodlust.

Well, she had a bloodlust of her own.

I'm coming for you, bastard.

LOUISVILLE, KENTUCKY

"Lambell?" Caleb shook his head. "Dorgal gave me five names and locations here in Louisville. None of them was Lambell, Hu Chang."

"Then he lied," Hu Chang said. "And it doesn't matter. Catherine says that he exists and is a danger." He headed for the door. "A Victorian house that's at least a thousand feet from this one. Do you recall such a house, Sam?"

"Two blocks away. Three-story. Green shutters and trim," Sam said. "It's the only one within that distance."

"I'm on my way," Caleb said as he headed for the door. "Call me if you hear anything more from Catherine."

"She called and asked my assistance," Hu Chang said. "I do not appreciate being told to monitor the phone."

"She told you to take care of Luke," Caleb said. "How can you do that if you're busy cutting that bastard's throat? And Sam's got to protect the house. I'm the outsider. Much better that you leave Lambell to me. I was getting restless anyway."

"How could we tell that? Just because you've been prowling like a panther since you arrived here?" Hu Chang said. "Outsider. Yes, that describes you." He shrugged. "Very well. I'm disappointed, but I yield to logic if not to your selfish desire to indulge yourself." He stared him in the eye. "But do not fail her, Caleb. You do not want me to be displeased with you."

"You won't be." Caleb smiled recklessly. "I've got it. Victorian house. Green trim. One shooter soon to be deceased."

The door slammed behind him.

CHAPTER
16

I'll give you four minutes." Cameron pushed Catherine back against the tomb. His face was taut, his eyes glittering as he stared down at her. "And that's cutting it close. Then I'm coming in after you."

"Whatever." She met his eyes. "It should all be settled by that time anyway." She smiled faintly. "Or it will be two minutes later."

"Not funny."

"No, you're very serious. Not like you at all. You usually have a lighter touch."

"I'm having a problem with watching you walk into that tomb when we don't know what's waiting for you."

"Santos's gun is lying there on the ground. He has my dagger, but he'll have a tough time using it with that wounded hand." She held up her Luger. "And I have a gun, and I'll have no trouble using it."

"Santos may have run back into that tomb for a reason."

She shrugged. "Maybe he feels safe with his Delores."

"Or maybe he's setting a trap for you."

"Possible." She knew it was more than possible that Santos might have other weapons in that tomb. But she'd tried to distract Cameron from dwelling on it. Obviously not with any degree of success. "But I won't know if you keep me pinned to this tomb instead of letting me go inside." She pushed him away from her and slipped away. "It's going to be all right, Cameron. It's not as if we didn't know this was going to happen. It was always in the cards. Now stop treating me as if I don't know what I'm doing." She moved quickly toward the bronze door. "Four minutes."

"And I won't forgive you if you get yourself killed before that," he said roughly. "You be careful, you stay alive. Do you hear me?"

"I hear you." She gave him a faint smile over her shoulder. "I'll do my best to obey. Now get out of here and do your job." She pressed to one side of the door and drew a deep breath.

Throw the door wide.

Go in low and fast.

Count to three.

One.

Her hand closed on the bronze handle.

Two.

Position.

Three.

She threw the door wide, bent low, and dove through the doorway! She rolled on the floor behind the shelter of one of the gilt throne chairs.

And a bullet splintered the wood next to her head!

Santos did have a gun.

"Welcome, Catherine, I've been waiting for you. You took long enough." Santos's voice was mocking. "Were you afraid?"

"Of whom? You? That corpse?" She moved to the side. "You're cornered like the rat you are. Your Delores is nothing, nonexistent."

"Liar. Stupid bitch. She does exist."

Another shot, this time striking the floor beside her leg.

The shot had come from somewhere behind that glass coffin. Make him speak so that she could judge the exact direction.

"Where did you get the gun, Santos?"

"Delores. Do you think I'd put her to rest without her favorite weapon? She loved this gun. I bought it for her in Paris, then gave her a target to practice on. She made him last four days, almost tore him apart." He paused. "She had it the day you killed her. It took Dorgal weeks to negotiate that gun away from the police. But I placed it in a pearl-and-gold case on the table by the coffin."

From the sound of his voice, Santos had to be near the foot of the coffin.

"Touching. Very touching. I'm sure she wouldn't mind your using it as she would." She got off a shot.

He muttered a curse.

She must have been close.

She heard him moving. To the left, perhaps beside that oak table . . .

Bring him out in the open.

"Let's see how durable that coffin is," she said. "How does it withstand bullets?"

She fired four shots in rapid succession at the coffin.

They pinged, then flew off the transparent surface in all directions.

"Did you think I'd leave her vulnerable?" he said scornfully. "Montez had orders to make sure it was indestructible. The worst that could happen is that Montez will have to polish that Plexiglas surface to get the scratches out."

"I don't believe you'll get Montez to do that service. He has other plans." She got off another shot. "And you won't be around to try to change them."

"Yes, I will. I could have been out of here a few minutes after I ran through that door. I was only waiting for you."

She tensed. "Bluffing?"

"No, that wonderful Persian carpet on the floor behind the coffin. It hides a trapdoor that leads past the cryogenic equipment to an underground passage ending at a boat dock. I'll be off the island five minutes after I kill you. Then I start over."

"How?"

"Bribes. Murder. Intimidation. It's a corrupt world. I'll survive and climb to the top again."

He believed it. And he was making Catherine believe it, too. He had survived her killing Delores and managed to get out of prison. He had caused the death of three of her friends and threatened others. If he got out of here, she had no doubt that threat would be realized.

"You wouldn't abandon your Delores."

"She will be fine until I can get her back. Montez's work is a breakthrough. There will be people standing in line who will want to make sure that the formula and process of what he did with Delores can be used on others." He added harshly, "But I'm not going to forgive or forget your making us go through this. I'll go down the list, and everyone you've tried to keep alive will die. Luke, first. Then Hu Chang. And I'll go from there. You might remember that in these last few minutes you have."

She could tell he had moved again. Was he heading for that trapdoor?

No! He was to her left. Very close.

And he had a clear shot.

She dove behind the chair.

Pain.

She cried out.

The bullet had burned the flesh of her right shoulder.

"Got you." Santos's voice was triumphant, then more

regretful. "I wish I had more time . . ." He was moving toward the trapdoor. "But if you're not dead, you will be. And I still may have the pleasure of doing those kills while you watch. Just a postponement . . ."

She heard the trapdoor open.

No! She struggled to her knees. "Not a postponement, Santos. You're through."

But he was disappearing down the steps to the tunnel. She jumped to her feet and ran toward the door. "Cameron, dammit, *do* it!" She called, "How long?"

"One minute. No more."

But in one minute, Santos could be out of danger and halfway to that dock.

She whirled back and ran toward the trapdoor. She could see Santos on the second landing of the spiral staircase. Make him stop. "Santos, come back here. I'm waiting for you. Delores is waiting for you. Do you know what's going to happen? You know all those explosions that blew up your hill? Cameron still had some of his clever little devices left over. So he set a few outside the tomb at strategic points. Montez helped him to make sure the blast would be strong enough to send this tomb straight to hell. To send Delores straight to hell."

"You're lying. He wouldn't destroy his work." But he had stopped and was looking back up at her. "He was proud of it. Proud of her."

"Maybe proud of his work, but he always knew what a monster he'd created."

Thirty more seconds.

Distract him. Keep him talking.

"I have a present for you." She took Jane's gold dog tag out of her pocket and threw it at him. He automatically reached out and caught it. "I promised Eve I'd give it to you after you had Jane shot."

He smiled. "And killed."

"No, she's still alive. You've been had, Santos."

His smile faded. "I don't believe you."

"Yes, you do. You've failed all around. Including with Delores. You said she'd never be vulnerable. That blast is going to do considerably more damage than a bullet to that pretty coffin."

"No." His eyes were wide, glaring with rage and panic as he turned to face her. "Stop it. They can't do that to her."

Ten seconds.

"Watch us. She's dead. So are you."

Five seconds.

"Catherine." Cameron had burst through the door and was by her side. "Get the hell out of here." He was dragging her toward the entrance. "Leave him."

"I am." It was safe now. She had kept Santos away from the tunnel.

And time had run out.

As they reached the bronze door, she glanced back over her shoulder at the gleaming coffin, where Delores lay in pagan splendor. At the gaping hole where Santos was probably now scrambling for safety.

"Out!" Cameron pushed her ahead of him out of the tomb.

The earth was rumbling beneath their feet.

"Down!"

Cameron jerked her down and fell on top of her.

Crack.

Kaboom.

Searing heat. Debris falling around them like missiles.

Kaboom.

Another blast.

More debris.

Granite. It was black granite. The tomb . . .

The heat was intense.

She could see patches of fire igniting the grass around them.

And burning sparks on the shoulder of Cameron's shirt next to her cheek.

She put them out, then pushed him away. "We've got to get out of here." She jumped to her feet. "Come on. We're too close."

"Tell me about it," Cameron said dryly, as they ran for the trail. "You're the one who ran back in there. You'd better have a damn good reason."

"Tunnel." She was coughing from the choking smoke. "Escape tunnel. I had to keep Santos from using it."

"And did you?"

She nodded as she looked back at the tomb.

Only there was no tomb.

It was a pile of granite rocks and blazing flames that were incinerating everything around them.

"She's gone," Catherine whispered. "Even Montez's coffin couldn't survive those blasts."

"He made sure of it," Cameron said. "He did the calculations even before I told him what we wanted. He was going to find a way to destroy them himself if we couldn't do it. He told me that Santos and his Delores would probably be vaporized by the force of those explosions."

"As you both almost were," Dario said grimly as he strode down the hill from the bunkhouse. "You look like hell, Catherine. Blood . . ." He took a step closer and examined her shoulder. "Bullet wound. Do we need to get you back to Port of Spain for medical attention?"

She shook her head. "It's only a flesh wound. I'm not going anywhere for a while."

"Why not? We've about wrapped everything up here."

"Not everything." Her gaze went back to the burning pyre that had been Delores's tomb. "I didn't see him die. I can't leave here until I know that Santos is dead." She glanced at Dario. "There's a tunnel beneath the tomb that leads down the hill to a boat dock. Will you have it checked to make sure that boat is still at the dock?"

He nodded. "Right away." He turned and headed toward the beach.

"Come on," Cameron said. "We need to find water and a first-aid kit to bandage that shoulder. It's at least got to be cleaned if not—" The text ring on his phone went off, and he glanced down for the message. "It's from Hu Chang." He read her the text. "Situation resolved. Seth Caleb enjoyed his visit to the Victorian house. Lambell did not."

Catherine drew a relieved breath. "Luke's safe?"

"So it would seem. Now, as I was saying, let's go take care of that wound."

"Not now."

"You're just going to sit here and wait?"

She nodded grimly. "And hope to hell that Montez was wrong about Santos's probably being vaporized. I need to *know*."

He didn't argue. He dropped to the ground and pulled her down beside him. "Then we'd better get comfortable. It's going to take a long time before we can get back into that tomb."

"You don't have to stay with me. Dario may need you."

"I don't have to do anything. It's pure choice. And I choose you." He drew her closer and tucked her head into the hollow of his shoulder. "And you may never admit that you need me, but someday I'll make you admit that you want me for something other than sex. For some reason that's becoming important to me. Isn't that strange?"

"Completely." Strange and warm and frightening all at the same time. She didn't want to deal with any of those emotions in connection with Cameron. She didn't have to do it. Pure choice, as Cameron had said.

But at least she could yield a little of herself to him in this moment of weariness and relief and hope. He had claimed that part of her anyway during these past days of fighting at her side. Would she be able to get it back? She didn't know. But it would do no harm to relax now and worry about it later.

Maybe. Cameron was always an emotional threat and a danger to her.

That was okay, she could handle it. Right now, he was only giving her comfort and companionship and the knowledge that he would not leave her.

She relaxed back against him, watching the leaping flames devour the tomb down the hill.

And, dammit, she was going to take that gift.

ATLANTA, GEORGIA
ONE DAY LATER

"Is Catherine sure? I can't believe Santos is really dead, Eve." Jane's lips twisted. "He's been hanging over my head like a hangman's noose for too long."

"Over all our heads," Eve said. "Catherine said that she was certain when she called last night. You can ask her yourself. She told me that she was coming here today and that she'd see us."

"I may do that. It's hard to believe the nightmare is over. But I have to believe it. I've got to go on, I have to move forward." She was silent a moment, thinking. "I'm going to need my sketchbook, Eve. Will you bring it next time?"

"Sure. But let's check with the doctor and make sure it's okay. You get pretty intense when you're working." Eve smiled. "Why not just read or watch television?"

"Because I'm going crazy since they cut the drugs."

Jane made a face. "I need to do something constructive. I can't just lie here and stare mindlessly."

"You're never mindless." But Eve could see that she was terribly restless, and that might be a healthy sign. Jane had always wanted to move, to search for that next adventure, to find the key that had been lost. It had only been after Trevor had died that she seemed to turn her back on that essential part of her character. "I'll talk to the doctor and see what I can do. Maybe you should wait until Joe and I take you home with us to heal. You'll have more leisure time."

She shook her head. "I need to start now. And I'll only need to be at the lake cottage for a week or so. After that, I'll go back to London and be out of your hair."

Eve looked away. "That soon? I kind of like the thought of your hanging around and being in my hair."

"Me, too." Jane reached out and covered Eve's hand, lying on the bed. "That's why I have to leave. I want it too much. I always want to stay with you and Joe. It's home. It's the place I love. If I didn't force myself, I'd cuddle down forever and be the little girl you found in the streets all those years ago. But that's your life, that's Joe's life. I have to find a life of my own." Her hand tightened on Eve's. "I thought for a while I'd found it with Trevor, but that didn't happen. So I have to go on, don't I? Like you did when Bonnie died. You didn't hide. I can't either. Do you understand that, Eve?"

She nodded jerkily. "Though I really like the idea of all that cuddling down forever with Joe and me. London is too far away."

"It didn't stop me from flying back to you at the drop of a hat when you needed me." Her eyes were glittering with moisture as she smiled unsteadily. "London isn't home to me. *You're* home. Besides, I've been thinking about going up to McDuff's castle in Scotland after I fully recover. You remember McDuff?"

"How can anyone forget him?" she asked dryly. "Lord McDuff, who thinks he runs all the world, or at least Great Britain. Why would you go there?"

She shrugged. "McDuff is always trying to persuade me that I should come and go treasure hunting with him. As I was lying here, it occurred to me that would be the farthest thing from hiding that I could choose. McDuff would never permit it."

"And neither would I," Caleb said.

Jane tensed as her gaze flew to the door, where Caleb was leaning against the jamb. "Hello, Caleb. I haven't seen you lately."

"I had things to wrap up." He strolled into the room. "Did you miss me?"

"Let's say I noticed your absence."

"Which means you missed me." He smiled. "But not enough to keep you from trying to supplant me with McDuff. I admit I was surprised when I overheard you talking about him."

"Eavesdropping."

"Of course, I've never claimed to be honorable." He turned to Eve. "But I hope you agree that it's a good idea for Jane to go to McDuff's castle."

Her eyes narrowed. "Do you?"

"Yes, I'm all for any change that brings Jane out in the real world." He smiled. "Particularly since Edinburgh is one of my favorite stomping grounds. And to which destination I'm about to go as soon as I say my good-bye to Jane."

"You're leaving?" Eve got to her feet and held out her hand. "Thank you, Caleb. Joe and I owe you."

"No, you don't." Caleb shook her hand. "If anything, I

owe you for making that call. It's been an interesting challenge."

"So casual." Eve shook her head. "And so phony. I was here when you nearly went off the deep end when Jane was hovering between life and death." She took a step closer and gave him a brief hug before she turned and headed for the door. "But I'll make sure Jane lets me know if you behave yourself if she runs into you in Scotland."

Caleb chuckled. "Oh, she'll run into me. But she may not give you a report. She's very protective of you."

"Would you two stop talking about me as if I weren't here?" Jane said.

"I'm gone." Eve lifted her hand as she left the room. But her smile faded as soon as she closed the door.

And I think, in your heart, you may be gone, too, Jane.

I have to be grateful, she thought. Jane was coming back to them, and it was a stronger, more mature Jane, who was taking charge of her life.

Eve *was* grateful.

It was just going to take a little while for the ache to go away.

I gave Eve a bad time when I showed up here that first day." Caleb turned back to Jane as Eve was lost to view. "I'm lucky that she has a forgiving nature, or she would have tossed me out."

"Would you have let her?"

He smiled. "No, but she might have found a way. She's very smart."

"Yes, she is." She paused. "And she didn't argue with me about going to McDuff's castle. Neither of us needed your approval."

"I thought I'd give it anyway. I hate to be left out in the cold."

"And you believed I might change my mind if I thought you approved?"

He chuckled. "That's too complicated. Why not believe I meant what I said?"

"Did you?"

"Yes." He moved closer to the bed. "I'm not worried about McDuff. Sometimes I even like him. When he doesn't get in my way."

"It's you that would be in McDuff's way if you show up at the castle. I don't intend to invite you, and I don't believe he would."

"How rude." His eyes were gleaming with mischief. "Afraid, Jane?"

"Don't be ridiculous." She paused. "I'm grateful for what you did for me. But there's nothing easy about our relationship, and I won't pretend that I want the disturbance you always bring."

"People change. Sometime you might welcome it."

She gazed at him incredulously. "Not likely."

"When you were on those drugs, we were almost compatible. Perhaps you could get a refill."

He was joking. His expression was alive with amusement.

"You're in a very good mood," she said warily.

"Because you're getting well, and I don't have to force you to go the way I want you to go." He reached forward and touched her cheek. "And it may be a long road, but I can see that it will be an interesting journey." He added softly, "And, oh, when we reach that final destination . . ."

Darkness. Flame. Electricity.

She stared at him in fascination. Then she pulled her gaze away. "There's no final destination with you, Caleb."

"Of course there is." His hand dropped away from her cheek. "You just don't understand it's there yet." He turned and headed for the door. His step was springy and his voice light. "I'll see you in Scotland, Jane."

"Good God, you look terrible." Eve's eyes widened when Catherine walked into the waiting room. "You said you were okay when you called me yesterday to tell me that Santos was definitely dead. You didn't mention he'd used you as a punching bag." She glanced at Catherine's bandaged shoulder. "No problem with that wound?"

Catherine shook her head. "I told you, it's a minor flesh wound." She gingerly touched the bruises on her cheek and lip. "These hurt more."

"And you have deep circles under your eyes. You're exhausted. You shouldn't have stopped off here. Go home and get some rest."

"I will." She reached out and took Eve's hand. "But that's not true, I should have stopped off here. You were all in the front lines. Santos targeted you, and you came through for me. Hu Chang made sure everyone else was safe, but you were the center that let me move forward."

"Bullshit," Eve said baldly. "It was a team effort. I just rounded up the troops when you called and said that Dorgal was on the way. I handled persuading the doctors and nurses to go along with it. But, basically, we got a plan together and executed it. Joe, Caleb, even Jane, were part of it."

"How is Jane?"

"Better every day. She's in her own room now. We had her moved from the isolation area after you called me yesterday. We'll be able to take her home in a week." She shook her head. "Which is good and bad. She's been very much my own while she's been here in the hospital. It will change once she starts taking back her life." She added quickly, "Not that I don't know that's for the best. I want her to have her independence back. It will just seem . . . a little empty."

"I can understand. Luke is only twelve and I'm having issues." She paused. "I want to see her, Eve."

"By all means. Caleb is with her now, but I got the impression he wasn't going to stay long. Besides, she's getting restless. She'll be glad to have someone besides us to talk to." She smiled. "Though she may go into shock when she sees your face."

Catherine grimaced. "Maybe she'll think I deserve it after what I put her through." She held up her hand as Eve frowned. "Okay, no more apologies. I'll substitute gratitude and just say I owe you more than I can say." She gave her a hug and held her tight for a moment as she whispered, "This has been a terrible time, but I've learned from it, Eve. I thought I was a loner, and I am in many ways. But I didn't count my blessings, I didn't realize that the friends who surrounded me were so strong, so unique, that I am never alone." She hugged her again, then stepped back and turned away. "And that I'll never let you be alone either. You feel a little lonely or empty, give me a call. I'll be there for you."

Eve chuckled. Though she was very touched. "I don't need you to hold my hand, Catherine. I'll be fine. I'm just anticipating a little withdrawal syndrome. Go on and see Jane."

Catherine nodded. "I will." She took Eve's hand and turned it palm up. "Right after I give you this. It's not in nearly as good condition as when you gave it to me."

Eve looked down at the melted, blackened, gold dog tag chain that Catherine had poured into her hand. Only the LING were left of the letters.

"I didn't expect it back."

"It had Jane's blood on it. I decided I didn't want him

to be able to claim what he did to her even in death." She touched the chain. "It was in his hand when we found him at the bottom of the spiral staircase. He was burned and in a number of charred pieces, and he must have been clutching the dog tag when the blast hit. I thought I'd let you decide what you wanted done with it."

"I'll talk to Joe. He'll probably want to drop it into the nearest toilet."

"Good choice." She started down the hall. "And very Joe-like. I should have known it would have to be a joint decision."

"Always." She called after her. "What about Richard Cameron? You didn't mention him."

"What about him?" Catherine didn't look back. "He went on ahead to talk to Hu Chang and make sure that Erin was all right. Then I guess that he'll be on his way again. I'm sure his precious committee is very impatient to get him back on the job. I was an unwelcome distraction to them."

"But he was a very good friend to you. You've got all this warm and fuzzy viewpoint on friendship now. If he was in trouble, would you come if he needed you?"

Catherine stopped and turned around to face her. "Maybe. If he asked me, which he would probably never do. And friendship isn't what he—well, maybe it is, but it's much more complicated than— You're smiling."

"Yes, I am. I'm curious about Cameron, so I decided I'd probe a bit."

"Well, you probed." She grinned at her. "And the only concrete statement you'll get from me is concerning you, my friend. Through hell and high water, I'll always be there for you."

Eve watched as Catherine turned and continued down the hall.

* * *

I'll always be there for you. Those are nice words, aren't they, Mama?"

Bonnie.

Eve turned to see Bonnie curled up in one of the chairs across the waiting room. "Very nice. And the meaning is even nicer, young lady. I could have used having you here for me during the last few days. What good is a ghost if she's not on the job when you need her?"

Bonnie smiled. "Not much good at all. I've told you that I can't be with you all the time. It doesn't work that way. I have things I have to do. I'm lucky to be able to be with you at all. It doesn't usually happen."

"I know, I know. I just miss you. Sorry to complain. We managed without you. Santos is dead. Jane is getting well."

Bonnie nodded. "And Trevor is trying to keep busy and stay away from her. It's hard in the beginning. You want to stay where you know you're loved instead of sending out the love yourself."

"Was it hard for you, baby?"

"Oh, yes, but you needed me so badly that I was allowed to come to you and visit." Her smile deepened. "And it was wonderful, wasn't it, Mama?"

"Past tense?" She went still. She was sensing something that was making her uneasy. "I don't like this, Bonnie. Are you trying to tell me something?"

"I think so. I'm a little confused myself. You know I don't always understand what I'm supposed to do to help you. Most of the time, it's enough for me to be with you and let the love between us do the work." She paused. "I think something is going to happen, Mama."

"Something bad?"

She nodded. "Something bad, and terrible, and scary, and yet there's a light, too."

"Well, that's clear."

"I just wanted to warn you. Because I don't know if I'm going to be able to be with you again."

Eve felt a surge of panic. "No. Why shouldn't you be able to come? You thought that when we found your body and the man who took you, that you might not be able to come. But it wasn't true, you still managed to do it."

"This is different."

"How?"

Bonnie shrugged helplessly. "I don't know. It's just different. Things are going to . . . change. I don't know how, but they're going to change, and I don't think I'm going to be able to stop it."

Eve drew a deep, shaky breath. She said unsteadily, "You're being most unsatisfactory, and I don't want to waste my time with you worrying if you can't tell me what's happening. So just sit there and we'll talk about things that make us happy until you have to leave me. Okay?"

"Okay." Bonnie smiled her warm, luminous smile, which always seemed to light up the world. "I only wanted to make sure that even if someday you can't see me anymore like this, you'd know that I hadn't really left you."

I'll always be there for you.

Not a coincidence that Bonnie had echoed those words when she had come to Eve today.

"No, not a coincidence," Bonnie said softly.

"A promise?"

Bonnie nodded. "A promise that will last forever. You'll remember that, Mama?"

"I'll remember." She swallowed to ease the tightness of her throat. "But that doesn't mean I'll accept it. I'm not giving you up, baby. We've worked this ghost business out to a fine art. So you just go tell all those mysterious entities that think they can keep you from me for no apparent reason that it's not going to happen."

"Because you say so." Bonnie was suddenly chuckling. "Only you, Mama."

"Why not? I know the love goes both ways, and being with me is probably good for you, too." She smiled into her eyes. "So I don't intend to let you go. I don't care what kind of horror story you're sensing ahead. We'll make it through together." Her smile deepened with all the love she was feeling. "Because I'll always be there for you, too, Bonnie."

Read on for an excerpt from Iris Johansen's new book

SHADOW PLAY

Available in September 2015 in hardcover
from St. Martin's Press

CHAPTER 1

SONDERVILLE, CALIFORNIA

Walsh watched the detectives and forensic team milling around the open grave, their flashlight beams lighting the darkness. Stay in the back of the crowd, he told himself. The rest of these locals were only curiosity seekers and the cops were used to dealing with them. If he blended in and didn't call attention to himself, no one would notice or remember him.

Damn kid. The girl had been buried for years and might have never been recovered if those Boy Scouts hadn't chosen this area to set up camp. It must have been the recent rains that had washed away the top layers of dirt and revealed those old bones.

Or maybe not.

He remembered how strange that little girl had been, how he'd hated her before that final blow. And he'd heard there were weird stories about this wood where he'd buried her . . .

He felt a chill as he remembered those stories.

Forget it. They were just stories. He had come here to make sure that the report was true that the girl had been unearthed after all these years. He had carefully monitored the town and vineyards since the night she had been buried. Now that he was certain, he'd fade away for a while. He was good at fading away. He'd done it eight years ago and no one had connected him to anything that had happened in this valley.

And no one must connect him to that child the forensic team was so carefully taking out of her grave.

She had to remain unknown and lost as she had been all these years. It was too dangerous to him for her to be anything but the heap of bones she'd become after he'd thrown her into that grave. He would have to keep monitoring the situation to be sure that threat didn't become a reality.

It would be okay. Years had passed, life moved fast, no one would care about this child who had been lost so long . . .

LAKE COTTAGE
ATLANTA, GEORGIA

"You have a FedEx package," Joe Quinn said as Eve came into the cottage. "It's on your work table. It came from somewhere in California."

She nodded. "Yeah, Sonderville. Sheriff Nalchek called me last night and asked me to bump his reconstruction to the top of my list." She made a face. "I almost told him to forget it. I'm swamped right now and I don't need any more pressure."

"You're always swamped." Joe smiled teasingly. "You thrive on it. And it's natural that you're in demand. Everyone wants the world-famous forensic sculptor, Eve Duncan, to solve their problems."

"Bullshit." She went to the kitchen counter and popped a K-cup in the coffee machine. "There's usually no urgency about putting a face on a skull that's been buried for years anyway. It has to be done, but there's no reason that I can't do it in an orderly fashion. Every one of those children is important."

"So why did you give in to Sheriff Nalchek?"

"I don't know." She poured her coffee and came back to Joe. "He wore me down. He sounded young and eager and full of the horror that only comes the first time that you realize that there are vicious people out there who can do monstrous things to innocent children. I got the impression that he was an idealist who wanted to change the world." She sat down beside Joe and nestled close, her head against his shoulder. He was warm and strong and she loved the feel of him. She loved *him*. Lord, it was good to be home. That trip to the airport today had been achingly difficult. She had watched her adoptive daughter, Jane, fly away back to London and she had no idea when she would see her again. "He kept telling me that this little girl was different, that he was sure that he'd be able to find out who she was and who had killed her if I'd just give him a face to work with. Who knows? Maybe he's right. In cold cases like this the chances are always better if the officer in charge is enthusiastic and dedicated."

"Like you." Joe's lips brushed her forehead. "Maybe he thinks he's found a soul mate."

"Oh, I'm dedicated. Enthusiastic?" She wearily shook her head. "Not now. I'm too tired. There have been too many children in my life who have been killed and thrown away. I'm not as enthusiastic as that young officer is. I'm only determined . . . and sad."

"Sad?" Joe straightened and looked down at her. "Yes, I'm definitely feeling the sad part. But it's not only about that skull in the box over there, is it?" His hand gently cupped her cheek. "Jane? I could have taken her to the airport. I thought you wanted to do it."

"I did want to do it. It may be the last time we see her for a while. She's off to new adventures and finding a life of her own." She tried to steady her voice. "Just what we wanted for her. Look what happened when she came back from London to try to help me. She got shot and almost died. Now she's well and going on with her life." In her line of work, sometimes the evil came close to home. Most recently Jane had been one of the targets. Those weeks with her daughter, Jane MacGuire, while she had been recuperating had been strained and yet poignantly sweet. Jane had come to them when she was ten years old and she had been more best friend than daughter to Eve. But that hadn't changed the love that had bound them all these years. Now that Jane was out on her own and becoming a successful artist, it was terribly hard to adjust to the fact that most of the time she was thousands of miles away. "It's exactly what she should be doing. What's here for her? Hell, I'm a workaholic and always involved with a reconstruction. You're a police detective who they tap to work cases that don't give you normal hours either. It was just . . . difficult . . . to see her get on that plane."

"And you didn't let her see one bit of that pain," Joe said quietly. "You smiled and sent her on her way."

"That's what every parent does. It always comes down to letting them go."

"And more difficult for you than for others. First, you had to let go of Bonnie when she was killed. Now Jane is moving out of our lives."

"Not out, just away." She made a face. "And evidently I couldn't let go of Bonnie because I insisted on keeping her with me, alive or dead. I was so stubborn that whoever is in charge of the hereafter let me have my little girl's spirit visit me now and then." Though she had initially resisted that blessing. She had thought she was hallucinating, thought that grief had made her mind fly to any solace possible. She had only wanted to be with her Bonnie and was spiraling down to meet her when she had been stopped by the realization that the visits from Bonnie were no hallucination. She drew a deep breath and gave Joe a quick kiss. "Which makes me luckier than a lot of people. I refuse to feel sorry for myself. I have you. I sometimes have Bonnie. I'll have Jane when she moves in and out of our lives." She nodded at the FedEx box across the room. "And I have a chance to help the parents of that little girl find resolution." She got to her feet and took a sip before she put the cup down on the coffee table. "So slap me if you see me go broody on you." She headed for the kitchen. "How about lasagna for supper? There's something about the smell of baking garlic bread that lifts the spirits and makes everything seem alright."

"Besides outrageously tempting the taste buds. Sounds good. Need help?"

"Nah, you know my culinary expertise is nonexistent. I'll do frozen."

"Eve."

She glanced over her shoulder.

He was frowning and his gaze was narrowed. "It's just Jane leaving? You've been pretty quiet the last couple weeks. Nothing else is wrong?"

And Joe noticed everything. She was tempted to deny it and put him off, but she couldn't do it. They had been together for years and their relationship was based not only on love but honesty. "Nothing that can't be fixed." She shrugged. "I guess I'm just going through some kind of emotional adjustment. I wanted everything to stay the same. I wanted to keep Jane close to me. Mine. Though I always knew she didn't really belong to me. She was too independent and was ten going on thirty when we adopted her. And Bonnie was mine but then she was taken." She smiled. "And that spirit, Bonnie, who comes to visit me now and then is very much her own self now. Beloved, but only flashes of being mine." Her smile faded. "But I'll take it. I just want to keep her with me, too. I don't want anything to change."

"Why should that change?"

"It shouldn't change. That's what I told Bonnie. Nothing has to change."

His brows rose. "Ah, your Bonnie. She said something to disturb you? When?"

"A couple weeks ago. She scared me. She said she didn't know how long she'd be able to keep coming to me. She said everything was going to change."

"How? Why?"

"She didn't know. She just wanted to warn me."

"Very frustrating." He chuckled. "If your daughter has to pay you visits, I'd just as soon she not upset you like this."

"That's what I told her."

He got to his feet and took her in his arms. "And so you should. Send her to me and I'll reinforce it." He kissed her. "Though I doubt if that's going to happen. She only appeared to me a couple times just to make sure I knew that you weren't hallucinating." He looked directly into her eyes. "I know you need Bonnie. She's your anchor that keeps you here with me. You were spiraling downward and almost died before you had your ghost visits from Bonnie. She brought you back and I thank God for her." He paused. "But if for some reason she stopped coming, I want you to know that we'll make it alright. I have so much love for you, Eve. I'm full of it, you're my center. You always have been and always will be. If your Bonnie drifts away from you, I'll just pour more of that love toward you. I'll find a way to stop you from hurting. I promise you."

He meant every word. The knight was about to mount his stallion and launch himself into battle, she realized. God, she was lucky.

She gazed up into his face, the strong square contour, the well-shaped lips, the tea-colored eyes that held both warmth and intelligence. So familiar, yet so new, every time she looked at him. "Hey, I'm just having a few twinges, nothing major. It just seemed when Jane got on that plane that the changes were starting. A sort of harbinger of things to come." She pushed him away and turned back to the freezer. "But change can be good, too, can't it? After all, Bonnie wasn't definite about anything. Forget it." She took out the lasagna. "Jane told me she'd call me as soon as she got off the plane in London. I think I'll start working on the new reconstruction after dinner so that I'll be awake when she calls . . ."

But Eve's cell phone rang before she even finished loading the dishwasher after dinner.

"Sheriff Nalchek," she told Joe with a sigh. "You finish here. I may be more than a few minutes."

"Dedication and enthusiasm," Joe repeated with a grin. "At least he waited until after dinner."

"Not necessarily. California is three hours earlier." She punched the access button. "Eve Duncan."

"John Nalchek." His deep voice was brusque. "Sorry to bother you, Ms. Duncan. I just wanted to make sure that you'd received the skull for reconstruction today."

"Yes, FedEx is usually pretty reliable."

"What do you think of her?"

"I haven't opened the box yet, Sheriff Nalchek."

"Oh." A disappointed silence. "But you'll do it tonight?"

"Possibly." No promises or he might be calling her in the middle of the night. "Or tomorrow."

Another silence. "Okay. I don't want to rush you."

The hell he didn't. "There's no rushing a reconstruction, Sheriff. There are several stages, measuring and processes that have to be done before the actual sculpting. It will take as long as it takes."

"What stages?"

She tried to be patient. "The first stage is repairing, then I go to the measurement stage which is vitally important. I cut eraser sticks as markers to the proper measurements and glue them onto their specific points on the face. There are twenty points in a skull for which there are known tissue depths. Facial tissue depth has been found to be fairly consistent in people the same age, sex, race, and weight."

"What happens next?"

"I take strips of plasticine and apply them between the markers, then build up all the tissue depth points."

"It sounds kind of iffy, like connect the dots."

"If you wish to simplify it. I guarantee it's not simple, Nalchek. And that's only the beginning."

"Sorry, I wouldn't have sent her to you if I hadn't believed you could do the job. But you are going to put her before the others on your list?"

"I told you I would." Remember what she had told Joe. Dedication and enthusiasm might work miracles for that poor child. "I know that you probably had a shock when you found that skeleton. It's never pleasant. But you have to remember that we can do something about it if we work together. We can find her parents, we can find the person who killed her."

"I wasn't shocked, ma'am. I was in Afghanistan and I worked as an EMT before I went to work with law enforcement. There's nothing much I haven't seen." He paused. "And I told you yesterday that I know I can help her if you give me a face. I *know* it."

His voice was so passionate that Eve asked, "Really? And how do you know it?"

"Sometimes you just know. Sometimes you—" He

stopped. "Or maybe I just want it so bad. I looked down at that little girl's skeleton all covered in dirt and mud, and I felt as if she was calling to me. It was so damn strong, it rocked me. She was so . . . small and fragile. I wanted to pick her up and take her somewhere safe where no one would ever hurt her again. Crazy, huh?"

"Not so crazy." All her impatience had disappeared with his words. When her own daughter had disappeared, she would have wanted someone like Nalchek to be hunting for her. It was a cold world and men who cared were rare and to be valued. "What can you tell me about her?"

"Nothing much. We think she's nine or a little younger. She died of a blow to the head. She's Caucasian and she's been buried for a good eight years or more. I've checked the missing persons reports at the time and there's nothing that matches up to the location or the time frame."

"She might have been transported from almost anywhere in the state or beyond."

"I know that. You asked me what I knew. I didn't think you wanted guesses, ma'am."

"No, I don't." Nine years old. Buried eight years. If she'd lived, she'd have gone to high school proms by now. She might have had a boyfriend or had a crush on some rock star or movie actor. She'd missed so much during those eight years. "Thank you. It may help to know something about her."

"I thought it might. I read a couple articles about you before I sent you the skull. You were quoted as saying that you liked to do anything that brought you closer to the victim. You said for some reason it seemed to make the sculpting process easier. The reporter made a lot of that remark."

"He was looking for a hook for his story. I made the mistake of giving it to him."

"It was a good hook. It was what made me send the

skull to you. I liked the idea of someone caring enough to want to get close to a victim."

"I feel sympathy for any victim but the closeness of which I spoke only occurs during the actual sculpting process. That's really the only part of reconstruction that has the potential for creativity."

"And bonding?"

"You're putting words in my mouth."

"Maybe. I'm trying to make sure I did the right thing sending her to you. I feel responsible."

"Should I send that skull back to you?"

"No, ma'am. I didn't mean to offend you. I'd appreciate it if you'd get right on it, please."

"No offense taken. You just seem very possessive about this skull."

"That's what I thought about when I researched you, Ms. Duncan. Two of a kind?"

"No." Though those words were eerily close to what Joe had said, she thought. "Perhaps I do feel a responsibility and closeness to my work while I'm doing a reconstruction, but I'd never feel possessive. I only want to set them free."

Nalchek chuckled. "I haven't gotten there yet. I feel like that little girl still belongs to me just like the minute we pulled her out of that grave. Maybe after you get me a face, I'll be able to let her go. Good night, Ms. Duncan. You'll let me know how it goes?"

"I imagine that you'll make sure I do," she said dryly. "Good night, Sheriff." She hung up.

Nalchek wasn't entirely what she had thought. She would still bet that he was young, but he wasn't inexperienced and had a toughness that made his insistence about her doing the reconstruction all the more puzzling.

A nine-year-old girl, buried over eight years.

"I felt like she was calling to me."

"Eve." Joe was standing behind her in the doorway. He was carrying two cups of coffee. "Done?"

She nodded and took the cup he handed her. "For the time being." She moved toward the porch swing and curled up next to him as he sat down. She sighed with contentment as she gazed out at the lake. The fragrance of the pines, the moonlight on the lake, Joe beside her at this place they both loved. "Nalchek is very polite, very concerned. And he's going to be a thorn in my side until I finish her."

"Then don't take his calls."

"That's one solution."

A breeze was lifting her hair and it made everything in this moment all the more wonderful. This perfect place, this perfect man for her.

That little girl had not lived long enough to have a perfect anything. That took time and searching and the wisdom to know it when you found it.

"Then do it." Joe put his arm around her. "Why not?"

"I'll think about it."

But she knew she wouldn't do it.

"I felt like she was calling to me."

So did your bone lady come through for you, Nalchek?"

Nalchek looked up as Deputy Ron Carstairs came into the office. He was a friend as well as a co-worker, and Ron had been riding him since the night they'd found the little girl. He was a good guy and they'd worked together for five years, but he didn't understand why Nalchek hadn't just dropped this investigation and pushed it into the hands of the medical examiner. "She's not a bone lady. You're thinking of that TV show. She's a forensic sculptor and probably the best in the world."

"And she's rushing to give that kid a face just because you asked her to do it?" Ron dropped down in the visitor's chair. "Hell, then she couldn't be that good. We're small potatoes out here in the boonies."

"She's that good," Nalchek said. He tossed the Eve Duncan dossier to Carstairs. "Take a look for yourself." He pointed to the photo of Eve Duncan. Red-brown shoulder-length hair, hazel eyes, features that were more interesting than beautiful. "She was illegitimate and born in the slums of Atlanta and had a baby of her own by the time she was sixteen. She named the little girl Bonnie and the kid turned her life around. The kid became her whole life. She went back to school and then on to college. Then when the little girl was seven, she was kidnapped and killed. It was a terrible blow and Duncan went into shock. But then she rallied and started to rebuild her life. Duncan went back to college to study forensic sculpting. Since then she's become the most sought-after artist in forensic sculpting. She works for police, FBI, and private concerns." He pointed to the dossier underneath Eve Duncan's. "That's Joe Quinn, ex-SEAL, ex-FBI, currently a detective with ATLPD. They've been living together for years."

Ron only glanced at the dossier. "I'll look at them later. Nice-looking woman. Not my type. Too intense."

"She's my type. I want her intense." He grinned as he leaned back in his chair. "Though I'll probably stay away from Joe Quinn. His reputation is a little too lethal for me."

"You said he was a cop."

"There are cops and then there are cops. You know that as well as I do. He's supposed to be totally bonkers about Eve Duncan and very protective."

"Well, you shouldn't have to deal with either one of them now that you've turned the skull over to Duncan."

Nalchek's smile faded as he looked back down at the dossier. "Yeah, you could say that."

"Hey." Ron was shaking his head. "Drop it. Let it go, Nalchek."

"I have let it go. It's out of my hands."

"But not out of your mind. There's a lot of talk around town about how weird you've been behaving since we found that kid's skeleton. We all felt bad about what happened to that little girl but you overreacted."

"How can you overreact to the murder of a kid?"

"She's been dead over eight years. What're the chances we'll ever find her murderer?"

"Damn good, if we try hard enough." He got to his feet. "And I'm trying hard, real hard. I'll find the son of a bitch. I've got Eve Duncan and soon I'll have a face." He moved toward the door. "And right now, I'm going back to that grave site and taking another look to see if I can find anything more."

"You've been out there five times. Don't you think it's a little excessive?"

"No.

I felt like she was calling to me.

He had said that to Eve Duncan and he was still hearing that call even though the bones were long gone from that crime scene.

"You can never tell what you'll find if you look hard enough. Want to come along?"

"Waste of time." Ron grimaced. "Oh, what the hell." He got to his feet, grabbed the Duncan and Quinn dossiers, and followed him toward the door. "Why not?"

Are you still going to wait up for that call from Jane?" Joe asked as he paused before going back to their bedroom. "Want company?"

Eve chuckled. "I've got company." She moved across the room to her worktable where the FedEx box remained unopened. "No, you go on to bed. You've got to work tomorrow morning. I won't be too long. I'll just take care of the setup and preliminary measuring and then come to bed after I get Jane's call."

"Sounds like a plan." He still didn't move. "Sure you're okay?"

"Absolutely." She started to unfasten the box. "Stop hovering. You're acting like a grandma with her first grandkid."

"I beg your pardon." Joe's voice was suddenly deep, silky smooth, and infinitely sensual. "Grandma? Me? I think we're going to have to address that insult when you come to bed."

She glanced up at him and suddenly lost her breath. Thigh muscles that were compact and yet sleek and full of leashed power. Tight stomach and buttocks. In this moment he was totally male, completely sexual, and she could feel her own body respond. Even after all these years together, their sexual chemistry was just as explosive as when they had come together when he had been the FBI agent sent to investigate Bonnie's death. "I'll look forward to it," she said softly.

He grinned. "That was my intention. Anticipation is the name of the game." The next moment he'd disappeared down the hall.

She stared after him for a moment before she ruefully shook her head. She was tempted to go after him, but he could just wait until she got the call from Jane. Anticipation worked both ways.

She looked back down at the box and completed opening it. Then she carefully removed the plastic ties that held the skull in place and the protective plastic wrap around the skull itself. "Let's see you," she murmured as she took the skull in her hands. She always talked to these lost children when she first started the reconstructions. It seemed to aid her in making a connection and helped her over the first painful shock of seeing their remains. She never got used to that moment. She held the skull under the light. "Small. You were small for nine. I wonder if they were wrong about you . . ." Small, delicate features . . . fragile. She looked so fragile and vulnerable. Nothing appeared to be broken or devoured by animals.

If you discounted the crushed side of her right temple where her killer had struck the fatal blow.

She'd have to repair that immediately so that she could concentrate on the actual reconstruction. Her fingers gently touched the crushed bones. "Bastard." She felt a sudden surge of rage that was as intense as it was unusual. She always felt sad, but it was difficult to focus rage on a faceless predator. She was having no trouble focusing now. This child's killer may only have been a shadow figure, but it was malignant and evil and Eve felt as if she could reach out and touch him. "But I don't think it could have hurt you for more than a few seconds. That's a mercy. Though I'm sure he didn't mean it to be." She tossed the box in the trash and spent a few minutes setting up the skull on her worktable. "There you are. Now I'll clean you up and start the measuring. I have to do a lot of measuring before I can start bringing you back the way you were. Were you a pretty little girl? Not that it matters. I've always liked interesting more than pretty anyway. I've had two children of my own in my life. My Bonnie was both pretty and interesting and Jane is very beautiful. But they both know that it's what's inside that counts." She was done with the cleaning and tossed the cloth aside. "What's inside you? Maybe we'll be able to see after I finish. Right now it's difficult, but I've gone down this road before. Okay, that's all. I just had to establish a sense of what we have to do together to find a way to get you back home. From now on I just work and maybe you help a little." She leaned back in her chair and gazed thoughtfully at the delicate skull. "One last thing. I always name my reconstructions. No offense. You can have your own name back once that sheriff finds out who you are. But I have to call you something besides 'Hey, you,' when I talk to you or about you. It's just the way I work." She tilted her head. "What name. . . . Linda? Penny? Samantha is a good name. It's got substance. Do you like it? Maybe too heavy. How about Carrie? Short and sweet. I kind of like that for—"

Jenny. I . . . think . . . my name is Jenny.

Eve went still. Out of the blue, out of the darkness, those words had come to her. Weird. Imagination? Or had she been concentrating so hard on this little girl that the name had just popped into her head and she'd mentally couched it in terms that the child might use? It didn't matter. The name was there and she might as well use it. "Jenny. I like it. And it seems to suit you. Much better than Samantha." She opened the drawer of the desk and drew out her measuring tools. "And now that we've got that out of the way it's time to get to work. Let's see if we can get the basic stuff done before I have to leave you and get to bed. . . ."

delicate [illegible] I always [illegible]
structures. [illegible] you can have your [illegible]
once [illegible] who you are. But I [illegible]
you something [illegible] when I [illegible] you or
about [illegible]

[illegible]